MW01106198

Irish Twins

A Novel of The Troubles

By Bob Huerter

Copyright © 2010 Bob Huerter

ISBN 978-1-60910-260-9

All rights reserved. No part of this publication may be reproduced, stored in a retrieval system, or transmitted in any form or by any means, electronic, mechanical, recording or otherwise, without the prior written permission of the author.

Printed in the United States of America.

The characters and events in this book are fictitious. Any similarity to real persons, living or dead, is coincidental and not intended by the author. The exception being those actual public figures mentioned by the author, Margaret Thatcher, Bik McFarland, Bobby Sands and all the rest of men who died on hunger strike in Northern Ireland in 1981.

BookLocker.com, Inc.
2010

Acknowledgements

One does not write a book alone, it takes a village. So I'd like to thank the members of the village who made this possible for me. I'd like to thank the following: My brother John Huerter and my dad Jim Huerter for their support and belief in this work. My wife Maureen for reading it more than she wanted to and "hoinking" it up, her suggestions were invaluable, I love you. Then Erin and Lewis Moore got a hold of the manuscript and their enthusiasm bowled me over, now it is not quite so Irish. My Daughter Clare for the line editing, thank you so much. My son Mick for letting me use his name, you really are a Quinlan. My daughter Molly for always believing, even when I didn't. My son Frank, my one and only reading buddy. Mike Sterba and Marty McCaslin, my writing buddies, who were there when there were no words on the page, who taught me more than I can ever put into words. My agent Paul Feldstein, the first to believe outside the inner circle and still does. I'd like to thank the following authors who I have not met but without whom this book would have been impossible. David Beresford for his book **Ten Men Dead**, Paddy Hayes for his book, **Break Out**, Johnston Brown for his book **Into The Dark,** Steve Bruce for his book **The Red Hand: Protestant Paramilitaries in Northern Ireland.** Seamus McManus for his book **The History of The Irish Race**. Leon Uris for his book **Trinity**, that was the beginning for me. I would also like to thank the publishers of **IRIS** for their special addition re-issue of **The Greatest Escape. A** Yank like me would've never known without all of these people and their passion for their work. I'd like to thank the Omaha Public Library, especially The Willa Cather branch. All my friends in and out of the rooms, you know who you are. Also I would like to thank my good friends Bill Gray, Joe and Nancy Casey, Carl and Vince Finocchiaro, John Berigan and John "Fry" Ryan for letting me use their names, unbeknownst to them. Don't worry guys, it's all good. I would also like to thank my friends in Upperchurch, Niebh Kinnane, Jimmy and Siobhan Butler, Packy Purcell and Johnny Gleason for letting me use your names, your village and thank you for your hospitality, I will never forget. And my acknowledgements wouldn't be complete without thanking my angel in heaven, Therese Ann Quinlan Huerter, me Mum, for giving me the love of all things Irish.

Dedication

This work is dedicated to my father, James V. Huerter, Sr. He was there from the beginning, he always believed and I could have no more gratitude than I have for all he has done for me. Thanks, Dad.

CONTENTS

Abbreviations and Definitions

In studying the Irish story of The Troubles in Northern Ireland I found that there are so many acronyms that I got confused. So I wanted to make sure I listed and defined them for you so that as you read you won't find them confusing.

Ulster: Ireland is made up of four provinces. Ulster is the northern most province.

Derry: City in Ulster as referred to by Nationalists

Londonderry: Same city in Ulster as referred to by Loyalist.

Loyalist: The Scotch Irish Protestants who live in the six counties in Ulster that make up Northern Ireland who consider themselves British citizens and are loyal to the UK.

Nationalists: The Irish Catholics who live in Northern Ireland and are interested in uniting Ireland without the presence of a foreign sovereignty.

Unionists: Members of Ulster Unions with the same leanings as Loyalists.

Peeler: Nickname for the Irish Police in the Republic of Ireland*

RUC: The Royal Ulster Constabulary, the police force in Northern Ireland

CID: Criminal Investigation Department of the RUC.

MI5: Military Intelligence, Section 5, is the United Kingdom's counter-intelligence and security agency.

UDR: The Ulster Defense Regiment is the Government Army of Northern Ireland

UDA: The Ulster Defense Association is a loyalist paramilitary group in Northern Ireland.

IRA: The Irish Republican Army, Nationalist Paramilitary

PIRA: Also known as the Provos, is the Provisional Irish Republican Army.

INLA: Irish National Liberation Army, a radical paramilitary off shoot of the PIRA

NORTIP: Northern Tipperary Republicans

UVF: Ulster Volunteer Force, Loyalist Paramilitary

UFF: Ulster Freedom Fighters, Loyalist paramilitary

Cuchullain: Ancient Irish Warrior hero pronounced Ka-Who-lan

Craic: Irish term for fun, the fun of it.

Shyte: How the Irish say shit, don't ask me why, I don't know.

Sir Robert "Bobbie" Peel, British Home Secretary started the Royal Irish Constabulary which hired Irish to police Irish in the early 19th century, they became known as Peelers. He then went on to create the Constables in London and thus the Bobbies.

“It is not those who inflict the most, but those who endure the most who will conquer in the end.”

Terence McSweeney

IRA Ballingeary Brigade from 1916 - 1920

“They won't break me because the desire for freedom, and the freedom of the Irish people, is in my heart. The day will dawn when all the people of Ireland will have the desire for freedom to show. It is then that we will see the rising of the moon.”

Bobby Sands

First Member of the IRA to die on Hunger Strike in 1981

“Let no man write my epitaph; for no man who knows my motives dares now to vindicate them. Let not prejudice or ignorance asperse them. When my country takes her place among nations of the earth, then and only then, let my epitaph be written.”

Robert Emmet

Irish National Rebel Leader who led the rising of 1803,

was caught and hung for high treason

Prologue

May 5, 1981

Creighton University

Omaha, Nebraska

Frank McGrath's head pounded, it was so bad that even in his dreams his head ached. Then there was the rattle of the keys and he felt the excitement coming that he didn't need but couldn't avoid.

Eddie McMahon said, "Frank! Frank! Wake up, damn it! Are you awake?"

Frank McGrath rolled over in his dorm room bed and said, "Eddie, what the hell do you want?"

"Look at this!"

"Holy shit, its seven a.m. Eddie, we didn't get in until two."

"I know, I know, I feel like shit, too. But my dad called, Frank. Look at this."

Eddie opened the morning edition of the Omaha World Herald to the World News section and Frank squinted through the dirty, yellow light of their early morning dorm room and read, "BOBBY SANDS DEAD AFTER 66 DAYS." Frank sat up and felt real grief for only the second time in his life. His granddad had been killed four years before in a car accident in which Frank had been driving. The awful sick feeling he had when he woke in the ICU to the news of his granddad's demise, he thought it might never go away. He felt the same way now and without ever having met Sands, he felt as if he had just lost a close friend.

Frank and Eddie had been following the hunger strike of the Irish Republican prisoners in Long Kesh prison southwest of Belfast, since the prisoners had announced their plans in February.

They knew about the five demands of the prisoners and their request for political status versus criminal status and they had debated with other students throughout the early parts of the strike.

Frank said, "Do you think Thatcher is going to allow more prisoners to die?"

"Frank, my dad says the mistake the Republican prisoners are making is that they're assuming the Brits will place as much significance on a hunger strike as the Irish do."

"What do you mean?"

"He told me that in ancient Ireland under Brehon law. . ."

"Brehon law?"

"Yeah, ancient Irish law. Anyway, under Brehon law a hunger strike was a legal method of protest used by the poor."

"Like?"

"Let's say that a wealthy merchant cheats a poor guy out of some money."

"Yeah."

"The poor guy could go to the wealthy merchant's home or place of business and begin a hunger strike. If the wealthy merchant let the poor guy die, by Brehon law, the wealthy merchant had to take care of the poor guy's wife and kids. Most times the hunger strike was settled before anyone died. The Brits don't look at it like the Irish do and dad thinks this could get really ugly."

Frank lit a cigarette and said, "Eddie, your dad was right, they don't understand the Irish. Those fuckers let him die."

"And there are more behind him, Frank."

Frank put his head down and tears welled in his eyes and dropped to the tile of his dorm room floor. He missed his granddad more now than he had in the last four years since he died.

Frank was a senior in high school at the time of his granddad's death, and after a nasty confrontation with his father, Frank was forced to drive his eighty-three-year-old granddad, Liam O'Conlan, to his childhood home in eastern Iowa. Liam, wanting to put some demons down from a bit of a sordid past, needed a ride. It was eight hours there and eight hours back and Frank was a captive audience to a particularly talented Irish story teller who captured his mind and heart, someone who, in the old country, they would call a Seanachie.

As the journey was ending they were crossing the Missouri River Bridge that connected Iowa and Nebraska. The bridge became slick with ice and their car careened out of control and collided with a semi truck, killing Liam and sending Frank to the ICU.

Frank found himself going back to that period in his life often because of an odd occurrence that happened to him a month or so after he was released from the hospital. He still debated with himself as to whether it had been a dream or had actually happened.

One evening, after Frank had fallen asleep, he awoke suddenly from a nightmare, and there on his bed sat his granddad. The question was always the same. Had he still been dreaming or had his granddad come back from the grave as a ghost? It was so real. What was crazier than the ghost was the fact that Frank found himself witnessing his family's immigration from Ireland to American during the potato blight of 1846. So was it a journey or a great dream? Once again it was so real, and after some research, he found he knew more than he should've known, that no one ever taught him. He knew historical facts that no one in his family or in this world had ever told him before that night, that dream, that experience or whatever it was. The debate raged within him and he couldn't tell anyone, they would think he was crazy. Sometimes he thought of telling Eddie, but the time was never right.

As the spring of 1981 moved into the summer, one hunger striker after another was allowed to die until ten Irish Republican prisoners had been buried; all of them denied their lives and their political status. Frank felt a sense of despair and helplessness as the British Government, under the leadership of Margaret Thatcher, once again turned a blind eye to the plight of the Irish nation.

Eddie McMahon was studying for a pre-med degree and had just found out he had been accepted into Creighton's medical school. He had grown up in Butte, Montana and came from a long line of copper miners. They were Irish Republican supporters and Clan na Gael members, the Irish-American clan supporting the brotherhood in the fight for freedom in Ireland.

Eddie's father, Barry McMahon, had broken the family chain of miners by sneaking away to Creighton University and graduating with a business degree in 1958. Barry ran the Montana branch of the clan for many years until an Irish national upstart named Paddy Quinlan, who had immigrated to America and made it big in the ranching business, took over for him.

Eddie had every intention of graduating from medical school and heading back to Butte to practice his profession. But, in the meantime, he stayed close to his dad and the American clan's support of the fight in Northern Ireland.

In the summer of 1981, Eddie and Frank had rented a small apartment while bartending and waiting tables at Barrett's Barleycorn Irish Pub, the hunger strike and the political clime in Ireland being a key topic of conversation there. One evening Eddie walked in out of breath and said, "Where's Frank?"

Ruthie Barrett, the owner, said, "He's stocking the back bar, like you should be. Eddie McMahon, you're late as usual. Get clocked in we've got work to do. Its going to be busy tonight, damn it."

Eddie, ignoring his boss, walked back to Frank and said, "You're not going to believe this."

Frank looked up from the case of beer he had been stocking and said, "Believe what?"

"You and I are going to have company."

"Who?"

"Irish Twins."

Frank, used to puzzling together conversations with his best friend said, "Eddie, what're you talking about?"

Ruthie Barrett screamed, "Eddie, where are you?"

Eddie said, "Coming, Mrs. Barrett. Frank, you know how these hunger strikers have been dying in Long Kesh prison?"

"Yeah."

"Eddie McMahon, do you like working here?"

"Yes, Mrs. Barrett, I love working here. Anyway, I don't know all the details but one of these guys busted the other out of Long Kesh and they're now on the lamb."

Frank laughed and said, "On the lamb?"

"Yeah, fugitives, hiding from the law and they're heading to Omaha."

Frank, suddenly serious, said, "No shit?"

Eddie said, "No shit and dad wants me to put them up at our place and then drive them to Montana."

"Not without me you're not."

"You're going to have to take a semester off."

"And where's the problem?"

"Edward McMahon if you're not clocked-in in exactly three seconds you're fired!"

Eddie smiled, winked at Frank, and walked away.

Chapter 1
The Right Foot

1925 Upperchurch

County Tipperary, The Republic of Ireland

The cool night air blew in through the farmhouse window, it was empty except for a screaming woman in labor and the midwife helping her. The cool air felt good as the sweat ran down the woman's face.

In between contractions she said, "Oh my God I'm heartily sorry for having offended thee. . ."

Contraction, "Hail Mary full of Grace the Lord is with thee. . ." Contraction, "I Believe in God the Father thee Almighty Creator of heaven and earth. . ."

Time passed stubbornly and the pain swept through her body as if purging her of past iniquities. The midwife continually wiped her brow and whispered words of encouragement; she came from a long line of Druids, the earth her religion, nature her god and she never understood these foolish prayers.

Under her breath she said, "And they call what I do magik?"

The stubborn child in her womb, comfortable and content there, moved to the birth canal with the utmost reluctance. It fought like a Celtic warrior from ages past and wreaked carnage inch by inch until it acquiesced, like a prisoner of war brought into a cold hard world it did not recognize.

The midwife said, "You're ready darling, next time push."

She screamed, "St. Michael the Archangel defend us in battle, be our protection against the wickedness and snares of the devil!" And pushed like she was at war; the head began to crown a thick tuft of jet-black hair.

"It's on its way. That's it, there's a good girl."

The struggle was underway once more, but the woman lying in pain would not be turned away. The purple and bloody head witnessed the world for the first time. She pushed. "May God rebuke him we humbly pray!" The shoulders and arms slid forth. She pushed. "And do though oh Prince of the Heavenly hosts by the Divine power of God!" The belly slipped by. She pushed.

"Cast in to hell Satan and all the evil spirits who roam throughout the world seeking the ruin of souls. Amen!" The baby found itself in the arms of the midwife as she walked away shaking her head.

The mother said, "What's wrong?"

The midwife just shook her head again and cut the umbilical cord. She then held the child up and spanked it on his bum. The baby boy let out a scream that only a mother could love and she wanted to smile but the aftermath of the delivery was too painful.

The woman looked up from the bed, tears streaming down her face and said, "I asked what was wrong? How is he?"

The midwife said, "I'm so sorry darling. He's a club foot. He'll be nothing but a burden to you. Best to be rid of it now."

She set the baby in the dustbin and went to clean up the mother.

The baby cried out.

The woman looked at the midwife with stiletto eyes that would have slashed and wounded if she had her way and said, "What did you do? How dare you! Get away! Get away from me, now!"

The midwife was not to be pushed away so easily and said, "You're delirious, darling. Now you listen to me. I've delivered many a child and it's hard enough for the healthiest of them. It's for the best."

The woman pulled her nightdress down to cover herself, pushed the midwife aside, and said, "I don't care how many you've delivered, get out now!"

"Have it your way, lass. You'll regret it."

"You'll be the one to regret it. You'll rue the day you tossed away a Quinlan like so much garbage, now leave!"

The midwife shrugged as if she had just tossed scraps to the pigs and left the room.

The mother cried out again as overwhelming pain shot through her like stab wounds from the slightest movement. But she had to get to him. Pain be damned she scrambled from her bed, crawled to the dustbin, reached in and pulled the precious child from its heap and held it close. Instinct led the wee one to her breast, she reached up to the bed and grabbed a blanket to cover him and he was content once more.

She sat on the floor and rocked the child back and forth crying as he fed. She said, "As strong an appetite as you've got, of course you'll be a burden, but no more than any of the rest of them. She's a foolish old hag, I'll run her out of this village, I will."

Suddenly the pain seemed to vanish, like a wisp of steam over an early morning pond. She stared at the miracle she held and said, "It's not a club foot darling, it's the right foot. I think we'll call you Padraig. Yes, after our patron saint. People of little faith tried to kill him too. Padraig Vincent Quinlan, you'll do great things one day, lad. I'll see to that."

Chapter 2
The Walking Nun

1950 Ballycraig

County Kilkenny, The Republic of Ireland

Clare Eva White stopped for a moment. She had the gift. The intuition that the women of rural Ireland used just like they used sight, sound and smell. Since she was a little girl her mom told her to be aware of and nurture that intuition and she had. And it never failed her.

The October wind blew clean and cold around her but something wasn't right. She could feel it in her bones as sure as she could see the red and purple leaves that fluttered to the ground in front of her, as sure as she knew that pigs could see the wind. She remembered the village women working together to churn butter or sew patchwork quilts while the wee ones played nearby and listened. It was all too often that they would warn one another to keep on eye on the pigs; they could see the wind and any malevolence it brought with it. If they started to the barn for no reason, beware. Clare looked for the pigs and there were none to be seen. She whimpered and prayed, begging the Blessed Virgin to allow her to see the wind just this once. But she hesitated, if only for a moment, knowing certain if her prayer was answered what she would see there.

The feeling formed a black pit in her stomach and the evil seemed inexorable, like a single black crow on a gust, unable to stop itself. Clare moved once again, only her pace quickened and, with no little resolve, forced herself to stay calm. She wondered if the October temperature had just dropped ten degrees or if it was the chill of her inner senses, warning of an ill wind blowing in and harboring some unknown malice. All Clare had wanted was to get away from home, her endless chores and her mom's doting on her to frolic with her best friend, Cassie Kenny. Saturdays only came once a week, she thought, and she was out to make the best of it. But now the doubt was as real and menacing as a banshee screaming in the middle of the night. The chill forced her to fold her arms tighter in her sweater.

Rosemary Kenny came to the door and looked suspiciously at Clare as she did with all children.

Clare shrugged and said, "Hello, Mrs. Kenny, is Cassie about?"

With a note of frustration in her voice she said, "She disappeared an hour ago and I haven't seen her since. She's not finished her chores. When you see her, tell her I'm after finding her."

"Aye, ma'am, I will."

The two girls liked to play in the woods near the back road in Ballycraig, the road that the tinkers used. The Irish gypsies would travel it in their covered wagons peddling their trinkets, sharpening knives and mending pots or pans for cheap. The girls were fascinated and terrified by the traveling nomads. So they hid in the trees to watch as they passed.

Clare ran to the spot that they usually gathered in the woods when she heard a scream that sounded like Cassie. She then heard a man's voice, loud and booming. It hit her hard and her breath was taken from her as if someone had doused her with ice water. The voice spoke in Shelta, the language of the Irish travelers, and she wanted to vomit. Her intuition proved itself once again, and there would never again be even a shadow of a doubt about it.

Willing herself beyond her own fear she ran and by the time she reached the road, it was deserted except for the familiar jacket, which Cassie always wore, lying in the ditch. She looked around for a few seconds and was disoriented. She wanted to scream for help but knew no one would hear. Besides, she thought, there's no time. She looked down at the dusty road and saw the tracks of the tinker's covered wagon and she began to run. She ran for twenty minutes or so and just when she was ready to give up, thinking maybe she went the wrong way, she saw the small chimney on the tinker's wagon disappear around the bend in the road a half a mile ahead.

Clare ran harder now than she had ever run in her life. She knew in her heart that she could run forever if she had to. When she finally got close, she moved with stealth in the woods nearby.

The sun finally began to set in the west and the gypsy, traveling alone, made camp. She watched as he built a small fire, made some dinner and pulled on a jug of what she guessed was poteen, potato whisky. She began to wonder where Cassie was when he stood precariously and ambled to the back of the wagon. He stepped up and in and pulled Cassie out by the hair, bound and gagged. He dragged her near the fire, pulled her skirt up and began to pull her underwear off.

Clare's heart raced in her chest, trying to find the courage. Cassie, now half naked, defenseless and terrified, lay in the dirt by the fire. The man stood and began to unbuckle his trousers. Clare, feeling every bit as naked, walked slowly and quietly from the shadows and when Cassie looked over at her, with tears streaming down her face, Clare put her fingers to her lips to motion Cassie to lay quiet. Clare moved closer, the tinker's back to her, talking to himself and more intent on his prey than watching for intruders.

He dropped his pants and when they came to rest around his ankles Clare charged. Before he knew it ninety pounds of fury hit him sending him sprawling face first into his campfire. She landed on top of him and looked up at the iron skillet that had been resting on a grate above the fire, which now clanked near by spilling its contents. She grabbed for it. The tinker came up to his knees roaring with frustration and pain, trying to put out the fire in his hair and beard. He then grabbed Clare around the waste, howling a blood-curdling curse she couldn't understand, as the smell of burnt hair, flesh and whiskey sickened her. She wielded the skillet now firmly in her grip, the adrenaline keeping her from dropping it as her skin broiled and blister under the heat of the iron handle. She hit the man squarely across the face, knocking him back to the ground. She then turned it sideways as if to use it like a hatchet and before he could come to his senses she crashed it down once more upon his head, splitting it wide and sending his blood up her arm and on to her face.

She looked down at Cassie, who was now hysterical, and said, "Hush now, let's get you out of here."

She grabbed a sharp knife from the man's cooking gear, and as she cut loose the ties that bound Cassie, which became the ties that bind, which bound them forever and they ran away into the night.

* * *

Sister Maria St. John walked slowly through the tenebrous Irish countryside, carpet bag in hand, her pipe hanging from her lips, sending the sweet smell of pipe weed into the night air. She hummed ditties in between decades of her rosary as she went about her missionary work. She walked about her country visiting prisons, hospitals, homes as well as the marginalized tinkers who shared the road with her. Since she was a wee lass she had watched those travelers. She had watched as they wandered the highways and byways of Ireland, reading a palm or two, telling a fortune or just swindling whoever they might and occasionally showing up for Mass on Sunday.

As with most youngsters in rural Ireland she would watch them pass on their eternal road, but unlike her young friends who feared them she was infatuated with the Tinkers. She would spend hours assimilating their ways, even beginning to understand their secret language. She witnessed them as they set up along the road selling snake oils and health potions taking advantage of the naïve when it was to their advantage and then move on down that gypsy road of the outsider, unwelcome to stay too long.

Sister Maria St. John was an anomaly working among the often double-dealing nomads, but found their trust and respect as she spoke their language. She had been moved to work with them at the beginning of her vocation quite by accident. She simply went about making her calls on those left behind and ran into them as she walked about the country.

She walked along the road and heard the two frantic voices off in the distance. She walked, calmly waiting for them to come upon her, not wishing to startle them further if they were in trouble.

They walked arm in arm to support one another and when they saw the dark figure standing in the shadows up ahead they stopped. The nun looked at the girls, seeing them plainly in the light from the harvest moon.

Clare said, "And who are you?"

"Sister Maria St. John, I'm a Mercy nun."

Clare said, "What's a nun doing on the road at night?"

"I work with the travelers and this is where they roam."

Clare said, "Then go away and leave us be, we want nothing to do with them."

"With who?"

"Never mind, just leave us be."

The girls began to make their way to the woods and the nun, seeing the blood covering Clare, said, "No, wait. I can help. Please, give me a chance, you're hurt."

They stopped for a moment and gave the nun a chance to approach.

She said, "My God, lass, what has happened here?"

Cassie, now hysterical, ran into the nun's arms and said, "Oh, Sister."

Sister Maria hugged her tight and said, "What has happened?"

Clare said, "A tinker took Cassie and tied her up. I followed and after he had his supper and drank too much, he pulled her out of his wagon, hiked up her skirts and was ready to have his way."

She stopped briefly, sucking her breath through her teeth, and with an intense clarity the moment hit her, she dropped to her knees in anguish and said, "And I killed him. I killed a man, Sweet Lord Jaysus. He's dead and I killed him."

The nun gathered the two girls in her arms and gave what comfort she could then said, "He was by himself, then?"

Clare said, "Aye."

The nun said, "He's an odd one, 'tis rare they travel alone, but this one, I think I know who we're talking about here. Will you girls be okay, if I go up ahead and have a look?"

Cassie said, "No! Don't leave us, Sister."

Clare said, "Can we walk with you? We'll wait back, but we don't want to be alone."

The nun smiled gently and said, "That would be fine."

The fire sparked and cracked and sent daunting shadows dancing among the trees in the nearby wood. Cassie shivered as she sat close to the fire. Clare sat in her underwear with a blanket around her, her dress on a line tied to two trees over the fire to dry.When Sister Maria had made a fire, she took Clare to a nearby running brook to wash the blood from her arms, face and clothing.

Clare shivered and said, "Sister, our parents are going to worry and then they'll be furious."

The nun said, "Hush, drink your tea and don't worry about your parents. In a few hours your dress'll be dry and we can take you home. I'll explain everything and no one need be the wiser."

Two weeks later

McMahon's Pub
Ballycraig

Will White and Sean Kenny sat sharing a pint and small talk at the end of a long day in the peat fields.

Sean said, "Have you given much thought to where those two wild ones were off to that night?"

Will said, "My Clare can be as wild as a March hare, I don't think there's any stopping her."

"You know who that nun is?"

"Aye, she's the crazy one who works with the tinkers."

"Do you believe her story?"

"Are you serious? You think those two just fell asleep out there and she just happened upon them?"

"You heard about the dead tinker, then, on the back road?"

"I have."

"That was the same night."

"Aye."

"Do you think those two had anything to do with it?"

"I do."

"How?"

"The wife found a blood stain on Clare's undershirt."

"Is that so."

"'Tis. But it, as well as the dress, was burned."

"Why?"

"Even with a tinker, the peelers are sure to start nosing around. The lass can be mean as a hornet when provoked, Sean."

"I wonder what he was up to?"

Will thought back to the night a few days back when Clare had broken down and told her parents what had happened and what she had done when her mother questioned her about the bloodstain.

Kate White said, "Will, she needs to see a priest and a confessional. Killing's a mortal sin."

Will said, "There'll be no confessing anything. The man got exactly what he deserved, Clare saved Cassie's life. This matter is closed."

Will White looked carefully at his best friend and decided to leave it at that.

Chapter 3
The Hurling Midfielder

Nine Years later

Ballycraig, County Kilkenny, The Republic of Ireland

The spring of 1959 in southern Ireland was exceptional. It had been a long, cold, wet winter and spring fever was running high. It was no different in Ballycraig, a small village in county Kilkenny, The Republic of Ireland.

Clare Eva White had blossomed into a beautiful twenty-one year old woman. Her plans to follow Cassie Kenny, who had been gone for nearly three years now, had been foiled, as something always came up that kept her home.

Clare's mother doted on her. She had nearly died giving birth to her daughter and was left barren afterward. Clare was the rare only child and her mother was disinclined to let her go anywhere.

At dinner one night, Will White said, "We've a young new priest coming in a week."

His wife Katie said, "Now where did you hear that?"

"McMahon's pub Thursday last. Fr. O'Keefe, Ruari O'Keefe, fresh from the seminary in Maynooth."

Clare said, "Well, I'm sure Widow Buggy will be relieved. Old Father Egan quit showing up when she called for last rites. Now she'll have someone to give her the sacrament three times a week again."

Will looked at his daughter and said, "If I looked like Widow Buggy I'd be calling three times a week myself."

Kate White said, "You two should be ashamed of yourselves, standing in judgment over a poor lonely old soul like Genevieve Buggy."

Will said, "Lonely? What about Colm?"

Clare said, "That son of hers is worthless as a fiddle without strings. He should've taken the pledge years ago; instead he's a pickled old goat at fifty."

Will winked at them both and said, "I could think of worse things."

Clare was tired and out of sorts that Sunday morning. Life had become dull. The village held no excitement for her anymore. She had become fed up. Dublin was just over sixty kilometers away and she dreamed of it every night. Known as the alien port in Ireland, people from all walks of life and from all over the world lived there. Artists, poets, actors, musicians, writers, playwrights, the pubs, the theater, that was the life she wanted..

She was half-asleep during High Mass and paid little or no attention to the service or the new young priest saying Mass. She was daydreaming of a life far away and she was languid in her movement to the communion railing to receive the Holy Eucharist, as if some unknown power was holding her back, uninterested in any type of guilt and shame-ridden redemption.

"The Body of Christ."

"Amen."

"The Body of Christ."

"Amen."

The monotonous drone made her crazy. When at last she had made her way to the communion rail, she knelt down and pulled the communion clothe that stretched the length of the railing to below her chin, the church's way of ensuring that the host did not fall. The second line of defense was the altar boy who held the gold paten below the hand of the priest that held the Body of Christ.

The young priest looked at her and said, "The Body of Christ."

His eyes, the color of gunmetal, held her gaze. They were penetrating and knowing, as if they saw things mere mortals did not.

She said, "Amen." And thought, isn't that how it always works? The best-looking man in the village is a Catholic Priest.

In the church vestibule after Mass, young Father Ruari O'Keefe stood shaking hands with all the parishioners.

"Welcome Father, nice sermon."

"Thank you."

"You're a breath of fresh air, you are, Father."

"Thank you."

"Don't worry about falling on your way to the altar, Father, first day on the job nerves. Welcome."

"Thank you."

When it was Will White's turn he said, "Hello Father. The name's William White, but you can call me Will."

"Nice to meet you, Will."

"Likewise Father, and this is me wife Kate."

"Pleased to meet you, Father. Would you join us for supper on this beautiful Sunday?"

Startled at the sudden invitation he said, "That would be grand."

Will then said, "And this is me daughter, Clare Eva."

Clare's short blond hair blew in the wind and she smiled as she reached for Ruari's hand and said, "Welcome to Ballycraig, Father. I'm sure you're overjoyed to be here."

Kate said, "Clare Eva White, what kind of smart thing is that to say to our new Father?"

Father Ruari O'Keefe laughed and said, "Don't worry Mrs. White, I've been in far worse places than Ballycraig and I'm finding that the view here is quite remarkable at times."

Clare was about to ask what he meant by that when his statement registered in her mind. She stared at him a bit bemused; convinced she saw a glint in his eye, however slight.

"Thank you for the invitation to dinner. What time should you expect me?"

Kate said, "4:00 should do it, Father."

Ruari O'Keefe was finally back in the sacristy giving the altar boys last minute instruction on how he wanted things cleaned up after Mass. He removed his garments and hung them up. He stood in front of the mirror, which hung above the washbowl. He rinsed his hands and face and toweled them off.

The late morning light began to shift and his shadow grew longer. He looked into the mirror, only this time he saw the old demon rising again. In his youth he knew the minute he stepped into the sacristy as an altar boy that he wanted to be a priest. The smells of burning bee's wax, incense, altar wine and the great quiet calm that the church held were all a source of comfort to him. He knew.

As he grew into a young man his athletic prowess became increasingly more apparent, hurling, Gaelic football and rugby. He loved the competition, the physical contact, and he was good.

Hurling became his true love. He started playing on the local clubs in and around Derry, in the Bogside neighborhood where he grew up. Word spread about this kid who was one hell of a midfielder. Scouts came around and pretty soon Ruari found himself playing for the Irish National Hurling Team with lads from Kilkenny and Tipperary, where the sport was huge. He became known as old number nine and the press loved him.

Ruari's thoughts of the ascetic life the church had to offer began to fade as the adulation of the women in the pubs increased, more and more finding himself hung over and in a strange woman's bed. A further distraction was his seeming inability to stop. As his reputation grew so did the demand for his time and attention. The word "no" had never registered with Ruari so it was night after night in the pubs and morning after morning of growing despair and regret.

"Father?"

Coming out of his thoughts Ruari turned around and one of the altar boys was standing in front of him.

He said, "Sorry to interrupt, but I forgot me cap and me mum will be after me if I show up without it."

Ruari smiled with relief and said, "That's a good lad."

As the young altar boy walked out of the sacristy Ruari winced remembering back on the night his life had changed. He had been spinning out of control for a while and he figured he had had it coming. The punch came out of nowhere, but it was only the pebble that started the avalanche. When Ruari pulled himself off the floor, he flew into a rage that hurling circles would talk about for years. He had been pursuing the favors of a married woman when her jealous husband had had enough and hit him.

He woke up on the floor of a crowded jail cell with handcuffs holding him behind his back. When he looked up he saw a familiar, if not somewhat welcome, sight. The prison chaplain, Father Byrne, a priest Ruari knew in his youth, had come to bail him out.

He said, "Well, if you aren't a sight."

Ruari winced as he tried to smile. He looked at the priest through swollen and black eyes said, "Aye, had a bit of a row last night."

"A bit of? You made the papers."

"I've what?"

"Aye, when a celebrity makes trouble it makes the papers."

"Celebrity my arse."

"So they've given you the boot, eh?"

"Who has?"

"The National Hurling Team."

"What? For a little row?"

"You don't remember do you? It was hardly a little row."

"What do you mean? The guy hit me first."

"That may be, but according to eyewitness reports in the paper you flew into a maniacal rage."

"So what? I've seen other players get mad."

"Well, then maybe it was because you put three men in the hospital, or maybe when you broke the Peeler's jaw."

"I broke a peeler's jaw? Jaysus."

"Or maybe when you ripped the dress off the lady and pulled her bloomers down around her ankles. Or could it have been when you jumped up and decided to relieve yourself on the bar."

"No," He groaned. "No I didn't."

"Or, according to the paper, you single-handedly broke every table and chair in the pub as the local law enforcement closed in to take you away. And you pulled this whopper off in your birthday suit."

"Nude?"

"Nude."

"Bullshit."

"Why do you think you're the only one in this cell on the floor and handcuffed?"

"Where'd the clothes come from, then?"

"When they brought you in, kicking and screaming, mind you, they called me in. Once you passed out we took off the cuffs and dressed you. I told them they didn't need to re-apply the cuffs, but the bleeding and bruised officers of the law disagreed."

Ruari sat up with his back to the chaplain and said, "Lord have mercy."

At dinner that afternoon, Ruari found himself mounting with distraction and discomfort. He couldn't keep his eyes off Clare. Unable to put a firm finger on it, he surmised that she was taunting him. Whether intentional or not, he couldn't tell, but she seemed to sense his difficulty and was enjoying it.

The months following his explosion in the pub and his expulsion from the Irish National Hurling Team were dark and lonely times. The calls ceased and it seemed to him that he had been left behind, that his fifteen minutes of fame were up.

For the first time in his life he was directionless. He never fathomed that the competition would stop and when it did so abruptly it left a gaping black hole in his life, a void that he could not fill. Next to a bottle, fear, anxiety and despair were his only mates, which led to more drinking to ease the pain and the spiral downward began.

He became reclusive, rarely leaving his flat, except for the fifth of Paddy's, cigarettes or a few groceries, living on a dwindling pension from his playing days.

A knock came on the door. It startled Ruari. He took a pull from his bottle and said, "You've got the wrong door, go away."

The reply from the hall came, "I'll knock it down before I go away."

Ruari said, "Well fucksake." He stood and went to the door more out of curiosity than anything. Standing there in the hall was Fr. Byrne.

He said, "Lord have mercy, Ruari. You look worse than the night I found you on the floor of the pokey."

Ruari said, "Jaysus Father, it's good to see you too."

Father Byrne said, “Well, would you like to come out into the hall to have this conversation or would it be better to invite me in?”

Ruari said, “Och Father, can’t you see I want to be left alone?”

“Sure enough, lad. But left to your own devises I suppose you’ll be dead in a month.”

“And a right better world it would be.”

“Quit feeling sorry for yourself and let me in.”

They walked into the filth of a man who had lost hope or the prospect of ever finding any.

“Do you have a clean jar? I’d like to share a sip of your whiskey.”

“Aye.”

The priest glanced around at the misery that had wrapped its insidious cold and lifeless arms around this place, this life.

He said, “I’ve come to see you at the request of others and not a minute too soon, I might add.”

“I’m doing just fine.”

“Yes, like a fox in a trapper’s snare, you are. What’ll you do for an encore? Chew your own leg off?”

“Father, what do you want from me? I’m in no mood for a lecture.”

“I’ve got a job opportunity for you.”

“Oh, I see. The great Catholic priest comes to save a poor fucking soul. I’m not interested.”

“Knock it off. I baptized you, watched you grow up and watched as you enjoyed grand success. You’re a talented man with a lot to offer the world and the first time adversity plays a part you run like a coward. Are you a coward?”

“You know better.”

“Do I? You seem to be fooling a lot of people. And I, for one, won’t stand by and watch you throw it all away.”

The priest shot the whiskey in the jar down with one gulp and said, “The mercy nuns have an opening for a janitor.”

“Jaysus father, are you serious?”

“Yes. They’ll feed you, give you a room and pay you a fair wage. A lad could do worse.”

“He could?”

Ruari smiled at the memory. At the time he was forced to comply, he was like a mule forcing his hooves into the dirt as they drug him into the place. After eighteen months, though, the calming effect of the serene bastion of nuns took hold of him. He somehow exorcised the demons that haunted his past and after two years, cloistered in the convent, he applied for the seminary in Maynooth and, with a letter of recommendation from Fr. Byrne, was accepted.

As years passed in the seminary, Ruari knew that he had made the right decision. He loved it at Maynooth and looked forward to his ordination and his first parish assignment. However, like all men of flesh and blood, he had his physical struggles. Celibacy and sobriety were not his least bane and yet somehow, so far, he had managed to overcome his temptations. That was before he met Clare White.

Chapter 4
The Delusion

Clare lay in bed that night, after dinner with Ruari, tossing and turning. She kept seeing those piercing blue grey eyes, that strong jaw, the bald pate that looked good on so few men but perfect on him, and she kept hearing his soft voice that felt like a soft quilt fluttering down on her. What was it about him that was inescapably drawing her?

Once Ruari had left their home after dinner, Clare's father pulled out an old newspaper and said, "I knew it."

Kate said, "Knew what Will White?"

He said, "It's him. The infamous hurling bad boy, I knew the name sounded familiar when I heard he was coming and then I saw him and knew it had to be him. He ran into a bit of trouble one night in a pub and that was the last we heard about him…until now."

Clare said, "Da, what are you on about?"

He handed her the newspaper and she read the article of Ruari's last public drunken escapade from beginning to end. The hurling hero's final fall from grace and this man was now in their village. She could think of nothing else for the rest of the evening.

She wrestled with her covers and punched her pillow now for the eighth time, unable to get his face out of her mind's eye. Bad boy made good? Bullshit, she thought, he's hiding here from his past.

Whatever it was, just the thought of the man created a desire in her that made Clare feel like she had lost the control she had always cherished.

These were uncertain feelings for a woman like Clare White, who spent her life trying to control her circumstances. She was quite certain that she would choose her partner, she would make the decision, and then she'd wear the pants. Now it seemed to have been made for her, but it was all wrong. Just the thoughts were ignominious, unforgivable, and dangerously wrong.

And yet, she thought, as she stretched in a long luxurious motion while gently touching herself, it was deliciously right. She smiled demurely and rolled over, back in control, or so her delusion went.

* * *

Ruari O'Keefe was restless. It was the reason he was drawn to sport of any kind at such an early age. Coupled with a natural physical and athletic prowess and you had your recipe for a national sports hero. But the restlessness also created his demons, highlighted his personal weakness and brought with it the occasional bouts with despair.

Since getting sober and finding his way to the seminary, his way of overcoming these overwhelming character defects was still the physical activity he sought in his youth. It was familiar, he did it with ease, and it took his mind away from the illicit company he kept while idle.

He would do calisthenics, go for a run, coach the local hurling team, and on more than one Saturday afternoon, he could be found in the peat bogs working up a lather with the local lads.

But as was the case with bachelorhood there was the inevitable time alone where he simply could not get away from himself. And, as if he did not have enough personal ill wind blowing in his mind, now there was Miss Clare White haunting his every thought.

Ruari felt as if he were hanging off a shear cliff holding on with one hand, and she, that rarest of gems sparkling radiantly and resting on the ledge up above. To reach for her meant to fall into that deep, dark cavern below, not unfamiliar territory for this priest. He smiled, sweat dripping off his nose as he ran through the beautiful countryside, seemingly away from this hell recently created, when in actuality he had lost his sense of direction and was unknowingly heading directly to its gates.

After seeing Clare that Sunday afternoon, Ruari O'Keefe's hours, days and weeks began to elapse like viscous, arthritic old limbs moving uphill in painful slow motion.

Sleep came in fits and starts and never in eight, or even six-hour increments, staring out his bedroom window night after lonely night at the quarter, half and then full moon. Sweating as the lust consumed him, the burden of his cross, onerous at times and utterly intolerable at others, dropping him to his weary knees.

On the other side of the village, Clare's thoughts were much the same. More, her thoughts were preposterous; he was a Catholic priest after all. She moved from project to project in an effort to keep her mind from her hell. Careful in her movements around the village, feeling out of harm's way in facing this man only in the safety of Mass, a place she no longer loathed. Even there she found her mind in the bed of the man on the altar and it was good.

Clare knew she couldn't live like this for long. If she stayed in Ballycraig there would be trouble. She contacted Cassie Kenny and made plans to go. Her mother would just have to learn to adjust without her.

Around the dinner table one evening, Clare said, “I’ve decided to move to Dublin and make me way in the world. There’s nothing for me here, no future. Cassie Kenny has an apartment there and has invited me to come.”

Kate said, “What would you do? And that McCaslin Kenny is a wild one, smoking at eight, drinking at twelve and chasing the lads around all the time. What did we ever do to deserve this sudden change?”

“Oh Ma’am, you did nothing. But you’ve known how unhappy I am. You both are always on about my finding a husband and I won’t be finding one here. It’d be different if I had a man, but I don’t. It’s a sad state of affairs when the best looking man in the parish is a bloody priest.”

The house went quiet and Will said, “If you must you must. But you won’t be going until you’ve secured work.”

“So, just like that is it?”

“She’s a grown woman and she’s right when she says she has no future here,” Said Will

“And what about us, William Joseph White?”

“Woman, you knew this day would come.”

Katie went to her bedroom, shut her door, worked on her quilt and wept.

Clare said, “Da.”

Will said, “Shush. Jack Tobin is a friend from Dublin. He runs an Inn there on Baggot Street. I’ll send word. In the meantime get a hold of Cassie and make sure she’s serious.”

A month later Clare White was on her way to a new life in Dublin and running hard from a life she could never escape. As she was soon to find out, she could never move far enough to get away from herself.

Chapter 5
The Poem not The Pike

Mid June, 1959

Belfast, Northern Ireland

Sean O'Kane sat in The Shamrock pub on the corner of Flax and Ardoyne streets in the Ardoyne neighborhood of Belfast. He was a barstool volunteer, a Patriot in voice only. He was thirty-years-old, lived at home with his mother and worked at The Andersontown News, a paper that reported the Nationalist news. His father, Bobby O'Kane, on the other hand, couldn't have been more different than his son. In 1929, the year Sean was born, his father Bobby was arrested for Irish Republican Brotherhood activity, a precursor to the Irish Republican Army. He was an anti-treaty Republican wanting Great Britain out of Ireland altogether. At the time, he and his wife were living outside Dublin, and Bobby was sentenced without trial and sent to Dublin's Mountjoy prison on criminal status. Bobby, with permission from the IRA command, went on a hunger strike for political status. After thirty-six days he quit taking water as well and was dead after thirty-eight days.

Sean's mother moved them back to her hometown of Belfast and it became the only home he would ever know. Being a Catholic in Belfast during the first half of the twentieth century, Sean became all too familiar with hatred. As he grew up, he never understood why his mother would want to move back to Northern Ireland. The treaty of 1921 partitioned just six of the nine counties that made up the province of Ulster, gerrymandering the six made up of a majority Loyalist Protestants who wanted British rule. These were the people in Northern Ireland who controlled the wealth, the government, the factories, the unions and businesses and, as a result, the Catholic Nationalists were left unemployed, harassed and hated. He came to understand why his father died the way he did.

Sean and his mother moved into one rented flat after another, only to be forced out repeatedly by unfair discrimination practices, intimidation and scare tactics. Whenever they tried to take a stand their lives were threatened, a promise typically kept, so they would move once more.

They finally, depending on how one defines luck, found a flat in an area of Belfast called The Short Strand, a fenced-in ghetto containing no more than fourteen or so blocks, where three thousand Catholics lived in an island surrounded by ninety thousand or so Orange Protestants, loyal to the Crown of England. There were enough Catholics to at least feel a level of comfort most of the year, but in July and August, during the Orange marching season, protecting themselves from Orange harassment and hatred was another story.

But unlike his compatriots, who raged with hatred and the fight, Sean O'Kane was more reserved. He turned to the pen and away from the pike, preferring to write than fight. Along with his job as a reporter, he also wrote for a local underground Republican publication called *An Phoblacht* and was a student of poetry.

Sean knew, first hand, why his comrades hated the Protestant Loyalists. In July and August, the Orange Lodges emptied every year, as the Irish Protestants celebrated the victory of the Battle of the Boyne, when the English and Protestant King William of the Orange was victorious over the English and Catholic King James on the Irish River Boyne.

They would march proudly through Catholic neighborhoods, harassing the inhabitants, and the Short Strand, year in and year out, received the worst of the flogging. They heaved pipe bombs and Molotov cocktails at the small bungalows that lined the streets of the Short Strand, and the fire would illuminate the night. Sean would staff one of the fire hydrants in anticipation of the nightly attacks, spraying water on homes that would have otherwise burnt to the ground. The Royal Ulster Constabulary, the Northern Ireland Police force, stood watch to keep the peace, allowing the Loyalists to break their ranks, heave bombs and then retreat, undeterred to their parade. When the Catholics retaliated in any fashion, they were cut down with plastic bullets that were supposed to be less lethal than metal ones. Right, Sean thought, shaking his head at the memories, wondering what they would think if they got hit by one.

One of the great sacrifices that befell the residents of the Short Strand during the late summer marching season, young and old, sick and healthy, strong and weak, was that they were cut off from supermarkets, all health services, the post office and other critical portals of society necessary for well being. These services were all located on the Loyalists side of Albertbridge road, and to access them was to put one's life in harm's way.

Sean spent much of his time in quiet contemplation; soul-searching life's deeper meaning. Known in the pubs as a philosopher and Seanachie, not a fighter, he was legitimate in the brotherhood's eyes, and not just because his dad had been martyred for the cause. Year in and year out he would entertain and educate crowds with stories of martyrs past, Irish history and the occasional poem, both his and others. With each fresh pint his voice would rise an octave and the more outlandish the stories would come, the crowds roaring with laughter.

One night while the pub was quiet, Sean sat by himself nursing his pint and chasing it with a shot of Irish. When the alcohol met its mark, as was usual, he cursed himself for not having the courage to join the fight, never accepting that he showed as much courage by speaking out against the injustices in Northern Ireland through his writing, and then allowing his byline in the underground paper.

The injustice was a constant companion for a Catholic in Belfast, and his thoughts were never far from the brotherhood. He loved them and envied their courage. What bothered him most was that many of the volunteers were also writers, especially the men who rose up that Easter week of 1916, they called themselves poet patriots. So wasn't he?

He just knew that he hated the violence and maybe there was a better way. He thought, "Why couldn't the Protestants and Catholics live in peace and solidarity? One Ireland."

His long-time, off-and-on-again girlfriend, Patricia Brennan, interrupted his thoughts.

Patricia said, "Sean O'Kane, what are you doing here sitting all by yourself?"

Embarrassed and at a loss for words he said, "Patricia, I wasn't expecting you, lass."

"That's the problem, Sean O'Kane, you're never expecting me."

"That's not fair darling. I was just lost in me thoughts, that's all. Plus I never know when your brother is going to have you out doing something for the IRA."

Patricia and her brother Dermot were members of the IRA, neither a novice to violence or street fighting.

"You're a dreamer, Sean, always lost in there somewhere. Would you mind taking a booth with me in the back?"

Sean looked up at the burly owner of The Shamrock pub, Hugh Reilly, who was smiling mischievously at him. Reilly jerked his head toward the booths in the back and said, "Ms. Brennan, what can I get you?"

"Whiskey neat, Hugh. Thank you."

Sean put money on the bar to pay for the drink and carried them to privacy in the back.

Patricia said, "How long have we been seeing each other?"

Sean said, "Four years this October 12th."

"My God, you know the date?"

"Aye, it was one of the great moments of my life."

She blushed and looked up as the old wall clock delivered the seven o'clock hour. The pub began to fill.

She said, "So, what are your plans?"

"What do you mean, lass?"

"I mean that we're getting no younger, Sean O'Kane, and I'm done waiting."

"Done waiting for what?"

"Do I have to spell it out for you, Sean?"

"Spell what out?"

"Are you daft, man?"

"Where's this going?"

"My God, I love you, can't you see that? I want to spend the rest of my life with you. I want babies running around my house. I want a family and I want it with you, lad. But I'm not going to stand by and watch as you waste your life away on a pub stool. Do you love me?"

"Of course I do, Patricia. But how do I know when you go out on one of your runs that you're coming back?"

Ignoring him she said, "Then say it."

"Say what?"

She said, "Can't you, for once in your goddamn life, tell me that you love me. Tell me that you want me."

"I want you."

"Not like that, Lad."

She lowered her voice and whispered, "Like you want to take me away and, and. . ."

He cut her off and said, "I'm serious, you've done enough for the brotherhood. I don't want to wake up a widower or have our kids wake up motherless someday because some Orange bastard shot you dead in a street fight."

"Are you saying you want to marry me?"

"You're a true fucking romantic."

She laughed and said, "I'll back off a bit. We can be a safehouse for the lads and you can still write, that'll satisfy me for a while."

He said, "I love you."

She stopped and looked at him. She would remember this moment for the rest of her life. He had never said it before and she knew he wouldn't say it until he was ready to take her up the isle and make it permanent.

He pulled out a key and hung it in front of her. She said, "What's that?"

"The key to our new flat."

"What?"

"You know the one we'll live in after we're married." He pulled a chip of a diamond ring out of his jacket pocket and said, "It's as much as a newspaperman can afford. But will you marry me, Patricia?"

She spilled their drinks reaching over the table to kiss her man, sat back down laughing and looking at the ring. She said, "It's the most beautiful thing I've ever seen."

Chapter 6
The Mullen House

1945 Butte, Montana

Paddy Quinlan walked off the train onto the platform of the Anaconda, Butte & Pacific Railway station, which sat on the corner of 3rd street and Utah Avenue in Butte.

Except for those picking up passengers, the area was quiet on this Sunday morning. Church bells called out to local sinners, but the sound was not the clean clear ring one would expect in a mountainous region. Instead, it sounded to Paddy like it was muted, as if the sound waves struggled against the filthy pall aborted by the copper smelters throughout town.

As Paddy stood on the platform he felt a heaviness, maybe a weariness come over him and his first thought was to get back on the train and leave. A genuine sadness seemed to hang over this town like a damp, musty, old quilt smothering the light and life out of everything.

His eyes burned and he became short of breath and he suddenly had an overwhelming desire to be back home in Ireland. To say that, in his heart, he knew he had made a big mistake by coming here was like saying to the drowning man he shouldn't have gone for that swim. He didn't care that it was Sunday morning, he needed a drink.

A man named George O'Halloran approached Paddy as he stood on the train platform and said, "Paddy Quinlan?"

"Aye. And how would you know to ask that?"

"Part Druid Seer and part Leprechaun, I guess. Welcome to beautiful Butte, Montana."

"I guess it's all in how you interpret that."

"Barry McMahon sent me to help you get settled in."

"Barry McMahon?"

"Aye, a friend of your brother."

"Thank you, I appreciate that."

"Where you from, Paddy?"

"Upperchurch, Tipperary."

"We won't hold that against you."

"You said we, you got a friend somewhere I can't see?"

O'Halloran laughed and said, "No, I meant that most of us are from Cork, miners from Castletownbere, at least at The Mullen House."

"The Mullen House?"

"Aye, it's a boarding house up in Centerville for single men like us, run by Nonie Harrington. It comes highly recommended, by Barry McMahon, if you take my meaning."

"Aye, I do. What's Centerville?"

"Just the name of an area in town full of Irish miners."

The two men jumped into a new 1945 Ford pick up truck with the Anaconda mining company logo on the door. As they drove north up Utah Ave Paddy said, "So, is Anaconda Mining who I'm going to work for?"

George laughed and said, "It's the only one left."

Paddy said, "How can you stand this?"

"Stand what?"

"Are you serious?"

George raised his left eyebrow and stared at his new companion.

"The air? The smell? It's horrible. I'm not sure I'm staying."

"Oh, that. You'll get used to it. Plus there are a lot of us and that seems to help."

"Us?"

"Yeah, you know, Irish."

"Makes me wonder how bright we really are."

"Listen, lad. Most of us grew up miners in Castletownbere back home. We're familiar with the work and the money is much better than back home."

Paddy stared ahead and as they moved further north his heart sunk further south. He noticed that the streets running perpendicular to Utah Avenue were named after minerals and metals, Iron, Aluminum, Platinum, Silver, Gold and Porphyry streets.

Paddy said, "Porphyry? Wasn't he a Greek philosopher?"

George said, "What?"

"Yeah, I'd bet on it."

"I don't know about that. But around here it's a mineral they pull out of the ground."

"Is it purple?"

"Huh?"

"Never mind."

"Whatever you say."

When Utah Avenue met Mercury Street they took a left and headed west to Main Street where they took a right and headed North once more up a steep incline.

Paddy said, "How the hell do you get up this street in the winter?"

George simply said, "Sometimes we don't."

The mineral and metal streets stopped for three or four blocks when Paddy noticed that they started up again as the automatic engine bore down to make the steep grade, Quartz, Copper and Granite streets.

Paddy said, “I was wondering when I’d see Copper.”

George said, “Huh?”

Paddy said, “Jaysus, man. The street, Copper Street.”

George said, “Oh.”

Centerville was a section of town that rose up North of Butte overlooking the Butte valley below. The area was mostly made up of the poorer shanty Irish who dreamed of one day crossing the Missoula Gulch on to the West Side to build a Victorian home and be revered by their neighbors. Homes in Centerville and Dublin Gulch were built anywhere they could find room; the only city planning consideration seemed to be that they were close to the mines. All of the miners trudged off on foot to the filth, the danger and the heat of the deep, damp mines run by the Anaconda mining company.

George pulled the truck off Main Street onto Mullin Street, stopped, and said, “There she is.”

Paddy said, “Who?” Looking around with question.

George said, “The Mullen House.”

“Oh yeah, right.”

“Head on in and ask for Nonie Harrington. I’ll park out back and meet you inside.”

“All right then.”

He opened the door to the truck, got out, grabbed his bag from the truck bed, and waited for George to move the vehicle.

As he drove away, Paddy said, “I hope the rest of the lads from Castletownbere are brighter than that idiot.”

Paddy studied the front of the building, a three-story red brick structure that was originally The Union Hotel. Paddy walked up cement steps cut between a thick cobblestone retaining wall. A single large black crow sat upon the rain gutter of the boarding house and cawed odiously at him as he walked up. Paddy picked up an errant rock and tossed it at him and watched as he flew away unconcerned.

The porch stretched the entire front of the now boarding house with four large pillars holding up the heavy awning. They stood straight and strong like four sentries staring into the valley below while guarding the entrance.

He walked into the prodigious lodgings and found a large, ornate front desk made of some sort of dark, polished wood, watching over the foyer. The square mailboxes on the wall to its rear were numbered and held keys, notes and letters for boarders. No one was behind the desk and so he walked to the rear of the entrance and looked left into a long wide dining room filled with miners eating or waiting to do so. To the rear of the room was a swinging door that he surmised was the kitchen, as waitresses moved in and out carrying trays of what looked like both breakfast and supper dishes and that, he thought, was odd.

To his right was a great room filled with comfortable chairs, couches and coffee tables. A simple crystal chandelier hung from the center of the room and a stand up piano stood as if smiling with old yellow teeth at the far end of the room.

Drawn to the great room and knowing no one in the busy dining room, he felt uncomfortable in the foyer as if he stood in a stranger's home before they knew he was there. So he entered the great room and an immediate comfort descended on him as he sat in one of the lounge chairs. That was when he noticed the formal staircase ascending from the great room to the rooms on the second and third landings.

He was settling in when he heard, "May I help you?"

He quickly looked up and before him stood a plump, fair-skinned woman, with long thick dark hair pulled back in a tight bun, drying her hands on an apron that covered her white linen blouse and floor length skirt. The smatterings of flour in her hair and on her cheeks and the wonderful aromas wafting in behind her reminded Paddy of his own mother on a typical Saturday afternoon back home. Her sparkling blue eyes danced and her rosy cheeks spoke volumes.

Before Paddy got a chance to say anything George O'Halloran walked in and said, "Good afternoon, Mrs. Harrington. My friend here needs a room."

Nonie Harrington looked at Paddy and said. "And who might that be?"

Paddy reached out his hand and said, "Paddy Quinlan, ma'am."

"Where abouts are you from, Mr. Paddy Quinlan?"

"Ireland."

Her infectious laugh filled the room and said, "Ask a stupid question. Where in Ireland?"

"Upperchurch."

"Ah, County Tipperary. Well, I won't hold that against you."

"Aye ma'am, that seems to be the general consensus around here."

"Lot of Cork people, Mr. Quinlan, and maybe a bit too proud of it. Quinlan, huh?"

"Aye, ma'am."

"You're not related to that rascal Dinty Quinlan?"

"Aye ma'am."

"Well, I won't hold that against you either, but how?"

"Dinty's me older brother."

"Strong family resemblance."

"That's what they say."

"Can you tell a story like him?"

"No, ma'am, I'm no Seanachie. I love the history but storytelling's not one of me strong suits."

"Well, that's a shame. That Dinty can hold an audience. So you need a room?"

"Aye."

"Thirty-five dollars a month. Includes room with breakfast and supper, paid in advance. Third meals are available to go for two bits a day, give me notice after supper, times depend on your shift."

"That's why some of the lads are eating supper and some breakfast."

"Very astute, Mr. Quinlan." Nonie said, tongue in cheek. "We've got two hundred and forty seven rooms at The Mullen house and we need every one of them. My kitchen is open twenty-four hours a day, seven days a week, three hundred and sixty five days a year. Those smelters are going the same and we need to take care of the lads as they come in off three eight-hour shifts."

Paddy said, "Aye, it seems to be a busy place."

Three men walked in singing songs and seemed to be having an exceptionally good time.

Paddy smiled at them and said, "Well, thank you ma'am for the hospitality and it was nice to meet you."

Nonie looked at George and said, "And the lad has manners to boot."

She smiled and walked back into her kitchen.

Paddy checked into room number twelve, the corner room on the second floor, vacated recently. Entering he saw a window to the west and another to the north overlooking Wells Street to the back, a bed, a small desk and a crucifix hung on the wall. He sat on the side of the bed and stared out the window at a landscape of A-shaped head frames delivering miners to and from the mines below as well as smelters spewing the yellow and black filth into a neon orange sky. His heart sunk and he wondered not for the last time whether he had made the biggest mistake of his life. He pulled out pen and paper and decided to send Dinty a note to let him know he had arrived in Butte, Montana.

In the meantime, George O'Halloran walked into The Finlan Hotel where O'Flaherty's pub was lively on this Sunday afternoon as miners on different shifts imbibed at different times. The morning shift had been there about an hour and it was starting to get loud.

Woody Costello was bartending when George walked in. Woody said, "What'll it be, Georgy lad?"

"Beer, Woodman. Hey, I'm looking for McMahon, you seen him?"

"Upstairs with the boys."

"Thanks." George threw two bits on the bar.

Barry McMahon sat with his feet square on the ground. Out of the corner of his mouth he ground a cigar stub between his molars. He was staring with nonchalance at the queens over sevens that made up the full house in his poker hand. The deadpan look on his face gave no indication of the power he wielded over the large ante laying at the center of the round table.

George walked with hesitation.

McMahon threw in a chip and said, "Raise, five dollars."

All the men around the table dropped their hands, surrendering another portion of last week's salary. No grumbling – McMahon would not allow it.

As he pulled his winnings toward himself, he said, "Gentlemen, it's been a pleasure."

He was getting ready to depart when George said, "Excuse me, Mr. McMahon, but Mr. Quinlan is set at The Mullen House."

Barry McMahon looked up and said, "And you're going to take him to the mines tomorrow and get him on?"

"Aye."

"That's a good lad."

McMahon stuffed a five-dollar bill in O'Halloran's shirt pocket and walked out.

Chapter 7
Clan Na Gael

Butte, Montana

The American Clan

Four days later

The sun settled behind the yellow haze and created a neon sunset. After washing up and eating dinner, Paddy, who had just finished his third day in the copper mine, sat on a rocking chair that rested on the porch in the front of The Mullen House. He sat and spit into a brass spittoon in between his boots from a plug of chewing tobacco and rubbed his sore muscles, bemoaning his tight lower back, he had somehow talked himself into a better attitude toward his recent plight. He was, after all, glad to have work and knew it was no more than a stepping stone to a better place. To keep his mind busy he continually visited with boarders as they moved in and out of the house.

Paddy yawned and looked forward to a good night sleep when a stranger walked up and said, "Come with me."

"And you would be?"

"Mr. McMahon sent me to fetch you."

Paddy stood and said, "Interesting."

Barry McMahon lived in a beautiful new ranch style home five miles outside of Butte. The house sat on ten acres of land in a valley and was surrounded by Aspen, White Pine and Oak trees. Barry McMahon was a private man whose house was a safe haven for Irish brothers on the run. He did not want nosy people sniffing around his private business.

The McMahons had a brood of children. His bank financed much of the industry in Butte and the fact that his friendship with Marcus Daily, owner of the largest and only copper mine still running Butte, was a big part of that, was not lost on him.

He sat at the head of a long dark hickory table in a large finished basement. Wet bar, one piece slate pool table, a dart board and poker table filled the room with the play things of men. Ten well dressed men sat at the table with McMahon smoking while nursing whiskeys.

The men who had escorted Paddy Quinlan into the large home disappeared and he stood there uncomfortably for a minute or so, then he smiled.

McMahon said, “Have a seat, lad.”

Paddy sat down and stared at each man at the table individually while they stared back. He smiled again in spite of himself and said, “What’s with all the formality and the last minute notice? I’m just a working stiff, nothing more. Well maybe a little more stiff these days.”

McMahon said, “We don’t know you and we have to be careful.”

“Well, that goes both ways.”

“How rude of me, my name is Barry McMahon.”

“I guessed as much. Barry McMahon, Carrowkeel, Donegal, Lough Foyle.”

The room went decidedly silent and Paddy got the attention of Barry McMahon who stood, walked around the table and sized up this stranger who had done his homework, and knew way more than he wanted him to. One way or another he was a bright lad and might be a welcome member of Clan-na-Gael, the Irish American Clan, in her efforts to support the fight to rid Ireland of her oppressor.

“So I get a call from Eamon Gainey and he tells me you’re coming. That’s a fairly infamous messenger. How do you know Eamon Gainey?”

“I don’t.”

The room muted further as eyes met one another in concern and breaths involuntarily held. Paddy grinned slightly as he looked around at his brethren.

“And I don’t know anyone who does, he keeps a rather low profile.”

, “Then the question begs asking, Mr. Quinlan, if you don’t know him, how was it that he called to do you such a favor?”

“We’ve done some work for him in the south. He knew he could count on us and when it was decided that I was to leave, me brother Dinty made a phone call, that’s all I know. That Mr. Gainey made a personal phone call on my behalf speaks volumes for me brother and not me.”

“What kind of work?”

“Oh, digging and trenching, mostly the graveyard shift.”

“For what?”

“That’s as far as it goes. I don’t see how that’s relevant.”

“It’s relevant insofar as, Eamon Gainey, assistant chief-of-staff of the standing IRA called on your behalf.”

“Look, Mr. McMahon, if that’s who you really are, I’ve seen men shot for saying less than I already have.”

Barry looked at the man standing next to him and said, “Seamus, the box.”

Paddy, guessing Seamus to be McMahon’s bodyguard, watched as the large, hairy man brought a small cardboard box wrapped in twine and laid it down in front of him.

McMahon stared at Paddy Quinlan and said, "This should put any question you have to rest."

Paddy opened the box and inside was a pair of bronzed baby shoes, one obviously misshapen. His mother hung them above her bed as reminder of the miracle of life, no matter which package it came in. The note attached said: *Paddy, you seemed to have forgotten to pack these and I think mam would've wanted you to have them. I also got to thinking that a skeptic like you might need a little proof. Dinty.* Paddy stood motionless for a second. A wave of homesickness brought on by any mention of Dinty, unexpectedly filled every fiber of his being and he had to physically will himself to hold back any show of emotion. He shook hands with Barry McMahon and said, "What would you like to know?"

From that night forward Paddy was a member of the secretive and surreptitious Clan-na –Gael, the American arm of the Irish volunteers.

Chapter 8
The Letter and The Request

Butte, Montana

Two Years Later

Paddy Quinlan met a rancher named Horace Mansfield on the train and as a result he had spent a couple of weeks on his ranch in the Flathead Valley before he made his way to Butte. Paddy fell in love with the area and swore to the man he would be back to buy land some day.

Paddy spent two miserable years in the mines of the Anaconda Mining Company. He stayed in touch with and sent money to friends and family back home while immersing himself in the activities of not only the Clan-na-Gael, but also the Ancient Order of Hibernians, another Irish society, but distinctly more social. He had languished in the mines long enough and wanted to get back to the Flathead Valley and the ranching business.

He wrote regularly to Horace Mansfield, who always wrote back to let him know that a job awaited him, should he change his mind. And he was sorely tempted to take the man up on his offer, on more than one occasion, but something held him back.

Paddy loved the man, but he had bigger plans and was thinking more of owning his own place rather than working for someone else. He continually made his feelings clear to Mansfield on this point.

One day he went to his mailbox, surprised to find a letter from Horace.

Dear Paddy:

I just received news that the Higgins place up the road is coming up for sale. Old Hank passed away last month, none of his kids want the place and his widow doesn't want to run it alone. It is 1,000 acres all fenced with two hundred head of cattle and 100 quality quarter horses. The land is worth thirteen dollars an acre and it will fetch that. On top of that, the buyer would have the option to buy the cattle, buildings and house. If you are interested you are probably looking at $50,000.00 for the whole shooting match.

Son, I know it's a lot of cash, but knew that you were thinking along those lines and thought you would like to know. An opportunity to own this kind of ranch isn't an everyday occurrence. But times are tough and people are not lining up. So this might be the opportunity you have been looking for. I believe it is an excellent long-term investment.

Regards,
Horace Mansfield.

Paddy's heart pounded wildly in his chest and his long fingers shook as he held the letter. He thought this could be it. Then he caught himself and said, "Ah, for Christ sake, Paddy, put your head on straight. Where are you going to come up with that kind of cash? You couldn't even come up with a down payment."

He sat down and put his head in his hands in deep thought. Then he looked up, slapped the letter with his free hand, and said, "It's just crazy enough to work."

That evening Paddy borrowed a friend's car and drove out to the McMahon place to pay Barry McMahon a visit.

"Good evening, Mrs. McMahon. I'm hoping to find Mr. McMahon at home."

"Sure, he's in his study, Mr.?"

"Quinlan, Padraig Quinlan."

"Oh, yes, I've heard Barry mention your name. Please come in."

Paddy stood in the McMahon foyer waiting nervously, shuffling his hugger cap, and watching some of the McMahon clan wrestling to show off in front of their new company.

"He'll see you in his study. Would you care for a drink?"

Being polite he said, "Thanks, no, Mrs. McMahon." Even though he would have loved a belt just about then.

Paddy walked into Barry's beautiful, hardwood study. The smell of whiskey and cigar smoke pervaded the fabric of the room and for a moment made Paddy yearn for Kinnane's pub back home. He stopped, filled his lungs with a deep breath, and smiled with pain.

Paddy said, "Ah, for a moment there I thought I was at Kinnane's pub in Upperchurch."

Barry said, "Aye, I don't think we ever fully recover from the homesickness."

They sat, as immigrants sometimes did at the mention of their homeland, while fond memories flooded their minds and for the briefest of moments they were there.

Barry broke the silence and said, "What can I do for you, lad?"

"I need a small favor."

"And what's that?"

"I need to borrow $50,000.00."

McMahon dropped his cigar in his ashtray and said, "Thank God it wasn't a large favor."

"I don't mean from you personally, Barry. I need your help securing a note from your bank."

"What for?"

"You've heard me talk of the beauty of the Flathead Valley."

"Aye."

"Well I've got a chance to buy a ranch up there."

"And?"

"I want you take it to the bank's board for me."

"What?"

"Barry, this is a business proposition. $50,000.00 sounds like a lot of money and it is, I guess."

"You guess?"

"Listen, in what little time I've had I was able to look at the books of this ranching operation and if I can get my hands on the capital I know I can operate this thing from the black day one. I won't take a salary for the first five years. Once I get this thing rolling, I know it'll be a cash cow. "

Impressed with Paddy's business acumen and always interested in landing a decent loan for the bank, Barry said, "You've got access to the books then?"

"Aye."

"So the board can take a look?"

"Aye."

"What do you have for collateral?"

"Barry, you know I don't have a pot to piss in. I've saved some money, but not enough for a down payment on the loan. But, please, just have a look at the books; I know I can make this work. We use the ranch for collateral and my good intentions."

Barry smiled, he knew what good intentions were worth. If nothing more, he thought, the lad could sell water to a drowning man. He's smart and he works like a draught horse. That may be collateral enough.

"Bring it to me tomorrow, I'll have a look. If I like what I see, I'll take it to the bank board. But don't get your hopes up."

Barry was also struck with Paddy's confidence. It was not a matter of making it or not, it was *when*.

Waiting to hear from the bank, the days waded slowly that month. The grind in the dark hole of the copper mine was endless drudgery. Paddy felt the walls of the mine begin to close in on him and he had to continually fight the urge to allow his imagination to give way to claustrophobic panic. The ninety-degree heat in the mine certainly didn't help.

As he chipped along his piece of the wall looking for the precious copper, he did, however, allow his mind to wander to that part of the

Flathead Valley that he hoped would soon be his. He could smell the fresh pine in the air and taste the clear, cold, running water from the mountain streams.

As the ceaseless days turned to seemingly infinite weeks, he became convinced that the bank had turned him down and he would be in this mine forever. And his stubborn pride would never allow him to ask; to him that was tantamount to begging. To describe Paddy Quinlan as irresolute would be like watching a two-toed sloth get riled. Whatever was to happen was to happen, he would just have to find another way.

After a month of waiting, his impatience, irritability and drinking all escalated, he became more and more inclined to challenge co-workers and friends alike to try and knock the chip off his shoulder. When one day in late December he walked out of the steam-cloud that was created when the mine's head frame elevator opened and the ninety-degree mine air collided with the ten-degree early winter air of Butte, a stranger approached him.

The man said, "Mr. Quinlan?"

Paddy said, "Who the hell wants to know?"

"Mr. McMahon, that's who, be at his house tonight at seven."

Paddy wanted to say thanks but couldn't bring himself to. He walked away and could feel that heart flutter of nerves reverberate in his chest. Exacerbated, he said to himself, "It's about time."

Chapter 9
The Unlikely Response

Paddy borrowed the car once again and Barry's wife once again showed Quinlan to the man's office where the cigar smoke wafted aimlessly. It moved toward the ceiling in an eternal sacrifice to some Druid god long since forgotten.

As Paddy walked in Barry stood, his ubiquitous cigar clinched to the left side of his mouth, shook Paddy's hand and said, "Thanks for coming, Paddy."

Paddy said, "You finally got news then?"

McMahon said, "Aye. No matter how much arm wrestling I did with the board, and I'm a member mind you, I couldn't get them to agree to the loan."

Paddy's heart sunk in his chest like a great anchor mooring a ship in harbor.

Barry said, "However."

Paddy looked up and his heart lightened slightly with that one wonderful word, but he did not get his hopes too high.

Barry continued, "I really believe in you Paddy . I've watched you the last two years. You enjoy a drink, but you're not a drunk. You show up to work every day. You've got nice savings developing in the bank, so you haven't been frivolous. You're a leader; people like you and you just won't give up. And no offense, but even with that clubfoot, I talked with your foreman and he says you work harder and get more done than most men in that hole in the ground. Management of Anaconda even have their eye on you for a foreman position and even greater things, so they're confirming what I already know."

Paddy eyes lit up said, "No shyte?"

Barry said, "Yes. As a matter of fact, two Vice Presidents at Anaconda are members of the bank board and were willing to vote in favor of your loan proposal."

Paddy said, "You're serious?"

Barry said, "Aye. But we needed three quarters of the board voting in favor and we didn't get it. They're a conservative bunch and if you don't have twenty percent down and your first born as collateral you can forget it."

Paddy stood turning his hugger cap dejectedly in his hands and said, "Well, thank you Barry, you did what you could. I'll be leaving now."

"Sit down, lad, I'm not finished. Would you care for a little whiskey?"

Paddy, not really in the mood now, but not wanting to offend the man said, "Aye."

McMahon went to his bar, poured two Middleton's Rare Irish whiskeys and handed one to Paddy smiling and said, "To your success, lad. Good luck Padraig, I think you're going to make a fine rancher and an even better community leader."

Paddy, not listening, raised his glass and said, "Aye." He shot the whiskey down, put the glass on the desk and it finally registered with him what McMahon had just said.

Paddy said, "Excuse me?"

Barry smiled and said, "Oh, did I forget to tell you?"

"Tell me what, sir?"

"An independent investor, who will remain anonymous, was willing to put up five thousand dollars. And then I put up the other five thousand. That's twenty percent down and, with our signatures to secure the note, we had enough to get the loan approved. You're in business, lad."

"Well blessed be the Holy Family."

His hands began to shake and Barry said, "Here, have a little more."

Paddy raised his glass with a shaky hand, nodded his head and drained more of the twenty-five-year-old contents in one gulp.

Paddy looked Barry McMahon in the eye and said, "And you're sure I can't find out who the investor is so I can shake his hand?"

"Quite sure," McMahon replied.

"Well then, sir, I just want to thank you for your belief in me. Oh, and make sure you thank the second lad for me. This is truly the greatest day in my life."

"Listen, lad. We believe in you but there is also a risk reward on this deal. We just happen to believe that you can make us a tidy sum on this investment."

"I won't let you down."

Barry winked at him and said, "We know."

The two men sat down and worked out the particulars.

When Paddy left McMahon picked up the phone and placed a call.

"Hello."

"Mr. Mansfield, this is Barry McMahon. It's a done deal, Mr. Quinlan is on his way. I think you made a smart investment."

He smiled and said, "Oh, I think I made one hell of an investment."

Within a month Paddy Quinlan stood watching as his ranch started spring branding. A month after that an outsider looking in would have had a hard time believing he didn't grow up on the ranch.

Horace Mansfield couldn't have been happier to have a neighbor like Paddy Quinlan. Paddy was never to find out that Horace was the second investor. He was a good friend who was always there for Paddy when he needed advice or just someone to listen.

Horace had met few men more competent. Paddy was savvy, worked long days and was loyal to a fault. Ranching, like Ireland, seemed to run in his veins and he loved it from the beginning. He hired new hands, fired old ones not interested in change and promoted those hands who had been around a while who showed some gumption and leadership. He paid them well, was a fair man and his reputation grew.

Within five years he was one of the wealthiest ranchers in Montana, rubbing noses with Senators, Congressmen, Governors and of course, local representatives taking care of ranching legislation. Paddy knew that it was hard work with more than a wee bit of good luck. He always said, "The harder you work the luckier you get." He was a man with endless energy. Away from the ranch he became treasurer for the statewide Ancient Order of Hibernians and then bumped Barry McMahon, who was ready to step down, from the top post of Clan-na-Gael Montana. His mind was never far from Ireland and neither would anyone's mind around him be.

He drove himself with a fury and a passion that was typical of first generation wealth, but there was something missing in his life. Paddy longed for a wife and a family. He needed someone with whom to share his wealth.

Chapter 10
The Discretion of a Rebel

December 1959

Dublin, Ireland

The teakettle whistled. Cassie Kenny stood and walked to the stove. She sat back down at the table with one leg resting easily under her bottom and poured two cups. As the tea steeped she looked at Clare and said, "Is Dublin everything you thought it'd be?"

Clare said, "It's a bit crowded, noisy and dirty, isn't it? But I suppose that adds to its charm."

"You'll get used to it."

"I do love the people, from all over it seems."

"What's on your mind? You seem distracted."

"Oh, I'm traveling back to Ballycraig this weekend. I told Da I'd drop in every once in a while, cheer up mum some."

"It's more than that isn't it?"

"What do you mean?"

"Come on Clare, it's me. You left home in an awful hurry six months ago."

"It wasn't such a huff."

"It wasn't? I tried for three years to get you to come to Dublin but you always came up with some excuse when we both knew it was your mum keeping you home."

Clare blanched.

"Then I get a sudden ring on the phone and within a week you're moving in. I've known you too long Clare Eva White. What is it then?"

Clare smiled and said, "Cassie, you're a shyte."

Cassie said, "I figured something was up. I've caught you a couple of times just staring out the window with that glazed look in your eye."

All Clare could do was smile as she suddenly began to look forward to her visit home with the prudence of a rebel.

The train seemed to move in slow motion, no hurry to get anywhere. Clare was excited to get home for the first time in a long while. As she watched the Irish countryside slip past, her resolve vacillated, her thoughts as capricious as an Irish fairy moving whimsically in her mind. The inevitability, she lied to herself, its going to happen and it's going to be okay. She was both frightened and excited, but refused to fast-forward the tape to contemplate the consequences; that was too big.

Clare walked into the cottage of her birth. The familiar smell home made her realize just how homesick she had been. Her mother had a stew on and the smell of her dad's pipe allowed Clare to put her anxiety behind her, at least for the moment.

Her dreams that night were unsettling and she slept little. In an effort to put her mind at ease she spent the whole of Saturday afternoon outdoors walking in her childhood stomping grounds, always careful not to get too close to the back road, even now.

A mist began to permeate the air and her attempts at serenity failed miserably. She felt like a startled rabbit being harassed by the world around it, and every time she turned her head to look she saw him, in her mind, standing there dripping from the mist, calling her. She felt a tap on her shoulder and turned her head so fast that she snapped her neck and felt the uncomfortable burn. Father Ruari O'Keefe stood smiling at her. At first she thought he was a dream and then he spoke.

"I heard you'd come to visit."

"Aye, to look in on Mum and Da."

"We need to talk."

"About what?"

"I think you know. You're being coy."

Clare smiled as the mist beaded on her upper lip and her soft blonde hair began to wilt.

Ruari said, "Look, I felt it the minute I met you and I don't think your leaving so abruptly was an accident. I felt it, I want it, but that doesn't mean I can have it."

Clare said, "Don't flatter yourself."

Ruari began to laugh, which caught Clare off guard. He then grabbed her by the shoulders and pulled her close. She could smell his clean aftershave and feel the utter power in his athletic arms. His eyes bore a hole in her outer shell as if they were shot from a rifle and she felt helpless.

He said, "I, for one, can't live like this. I'm not going anywhere and neither are your parents. So that means we're going to be seeing one another, unless you plan on never coming back."

She said, "So?"

Ruari said, "Stop it, Clare! There have been way too many nights I haven't slept thinking about you. Are you going to stand there and tell me you feel different?"

She pushed his arms away from her shoulders, moved in closer and said, "No." And she kissed him.

Seemingly unable to stop, he let the kiss go on longer than was safe. Coming to his senses he stepped back and said, “No. We can’t. This is quixotic. I’m a Catholic priest, or have you forgotten?”

She said quietly, no longer fighting, “Some things are just inevitable.”

He clenched his jaw and said, “This isn’t one of them.” And then he walked away.

Later that evening, Ruari O’Keefe sat in the darkness provided by the front room of the rectory, afraid to move. How could this be happening? He thought. A woman that I can’t resist is pursuing me.

A knock came on the door. He jumped at the unexpected interruption. His heart raced in his chest. He stood, turned on the hall light, walked to the door and then turned on the porch light as he pulled it open. There stood the widow Buggy; he guessed that she was just a few years younger than God. He looked down at the bent old woman. Her ancient arthritic hands clutched a walking stick and a rosary. She held up the rosary and said, “Father, you left this at me cottage after giving me the last rites.”

Ruari smiled gently and said, “Mrs. Buggy, you walked all the way over here to give me my rosary back?”

“No,” she shrugged, “I've me lad.”

Ruari looked out and widow Buggy’s fifty-year-old son Colm waved from the buckboard on which he sat, grinning toothlessly at the priest while cuddling a jug of poteen on the seat next to him. .

Widow Buggy said, “Aye, Father. You can’t be sleeping without saying your rosary first. The evil spirits will have a heyday.”

He wanted to ask her, but didn’t have the heart, if it had occurred to her that the beads were a mere tool and that he could say his rosary without them? Or that he might have a backup rosary somewhere in the rectory?

He said, “Come in here before you catch your death.”

He put on tea and asked if Colm would like to join them to which she replied, “No Father, he prefers his own company.” Ruari sat patiently listening to the forlorn soul droning on endlessly about nothing. After an hour of this penance he escorted her to the buckboard, helped her into her seat and said, “Colm, drive safely.”

To which the old woman said, “Hardly, Father.” She then took the reins, snapped the back of their nag with them and they made their way down the lane. All he could do was smile.

It was another endless night of restlessness. He stared silently out the window of his bedroom, envying the serenity and seeming orderliness of nature while he fought the internal struggle of chaos and despair. He cursed his weakness and prayed for a strength that wouldn’t come. He dropped to the floor and wept.

"Shhh."

He looked up, silhouetted in the doorframe stood Clare White. She walked to him and held out her hand. Ruari, sitting on the bedside, looked up. She smiled at him. His fingers touched hers and he felt suddenly weightless. He raised himself with the ease and grace of an athlete. He no longer cursed his weakness but paid tribute to his humanity. She pulled him close and he rested his weary head upon her shoulder, aware of her great tenderness. He kissed her neck and she moaned so softly that only he could have heard it. She laid down on the bed, as he dropped down beside her and it was over.

Chapter 11
Foolish Talk

Two Months Later

Dublin, Ireland

It had been a long day and Clare White was tired. Her roommate, Cassie Kenny got home, poured a glass of red wine, looked across the table from Clare and said, "How was your day?"

Clare sighed, "Long."

"Are you working tonight?"

"No."

"Why not?"

"I'm too tired. I decided to take the night off."

They sat staring at one another and Cassie said, "When were you planning on telling me?"

Clare said, "Telling you what?"

"That you're pregnant."

Clare blushed furiously and then began to cry. She said, "I didn't want to believe it myself, how did you know?"

"Maybe the fact that you're eating us out of house and home and your secretly throwing up in the morning while running the tub were pretty solid tips."

"My God, is it that obvious?"

"Come on Clare, pregnant women were more common in Ballycraig than butter churns."

"Okay, so I'm pregnant. So what?"

"Clare, it's Cassie here, darling. I'm not here to condemn you. I just want to help."

"Well I've made a right mess of things."

"Who hasn't at one time or another? What're you going to do?"

"I don't know."

"Can I ask who?"

"You already know."

"Oh, Lord."

"Oh Lord is right."

"Does he know?"

"No! And I'm not going to tell him. No use in ruining two lives over this. It's entirely my fault."

"What?"

"I seduced him, Cassie. He tried to stop it but I wouldn't let him. God in heaven, I love him, I want him, and I want this child."

"Have you told him that?"

"Good Lord, no."

"Clare, I know he's a priest, but you owe it to yourself to at least tell the man and then let him decide."

"What? And be known as the whore that seduced the priest and caused his fall? No thank you. I'd be a fucking pariah."

"So that's it?"

"As I see it, yes, that's it."

Clare put her head in her hands and winced as a searing pain had shot through the back of her eyes. The flat became eerily quiet and the clock that hung on the wall above the kitchen table began to tick as if it were amplified and in a cadence with their slow heartbeats.

Cassie took Clare's hands and said, "Clare, everything will work out all right."

"How can you say that? Not only am I pregnant out of wedlock, the father is a man of the cloth. May God have Mercy on me, 'tis a sin so grave there can be no forgiveness."

"Stop this foolish talk. Do you think the child you carry is any less a miracle than a child created within the bonds of marriage?"

"No."

"And it sounds to me like it was created out of love."

"Aye, it was."

"Then stop berating yourself, it's doing no good."

"And what would you have me do?"

"I've got a cousin who's a Mercy nun. She's a midwife in the convent up on Baggot Street. They take care of unwed mothers until the baby is born and then they take care of the adoption. You rest now and I'll take care of everything."

"This is my problem and no one else need be involved."

"So the good Father Ruari O'Keefe has no responsibility then?"

"Cassie, I didn't say that. It was an accident; neither of us wanted this to happen."

"Well it did."

"You promise me that you'll let me handle this *my* way."

"Then you'll tell this Fr. O'Keefe?"

"No, I'll have the baby and have it adopted and no one needs to be the wiser."

Chapter 12
The Cleric and The Reporter

Ballycraig, County Kilkenny, Republic of Ireland

One week later

Cassie paid a quiet and unexpected visit to Ballycraig, the village south of Dublin. She had left three years earlier and had not been back since. The broil she had had with her parents before her departure was already legendary within village lore. No one in the village, especially her folks, ever thought they would see her again.

Cassie was number seven of twelve children and was born with the whiskey burning in her throat. By the time she was old enough to know better, she was chasing the boys, nipping at her Da's poteen and filling his old used pipes with stolen pipe weed.

As with most villages in Ireland, the locals in Ballycraig were tight knit, and when necessary, they would close ranks. Cassie and Clare's confrontation with the tinker was now also legendary, never talked about with outsiders, but a mark of pride locally. Time and again they had proven themselves ladies not to be taken lightly and anyone who did, lived to regret it.

Cassie had been attracted to writing since she was a child. When she first arrived in Dublin she applied for a job as a cub reporter for the Dublin Times. After some arm wrestling over her gender, she got the job. The editor decided that if she were that hard on him she'd get any story he wanted her to. Cassie was fearless and that courage made her one of the best reporters in Dublin. She loved to write, was good at it and wasn't afraid to take on anyone, including the upper echelon Brits who occupied Stormont, the building where the government of Northern Ireland resided.

She walked in and said, "Hello mum."

Cassie's mother, who could've been her twin twenty years earlier, turned around and stared at her daughter.

She said, "Well blessed be Jesus, Mary, Joseph and all the saints in heaven. This is a day I never expected to see."

With a dual purpose she said, "Neither did I mum, but I've come to set things right."

After an uncomfortable tea with her mother, Cassie went to take care of the real business for which she had come.

After a long contemplative walk she decided it was time. The sun was beginning its downward journey and as Cassie knocked on the door her shadow was outlined before her. Father Ruari O'Keefe answered the door and she understood for the first time how Clare had gotten herself into this mess. She felt a strange weakness in her knees. He was not handsome in a typical way, average height, bald, square jaw. But he was powerfully built, his eyes were piercing and yet kind and he was welcoming. She stared at him for a moment and realized he was oddly familiar and it bothered her that she couldn't place him.

He said, "Hello, may I help you?"

She cleared the dryness in her throat and said, "Aye Father, my name's Cassie Kenny, I was raised in Ballycraig, but now I live in Dublin. I heard you were new and thought I'd come by to introduce myself while I was home."

"Well that was nice of you, come in."

They walked into the front room and she sat down.

"May I offer you some tea, Miss Kenny."

"That would be grand."

"The woman who helps me around here is off to visit her mum today, so it may be a minute."

"Take all the time you need."

He walked away and she stared after him and suddenly she thought she remembered where she had seen him. She said in a whisper, "No, it couldn't be."

Ruari walked back in carrying a tray and set it down.

"Cream and sugar?"

"Aye."

He sat across from her and she smiled.

"So, what can I do for you?"

"You look so familiar. Can I ask you a question first?"

Cautious, he looked at her and said, "Okay."

"Did you play for the National Hurling team nine or ten years back?"

He stopped and cautiously said, "Aye."

"Then it is you."

"What're you on about?"

"In researching a story I ran across some articles written about you and your famous pub row."

"I don't know what you're talking about."

"Come on Father, don't be modest. If you did half of what they wrote about you!"

"I'm not sure what you're on about, but."

"It really is you. You're Ruari O'Keefe."

"So?"

"The man so tough and wild that he was kicked off the National Hurling team, that's got to look good on the old curriculum vitae huh?"

"Look, Miss Kenny."

"Please call me Cassie. Let's see, from handsome, hurling hero chasing women and whiskey to Catholic priest in a quiet village. I can see the headlines now."

The priest, not ready for this, stared at her and then it dawned on him. He said, "So what? You're a reporter from Dublin trying to make a name for herself"

"Not initially, but maybe now."

"I'm busy Miss Kenny."

"I'm not here to do a story on you, but now I might just because you want to stay anonymous. I didn't even realize who you were until I showed up here today. I'm a friend of Clare White, we're roommates in Dublin. Let's see, it might read 'Ex-Hurling champion turned priest knocks up innocent girl."

His teacup dropped to the floor and she heard a quiet, "Oh my God, she's. . .?"

Cassie finished his sentence with spite and said, "Pregnant? Yes, she is. Damn, Father, this could sell a few newspapers."

"You don't understand."

"Oh I think I understand all too well."

"How could you?"

"What are your plans?"

"Look, this is not what you think."

"What is it then, Father?"

"I've not slept in three months, I can't eat. Does she even know that you're here?"

"No, she'd be angry if she knew. She was actually telling me she didn't want to burden you, if you can possibly believe that. She's independent, but that's where I draw the line."

He looked at her knowing he deserved her contempt and feeling like he deserved the scorn of the whole world.

She stood, getting her Irish up, stared down at him and said, "The only reason the story won't go to print is because Clare Eva White is my best friend. I owe her my life and she'd be looked at like the whore that seduced the priest. You son of a bitch, how could you?"

He looked up at her and said, "How could I what?"

"Don't get cute with me, you know damn well *what*."

"Look, I know what I did was wrong and I don't need you to give me a course in ethics."

"You could've surprised me."

"I'm not sure why I'm even having this conversation with you; it's none of your damn business. But I've felt incredible shame over this. And it wasn't over whether she was pregnant or not because I had no idea."

"Well guess no more. Maybe you should bathe in a larger tub of Holy Water. That should cleanse you of all that shame and guilt."

"I'm not sure where you think this is going, but I'm not hiding behind this collar."

"You could've fooled me."

Losing his temper, at last, he stood menacingly and seemed to grow larger and said, "Who in the hell do you think you are?"

Witnessing this new demeanor she was now questioning her wisdom in poking the hornet's nest, she said, "I'm. . ."

He said, "I'm not finished! Coming in here and passing judgment against me. I told you I wasn't hiding behind any collar. I own up to my mistakes and I'll own up to this one. I don't need you or anybody else to tell me what to do. But how in the hell was I supposed to do anything when I didn't know anything for sure?"

"You could've come to Dublin."

"Oh, I see, you think that a priest six months into his first assignment can just drop everything and waltz off to Dublin to visit a woman?"

"I didn't think. . ."

"No you didn't!"

They sat quietly sizing up one another.

He said, "What is she going to do now?"

"Sister Mary de Angels is a cousin of mine in residence at the Mercy convent in Dublin. They take in unwed mothers and she's agreed to cloister Clare for six months until the baby is born. They'll then find a home for the child."

"Yes, I'm aware of what they do there."

"What are your plans now?"

"I don't know – God have Mercy, I don't know."

Chapter 13
The Visitation

Ballycraig

One week later

Clare White had come home to Ballycraig with a purpose. It happened most unexpectedly. She arrived in the morning and had spent the day walking throughout the Irish countryside, lost in her thoughts and scared.

Just before dusk she took a deep breath of the sweet country air, the *only* thing sweet, she thought, and opened the door to the cottage. Soup simmered in the cauldron over the peat fire in the fireplace, it gave her a moment's peace, bringing her to a safe place in her childhood. The rain that had begun to fill the night air as she walked in was kept at bay by the thatched roof that her father worked on incessantly.

It was cozy and secure, something she desperately needed now. The pit of fear that grew within her gave her little rest, but she was home now and those mischievous sprites that haunted her day and night would have to wait outside for now. This was a safe haven, a barrier keeping her from those dark and stormy seas that moved interminably in her mind.

Her mother Kate was putting on dinner while her Da Will nursed a small glass of Poteen, the potato Whiskey he'd bought from Widow Buggy.

Will said, "A tasty brew, Clare. Widow Buggy says Colm triple distilled this and I've got to believe it."

Kate said, " 'Tis the devils brew and it'll be the death of you."

"Och woman. Let a man have a few pleasures."

He winked and smiled at his daughter who'd walked in not paying any attention to what he said, lost in her thoughts.

They sat down to dinner.

Half way through their meal Will said, "Clare darling, you haven't said a word, what's on your mind?"

Clare looked up and said without pause, "I'm pregnant."

Silverware clattered upon stoneware as four eyes narrowed on Clare like mangy, underfed wolves closing in on a limping runt being left behind by the herd. As if not noticing the sudden attention, she stared at her plate and continued with great strength and calm, "I'm ashamed, scared, and sorry. 'Twas a mistake, for sure, but it'll not ruin me life. I'm not interested in bringing any shame to either of you from nosy, righteous neighbors or the Church."

Kate said, "But. . ."

Clare raised her hand and said, "Shush Mum. This isn't your problem, 'tis mine. You're both dears and I didn't want to hurt either of you like this. But this is sure to get out and I didn't want you to hear this from anyone else."

"Good Lord, lass, who's the father then?" Will said.

"I'll take that to me grave."

"He'll have no responsibility then?"

"Yes Da, more than you'll ever know."

Kate said, "And you say you won't let it ruin your life as if it hasn't already."

"Mum, don't start. I made a mistake, but I'm going to make it right and I won't live with the shame or the guilt. No one in Ballycraig ever need know."

"Well then, as long as you have the whole world figured out, what do you plan to do?" Kate said.

"Cassie's cousin is a dear and a Mercy nun as well as a midwife. She's arranged for the convent in Dublin to cloister me until it's over. They'll make sure the baby's adopted in a good home and that'll be that."

"'Tis a confessional you need, not a convent." And her mother walked from the table.

Chapter 14
He's Ours

June 1960

The Short Strand

Belfast, Northern Ireland

Sean O'Kane had a new lease on life. He no longer regretted his station and never looked back. Patricia made him understand just how important his writing was, how important writers had always been in Ireland's history, that it was a noble passion and thus he was a noble man. He now looked at himself in a different light and felt very much a part of the fight. His words triggered emotions and the courage to put his name on his words was as dangerous, at times, as carrying a gun.

Within six months of their engagement Sean and Patricia were married. Sean continued his work at the newspaper while Patricia made good on her promise to keep a low profile and stay out of trouble. But she would not be kept from being involved as an Irish Republican volunteer in other ways, helping her brother Dermot Brennan in his command post in the brotherhood with whatever they needed done. She was also deeply involved in anti-march activity, which at times turned violent, but she would never back down. She would not begrudge them their right to march; after all it was a free society. But if the Orange bastards insisted on marching through Nationalist neighborhoods taunting and scaring its residents, there was a price for admission. She told Sean she wouldn't go looking for trouble, but if it marched down her street she wasn't going to sit back and watch.

Her most prized possession from one of her more brutal confrontations was a blackjack. She always smiled at the memory while unconsciously rubbing the bump left by the scar on the back of her noggin. Stones were being thrown and firebombs were lighting up the night skies as homes flared in The Short Strand neighborhood in the heat of another mid-summer marching season. Fire hydrants were manned to keep the conflagration from getting too far out of control while Patricia and a band of brothers went on the attack. The large Ulster Defense soldier came out of nowhere and cracked her on the skull with the blackjack. Stunned for a moment her knees buckled and she stumbled to the ground, the large man laughed while blood dripped from the back of her head. With enough sense left she grabbed the club from his large unsuspecting hand and slammed it point first into his right kneecap, forcing his leg the wrong way. He went down like a freshly cut tree trunk, screaming in pain. She got to her feet and before he could move she crushed his jaw with one monumental stroke of the club and the snap of jawbone could be heard over the rioting in the street. She walked away smiling while he choked on his molars. The blackjack hung next to their crucifix in the kitchen, a mosaic of sorts to their struggle as Catholics and Nationalists.

As the months passed, it became increasingly more apparent that they couldn't have the baby that they wanted. One night when Sean came home from work Patricia said, "Sean, neither of us seems to want to talk about it, but I don't think we're able to have a baby."

Feeling his manhood being tested he said, "So?"

"So, a month ago I sent a letter to a girlhood friend, Sr. Evangeline, in Dublin. She told me a few years back that the Mercy nuns there took in unwed mothers, helped them deliver their babies and then saw to their adoption and I inquired as such."

"And?"

"You're interested in hearing more?"

"Aye?"

"A woman is there now and ready to have a baby. It's ours if we want it."

Chapter 15
The Surprise Delivery

September 4, 1960

Mercy Convent

Dublin, Ireland

Sister Mary de Angels, the midwife amongst the Mercy nuns in the Baggot Street convent, walked into the room. Clare White, as big as a house, screamed in pain.

"That's me girl." Sister Mary said.

"Oh shut your gob, this hurts like hell."

The large, sweet nun bent over her patient and wiped the sweat from her forehead and face and said, "Now you know one reason I took me vow of chastity."

"Thanks, but it's a little late for me."

She put some lubricating jelly on her hand and checked the dilation of Clare's cervix and said, "Nine centimeters, one more contraction lass and you'll be able to push."

"It's about time."

The contraction started and came on strong and fast, with pain so excruciating that she thought she was going to pass out. Sister Mary held Clare's hand throughout.

"Okay darling, you're ten centimeters, when you feel the next contraction coming on push like St. Michael fighting Lucifer, all right?"

"Aye, I will."

She felt the contraction coming. She hunkered down in the bed, grabbed the guardrails above her shoulders and pushed. She was amazed because all the pain seemed to momentarily go away and as she pushed it felt good.

A baby boy was born.

A contraction.

"Why am I contracting? The baby is born, right?"

"Sometimes that happens with the afterbirth, darl . . ."

The nun stopped, and looking startled said, "Lord Jesus in Heaven have mercy on us all. Sister Evangeline! Sister Evangeline, get in here I need help, please I need help!"

Sister Evangeline came running and said, "What is it?"

"Here take this one. Clare's delivering twins."

The second nun said, “Blessed be the Holy Family and all that’s good in Ireland.”

“I’m having what?” Clare said as the contraction came on like a twister.

“Push darling, push.”

A second beautiful baby boy was born. As they were whisked from the room she realized that she may never see them again.

Chapter 16
Coming Clean

Dublin

That Same Night Across Town

Bishop John Byrne came in late. He had been to a fundraiser on the north side and was tired, but he still had work to do so he headed to his office.

He opened the door and was assailed by a miasma of vomit and whiskey so offensive that he felt violated. He stepped back as if to protect himself from the adversary he knew in his youth, in the pubs by the docks where he went to rescue his father before he spent the family dole on the drink. He then covered his nose with his sleeve and, with no little resolve, moved across the floor of his office to his desk and its lamp when he came upon Ruari O'Keefe passed out on his office floor.

His mind went immediately to the morning he bailed Ruari out of jail where he found him in a pool of his own sick and handcuffed to the cell bars. He was not a pretty sight then and he was not a pretty sight now.

Exhausted and beyond irritation he said, "Dear God in heaven above, what has caused this? I've got more work than I can keep up with and now I've got to clean up this mess of a man."

The next morning Ruari woke with sawdust in his mouth and a ten-pound headache. He slowly lifted his head off the couch wondering where he was.

Upon seeing him stir, the Bishop said, "Do you mind telling me what in the hell you're doing here?"

Ruari got to his feet and looked around as if he were getting his bearings straight. Before answering, he walked to the tea service on the opposite side of the room and poured himself a strong cup. He then walked back to the chair in front of the large desk. He blew quietly on the steaming liquid and looked sheepishly at his boss who said, "You look like hell."

Ruari said, "Aye, thanks."

"I want an answer and it better be damn good."

"I came here to resign."

"You what?"

"I came to. . ."

"I heard you. Why?"

"I can't say. But it's unforgivable; let's just leave it at that, shall we? Nonetheless, I quit."

He got up to leave and find himself a little hair of the dog when the Bishop said, "Aye, go ahead, it's exactly what I'd expect from a coward. When life gets tough you run."

Ruari turned around and said, "Nice try, but I never expected you or anyone else to understand."

"Understand? How the hell can I understand when I don't know what the hell we're talking about here, man? Quit talking in riddles and tell me what this is about."

"I can't."

"You can't or you won't ?"

Ruari's shoulders heaved as the weight of his world came crumbling down around him.

The Bishop said, "Come back over here and sit down."

It was not a request. Ruari obeyed the command and found himself in the chair in front of the Bishop's desk.

The Bishop said, "I'm not sure what this is all about, but you can't tell me anything I haven't heard before, Ruari. And we're not leaving here until I get some answers. You don't just barge in here and tell me you're quitting and then waltz out of here without an explanation, boyo."

He then got on his office intercom and said, "Mrs. Murphy, hold my calls and cancel the rest of my appointments this morning, please."

She said, "Aye, Imminence."

Ruari looked at his boss and said, "I'm sick."

The Bishop understood. He got up, walked to his cabinet, poured a tumbler of whiskey, handed it to Ruari, and said, "This should be all the medicine you need. It'll stop your shaking."

Ruari poured it down and immediately thought it was coming back up. But after a few minutes of struggling he won and soon felt better.

"Now then, tell me what is going on here, Ruari."

Ruari shook his head in despair as he looked down at the empty glass that rested gingerly on the fingertips of both hands and said, "I, uh, I, well I uh, had sex with a woman in my parish."

The Bishop felt a bitter frost course his veins and he visibly stiffened. He had heard this before, usually in a confessional, and whether it was a man of the cloth or a married man it always shook him as to the pain it caused. He remembered only too well the carnal temptations of his life, some accidental, some intentional. His making it through unscathed was, he was convinced, only by the grace of God, nothing more. Even as an older man he had his moments. They were men, after all. Weren't they allowed to feel, be tempted, bleed and suffer like anyone else?

"Was she married?"

"No."

"I see."

"So, now you see, why I'm done, why I have to quit. I can't do this anymore, I've failed miserably. I was a fool to think I could be celibate *or* sober. It's keenly obvious that I can do neither."

The Bishop sat in quiet contemplation and then said, "Lad, God can do for us what we can't do for ourselves."

"So?"

"So it was a mistake to be certain and a mortal sin, no question. But you have to remember a couple of things here. To not forgive yourself after God *does* is a grave form of self pride, in other words, quit beating yourself up. You're a man of flesh and blood, you're going to make mistakes, some more serious than others. You're as vulnerable to sin as any man. The key is to come clean, admit your faults and pray that God will give you the strength not to do it again. God knows all of this, that's why He is so merciful with us. If you're sorry and show a bit of humility in asking for forgiveness, you're forgiven."

"You don't understand."

"What?"

"She got pregnant and delivered twin boys last night."

"Where?"

"The Mercy Convent."

"Sister Mary de Angels?"

"Aye."

They stared at one another, the Bishop saddened by the pain of human weakness and Ruari in a hell he never thought he could escape.

"So what now?"

"I want you back to your parish this afternoon. I'll call Sister St. John to find out the status of those babies and the mother. Then I want you back here in a week. You won't be able to stay in that parish. I'll have more for you then."

Chapter 17
The Adoption

September 5, 1960

The Four Clovers Ranch

Flathead Valley, Montana

Paddy sat stock still at his desk in his large study, his mind in quiet contemplation, feeling as alone as he'd ever felt in his life. For him it was usually six in the morning to late into the night, business, politics, the state legislature or whatever he was doing. The backroom politics he had grown up with were as much a part of his life now as they were back home in Upperchurch. Paddy had the money now, though, to accomplished what he needed or wanted.

But right now, in this rare moment, he didn't move, he didn't care about the papers on his desk or the deals he was working on. He just stared out his study window at the pines that swayed gently in the night breeze. He could hear them talking on the wind and he could feel their peace and realized he had none. He longed for the human touch, a kiss, a hug, a whisper, the healing that only a woman could bring. Not a fling or a one-night stand, but the love of a woman, that singular essence that would fill his home and his heart, but where was she? Did she even exist? And how? How would he ever come to that one person, that one lovely creature that would make him whole? He worked on a ranch with a bunch of men and it was the rare occasion at a function he attended when he would meet any available women at all, let alone one for which he felt anything.

He came out of his thoughts and said to himself, "Snap out of it lad, you've got work to do."

His downtime was spent at his desk in the evening, when the physical work was done and the house was quiet. This is when he would take care of endless paperwork, pay the bills and communicate with loved ones back home in Ireland. The majority of his letters, however, went to his brother Dinty, or to his cousin on his mother's side, Margaret O'Meara, or as she was known now, Sister Mary de Angels.

In his regular correspondence with Sister Mary de Angels he would share his thoughts. These were extremely private thoughts and regrets he couldn't or wouldn't share with anyone else. He had been so busy being successful that he completely fouled up his personal life. "Margaret," he wrote, "I have no one to blame but myself."

She would write back and try her best to help him through these difficulties and always thanked him for the large contributions he would send to the convent.

The quiet of his study was suddenly broken by a booming knock on his front door. The entire house staff was gone for the night so he got up to answer it.

Young Carl Finocchiaro, the son of the man who ran the post office and telegraph station stood smiling at Paddy and said, "Mr. Quinlan, Papa sent me up with this telegraph. He said it shouldn't wait until morning."

Paddy smiled back, pulled a five dollar bill out of his wallet, handed it to the young man and said, "Here Carl. But wait a minute while I read this."

My Dearest Padraig(stop):

It was grand, as always to hear from you(stop). You are in our daily thoughts and prayers(stop).

I am telegraphing instead of posting this because of its urgent nature(stop)Do you remember Cassie Kenny?(stop) She is my first cousin on my father's side of the family. (stop) She contacted me six months ago about a roommate of hers who is with child out of wedlock.(stop) We agreed at that time to cloister the young woman, deliver the baby and get it adopted.(stop) Another way we use your generosity.(stop)

Last night we delivered twins unexpectedly. (stop) I had already made arrangements for what I thought was to be one baby to be adopted by a family in Belfast. (Stop) But now that there are two, I thought this might be something in which you'd have an interest.(Stop) The baby needs a home.(Stop) And you need a son. (stop) Let us know as quickly as possible.(stop)

Love, Margaret(Stop)

Paddy looked at Carl and said, "Tell your da that I'll be there within the hour."

Carl nodded, thanked him for the five dollar tip and left without a word.

Paddy re-read the message sitting behind his desk, as the grandfather clock in the hall rang twelve times. It was late spring when he walked out the door, took a deep breath of the familiar pine, looked at the full moon reflect off the Flathead and walked to his car knowing he had made the right decision. Then he thought, "No." He walked to the stables and saddled up his favorite horse, who he named Tipperary, and rode her to town. As he rode and midnight covered the Montana sky he screamed out, stopped his horse and began to laugh. He laughed so hard he had to get off his horse. The feeling so overwhelmed him that the laughter turned to tears and he sat by the side of the road and cried.

The little Sicilian immigrant answered the door on the first knock and Paddy said, “Vince, you're right, this couldn’t wait.”

Vince said, “I thought that may be the case. Come in, come in.”

Vince Finocchiaro, who always liked Paddy said, “I’m always glad to help, Mr. Paddy.”

Vince went to his machine, sat down and said, “Where in Ireland?”

“Dublin.”

“Who to?”

“The Mercy convent on Baggot Street, attention Sister Mary de Angels.”

“Okay, we’re set, what do you want to say?”

“Got your message on the twin babies-stop-would like to adopt-stop-respond immediately-stop-Paddy.”

Vince Finocchiaro sent it off and said, “God Bless you, Mr. Paddy.”

“Thanks, Vince.”

At 3:00 a.m. Vince and Paddy were on their third glass of Sam’s home made Chianti when his machine started to run.

“Paddy received your telegram-stop-I have started paper work-stop-you have to arrange transport-stop-thought this might work-stop-God Bless.”

Paddy, with a tear in his eye said, “Sam, my friend, it’s time for a toast.”

They drank in silence when Paddy said, “Sam, let’s send this last telegram in reply.”

“Margaret, thank you for quick response-stop-Will arrange transportation-stop-Is there a young lady to travel with baby?-stop-Will be in touch.”

Chapter 18
The Nanny

September 6, 1960

Dublin, Ireland

Cassie Kenny sat in her apartment sipping a glass of red wine and getting ready to go visit Clare, knowing how distraught she had been, when a knock came on her door. She looked at her watch, it was 5:30 p.m. Her stomach had started to growl and she was irritated with the interruption.

The messenger left a note that Sister St John, who had recently been appointed head of the Mercy convent in Dublin, had sent word that she would like to meet with Cassie at seven O'clock that evening. Under normal circumstances she would have been a bit disgruntled, but not with this woman. She went immediately to the humiliation she felt that night, being stripped and almost raped. Helpless and lost when this small nun comes, seemingly out of nowhere, and rescues her and Clare. Cassie would walk to the gates of hell and back for her. The memory ruined her appetite. She reached for her umbrella, left the flat and walked out into the cold wet night.

Clare sat rocking slowly on the side of her bed as if she could somehow rid her mind of the torment that existed there and her body of its craving to hold the two souls that had nested there the last nine months. An ache existed there that could not be assuaged, an ache she was convinced that time would never heal. She felt dead and useless like so much garbage in the convent dumpster.

Cassie walked noiselessly into Clare's room and watched as her best friend rocked slowly back and forth seeking some kind of relief, her pain palpable. Cassie felt the anguish that filled the room as it surrounded her and tried to drag her down. But instead she embraced it with a strength she didn't know she possessed; it would not beat her and she would not allow it to win over Clare either. A love rose in her that emerged from the deepest recesses of her heart. She would not pity this woman; she would raise her from this deep, aphotic chasm in which she now existed.

Cassie put her hand upon Clare's shoulder and held it there. She looked down, not knowing what to say, her presence seeming to be sufficient. Clare did not look up, though she knew whose hand was there and it was enough.

Cassie whispered, "Clare, Sr. Maria has asked to see me this evening."

"I know. She came to see me earlier."

"What's this about?"

"One of the babies is going to America."

"And?"

"She wants you to escort the child safely there."

"What? No, I can't."

"It would be a comfort to me if you would."

"Have you thought this through?"

"Cass, I can't stand the thought of that wee baby on an airplane with a stranger. I know it's peculiar, but somehow you being there would bring me some peace of mind."

A small, elderly nun with a frown on her face showed Cassie into the living room at the convent. Cassie sat and looked around, then looked down trying to fight the awful memory, like she did every time she was reminded.

Cassie came to and looked around the sitting room once more. Outside of Cassie, Clare, Sister St John and Clare's parents, no one had ever found out what happened to the tinker and why. The other villagers had their suspicions once the peeler came around asking questions, and in the beginning, both parents were furious with the girls when the nun delivered them home. But it was all short lived and was an easy price to pay for the secrecy that the nun kept, endearing the girls to her forever.

At seven o'clock that evening Cassie walked into the large entryway with trepidation, a fear that came from some of the nuns of her childhood. She thought, "Oh Jaysus girl, you're full grown, she's not going to hit you with a ruler. Get over it."

A nun came into the front room and said, "Miss Kenny?"

Cassie said, "Aye."

The nun said in almost a whisper, "Please follow me."

Cassie walked into a large office and smelled the pipe weed that she smelled all those years ago and saw the pipe in the ash tray. She was greeted warmly by the petite woman in full habit. Cassie had always been taken with her beauty and piercing brown eyes.

The Reverend Mother said, "Cassie, you look worried, don't be. Would you care for tea?"

Cassie, rarely tongue-tied, could only respond, "Aye."

"Cream?"

"Thank you."

"Cassie, I'm sure you're wondering why I asked you here."

"Not anymore."

"You've talked to Clare, then?"

"Aye."

"And?"

"How could I say no to either of you?"

"I'm so glad to hear you say that, I know how stubborn you can be and thought I might be in for a bit of a struggle."

"Normally you would be, but this is different."

"As you may or may not know, your cousin, Sister Mary, has a cousin on the other side of the family; he lives on a ranch in Montana in America and has agreed to adopt the second baby."

"Oh yes, I've heard her speak of him."

"He's a good man."

"Is he married?"

"No."

"How is it that a single man is able to adopt a child?"

"He is well to do. He's an Irish immigrant. He is very generous with us. We know that he's a practicing Catholic and we're convinced, after the normal research we do, that he has the means to take care of the child's well being and that he is a good and decent man."

As if not listening, Cassie said, "Reverend Mother, my editor at the paper will never let me just run off to America. I had to work him hard to get the job and he's just looking for a reason to sack me because I'm a woman."

"I've already talked to your editor, he owes me a favor."

"What? He doesn't do favors for anyone. Did you catch the old sot screwing a goat or something?"

The minute it came out of her mouth, Cassie was sorry. But growing up in the slums of Dublin, The Reverend Mother had heard much worse.

"I'll just pretend I didn't hear that, young lady. Your boss has agreed to a three-month leave of absence and you'll have your job when you return."

"Three months, why so long?"

"Just in case."

"Just in case what?"

"He needs some help. He's a man, Cassie."

"I can come back earlier if I want, right?"

"Aye, I just wanted to make sure he had time to find the right help."

"Okay."

"Oh, and did I mention there's five thousand dollars in it for whoever accepts this job?"

"Five thousand dollars! That's more than a year's salary."

Chapter 19
Baptism of Fire and Blood

The Short Strand

Belfast, Northern Ireland

October 1960

The Royal Ulster Constabulary, RUC, Newton Abbey Station was quiet on this Saturday afternoon. Ian Wright, who had been a police officer for just over five years and had just been promoted to CID, the Criminal Investigations Department, was on the fast track. He was gunning for Special Branch. He had seen how the game was played and he learned quickly. He picked up the cigarette that was burning in his ashtray as he finished some paperwork. There was no one around. The Orange lodges were marching and raising hell on the Catholic neighborhoods and all his lads were out on the route making sure the fucking Taigs didn't start some shit. He smiled at the thought and blew a plume of smoke into the air.

The door opened and a gruff looking Benji Mason walked into his office.

Ian said, “All right there, Benji?”

“Just fine there, Ian.” Said Benji Mason.

“Good Lad.”

Seeing Benji reminded Ian of his first day with the RUC. They had traveled to the RUC training center at Enniskillen. They all lined up and in the middle of them all was Benji Mason. All of five foot two and maybe 100 pounds. There was some snickering. Benji looked the proverbial fish out of water and was bounced after two weeks.

Ian had heard he tried for the UDR, The Ulster Defense Regiment, Northern Ireland's infantry, but got bounced out of there as well. But not to be turned away so easily, Benji decided if he couldn't defend Ulster from those Papist bastards the legitimate way, he'd join the UDA, an outlawed Protestant paramilitary organization on the side of the Loyalist in defense of the Crown.

Ian said, “Sit down Benji, smoke?”

“Aye, thanks.”

Ian shook a cigarette from the pack and handed him his lighter as Benji put the smoke to his lips.

Ian said, “Benji, do you know who Dermot Brennan is?”

"Aye, Brigade commander for the RA, Devil's Triangle, I believe."

"Right. Sources tell me he's coming to Belfast for a baptism. He'll be at Holy Cross Church in Ardoyne tomorrow at two in the afternoon. Should be nice and quite, nice and easy for you lads. You know what to do."

The envelope of cash was slid across the desk and Benji Mason disappeared down the street.

Ian smiled again. The great chicken shit Benji Mason. He'd shoot woman and children if they were Taigs and there were a few extra quid in it for him.

He said, "Nice to have a lad like Benji now and again to count on. He'd better not fuck this thing up."

Sean and Patricia O'Kane brought their new baby boy, Martin Peder, home to their flat in the Short Strand neighborhood in Belfast. Outside the sound of the Orange lodges emptying into the streets and the lambeg drums sounding their percussive hatred could be heard. Orangemen celebrating their odium as if the battle of the Boyne had taken place earlier that month rather than in the year 1690.

The homecoming celebration of Martin Peder O'Kane consisted of hurled stones, Molotov cocktails and shouts of vile and profane antipathy. Sean worked the fire hoses in the evenings, sometimes sundown to sunup, to keep his flat and those in the neighborhood from burning to the ground.

One month after the new arrival, Patricia's brother Dermot and his wife Bridget Brennan came to Belfast from Portadown for Martin's christening as his Godparents.

Benji Mason and the five lads that made up his crew were part of the Ulster Volunteer Force, UVF, a rogue Loyalist paramilitary group that hated Catholics and Nationalists and fought anything to do with a united Ireland. Northern Ireland was a country unto itself and if they had anything to say about it, it would stay that way. They headed south out of Monkstown, a Belfast Suburb, where they made their home. The tension was high in the van as they made ready for the assault.

Benji said, "Lads, don't put the masks on until we come to a stop. We don't want to tip anyone off. Then slide the door open and start firing."

Each nervously checked their weapons as they drove through the light Sunday traffic.

The priest at Holy Cross Church in Ardoyne called the Godparents forward as well as Sean and Patricia. When all the blessings were over and it was time for the actual baptism, bullets suddenly began to riddle the church, finding their way into the wooden pews. Dermot knew he had been a key target of the Red Hand, the UDA and the UVF for some time now, and it was he they were after. He commanded his brigade out of Portadown, a Protestant and Loyalist stronghold, and his guerilla street tactics had become legendary. They hated him, they hated his success, and they wanted him dead.

Shards of stained glass, large splinters of wood and chunks of stone danced throughout. A shard skipped past Dermot Brennan, leaving a superficial cut across his forehead. Holding the baby at the time, he leaned forward by instinct to cover the child. Without realizing he'd been cut, several drops of blood fell into the baptismal font.

The small crowd in the church heard Benji scream, "Let's get the fuck out of here."

Dermot said to his second in command, "What the hell, their not coming in?"

"Maybe just a little welcome to Belfast for you."

Dermot, who never traveled without a unit of his men, had them check out the perimeter of the church when the excitement was over and they realized no one was hurt. His Second Lieutenant walked in and gave him the all clear nod. They finished the baptism of Martin Peder O'Kane.

As they headed north Benji screamed in jubilation and said, "They all have to be dead, right lads? Every fucking one of them Taigs dead in their own fucking church. Good work men."

* * *

Two days later Ian Wright walked in to The Brown Bear Pub in the Shankill area of Belfast where Benji Mason was holding court.

Benji said, "Did you lads see the news?"

"What about?"

"The shooting down at Holy Cross Church in Ardoyne?"

"Aye, we did see something."

Benji just smiled as he drank his pint.

"Was that you Benji?"

He looked at the lads sitting at the table and winked when he suddenly felt a presence standing behind him. He looked up and saw Ian Wright glaring down at him.

Ian said, "I need a word Benji."

"Sure, Ian, have a seat."

"Outside Benji."

"Sure."

Before he was all the way out the door three large men were punching him and kicking him as he lay on the ground trying to cover his head. He found himself suddenly on his feet as Ian Wright held him up by his jacket.

He put his face an inch from Benji's and said, "When I ask you to do a job for me I expect it to be done. When I tell you I want a man dead, I want the motherfucker dead. No one inside that church died…no one!"

He slammed Benji so hard against the wall that he saw stars and as he slid down the wall. Ian reached into Benji's jacket pocket and retrieved what was left of the money he had given him.

He then squatted down to talk to the man who sat there stunned and said, "If you and your lads fuck up like this again…let's just say there won't be another chance. Do you understand?"

All Benji could do was nod as the Ulster policemen walked away.

Two months after Martin had blessed their home, Sean came home from work tired and out of sorts, and Patricia ran to him and threw her arms around him and said, "I'm pregnant."

Chapter 20
Columbkille's Penance

Bishop John Byrne's office

Dublin

September 11, 1960

Ruari O'Keefe looked like a man who'd had no sleep. He had paced the nights away for a week. He had fought the thought of a bottle all week, some battles he won, some he lost. His old addictions aroused, wanting to run to those old haunts. He sat in the chair across from his boss, raised his head and fixed his gaze on the crucifix that hung on the wall above the Bishop's credenza. The man in the chair beneath looked encumbered.

The Bishop said, "You look like hell, O'Keefe."

"What'd you expect?"

"Don't start with me, you weren't the only one who didn't get much sleep this past week."

Ruari put his head down; it was not his intention to hand this burden to someone else. He could feel the weight build once more. His life, his vocation, his future, everything, teetering on the head of a pin, rocking back and forth, waiting for a nudge forcing him into the castigation he knew he deserved and yet was loath to carry out.

The Bishop continued, "However, it gave me a chance to pray and meditate. You'll be sorely missed."

Ruari winced. He knew it was over. Everything he dreamed of, everything for which he had worked, all of it washed down the drain. He'd traded five minutes for a lifetime.

He thought, "They can all kiss off, I'm going to O'Donahue's Pub. I'll get pissed and make plans to move to Australia where no one will know me."

Ruari stood to leave.

The Bishop said, "Where are you going? We're not done."

"I made my bed, Your Eminence. What's done is done and I can't take it back. But I'm man enough to take my punishment. I'll clear my things out of the rectory and figure out what to do from there. I'm thinking if I go to Australia, I can put the shame behind me and no one there need be the wiser."

"What? You think I'm relieving you of your duties?"

"You're not?"

"I guess you didn't hear me last week?"

Ruari looked puzzled and the Bishop smiled.

"I'm not taking your collar, Ruari, I've got plans for you. Your sin was grave, no doubt, and it certainly can't be overlooked nor dismissed as easily as you walking away."

"What do you mean?"

"The Columban priests have a missionary in Mindanao in the Philippines. You'll be living in a hut, eating bugs and fried bananas, while trying to convert pagans. The Columbans are dedicated men. You'll be around your own kind and you'll learn a lot."

"So I'm not done?"

"No, of course not."

"How long?"

"How long what?"

"How long will I be gone?"

"Twenty years."

Father Ruari O'Keefe fixed his gaze once more on the crucifix. Then he smiled as a thought dawned on him. He looked at the Bishop sitting patiently across the desk from him and said, "I'm keeping good company then."

The Bishop furrowed an eyebrow in question and said, "What?"

"St. Columbkille."

The Bishop smiled and said, "Aye, St. Molaise gave Columbkille the same penance, but his was forever. Yours is twenty-years."

The Bishop smiled. He *had* been a disciple of St. Columbkille since his days in the seminary. He had called on his intercession many times in the last forty years and the week before was no different, reading the Saint's poetry and writings, looking for an answer. Now he knew his prayers had been answered and he had done the right thing.

Chapter 21
That Wasn't So Tough

Mercy Convent, Dublin

Same Day

The window on the second floor of the convent was open and the shears on the inside floated as if dancing on the breeze as the wind blew softly along Baggot Street. Clare stared through them to the street as they caressed her face and wiped her tears.

Vitriolic and sad, she played the scene over and over again in her head. Tired, though she was, she had been wide-awake to watch Sister Mary and Sister Evangeline walk away with her babies. In total despair she thought, "How could they take my babies away?"

Sister Mary walked into the room with hot tea and cakes. Clare wanted neither.

"You've got to start eating sweetheart, you're going to get ill."

"I couldn't possibly be more ill than I am right now."

"Clare, I deliver babies all the time. I deal with married mothers and unwed mothers. Overwhelming sadness after the wee one is born is a big part of having babies for a great number of women."

"I wouldn't be sad if I had my babies."

"You can't say that, you really don't know."

"I know one is on its way to America, please tell me the other, at least, stayed in Ireland."

"Telling you won't help, it'll just make the longing worse."

Clare put her face into her hands and as she wept uncontrollably she said, "It couldn't get any worse. I want to die, I wish I were dead, goddamn it!"

Sister Mary got on her knees in front of Clare's rocker and hugged her as she bent over in agony.

She whispered, "Clare, I can't say."

"What do you mean you can't say? Or you won't say."

"Clare, please I could lose my habit over this, don't."

"Your habit? I just lost me twin boys."

Sister Mary stared at the picture of The Sacred Heart that hung above the bed where Clare slept, blessed herself, smiled and said in a whisper, "Yes."

"Yes, what?"

"Yes, the other stayed in Ireland."

"North or south?"

"Clare, please, I can't."

Clare glared at the nun with venom and she said, "I lost my goddamn babies, north or south?"

"North."

"Belfast?"

"Aye."

"Catholic or Protestant?"

"What difference does that make?"

"Have you read *any* Irish history?"

"What kind of family do you think a Mercy convent would put a child with?"

"So this baby is going to be raised a Catholic in Belfast?"

"Clare, what?"

"What do you mean what? Everyone knows the hardships of a Catholic in Belfast, how could you?"

"But…"

"But what?"

Sister Mary stood, her rosy cheeks now a burnt umber and her rarely lost temper no where to be found. Sister Evangeline walked in to deliver a message, saw her friend and walked quickly out.

She said, "That's some way you have of showing a little gratitude. And for all we've done for you. So that's it, is it?"

The two women stared at one another, locked in a fury. Clare suddenly realizing that she may have just crossed the threshold into a place she didn't want to be.

Without a thought, Sister Mary said, "The O'Kanes are a wonderful family, he'll be well taken care of."

"Can the O'Kanes stop a fucking bullet or a car bomb from blowing up?"

"Your gratitude is overwhelming. And why should I have even begun to believe that we were becoming good friends Clare Eva White."

With that the nun walked out and Clare smiled and thought, "The O'Kanes in Belfast. That wasn't so tough."

Chapter 22
The Door Between Them

Dublin, Ireland

Two Days later

After making amends with Sister Mary, who told her she needed a confessional after the string of profanities she had thrown out, and thanking Sister Evangeline and The Reverend Mother, Clare left the convent to resume her life in Dublin. Somehow she was to pick up the pieces of her miserable, lonely existence and get on with it.

She put the key in the lock in the door of her empty flat and the click echoed in the darkness that awaited her there. She knew that Cassie would be gone by now, but one way or another, she had hoped that just maybe she would be waiting for her on the other side of the door. A hug, a good word, an act of random kindness was all she wanted right now. The door swung open and squeaked on its hinges to a stop. That's what it was, she thought, nothingness that awaited her there and the thought was almost overwhelming.

Clare sat up hour after hour; the seconds seemed to move as if submersed in water. The ticks of the clock soon became a loud boom in her ears. As the night strolled to dawn, she felt nothing but a cold chill intensify within her, allowing a demon of hatred to possess her as if wrapping her in cellophane, she could see everything but couldn't breathe.

Day break began to invade her flat and she realized she hadn't even taken off her coat. She stood with effort and put the kettle on the boil. Just finishing up her second cup she heard a feeble knock on the door.

She opened it and stopped cold. She looked at the man outside her door and said, "Father O'Keefe."

Ruari could manage no more than a shy smile. After a moment they moved to shake hands with incredible awkwardness. He finally pulled her to him and they gently held each other. It felt as if he were custom made to hold her in his comfort and warmth. The cellophane fell away and she could breathe again in the safety of his strong arms. She, with her overcoat hanging on her shoulders like the bedclothes of an unmade bed and black bags under her eyes, he, breathing hard, trying to control the panic he felt.

He said, "Are you going somewhere?"

She said, "Ah, no."

He lowered his voice to just above a whisper and said, "May I come in?"

"Aye, I'm sorry for being rude. Please do."

She offered him a cup of tea, he said, "Thank you"

"So, how're you feeling?"

With a chill in her voice she said, "How do you think I'm feeling?"

"Fair enough."

"What are you doing in Dublin?

"Cassie came to see me."

"She did?"

"Aye."

"She wasn't supposed to."

"Clare, I had a right to know."

"That wasn't the point. I just felt it would've been far more devastating to you than me and no one need be the wiser. Ignorance is bliss."

"Do you think I didn't have maybe an inkling?"

"I didn't know and didn't care."

"Well, after I found out I couldn't live with myself, you going through all of this alone without any support from me. So, I went to see Bishop Byrne."

"And?"

"I told him everything. I couldn't live like this; it was time to own up to my actions."

"But Cassie made it clear that I wanted nothing from you, right?"

"Clare, you're stronger than me, trying to do this all by yourself. But it wasn't right for me to be left in the dark; I'm glad she told me. And for me to pretend like nothing happened when I knew in me heart that it had, well, it was all wrong. Had she not told me I would've come anyway, if only just to check on you to be sure."

"So what was the outcome?"

"What?"

"The outcome of your meeting with the Bishop?"

"Oh, that."

He thought for a moment and winced as if the sudden reminder were a shooting pain.

He said, "I'm to join the Columban missionaries in Mindanao in the Philippines."

"How long?"

"Twenty years."

She could hear her own breath being sucked in as if it were magnified. She could feel this cloak of derision pull her down further. She seemed to sag under its weight right in front of him. She thought she might fall under its enormous burden. Not only had she lost her babies, but now this man was going to do his penance for the next twenty years in the Philippines—all this pain, loss and misery for a few lousy minutes of pleasure. She thought she might lose her mind. Maybe that was it, her insanity, her loss of mind, *was* her penance. No, she thought, there could be no penance, she could not plead insanity, she was sane enough. It was much simpler than that; in her mind the sin was unforgivable.

They stared at one another sipping their tea, struggling for the next words. A light went off in her head and a flicker of hope shimmered there only momentarily and she said, "Ruari, don't go. Stay here, marry me, let's get the babies back and have a family. We can move to America where no one will know. All of us together."

The thought had crossed his mind during those long nights, even when he stood before the Bishop knowing his career as a priest was all but history. But then what? What about his penance? Hell was eternal. But, if he left the priesthood and made good as a father and a husband, didn't that own up to his responsibilities? Didn't that make up for his mistake? Wasn't that a form of penance? But what about his calling to do God's work?

He held her hand as she anticipated his response. He leaned back and said, "Saints in heaven save us, but I've made a mess of things."

"So have I but we can make up for it. It's not too late."

"Clare, don't make this harder than it already is. I can't. We can't."

Tears streaked her face. Any small flame of hope that had existed anywhere in her world was just covered by a heavy wet blanket, extinguished in a damp mildew of guilt and shame leaving her wondering if she would ever feel warm and dry again.

She put her finger to his mouth and said, "Shush, I know. 'Twas stupid of me to even bring it up."

"No it wasn't, lass. It was grand and for a moment this pain lifted off me chest and I felt a wave of relief."

Then he heard the words of Reinhold Niebuhr in the back of his mind saying, "Taking, as Jesus did, this sinful world as it is, not as I would have. Trusting that He will make all things right if I surrender to His will."

Then he thought, "But what was God's will? Was it that I leave this beautiful woman to go live with rodents, snakes and large bugs?" He poured more steaming water and shuddered a moment. Wanting with all his heart to stay, give up his vows and marry this woman now. But something tangible was tugging at him, something overwhelmed his mind, it was dark and yet blindingly bright. And he knew what he had to do; he hung his head and wept. The scourge of Ireland was about to be his. He was about to join the throngs who left her shores, and the pain was obvious.

He stood as if a heavy burden was strapped to his back. He stared down at Clare. She stood and they held each other in the cold morning light, desperate for things to be different. Frantically searching for something to say that would make it all go away, make the ache subside, if only for a moment. But the words never came and the pain never went away.

When the door shut, the silence of despair fell on them both, Ruari in the hall and Clare in the living room, both staring blindly from opposite sides, their hearts being torn apart, ripped from their chest, like the hopelessness of burying a lover, only eternal anguish up ahead.

Chapter 23
Deliverance

Montana, United States

Late September 1960

Paddy Quinlan waited restlessly for the baby to arrive. His large ranch house was so quiet it was deafening, and at times it became so unbearable that he went to sleep in the bunkhouse with his hired hands.

Horace Mansfield would come over in the evenings to lend comfort and have a drink with him, but it was all hard. Paddy worried about the safe arrival of this new child.

Horace said, “Paddy, you have got to stop this worrying boy. It’s going to kill you.”

Paddy said, “I know, I know. But that puddle-jumper from Denver into Butte is a bitch. What happens if the damn thing goes down?”

Horace laughed and said, “Yeah, and you could fall off your darned horse and break your damned neck the next time you ride. Relax son they’re going to be fine.”

The next day Horace came by Paddy’s house to have a cup of coffee. He and Paddy were driving to Butte to pick up the new arrivals. They walked out of Paddy’s house and when they got to the car Horace said, “Come to think of it, I’m driving. You’re acting like such a damn fool I’m afraid you’ll run us right off the road.”

Paddy laughed, threw the keys to his friend and relaxed for the first time in quite a while.

They drove out of Polson on the south end of Flathead Lake and headed south. Horace said, “Who you got lined up to take care of this baby. Unless you’re planning on giving up ranching and becoming a nurse maid.”

Paddy laughed and said, “No plans of doing that. I figured that the lass bringing him along can take care of the baby until I find the right nanny. I’ll pay her more than she could make back home.”

“Have you asked her about that?”

“No, but.”

Horace cackled.

Paddy said, “What?”

Horace said, “I’ve met my share of the Irish around these parts. Pigheaded comes to mind and you not the least.”

"So you assume that she will not want to stay and work?"

"Let's just say that I want you to know that I'll be here for whatever you need."

"Damn it, Horace, Now you've got me worried."

The two cowboys made it to the Butte airport and went straight to the gate designated for the Denver arrival. Paddy walked back in forth in front of the window unable to sit still, Horace laughed, pulled his hat down and took a snooze.

The plane landed and the last person off was a woman carrying a baby.

Paddy walked to her smiling and said, "McCaslin Kenny?"

She said, "Aye. But please call me Cassie."

Paddy said, "Okay Cassie. I'm Padraig Quinlan but you can call me Paddy and this is my good friend, Horace Mansfield."

She said, "Pleased to meet you both."

Horace tipped his cowboy hat forward and said, "Ma'am."

Chapter 24
The God of Beneficence

Four Clover Ranch

Two months later

Cassie sat in the great room at the Four Clovers ranch and sighed, thinking back on the last two months. On the second day out of Dublin on her way to Montana with the baby she began to regret taking on this task. She had begun to fall in love with the baby boy and knew there was going to be hell to pay walking away from him, and started to wonder now whether she would have the strength.

Since her humble beginnings, Cassie had shared everything from clothes to chores with eleven siblings for little more than three meager meals a day. But like many little girls, she dreamed of moving to a faraway land, being swept up by a handsome prince and living in a luxurious castle with servants. She realized now that she had finally crossed over that moat. The intoxicating wealth coupled with her powerful affection for the baby was a recipe for adulteration, ruining her friendship with Clare and any self-respect she had developed since leaving home and setting out into the world.

Cassie let the large sofa consume her and cooed softly at her good fortune and quietly thanked the god of fate for his beneficence. However, in her ignominy, she missed the god of prudence frowning at her naïveté.

The delicious aromas of dinner began to permeate the great room as she was giving the baby his bottle. Her stomach began to rumble.

Since Paddy had first come to the ranch he had renamed it, had torn down the original house and had built, in its place, this large seven-bedroom estate in anticipation of one day having a large family. It also served well when entertaining the Montana Rancher's Association, VIPs, government officials and visitors from Ireland.

Like every night since she had arrived with the baby, Cassie and the baby sat on a large comfortable sofa and stared at the luxury that surrounded them. Because of her studies in Irish Art History for a short while at Trinity College in Dublin, she was impressed with the artwork that graced the walls of this room.

Paddy clomped in, dusty from a day's work on the ranch, sat down beside Cassie, removed his boots and rubbed his sore feet. He looked at Cassie and the baby as she studied his impressive art collection and said, "Are you familiar with the Irish impressionists?"

She said, "Some. This is an impressive collection of work and even more so that they're hanging here."

"What's that supposed to mean?"

"I meant nothing derogatory. We're not exactly in a major metropolitan area here and these works would be the envy of any decent art museum."

She partially opened a door to allow him the opportunity to either slam a finger in his ignorance or walk in to discuss the work, why it moved him and why it was here. She hated it when wealthy people collected art for no other reason than to diversify their financial portfolios and couldn't give a damn, or worse yet, were not even aware of what it took, what the artist went through; it was an insult to them and their work.

He stepped over the threshold with more than a little trepidation, but with the grace of one who loved the work for what it was. He loved the Irish impressionists but had never had the opportunity to discuss them with anyone before and here suddenly was a student of art.

He finally let his guard down a little and said, "Look, you probably know a lot more than I do about Irish Art."

"Paddy, it's not necessarily about what you know as it is how the work makes you feel. How does it move you?"

He stopped and seemed to be thinking carefully about what he would say next. He looked at her and said, "When I was a lad, as poor as we were, my Da would recite poetry, his own and others. He went on about this creative process. He'd write his verse and then occasionally share it with us. He talked about the need for art, music, dance, poetry, storytelling, writing, you know, all these creative expressions and the great talent that Ireland had to offer the world in all these areas. My da had it, my brother Dinty had it, but I never really understood much of it because I don't seem to have much of it in me, at least like da talked."

"Have what in you?"

"This creative thing that Da and Dinty have. I've never had a desire, even inkling, to create anything. I just had a desire to find good honest work and do it well."

"There's nothing wrong with that. It takes all kinds."

"Exactly. So when I started to make some extra cash I wanted to spread it around a bit. I thought if I didn't have it in me to create something, I could at least support the arts and those starving while trying. "

"Sure."

"So, I sent away for a book on Irish art."

"I noticed that on the coffee table."

"Aye. Each piece covers the page with a small blurb about the artist at the bottom. I was intrigued by the section on the impressionists, or as you put it, moved, I guess. There were paintings that I really loved, so I got in touch with this art broker and the first one I purchased was this one."

Paddy pointed to a painting and Cassie said, "*Temptation*, Walter Osborne."

Paddy raised an eyebrow and said, "They could be twins couldn't they?"

She stared at him for a minute and said, "They're not, but could be. Actually they can be anything you want them to be."

He said, "In that case, I prefer twin boys."

Then she nodded at another Osborne as she held the baby and said, "*Apple Gatherings.*"

He looked at the painting and then at her, impressed and not at all displeased to have someone around who appreciated this work that he had spent time and money to bring here to raise the cultural level, at least a little.

Cassie's initial take on Paddy was one of new wealth and arrogance, however hard working. She had tested him to find out if the art was here to impress people, to diversify his portfolio or if it was truly from the heart and said, "What is it about Osborne that moves you? Having two pieces hanging here, that must have set you back."

He smiled diffidently looking at her and seeing something in her eye, not so much a glance as a shimmering glint that told him he was being appraised.

He said, "The children."

She was looking at the baby and expected him to expound. When he didn't she said, "Go on."

He said, "He's obviously a very talented artist, and when I found out he was an impressionist I wanted to know what was meant by impressionism, what was the impressionist movement, you know, in the art world. I did a little research, it didn't make much sense but I liked the art and I happen to love children, always have. He obviously does too or one would guess he does or why would he spend so much time painting them? And so here we are."

He passed the test.

The room fell silent while the baby slept and Cassie put him in his bassinette.

Paddy said, "Enough about art. What are your plans?"

"Honestly, I've fallen head-over-heels in love with this baby."

"That settles it then, you'll stay on as nanny."

"That settles nothing."

He stared at her with knowing eyes, remembering his conversation with Horace.

She said, "You really are a pompous, arrogant son of a bitch."

"Wait a minute."

"No, you wait a minute. I'm not here to be your damned maid or to serve you your supper. I shouldn't even be here at all. I have simply fallen in love with this baby and all I'm saying is that it would be difficult to leave him. I never said I'd go to work for you and I never said I wouldn't go back to Ireland where I belong, where I should be heading to already."

"You seem to be enjoying the accommodations well enough."

She looked at him a moment longer than she wanted.

He said, "Well then you want to tell me what you did say?"

"I said you were a pompous. . ."

"Yes, I heard that."

"Where do you get off? You come from poverty, like ninety-nine percent of us. You came to this country and made it big. So what? Did you forget where you came from? Have you gotten maybe a little too big for your own damn britches?"

"How do you know I came from poverty?"

"Well if I'm not mistaken you already told me. But it doesn't matter, it's written all over you."

He stopped and thought for a minute and knew she was right, but he would be damned if he would admit that to her. Besides, as this Irish beauty flared up she became more striking and intriguing than she already was and Paddy knew she could fill that empty place in his heart. She may be just the feisty companion he longed for. He didn't want a wallflower; he wanted someone with passion and fire, someone who would challenge him, fight with him, air her own opinions and let him know when she disagreed.

But he sensed that she was using him as a bucket of well water for some other conflagration she was struggling to extinguish.

He said quietly, "You've known me for two months and we spend maybe an hour a day together and you pass such harsh judgment. Do you really know me well enough to do that?"

He had successfully taken the wind from her sails and it was the last thing she expected. At the worst she thought he may strike her, at best she'd get a hell of a tongue-lashing.

She looked up with surprise in her eyes and said, "Well. . ."

He picked up the baby and kissed him softly on the cheek. He did love the smell of a freshly bathed infant. He thought, "Who didn't?"

Leaving her ship stranded on a windless sea he said, "You've had a long day with this wee one. Take some time to yourself. Check the library, there's some great literature that you may like. I'll take him from here."

Close to speechless she said, "Do you know where everything is?"

"No, but if I can't find what I need I'll holler. I've always been pretty good with the little ones. By the way I'll pay for your trip back to Ireland if that's what you want. The island is like a magnet, always gently tugging at us, I know just how you feel. Oh, and that reminds me, I owe you five thousand dollars, I'll have a check for you tomorrow, whatever you decide."

She stood and stared at him while he held the baby boy over his head and cooed at him further.

Paddy said, "By the way, his name is Michael Padraig but I think we'll call him Mick. The christening is on Sunday. Father John O'Connor is a friend of mine from Butte, and he's coming up this weekend. I think you'll like him."

He held the infant on his shoulder and stared at Cassie for a brief moment. She nodded her head and silently walked from the room, more puzzled than before, and heard Paddy say, "Michael Patrick Quinlan, have you ever heard of the great Irish Patriot Napper Tandy. . ."

Chapter 25
La Femme Au Drap Rouge

Four Clovers ranch

Two weeks later

Cassie could not leave, especially after the last episode with Paddy. She tried to get tough with him and found out he wasn't the arrogant nouveau riche jerk she wanted him to be. He worked hard and earned every penny. She found that he was good to all the people that worked for him and all the people he did business with.

She was settling in and the quandary played out in her mind day in and day out. The longer she stayed the harder it was to leave and the greater her guilt for betraying Clare. She began to enjoy the wealth that surrounded her more than she wanted to. After her irrational outburst, or at least what she thought was irrational, she felt a substantial remorse and even shame at the kiss of Judas she had lain on the cheek of her best friend in Ireland.

In her justification, she had warmed up to Paddy immeasurably. But with more a specious demeanor she would approach him as he walked in dusty from his day's duties on the ranch and pretend to be interested in his life. Her new behavior seemed to further confuse the issue of disloyalty to Mick's biological mother.

Cassie was in the great room late one evening, after Mick was in bed, listening to Mozart and sipping a glass of cabernet when Paddy walked in. She had discovered Paddy's wine cellar and had acquired a taste for some of the better vintages, which she found had eliminated the inner tension she had created, at least for a while.

She stood admiring a painting. It was a nude done by another Irish impressionist, Roderic O'Connor, who spent most of his adult life studying in France. She guessed, after spending a month with him, that Paddy considered himself a man's man and conjectured that he may have struggled exposing this softer, more cultured side of himself to anyone who might venture into his home.

Paddy walked in and pulled a clean wine glass from the china hutch in the corner and poured himself a glass of the cabernet and walked to Cassie's shoulder and said, "What do you think?"

She said, "It's amazing. How did you get this? I thought all of O'Connor's works were in collections in France?"

He said, "I didn't know that."

She said, "Yeah, the French who couldn't get their hands on a Monet, Cezanne or Matisse went after the lesser known Irish impressionists who studied there, especially O'Connor."

"Well, a Frenchman did own it but everything's for sale."

They both sipped the red wine studying the curves and voluptuous breasts of the beautiful French model. Her soft buttocks and backside were reflected in a mirror in the background that also replicated the artist who painted her, pallet in hand. She lay on a full red drape looking as if she was waiting patiently for her lover. O'Connor's look in the reflection gave the admirer the subtle idea that he was in love with the woman, yet had been yielding to his urge to make love to her until the work was finished, all adding to the sexual tension emanating from each stroke of his brush.

She smiled at her correct supposition when he said, "I fell in love with the work the moment I laid eyes on it and wondered if it was appropriate to hang in here. You know how people are around here. I knew I had to have it and originally thought I'd hang it in my bedroom."

She nodded and said, "Well, it's not exactly Paris."

He smiled and said, "After the decision was made, my art broker tracked it down. The negotiations were long and drawn out and I ended up paying way more than I wanted to a Frenchman who considered a rancher in Montana too unsophisticated to own something like this. I believe his exact words were, 'I don't care how rich he is, anyone who walks into his home with cow shit on his boots night after night is both gauche and totally beneath me. I will not sell it no matter how much he offers.' And I, of course, made the man an offer he couldn't refuse."

Cassie laughed and said, "You know, I think I remember reading about this in the Dublin paper."

Paddy raised an eyebrow and said, "Yeah?"

"Aye. The Irish were delighted that one of their own, even if he lived across the pond, got his hands on an O'Connor."

"Well, it's just further proof that everyone's a whore. So you tell me *now* who's gauche and beneath who?"

Cassie said, "Don't take it too personally. The French can be rather truculent and not just with Montana ranchers. They think that they invented sophistication and they may be right. But they don't have to be so haughty."

A moment of silence followed as they both sipped their wine staring at the painting. Paddy hadn't realized until now the sexual tension the work created in him. Maybe, he thought, it was the reason he had to have this work in the first place, why it became so important to him. His inhibitions started to float away in a river of desire, as the wine began to swirl in gentle whirlpools in his mind.

Cassie turned to him to say something and stopped suddenly as they stared at one another. Paddy leaned very subtlety toward her and without further reflection they fell into one another's arms in a passionate kiss. Cassie had expected an awkward dispassionate sensuality and was surprised at Paddy's gentleness. He touched her delicately as if she were a precious porcelain figurine, easily broken.

Paddy smiled at her and said, “La Femme Au Drap Rouge.”

“What?”

“The painting, it's called La Femme Au Drap Rouge.”

She said, “Aye, Woman On a Red Drape.”

Chapter 26
The Letter

Four Clovers Ranch

One month later.

Light began to force itself through the outer membrane of Paddy's heart and it began to float like air in the resulting radiance. Herding cattle, breaking horses, mending fence or walking through manure, it didn't matter; he could smell her bittersweet perfume, taste the wine on her lips and feel her supple, columbine breast against his rough hands.

His mind wandered to her face, her touch, her smile and even her petulance. The thought left him spent as though he could take not one more step.

Darkness sucked the life from her once vibrant soul; Cassie sat in the shadowy prison cell that had incarcerated her mind. The self-loathing permeated every fiber of her body and, even after the letter from Clare, the exoneration she sought would never come, it was all wrong.

The second glass of wine after lunch, which would become three and then four, temporarily washing away her iniquities and her absolution had been momentarily realized, however false.

She thought, "And why the hell not? Everybody else was getting theirs." It was her turn.

"All the wealth," She cooed softly. "All of it could be mine and that beautiful blond haired boy napping upstairs was icing on the cake. Fuck Clare if she couldn't understand."

The darkness clouded her mind again and the chains of despair, hopelessness and betrayal became so heavy she was loath to move.

Try as she might to build the proper façade for Paddy's arrival each evening for supper, he sensed something was not right. And as much as he thought he loved her, he debated the possibility of infatuation. Love or no, intuition told him that Cassie would not reciprocate that feeling, not now, not ever. She loved the large home, the money, the material, but not him. But he knew that whatever it was that bothered her, the boy would moor her like an anchor in the harbor of her justification.

"What was it?" He thought. "What was she running from? What unseen enemy was attacking her?" At rare moments he allowed himself to focus, really focus on this complex woman. He wanted to know what was bothering her and then he didn't. Knowing all of this as sure as he knew he was Irish, he couldn't bring it up to her, couldn't ask. Paddy lost the courage for the first time in his life. He would give away all he had to change how she felt about him, more afraid of losing her than anything in his life, a novel feeling for him.

His suspicion about her demons were confirmed when he ran across a letter from Ireland, lying opened and addressed to Cassie, that she had inadvertently left on his desk. He picked it up, looked at it and knew he shouldn't read it so he put it down. But after an hour of not being able to concentrate on his work he gave in to the temptation and read the letter.

It had been from a woman named Clare White, who he now knew to be Mick's biological mother. It was a scathing reply to a letter Cassie had initiated, apparently hoping to get Clare's approval of her staying in Montana to take care of Mick. There was nothing ostensible in the reply:

Cassie:

I received your letter in today's post and am shocked and hurt. I would expect a letter like this from an enemy, but my supposed best friend? And what was the five thousand dollars, ransom for the little one you took on errand?

But now you write and what? Ask my permission to raise my child, my flesh and blood? Imagine my shock and horror at reading that?

I thought, for a fleeting moment, that you cherished our friendship as much as I. If you did it would be easy to show the kind of empathy necessary to make the right decision and come back home. And now I am supposed to live my life thinking every day of my best friend raising my child. The child that spent nine months developing in my very own womb, who I suffered dearly to deliver into this god awful world, who will know you as his mother and won't even know I exist? Don't you dare ask such sacrifice of me.

Since we were children it was all about you. You have always been a selfish, self-centered git, but I always overlooked that due to your gregarious personality and the sparkle you carried that lit up every room you walked into.

But knowing you as I do leads me to believe that you would justify this horrific blunder to gain the creature comforts provided by another's wealth.

If your decision is to stay in America and live this lie, I can do nothing to stop you. I can only say that I, at least, will be able to stare at my reflection in the mirror everyday and know that I have done the right thing, including saving your sorry arse from the tinker. Did you think I wouldn't take such aim at guilt? It is not beneath me.

With that said, I do not condone this decision of yours to stay, but pray that God will give me the strength to forgive you, so that the hatred I feel for you at this moment will not consume me and ruin my life further.

If I do not see you in Dublin in the next few months I will know what your decision was. In that case please do not write or try to contact me again. . . ever.

Clare.

Paddy stared at the letter and was stunned, this was the problem with Cassie, this was what she had struggled so hard with. He did not know what to do. And who was the tinker?

Chapter 27
The Truth Serum

Four Clovers Ranch

August 1961

Cassie Kenny had found herself lost in the middle of nowhere. She had become a glorified nanny by letting herself become inebriated with the false pretense of wealth. One day she loved Paddy and the next she hated him. One moment she was staying, the next she was leaving. Mick was just beginning to walk and she loved him so much her heart ached. But his short blonde hair and deep brown eyes, echoing a reflection of Clare in his every move or facial expression, reminded her daily of her illusory machinations.

She missed Clare so much that, at times, she felt a physical pain shoot through her body. The question of why constantly nagged her conscience. When Mick first sat up, said his first word, laughed for the first time or took his first step, her first instinct was to send Clare a note. Then she would see a brief reflection of herself in a mirror or window; see the thief standing their robbing her best friend of these moments, which merely continued nurturing the self-loathing that plagued her this past year, a feeling that only a good bottle of wine or strong Irish whiskey could temporarily eradicate.

Paddy had been in Butte on business all day and had walked into the house at around eight p.m. Mick was down for the night and Cassie sat with a glass of wine in the great room listening to Chopin.

Paddy walked in, poured himself a tumbler of whiskey and sat down next to her.

He said, "How was your day?"

"How are any of my days?"

Vileness in her tone, he approached her now with vigilance.

"Well, you know what I think you should do."

"Oh, the great, wealthy Irish immigrant is going to pontificate on what he thinks I ought to do."

"What's that supposed to mean?"

"It's *supposed* to mean that you don't even know me. So how the hell can you tell me what you think I ought to do?"

The truth serum contained in a bottle of cabernet was coursing her veins now and the resentments that she had been constructing over the past months were ready to be unveiled in all their elaborate architecture.

"That's unfair, Cassie," Paddy said, "I just wanted you to be happy."

"Happy?" she said. "How? I feel like a fucking prisoner here. We're in the middle of nowhere and I have no friends. Your work is your love, your marriage, not me."

"I'm not sure what you'd have me say? I've asked you to marry me, but you won't. I can't make you happy, Cassie. I have trouble enough with myself."

"I shouldn't even be here," Cassie said. "I betrayed my best friend, who couldn't possibly forgive me. I should've gone back right after delivering Mick and made it right with her, but I didn't, which was my first mistake. It was the allure of the damn money, all this wealth. I was drawn to it like some stupid moth drawn to one of your ranch hands campfires and didn't think it all the way through. I just flew to the heat of the fire like it was instinct and now I'm burning up here."

"Why won't you marry me? We could be happy raising Mick and having a few of our own."

"I don't love you and you don't love me. It's been a relationship of convenience. I thought maybe, if we worked at it, we would fall in love, but we didn't.

Paddy said, "Cassie, I love you."

Cassie laughed contemptuously at this lame attempt to sweep all her feelings under the rug with the limp remark. Paddy's face reddened with embarrassment and hurt.

She said, "You don't love me, Paddy Quinlan. You love power, money and the prestige it brings you. Marrying me would be nothing more than a façade, a false front that's grand to an outsider looking in. I'd look good on your arm at social events and then we'd have to come home and face this all over again."

He looked at her with a sadness that the truth often brings. The venom in her words oozed off of her lips as easily as the snake spits before it bites, and the sting of the fangs breaking unsuspecting skin made Paddy wince. He saw his personal life falling helplessly, once more, like a water drop in a cascade. He had everything except what he wanted most, true love and a family borne from that fruit.

"Cassie," he said with true sincerity, "I had no idea you were so unhappy."

"No, you wouldn't."

"I'll make sure you want for nothing the rest of your life."

"Oh, the easy way out."

"That's not what I meant."

In a whisper she said, "I know."

Cassie's impasse created a vast black crevice in her essence, a banquet of delectable fodder upon which her demons would feast and grow fat.

She leaned forward now and cried in a slump and said, “As much as I love him, I can’t even look at him without seeing his mother and reliving over and over again my betrayal. I’ve built nothing more than a road to hell here, one lousy cobblestone at a time and I can’t do it anymore.”

“Where's the lad's mother now?”

“In Dublin. A woman, who in good faith asked me to bring the child to America so nothing would happen to him, sent him with me because she had the trust of a best friend. And I repay her by shitting all over her fresh laundry.”

Paddy put his hand gently on her back and said, “What is it then? What do you want?”

“I have to go back. I have to go to Clare and make it right. I have to start over.”

“I’ll see to it that you both have what you need.”

She nestled her head into the nape of his neck and cried like she hadn’t since she had secretly shed her tears in the loneliness of her flat in Dublin after leaving Ballycraig at eighteen. It was an eternity ago.

Chapter 28
Taylor Made

1958 Belfast

Northern Ireland

Ansel Fane Taylor was born in the backroom of a rat infested, terraced flat no with indoor plumbing on the Shankill Road.

His sixteen-year-old mother, Lindy, lay on a lice ridden mattress, with eighty-year-old Shankill midwife Gurty Brown, who had been hired to hide the girl and deliver the baby, by her side.

The baby was named after his prominent grandfather, who he would never know. Fane Taylor was a well respected foreman at Harland & Wolf shipbuilders, a secret member of the UVF and a member in good standing of his local Orange Order. In order to maintain his good name and quash any embarrassing rumors, he disowned his daughter and threw her out of the house when she came home pregnant, and then hired out her death when it was confirmed that the father was a local Catholic boy.

Lindy's mother Sarah found out about her husband's plan, picked Lindy up from school and hid her with Gurty until the birth of the baby.

Lindy grew up spoiled in upper middle class Belfast, where work and religion ruled. Sundays were church service days as well as large dinners with extended family and church members. Wednesday evenings were three hour tent revivals, offering the latest Evangelical revivalist itinerant preacher come to spread the gospel of anti-Catholic, anti-Pope, anti-ecumenical militant rhetoric, getting the local rabble worked up to lead the fight.

Then there were the Orange members and Unionist that would come to visit her father, and more than a few had sniffed around her then thirteen-year-old virginity.

To the community they lived in, her father walked on water and her mother was so proper with her religious clubs and afternoon teas. What the community didn't see, or maybe refused to see, were the beatings. He would come home, eat his dinner and start in on the Bushmill's. As the bottle slowly disappeared the strain would grow on her mother's face. He would start to complain about work and the worthless louts who worked for him, then on to the papist bastards who thought they deserved work at Harland & Wolf, and finally the fists would fly.

Lindy would rush to her mother's aid, never to any avail, blood would spill, dignity would vanish, and still he would drink his whiskey until he passed out cold. Sarah would take Lindy to her room and hold her tight, whispering sweet lies that she need not worry, the drinking and the hitting would stop, everything would be okay.

And then came John Berigan. He was the forbidden fruit. She fell in love with him the minute she laid eyes on him and within a month she was carrying his baby. After finding out about his handy work, John disappeared like an apparition in a fog and Lindy's life was about to change forever.

Sarah Taylor waited for her husband to come home from work. She sat properly at the head of the table with a Colt .45 handgun on her lap, one that she had retrieved from her husband's handsome collection.

He walked in and noticed she was not in the kitchen making his dinner and that his bottle of Bushmill's in the glass cabinet was empty.

"Where's my dinner?"

"There is none."

"Well then what the hell happened to my whiskey?"

"You ask about your fucking dinner and your fucking whiskey, how about your daughter?"

"How dare you speak profane in this house."

He took a step toward her, raising his hand as he went.

She pulled the gun from beneath the lace tablecloth, pointed it at him and said, "Take another step and you'll be having this conversation with your Maker."

He stopped.

"Before you die, though, I want you to know two things. First, I found out about your sickening plan to have your own daughter murdered."

"So? If you think I'm going to allow her to have a child that's half papist with my last name you're sadly mistaken."

Getting worked up he took another step but the click of the gun cocking stopped him cold.

"Did you ever wonder what happened to her?"

"Not for a minute. Her getting pregnant was unforgivable. Her getting knocked up by a filthy Catholic well that's…"

"You hypocritical bastard. You come home every night, get drunk, beat your wife and daughter, and now you're worried about what the neighbors might think? Have you ever stopped to consider that they may have overheard your ranting and raving while you were beating the shyte out of me and Lindy? Well I made sure she was taken care of and your grandson Ansel Fane Taylor was born this morning. The lad is happy and healthy. And so is the mother."

A certain light came on in his eyes; he hesitated.

She continued, "Now, if you can put your foolish pride aside, we can bring them here or at least set them up some place where no one would be the wiser."

A moment of sanity rested there and then he came back to his senses and said, "Never, my grandchild will not be a Taig. Never!"

She said, "You foolish man. The lad's father disappeared."

"I would expect as much from that filth."

"So the child is not Catholic. You act as if he will have a large C imprinted on his forehead for everyone to see."

"Might as well have."

"Listen to me for once in your life. I can't lose my daughter and I won't live with the drinking and the beatings one more night. Either they come or I go."

He took one last step and she said, "One more step toward me, Fane, and I swear I'll blow you off your feet."

He smiled and said, "You're bluffing. You don't have it in you. You're weak."

The condescending smile on his face created that one second of insane hatred and that was all that was needed.

The bullet smashed through his sternum at close range and Ansel Fane Taylor was a dead man before his body rested on the floor. When the RUC came to the house to investigate the missing Taylors, they found Fane prone and Sarah's brains on the wall behind her dead body. Funny thing, the RUC man commented that it looked like there was a smile on her face.

Chapter 29
The Militant Custodian

Belfast

1963

Lindy Taylor thought back on that time as she got older. It was hazy, hard to remember. She had gotten pregnant, kicked out of her parent's home, lived in a rundown flat on the Shankill, delivered a baby there, and received the news of her parent's demise. She never quite believed her mother pulled the trigger, she was so delicate, so proper. But then she would go back to the nights of sitting on her mother's lap, hiding from her father in her bedroom, listening to his drunken shouts, feeling the hatred seethe in her mother's fast pumping heart and she wasn't surprised. Lindy never missed her dad, but still, at times, she desperately missed her mother.

When she received the news from the family barrister, it took her two months to meet with the man and finally settle the estate. She sold the family home, cleared out the bank accounts and moved to Glencairn, a neighborhood in North Belfast, and started over as best she could.

She never had the religious fervor of her father. She looked back on it and it seemed a front for her father's darker side. Here was this good and decent man in the public eye who went to services on Sunday and never missed a good tent revival. But he came home nightly, got drunk and beat his wife and daughter. Lindy could never get the two sides to meet, it didn't make sense.

Then she reached out to a young Catholic boy who she thought could save her, offered him her virginity in love and he trampled on her like so much dirt. Her one Catholic experience created a glowing ember of hatred that never grew cold. She loathed Catholics as much as she loathed Presbyterian services.

By 1963 she had been cleaning schools in Belfast for five years. It wasn't the most glamorous work, but it was steady and she didn't have anyone looking over her shoulder. She knew what to do, did it well and took home her pay check; that coupled with her inheritance allowed her and Fane a decent life.

It was at this time that she became acquainted with Dottie King, a heavy set, loud, opinionated woman with a dry sense of humor that brought many laughs while working with her. But Dottie had a dark side. Lindy had heard her say on more that one occasion, "The only good Taig is a dead Taig." She would then laughed her throaty smokers laugh and walk away.

This ruffled a few of Lindy's feathers. She didn't care for the Nationalists anymore than the next Loyalist, but she had no interest in hurting anyone, so she kept her opinion safely in her head. She now guessed what Dottie was capable of and she decided it best to stay on her good side.

One afternoon while working together, Dottie said, "Lindy, where do you go to church?"

Lindy said, "I don't."

Dottie said, "Tch, tch."

"What?"

"You've got to think about the hereafter some time."

"Och, Catholics killing Protestants and us killing them. That's not the kind of religion I'm interested in."

"Listen, there's a new minister coming Wednesday night. Might change your view after you hear what he has to say."

"I don't know."

"Brilliant young preacher, I've heard him. He'll change your mind."

"What's his name?"

"Reverend Jeremy Brown, down from Ballymena."

"Oh no thanks, that lot from Ballymena are a little too rambunctious for the likes of me."

"Do you trust me?"

"Aye."

"Then come with me just this once, if you don't like it then that's that."

Lindy shook hands with the sweaty, highly excited Reverend and walked from the tent gulping the fresh air away from the hot thick tent atmosphere and body odor. She stared up at the dark sky looking for answers, answers she did not get from the wild man on stage. She found no comfort in his words. If he wanted to scare her to God then it worked, but her God wasn't a scary, judgmental God and He wasn't short of cash. He seemed intent on preying upon people's fear with a message of divisiveness and hate. She felt like she needed to bathe.

Dottie startled her out of her thoughts and said, "So what do you think?"

"Rather intense isn't he?"

"Aye, but he needs to be. People need to be jerked out of their lethargy. If we don't look out for ourselves, the Catholics will take over. If we get cozy with them they'll try to talk us into uniting Ireland and pretty soon we'll be taking orders from the Pope. Next thing you know they'll be after our jobs."

A week later Dottie met Lindy at the door of her school as she made her way to work. She had this crazy look in her eye that scared Lindy.

"Dottie, what is it?"

"The company is talking about hiring Taigs to work with us."

"Is that so?"

"Aye, it is. We open the door a crack and the bastards will stampede in. They'll break the fucking door down, they will. Pretty soon we'll be out of work with them taking all of it for themselves. How are you going to feed wee Fane with the likes of that?"

"Well, I don't know about all of that."

A rage of hatred shot from Dottie's stare, shards of broken glass that Lindy felt as she blushed from being threatened.

Dottie said, "And what the hell is that suppose to mean? Listen you prissy little bitch, and you listen good because our livelihoods depend on this. We're marching, the lot of us, and it ain't going to be peaceful and it ain't going unnoticed. We're going right down Falls Road, right into the heart of fucking Taigville."

Lindy's heart was pounding now, this was the last thing she wanted.

Dottie said, "I know lads in both the UDR and the UVF, and they'll keep an eye on us in case the Taigs get a bit uppity with us marching down their streets. We'll be carrying stones, some petrol bombs, a Union Jack and maybe a three or four banners so they know exactly why we're there. Light up a couple Taig flats, knock a few of the bastards off their feet, even take a few out for good measure. That's what we'll do. Then even if the bastards that run this company get the idea of hiring Taigs, not a one of them'll apply."

She was damn near out of breath when she finished, then she poked Lindy hard in the chest and said, "Got it?"

As Lindy had expected the Catholics did not take kindly to these militant Loyalist Protestants marching down their street, nor did they lie down and watch. It was a battle and the most violent affair Lindy had ever seen. She wanted to run, but Dottie had her by the nape of her neck. She barely made it out alive and ended up at the local hospital to have her wounds attended to.

Lindy Taylor lost Dottie King's trust that day. She kept a wary eye out from that day on; expecting the errant pipe bomb through the picture window of her flat.

Ten Years Later
1973

Dottie King had become known as the militant cleaning lady throughout Belfast and through intimidation and violence, kept Catholics out of the public schools' custodial work.

Lindy never marched again and was ostracized for it. She did not mind though, she worked by herself and soon they forgot about her and left her alone. She was glad that she had distanced herself from Dottie, it was painful and ugly at times, but now it was over and Lindy avoided Dottie like a bad chest cold. Lindy's interest was solely her son Fane and that was it.

Fane was fifteen now and showed a propensity toward mechanics and machinery in his school shop class. Many of his mates' parents were forcing them to drop out and go to work at one of the local plants to offset some family expenses.

One morning at breakfast Fane broached the subject delicately with his mother to see how she might react. He said, "Mum, you know who Mr. Dade is?"

"Aye, your shop teacher."

"That's it. He likes me and says I've an aptitude for mechanics and machinery."

"I'd expect nothing less from a son of mine. That's a good lad."

"Morning paper says the Rolls Royce plant on the outskirts has openings for machinist apprentices, pays good, mum."

Lost in her thoughts and getting ready for the day she said, "That's good dear…wait a minute, what're you getting at, love?"

"If I got a job now, by the time I was twenty I could be a full blown Machinist, join the union. If that's my path, why do I need to finish school? Besides a second income would help out around here. You wouldn't have to work so hard or maybe you could go do something else. I know that Dottie's been a pain in your arse."

"But that's not the path that we agreed upon. I wanted you to go to University, do a little better for yourself."

"Come on mum, none of my friends are going to University."

"Are we playing follow the loser or follow the leader?"

"You think these lads at Rolls Royce or Bombardier are losers?"

"No, love, you know better. I just don't want you putting your back into your living. I want you putting your brain into it. How about being an engineer at Rolls Royce with twice or three times the salary. That's what I'm saying. But what are we talking about here? I won't hear any more of this nonsense. You're finishing school and that means I got two more years to talk you out of an apprenticeship and to talk you into University. Your grandparents left us a little and that's what I've been saving it for."

Fane didn't argue further. He knew he wouldn't win. His mother wanted him to go on to University and like she said there was two more years of school to talk her out of it.

Two Months later

The Abercorn, a popular pub restaurant in the Belfast Centre, was busy on a Saturday afternoon in March. It had been a long, cold wet and grey winter and people had the itch to get out, take a load off, have a few drinks and maybe a bite.

Lindy Taylor had been invited on a date by a gentleman she had been recently seeing. She had been happy for the first time in a very long while, dating a man, she thought, might be the lad, maybe a future. Fane even liked him.

Their time at the Abercorn had been leisurely. They started with a few drinks and some small talk. They ordered hors 'devourers, a bottle of wine and then dinner. The plan was to see a show following and then maybe a slow walk home.

He looked at her and said something funny when an explosion suddenly ripped through the restaurant. Lindy had been knocked to the floor. She looked up as people ran helter skelter, kicking her and tripping over her in their panic, but she felt nothing and heard nothing, all she could do was lay there on the floor where she fell helplessly. She tried to move to find her date. She looked a few feet away and saw him with half his skull gone and when she tried to get to him she found she couldn't move. She thought of death. She couldn't hear any of the ruckus around her and she couldn't feel anything. She closed her eyes and the confusion was over.

Chapter 30
Fane

Later that same afternoon

Dottie King and her boyfriend Dusty Smith, a local union machinist, knocked on the door of the Taylor flat in Glencairn. Fane looked through the lace curtains and reluctantly opened the door. He didn't like her and didn't like the way she treated his mum.

She said, "Lad, we need to talk."

He said, "Mum's not about just now."

"Lad, we need to talk, it's about your mum."

His stomach sank as they walked into the living room. It wasn't fancy but it was immaculate.

Fane said, "What is it?"

"Sit, sit, sit you two."

The two men sat and they all stared for an uncomfortable second.

Fane said, "Mum had a date. She'll be back after the show."

Dusty said, "Lad, there was a bomb blast at The Abercorn."

It took a minute for it to sink in and then his eyes went wide and said, "But that's where..."

Dottie said, "Your mum got hurt bad, Fane. She's at the hospital now in intensive care. Her boyfriend wasn't so lucky, he died."

Fane stood and grabbed his coat.

Dottie said, "Wait."

"No way. I'm out of here."

Fane walked out of the house across the yard and ran down the street.

He took short cuts through alleys and back yards and made it to the hospital in less than a half hour. He walked into her room in the ICU, took her hand, told her he loved her and within the hour she died.

The nurse looked at him and said, "I see it all the time lad."

He said, "What?"

"She held on for you."

* * *

Fane Taylor sat in his mother's flat in the dark when the knock came on the door. He looked through the curtain and saw that it was Dusty Smith and Dottie King again.

He said through the door, "Go away and leave me the fuck alone."

The two visitors walked away.

Dusty said, "Do you know Ian Wright?"

Dottie said, "RUC, special branch?"

"That's him. I'm guessing he'll be in on this, especially because the word is this was an IRA bomb."

"So, what are you getting at?"

"This Fane has the stones to be good. John Dade his shop teacher keeps me up on all the talented shop kids, he's one of them."

"So you're saying that Wright might want to pay the lad a visit, do a little recruiting."

"That's exactly what I'm saying."

* * *

The next day RUC Special Branch officer Ian Wright knocked on the door of the Taylor home. Fane Taylor, eyes red and swollen answered the door.

Fane opened the door and stood there as if he did not know what to do next. A fifteen-year-old boy who had just lost his mother, the only family he had in the world, stood there as if he moved an inch he would turn to powder and blow away.

Ian Wright recognized this for what it was and said, "Lad, I'm Detective Ian Wright, with the Royal Ulster Constabulary, Special Branch. I'm here to investigate the bombing that took place yesterday at The Abercorn down in Belfast Centre."

He showed the boy his credentials and said, "May I come in to talk?"

"I don't care."

"Lad, I'm sorry to hear about your mum."

"Whatever."

Ian asked Fane several questions, knowing his mother was simply an innocent bystander, but they had to be asked.

He stood to leave and Fane finally broke. Ian sat back down and allowed the boy to cut lose. It suddenly dawned on him how all alone the boy was. No one had come, he thought, except Dottie and Dusty and they did because Dottie is a nosey prat who has Dusty by the short hairs.

Ian finally said, "Lad, who'd your next of kin be?"

"What?"

"Your closest relatives."

"No one."

"No aunts uncles, cousins, grandparents?"

"No. None."

"So do you have any idea what to do next?"

"No. Where's me mum's body?"

"The city morgue, lad."

There was an uncomfortable quiet in the room, as if the truth were cold bony hands gripping at Fane's throat keeping him from talking.

Ian said, "Okay, lad. Look I need to make a call and then I'll help you with this."

He called the police station and told them he would be a bit. Ian then called a local mortician and Presbyterian Minister. He then asked the boy for permission to look through his mother's private papers. Fane went to the Living room curio cabinet and opened the bottom drawer withdrawing a black vinyl folder and handed it to the policeman and said, "Mum always told me that if anything happened to her, this is where all her papers would be."

Ian went through it and found her bankbook, stocks and insurance papers with names and numbers of all those with the answers he sought. He found that Lindy to be organized and forward thinking and had a sizable amount of money. Knowing bits and pieces of her story he figured she still had some inheritance from her parents when they died. Now, he just wanted to make sure none of these adults took advantage of a naïve fifteen-year-old.

"Lad, your mother was a very organized person and she obviously cared a great deal about your future in the unfortunate event that her life would be taken from her."

Fane nodded tentatively.

Ian said, "Wait here a minute I need to make a phone call."

Five minutes later he walked back in from the kitchen and the phone that hung on the wall there and said, "Lad, would you like to come live with my wife and I? We don't have any children and plenty of room. At least until we get all this straightened out."

There was a light that shone in Fane's eyes. For the first time since Ian Wright had laid eyes on the boy, a ray of hope existed there. Fane Taylor smiled as if the burden of a worrisome problem had been solved and he could move again.

Two weeks later

Ian Wright met Dusty Smith at The Brown Bear Pub in the Shankill for a pint.

"So the lad's still with you?"

"Aye, poor sot."

Dusty ordered another round and said, "You know his story then?"

"I knew the lads grandda, mean bastard. He was me Da's foreman at Harland. I was a rookie then, you know on the beat. I was the first one on the scene. Walked in on he and his wife, sickening business, that."

"The lad's a bit of his Grandda in him, then?"

"That right?"

"Aye, he can get a temper up in a hurry as I understand it."

"He's a good sized lad, that one. I suppose he could be a handful."

"Strong as an anchorman and I hear he's an aptitude for the engines and machines."

"Who's that coming from, then?"

"Mr. Dade, his shop teacher up at school. I try to stay in touch with him to get the good recruits out at the Rolls plant."

"So you think you could get him on at Rolls Royce?"

"Aye, as a Machinist apprentice, in a heart beat. We're hiring just now. He's strong, has a mind for it, you bet."

"Problem is my wife is on me about the lad finishing up his education. You'd think he was hers the way she dotes on him."

"Och. What's finishing school going to get a lad like that? We need him in the Union, The Orange Order and the UVF."

"I know. I know."

"Plus he's got the stones and the right motivation."

"I suppose with the right direction he could be good for us."

Dusty laughed and said, "Yes, he could."

"Go to work on getting him on out at the plant and I'll go to work on the wife."

At age fifteen, Ansel Fane Taylor II was hired on at the Rolls Royce plant in Belfast as an apprentice machinist working on large jet engines. By eighteen, he was a member in the 1st Degree in his local Orange order. By nineteen, he was member of the Woodbridge UVF unit. By twenty, he had killed his first Catholic businessman, under orders of his unit leader. He caught the man outside some high end Catholic club one evening. The man had had too much to drink which made him an easy target. Fane put a bike chain wrapped in white medical tape around his scrawny neck, pulled him into an alley and strangled him. He had never felt the powerful high that came with that first death. By twenty-two, he was unit leader of the Woodbridge unit of the UVF. The argument that led to his rise in the unit, led to the death of the previous leader. Six months later Fane became the youngest foreman on the machine floor at Rolls Royce. Life was good and his reputation was growing as a man who could get the job done. He had never forgotten the day he heard the news about his mother. The void that was left from her death was filled with a hatred for all things Nationalist and all things Catholic.

Chapter 31
Cassie and Clare

Dublin

December 1961

Clare Eva White wandered aimlessly through life the years following the birth of her twin boys and the betrayal of her best friend Cassie Kenny. She worked nights at Big Jacks' Baggot Street Inn and slept in the day. Life wasn't worth living and she didn't give a damn. She felt the only redeeming factor during that time in her life was that she wrote her mother once a week and went to visit every couple of months.

She wasn't sure whether there was a God anymore, but acted like there was one just in case, and prayed every morning that the hatred she felt for her once best friend would some how subside. Sometimes it was all consuming.

One morning the week before Christmas a knock came on the door. She was expecting no one and was surprised because no one ever knocked on her door anymore, except Mrs. Celeste Ryan, her nosy neighbor and resident gossip. She walked to the door thinking, "If that fucking Mrs. Ryan is. . ." She swung the door open ready to scream when a sudden tightness filled her chest and angst swept through her veins like the poison of a venomous spider, moving quickly and thoroughly. Cassie Kenny had come home.

Clare took a deep breath and stared. Cassie stared back. It was a long minute and a half before Clare broke the silence and said, "What are you doing here?"

Cassie said, "I made an awful mistake and I've come back to make amends."

"It's a little late for that."

"Is it ever too late?"

"Fucksake Cassie, you. . ."

The door to the flat across the hall opened and Mrs. Ryan stuck her head out and said, "Cassie Kenny, you've returned."

"Aye, Mrs. Ryan I've come home."

"And you're visiting in the hall?"

Clare rolled her eyes, wanting to ring the nosy old bag's neck when she grabbed Cassie by the coat and pulled her into the apartment slamming the door behind her.

She turned around and said, "The only way you're even standing in here is because I like that nosy old fool less than I like you. I don't know why you came, there's no forgiveness left in me for the likes of you."

"It doesn't matter."

"What doesn't matter?"

"That you've no forgiveness left for me. You've done nothing wrong, I have. I've no more control over your thoughts, actions or reactions than the man in the moon. I came here to apologize to you for my awful behavior because it was the right thing to do. My hope, though, is that you're able to forgive, but if not then I have to accept that and move on knowing that I did everything I could to make this right.

"Clare, I made as big a mistake as anyone can make. But I guess I never expected your forgiveness. Trading shoes with you, I'm not sure I could forgive you. And to make this whole mess worse, you saved my life and this is how I repaid you."

"Are you trying to get off the hook?"

"No. It's not that easy. If you won't forgive me then I'll pay for this the rest of my life. Getting off the hook would've been to stay in America. But it was all a lie. I got sucked into it, the wealth, the luxury."

"Sure as hell took your time."

"Look Clare, I know you're pissed and sore as hell as well you should be. But I didn't come here to kiss your arse. I came here to apologize and make my amends. If you won't accept that or choose not to then there's not much I can do about that. I'm doing what I feel is right. I got my job back at the paper."

"Who'd you blow to get that back?"

"You know, you're not the only one who suffered the last two years. You were the one who made a conscious decision to bed a man of the cloth with no thought to the possible outcome. You were the one who worked out this little plan with the good Sister to send me with the baby when I really didn't think it was a good idea, and you're the one who has been feeling sorry for yourself for the last two and half years. It was all your doing, so fuck off."

"Are your done?"

"Aye."

"Good. Then get the fuck out and don't ever come back."

"No. Now you're the one not getting off that easy."

"I'm not getting off that easy? Are you fucking daft? Have you been paying attention at all for the past two years? I trusted you to take my lovely lad to America and then come straight back! Did I have to spell that out in a fucking contract before you left? Did you even for one moment, while you were resting in the lap of someone else's luxury, imagine how lonely I was?

I had no one! I lost my babies, the man I loved and my best friend in one fell swoop."

Bitter tears flowed endlessly from Clare's eyes blurring her vision. Sorrow rested in familiar comfort upon her ragged visage and in slow whispering malice she said, "Now, I want you to get out."

There was nothing Cassie could say to defend herself but something deep inside her would not allow her to leave, she had to make this right.

"Clare, I'm not leaving until we talk this through. You're my best friend and I won't let it end like this, we have way too much history."

Chapter 32
Eamon

Dublin

February 1964

It had been two years since Cassie's return from Montana. It had taken much time and work but she and Clare had re-established that rare friendship that can be stretched, even to an unrecognizable shape, but never broken.

Cassie had gone back to work for The Irish Times Newspaper and was doing some freelance work for an underground newspaper who's tentacles reached from Cobh in Cork to the Giant's Causeway in Antrim, keeping Republicans from North to South aware of all rebel activity. On occasion she would collaborate with one Sean O'Kane, a writer in the North, who kept her connected to the troubles there. She had never met the man but had become very fond of him and guessed that one day the troubles in the north would escalate to the point that her paper would send her north to cover it and that she would meet the man whose writing she had so admired. When she had come back she found a small one bedroom flat, but in the past two years it became apparent that Clare needed someone who loved her to keep an eye on her as she constantly strayed toward the deep end, so Cassie and Clare found a place together.

After losing the babies, then losing Ruari, then facing her the abandonment of her best friend Clare had, Cassie observed, become a bit mad.

In the past four years, Clare worked nights at Big Jacks' Baggot Inn for a meager wage but good tips, servicing obnoxious drunks and ass pinching American tourists who knew everything. But the money was good and Jack Tobin, the Inn's proprietor, couldn't have been a kinder soul.

During the day and the wee hours after work she ran around with beatniks and poets, playwrights and Republicans, sailors and dock workers. Clare drank and smoked too much, she ate and slept too little while running herself ragged in search of her life's meaning. One day Cassie would find her smoking weed while reading Nietsche or Camus. The next day she'd be donning the black Doc Marten Jack boots that the soldiers in the brotherhood preferred, drinking Paddy's and sporting a new anchor tattoo on her right ass check that she'd gotten on a lost bet during a drunken binge.

It had now been just over four years since her twins were taken from her. The days, weeks and years hadn't diluted her pain, and she now understood the quiet desperation of the Republican standing in the shadows of an English gallows. So when the message came from her Da that her Mum had a stroke, she was too numb to be shaken. In recent months she had kept close company with depression, hopelessness and solitude. So, she thought, "Why not pile fear and sorrow on the heap?"

She remembered her mum saying, "The Father in Heaven won't weigh you down with one more ounce than you can bear." "Right," She thought as she crumbled to the floor shaking uncontrollably. That was the way Cassie had found her, coming home from work that afternoon.

Cassie ran to her and said, "Darling, what is it?"

She stuttered "Mum's had a stroke. Da rang me up and told me it was serious and that I was to be getting home."

"Jaysus, Clare, I'm so sorry. Let's get you packed, I'll come with you."

"Cassie, its Friday night. I can't be leaving Jack high and dry."

"Clare he'll understand."

"Sure he would, but it still wouldn't be the thing to do. They won't be able to keep up and us leaving for Ballycraig twelve hours from now won't change anything."

"I don't know."

Clare made it to work that night by a will greater than her own. She knew on a Friday night, if she hadn't gone to work, that Jack would be left short-handed and overwhelmed, and he had been too good to her.

In the back of the pub a group of Republicans had just taken up residence at a large table, and when Clare walked in the relief on Jack Tobin's face was plain to see. He was frantic behind the bar and said, "Thank God, Clare, there's a large group to the back that I want you to personally take good care of."

"Why, Jack, who are they?"

"Don't ask, lass, just do it; it'll be worth your while."

As Clare walked to the back of the pub through the growing Friday night crowd she saw the table of eleven men. They all were leaning forward in what looked like some intense discussion. It seemed odd to her that the crowd seemed to know to stay away, as if an unseen beacon emitted a privacy warning. She walked up and said, "What'll be, lads?"

They looked up and she said, "Well, don't look so surprised, it is a pub you know."

The last guy to order was a good looking man that Clare guessed was about her age. He was soft spoken with a hard edge around it, and his penetrating green eyes gave away nothing.

She got to him and said, "And you, sir?"

He said, "Uh, what?"

The man next to him nudged him and said, “What’re you drinking, Eamon. The lass would like to know.”

He said, “Oh yeah, Christ Bless us. Ah, a pint would be grand, thanks.”

She smiled at him and walked away and all he could do was watch.

An hour later, six police officers in combat gear burst in and ran to the back. The crowd went dead and Clare got up on the bar and looked to the rear and the table of eleven was deserted. The police looked around a bit embarrassed and walked out in silence.

Clare stood at the wait station while Jack Tobin cleaned glasses, shook his head and said to no one in particular, “Thank God for good luck. Would’ve ruined me night.”

Clare looked at the publican while sweat poured off his brow.

They shoved the last customer out just past closing, only after the touchy, feely American tourist had asked Clare to marry him for the fifth time. The staff went to work to clean the pub so they could sit, rest their sore feet and have a drink.

“Jack, before I’m off, do you have a moment?”

“Clare, I’ve always a moment for you, lass. Come upstairs to me room.”

The room, as Jack called it, was a small cramped office where Jack paid his bills, ordered his booze and kegs of beer and chain smoked cigarette after cigarette.

Clare sat on a fold out chair and Jack took his seat behind the desk poured some whiskey into an empty jar and offered it to Clare. She took it and said, “Jack, I’m sorry I was late tonight. I just found out me Mum had a stroke.”

“Jaysus, Clare. What’re you doing here?”

“It’s Friday night and you wouldn’t have made it tonight without my help.”

“Malarkey, its all malarkey.”

“Hardly. You didn’t see the look on your face when I walked in tonight. Anyway, I’m heading to Ballycraig in the morning and don’t know when I’ll be back.”

“Take all the time you need. How’s Will?”

“I’m guessing not well. He’d never tell me anyway.”

“Do you need any money? Or anything else?”

“No, I’m fine. But there is one thing.”

“What is it?”

“When I walked in tonight, you sent me straight back to that large table of men?”

Jack shook his head.

"You asked me to personally see to them. Who were they?"

"Why do you ask?"

"Well, it would've been out of sheer curiosity because of the anxious way you acted toward them when I first walked in. Then I walked back there and people were keeping their distance in a crowded barroom, like they knew to stay away. Then the bloody peelers charging in and them disappearing out the back before they got to them."

Jack stood, shut his door, drew the blinds and sat back down. He picked up his half-smoked cigarette and stared at Clare for a moment. Finally making up his mind he said, "Clare, the only reason I'm telling you this is because I've known your Da since we were young and you've worked for me long enough and I know that you can be trusted."

Clare sat up at this and listened intently.

"Eight of the men were some of the top men in the local arm of Sinn Féin. You know who they are?"

"The political wing of the IRA."

"Aye. Anyway, they weren't the reason for the police."

"Who was then?"

"The three men sitting closest to you when you waited on them. That was Eamon Gainey, Chief of Staff of the standing IRA, and two of his brigade commanders, Dermot Brennan and Daithi O'Connor. They're wanted men in the North and the bloody peelers in the south are working with those monsters in the RUC up north to round them up."

Clare said, as if to no one, "That's what the man called him, Eamon."

Jack said, "What?"

"I took the table's order and when it got to the last man, he seemed in a trance or something, like some heavy burden consumed his thoughts."

"Aye, that would be Eamon."

"So he's the reason the peelers came crashing in?"

"Aye, and they say the man has a sixth sense. He can sense danger a kilometer away and it's a good thing too."

"Why?"

"Because the bloody peelers busting up my place tonight would've made life rough."

"So you're saying that he knew the law was coming?"

"They say that's how the lad made it to the top spot of the Republican Army."

"This is a man I'd like to get to know."

"Don't count on it. He's elusive."

Clare raised an eyebrow and said, "Thanks for everything Jack, you're a love." And she walked to the door.

Chapter 33
Cutting the Ties

The next day

The early morning train headed south and it seemed to Clare like she was in a time tunnel moving in slow motion. Her head ached and her eyes throbbed from a night of crying and waiting to get on the train.

Suddenly that familiar feeling of malevolence, the intuition that gave her warning, brought her back to the day Cassie disappeared. Something was wrong, really wrong and she knew it as sure as she knew she was on a train heading south. Then without warning, the thought invaded her mind and played over and over, "It's worse than a stroke, it's worse than a stroke."

Clare screamed, "Mum!" The car went silent as passengers stared.

Cassie, sitting next to her friend, awoke as if from a bad dream and reached for her and said, "What is it, Clare?"

"Oh Cassie, its mum, she's dead. She's dead and I wasn't there."

"You don't know that."

"I know it and you know that I know it. Sure as the pigs seeing the wind and sure as I knew the tinker had grabbed you."

Cassie looked at Clare and knew the truth now; she hung her head and said no more.

By the time Clare and Cassie got to Ballycraig, later that afternoon, the women of the village had laid Kate White out on the table of their cottage. She had died in the night. When they walked in the Irish wake was on, women wailed, jugs of poteen passed, stories told, rosaries said. Kate White's best friend, Bridget Casey, walked up to the girls and handed them each a pinch of salt that they both threw over their shoulder to keep away the evil spirits, of course.

Bridget looked at Clare and said, "You'll be glad to know that I sent me lads to the beehives and cattle pens to let them know Kate got away from us. The faeries came to me in me sleep last night so we know the bees let them know, and the wee people too."

Clare hugged Bridget and said, "Thank you darling, I knew I could count in you,"

She looked over to see her da sitting against the wall with the men. She walked to him, knelt down and said, "I'm sorry da that I wasn't here when she got away from us."

He stroked her hair and said, “That's me girl.”

To the men’s surprise and secret delight she grabbed the jug as it passed and took a pull. The women, startled, would discuss it later and blame the devil for working on the bereaved.

The Irish wake was reaching a fevered pitch, rosary in full swing properly sending Kate White off to meet her maker. Clare’s heart sunk when she had the thought that she had let her mum down for the last time. She said, “I could have, I should have come last night and then I would’ve at least been here to see her off.”

Cassie said, “You can’t blame yourself for that. You’ve got a job, a life, responsibility and if anyone in this world understood that it was Kate White.”

"That's where you're wrong Cass."

“Da, I’m so sorry.”

He said, “Och, would you stop it now, you’ve a job and you can’t just leave a man high and dry. None of us knew she was going to go so quick.”

“I let her down, I always did.”

“Stop that talk. Your mum loved you, lass.”

“Oh and I her.”

“No, you don’t understand.”

“What?”

He walked his daughter outside away from earshot of clergy and nosy neighbors and said, “She almost died giving birth to you. We thought we were going to lose her and I didn’t know what I was going to do. Father Whelan, our pastor at the time, came around and made it clear that if a choice was to be made it was to be made in favor of the child. I told him to go to hell and get out. I didn’t see the inside of our church for five years after that. When your mum came around she was ashamed.”

“For God sakes why?”

“Because in her mind women we’re supposed to be stronger than that. She was also ashamed that she could bear no more children. The stares of awful pity she’d get from neighbors.”

“I know, it was almost embarrassing at times.”

“The hardest day of her life was the day you left, but she understood that you had to go, there was nothing left for you here. But she loved your letters home and your visits most of all. She called out your name with her last breath.”

“Did she ever get over my babies?”

“Aye, her only regret was never getting to see them.”

Clare gulped air as if her breath was involuntary at what her Da just said. She only thought of herself and never her parents. She thought her mom was ashamed of her.

They sat quietly mislaid in their thoughts when Will White said, "I honestly don't know what I'm going to do without her." He bent over and wept until Clare thought he was going to pass out. She held his hand and rubbed his back as he grieved she comforted him as best she could.

Six months later they found Will White passed away in his bed. Bridget Casey sent a telegram and the village was convinced he died of a broken heart. He just hadn't been the same since.

Clare stood next to Cassie over the freshly dug burial place of her father, next to the six-month-old grave of her mother, and realized that with them dead her ties to Ballycraig were cut. People walked one by one from the sepulcher and she said to Cassie, "Is this as good as it gets? People you love leave you, are taken from you, sent away from you, betray you or die. Is that all there is in this godforsaken life?"

As the shovels of dirt began to pile upon her father's burial place, Clare's resolve changed that day. She said, "Cassie, I'll no longer be the victim, this is my time."

She stared into the eyes of her best friend and Cassie stared back, seeing a look of anger and determination she had seen only one time before.

Chapter 34
An Phoblacht

The Republican News

An Phoblacht, The Republican News, was first published out of the Dungannon Clubs of Belfast in 1906 and because of English harassment died out until the Irish War of Independence. In 1920 it was brought back in both Northern and Southern Ireland until 1935 when funds ran out and public opinion was running low on the IRA.

Then in 1970, Jimmy Steele reissued the modern version of the paper and Sean O'Kane was one of the early writers for An Phoblacht during the troubles of the North. But the British, with their world-class propaganda machine, well oiled and moving at high speed, had the world believing the men and women fighting the oppression of a foreign invader to be terrorists. And in that same vein, they outlawed the publication of the Republican newspaper. It was freedom of the press for everyone but the Republicans.

As such, British soldiers were sent on search and destroy missions, looking for the Republican press room. So it was that the An Phoblacht press was constantly being moved from one location to another, usually in the dead of night.

The Republican journalists successfully published their paper, but not without duress. If they were caught they would be remanded to internment camps for men and women without trial.

It was with courage and conviction that they delivered their news, as they saw it.

UK Forces deployed to Ulster

Sean O'Kane

August 16, 1969

(UPI) Great Britain's Home Secretary James Callaghan announced today the deployment of British Army forces into Northern Ireland in an effort to gain control of a situation that is anything but. Sources say that London is beginning to question Stormont's ability to govern Northern Ireland.

UK taking Control of Northern Ireland Security
Sean O'Kane
August 30, 1969

(UPI) Great Britain's Home Secretary James Callaghan announced today that Control of Security of the six counties of Northern Ireland under British rule will now be Her Majesties responsibility under General Ian Freeland. Another move to show the lack of confidence London has in Stormont.

Falls Road Curfew
Sean O'Kane
July 3, 1970

(UPI) After a period of relative quiet, tension is rising once again. Only this time, it's between the Nationalists in Belfast and The British Army over a curfew enacted today over The Falls Road. Sources say that Great Britain suspects IRA safehouses and general activity in the area that they would like curtailed. Nationalists see it as more oppression of their freedoms.

Operation Demetrius Launched
Sean O'Kane
August 9, 1971

(UPI) As another violent marching season of the Orange order through Catholic neighborhoods comes to a crescendo and violence erupts throughout Ulster, Northern Ireland Security forces last night launched what sources say was "Operation Demetrius." Sources say that by daylight 432 known Republicans were arrested due to suspected IRA activity. Sources also say that due to reasonable intelligence within the brotherhood most key IRA members escaped.

Demetrius a Failure
Sean O'Kane
August 12, 1971

(UPI) Within forty-eight hours, a third of the those rounded up in Operation Demetrius were released due to bad information, and most key members of the IRA escaped before the operation got under way. The operation intention was "to smash the IRA," said Northern Ireland Prime Minister Brian Faulkner. Instead it managed to further intensify the violence, while twenty three people lost their lives in three days of rioting.

Chapter 35
The Ard Righ

The Short Strand

Belfast, Northern Ireland

July 1970

Eleven months after Martin O'Kane was brought home, as often happens, Patricia O'Kane delivered her first baby, Fergal Vincent O'Kane.

Martin and Fergal O'Kane grew up in The Short Strand and wore it like a badge of honor. The Loyalist Protestants hated the Nationalists Catholics and vice versa. Fighting was a part of life.

Religion was a part of the O'Kane household because it was part of their heritage and gave them an identity. But the O'Kane's were not like some of the other Catholic homes they had been in where the Angelus was said at noon and six o'clock and the Rosary said every night, with small fonts outside each room filled with holy water. The O'Kanes prayed before meals and went to Mass on Sunday, but that was about the extent of it. The blackjack that hung next to the crucifix in the kitchen summed up their religion.

What the boys loved the most growing up was listening to their Da's stories of Irish history, the Irish Republican Army, their Grandda's martyrdom in Dublin, the Brotherhood and The Trouble, as he called it.

As an adult, wherever Martin was, especially when he was lonely, he would always recall the times when his father, Sean O'Kane, had come home from the pub with a pint or two in him and sat with his boys in the living room to tell stories.

Sean said, "'Tis an ancient land we live in, lads, ancient. It used to be that we had five provinces, each with its own king."

Martin said, "Da, everyone knows that Ireland has four provinces, not five."

Sean said, "Martin, what does the Irish term Co'iceda mean?"

Martin said, "Provinces."

Sean smiled at that and said, "Well, you have been listening, good. But the exact translation is fifths. Originally Ireland was split into fifths or five provinces. There were the four we know now, Ulster, Munster, Leinster, Connacht and then there was Meath."

Martin said, "Meath is a county not a province."

"Aye, now it is. But in ancient times, Meath was a place of great power. It was the home of the ancient capital of Tara and it was the home of Niall of the nine hostages, the Patriarch of the great Ui' Neill clan, or as we know them today, the O'Neills."

Martin and Fergal nodded, once again engrossed in the magic of Sean's stories.

He continued, "Each of these provinces typically had a clan that dominated and from that clan came the provincial king, but never without a fight. The strongest and smartest made it to the top."

Sean lit a cigarette and his eyes gleamed. He loved Ireland more than anything in his life and he cherished her history, ancient and resplendent. He blew a plume of smoke into the night and continued, "Lads, during this time, there was also the Ard Righ."

Fergal said, "Ard Righ?"

Sean said, "Aye. Ard Righ, in Irish it means High King. Ireland had four kings that ruled over the four provinces and then the High King to rule over the whole island."

Fergal said, "So was the Ard Righ High King over all of Ireland and his Province as well?"

"That's right, lad. He was High King over all the land, including his own home Province. Once again it was survival of the fittest. Ard Righ was typically a man not content with being just a provincial king; he wanted it all and went to war to get it. Once there, the provincial kings had to pay him tribute."

Martin said, "Tribute? You mean like respect."

"Aye, but it was more than that. The provincial Kings had to pay tribute to the Ard Righ in livestock, gold or something of value once a year, if not he'd come and take it. One of the greatest Ard Righ was Brian Boru, which is short for Boruma which means cattle counter. When he took power around 1000 a.d., Brian ruled Southern Ireland and the O'Neills the North. He first took Munster and later Connacht, Meath and Leinster. After that he went after Dublin, took it and by then the O'Neills had Ulster and their King, a man named Mael Sechnaill, recognized Brian as Ard Righ by what they called a right of conquest. Brian is the patriarch of the clan we now know as the O'Briens."

Martin said, "So we've always been fighting."

"That's correct. We've always recognized that if it's worth having, it's worth fighting for."

Fergal said, "So now we fight the Protestants?"

Sean said, "No lads, not the Protestants, but the Loyalists who all happen to be Protestant and loyal to the English Crown."

Martin said, "What's the difference?"

"The difference is this. As free Irishmen we don't care what religion you are. Some of the greatest Irish patriots we've ever known like Napper Tandy, Theobold Wolfe Tone and Charles Stewart Parnell were Protestant. They wanted a free Ireland ruled by the Irish, the whole island, no outside rule. They were Republicans and died for that right just like any Catholic, Agnostic or Atheist republican for that matter. But let me rephrase that."

"Rephrase what?"

"I said the English when what I meant to say was the English government. All we want is a free and united Ireland. Ruled by the Irish, no matter what religion you are. The problem is these Orangemen who march every summer wreaking havoc in Catholic neighborhoods. They are loyal to the crown in England and want no unification here. They've lived here for three hundred years and they continue to hate the Irish and Catholics. So once again we will fight for what we want. And lads, what we want is freedom."

Martin said, "Da, tell us why exactly the Orangemen hate us so much and march through our neighborhoods screaming at us every July 12th?"

"The Orange saga all began in what they called the Williamite Wars in Ireland during the mid 15th Century. You see, lads, there was an English and Catholic King named James II. He was usurped by his son-in-law William the III."

"Usurped?"

"Ousted or overthrown by force. Good question. Anyway, William three sticks was more prominently known as William of Orange. When the Prods are marching through the yard in July you hear them singing about King Billy?"

They both nodded and said, "Aye?"

"That's William of Orange."

Fergal said, "Why Orange?"

"He was born to it, a Dutch Prince in the Orange lineage. William of Orange married King James' daughter Mary II and they, in cahoots with the English Parliament, who were also mainly Protestant, ran James off the throne. So James ran off to France, regrouped with King Louis XIV, who was also Catholic, and came back a year later to battle William in Ireland. He lined up on one side of the Boyne River outside Drogheda with 25,000 mainly poor Catholic croppies, who were under-trained and under-armed men. William, on the other hand, lined up on the other side with 36,000 mainly Scottish, mainly Protestant, well-trained and well-armed soldiers. The battle commenced on July 1, 1690 and, as all history books will tell you lads, the Proddies won the day and old King James ran away again. They say he ran away so fast that he beat his messengers back to Limerick with the news of the defeat.

"His soldiers and the rest of Ireland considered him a bloody coward nicknaming him Seamus Na' Chaca, or James the Shit."

The boys laughed out loud at that while Sean lit another cigarette.

The Martin said, "Wait a minute, Da, you said that The Battle of The Boyne was on July 1st but the prods march on July 12th?"

"Well, a year and eleven days after the battle of the Boyne was the battle of Aughrim. But unlike the Boyne the Catholics and their leaders didn't turn away this time and, as a result, it was a one-sided slaughter in which the Williamites ran the Catholics, both nobles and croppies, off their land while the soil ran blood red. So, it's The Battle of the Boyne they like to remember as the Catholics running away like cowards, and the 12th they like to remember because of their total victory."

Fergal said, "So every year the bastards have to rub our noses in it as if it happened only yesterday."

They all put their heads down as if the reality of it were a burden too heavy to lift at this late hour.

The father and sons spent many nights talking to the wee hours. The boys learned bits and pieces of the long Irish history from their father and developed his perspective on life in Northern Ireland.

The stories, coupled with the harsh realities of daily life, like fighting their way to and from school, continued to mold and form them. The Loyalist Protestant boys lined up on Newtonards Road or Albertbridge road, the roads dividing the Catholic Short Strand from its Protestant neighbors. The Catholics had to cross these streets to get to and from school. The cry went up "Taig!" The derogatory name the Loyalist Protestants used to describe Catholics in Northern Ireland. The two began to hate the Protestants, but they kept their thoughts deep within their own consciousness, and shared them only with a small crew of Catholic friends in the neighborhood.

The scream could be heard throughout the neighborhood, "Taig!" Their blood would run cold and their fists would clench. They fought their way to their front porch many days. The two would be bloody, bruised and their clothes torn. They never understood the hate in the eyes of their attackers, never understood why. They just knew that it was the way life was and the only way to survive was to be smart, tough and aware of their surroundings at all times.

Chapter 36
Martin and Fergal's Turn

Portadown, County Armagh, Northern Ireland

1976

Martin, as thick as he was with Fergal, more often than not, was a loner. He was popular and had friends, but he found solace in quiet seclusion and he liked it there. Fergal, on the other hand, wanted nothing to do with solitude. He was gregarious and was usually looking for friends and fun.

The same internal struggle that took up in many Irishmen took up in Martin. His instinct from an early age was to fight; yet he hated it. Freedom was not something that was given freely, he knew. One had to fight for the right to be free.

Martin grew to be tall with light features, blonde hair and towered over his Mother and Father, while Fergal was of average height, fair skinned, freckled faced and fiery red hair; a mirror image if his father, Sean.

In his solitude, Martin, heavily influenced by his father, found the writing and poetry that many Irish poet patriots discovered. It was a creative release that refreshed his soul from the daily grind of Belfast.

But on the street he had the fight of his mother in him. During every marching season of his youth he never once saw her back down even from the largest soldier. He saw her bruised and bloodied at times and the hate welled even greater in him. But she carried her black jack with pride and it hung in their kitchen for all guests to question and everyone to get the story of the day the UDR soldier met Patricia Brennan O'Kane.

There was a great, silent and complete understanding between the O'Kane brothers that came like a gift from their parents. When Martin needed his time, Fergal knew and would back away and when Fergal was restless and needed to go, Martin was ready and waiting.

What Martin O'Kane felt most, but voiced least, was a sense of loss. He couldn't put his finger on it. At times of solitude and contemplation, it was a vague tug at his heart. Other times, holidays and in particular his birthday, it was an all out assault on his person.

Something was missing in his life; there was a black hole, a large void that plagued him. At times of quiet loneliness, this feeling helped him to write and express things that would otherwise be left unsaid. But during the head-on attacks, it was like fighting a well-armed demon that he couldn't see. The beatings were often severe; leaving unnoticed, but very real scars.

The internal struggle about whether to join the fight or not, like so many decisions, was decided for him.

It was Christmas time and the O'Kanes went to spend the holidays with Aunt Siobhan and Uncle Dermot in Portadown, in County Armagh. The boys loved to visit, not only because the Brennans were their favorite cousins, but also because their uncle Dermot, they had found out quite by accident, was a brigade commander within the brotherhood.

One night during their stay, Martin and Fergal's cousin Thomas asked them to go to a local Christmas dance. They were off into the night for fun with some local girls. On their way home at just after midnight, Thomas said, "Lads, keep an eye out for the UDA."

Fergal said, "The UDA?"

"Yeah these cocksuckers who couldn't make the grade in the UDR or the RUC. They dress up like soldiers and scare old women and little kids. There's a sawed off little fucker named Benji Mason who left Belfast and came down here to cause trouble. He plays in the UVF in Belfast and the UDR down here."

Fergal said, "The name sounds familiar."

As they walked, a lorrie pulled up next to them and skidded to a sudden stop, six men carrying black jacks surrounded them.

One of them said, "Benji, it's the Brennan lad, nothing but trouble he is."

Benji stopped for a minute, knowing who Thomas' father was and then said, "Fucking Taig. Lads you know what we do with Taigs."

Martin said, "What's a short little fucker like you going to do?"

Benji pulled out his black jack and quickly struck Martin on his collar bone and he went down.

So used to the violence and reacting to it, as if by an involuntary reaction, Fergal's fist crashed into the side of the face of the soldier who stood closest to him. The clenched hand came out of nowhere with such speed and force that none of the soldiers saw it coming. With a loud snap the man's jaw broke and popped out of place. Before the soldier hit the ground, responding as naturally as a bird to flight, Fergal turned and kicked a second man in the groin and, as he bent in pain, Fergal's knee met the startled soldier's nose with an ugly crunch. In brutal retaliation a black jack came down on Fergal's head so hard he stood, looked at his cousin and passed out.

Martin, who was unable to lift his right arm, and Thomas stood their ground, but the blackjacks came too fast and furiously to fend off with their bare fists, leaving them bleeding and barely conscious at the side of the road. Benji, who had watched with glee after striking Martin, went down on one knee between them, lifted their heads by their hair and with the potent smell of whiskey and tobacco on his breath said, "Taigs shouldn't be out sightseeing after dark. Your other friend here is dead; you'd better find a place to bury him." He slammed their faces into the gravel and laughed as he walked away.

They dragged Fergal home, a gash in the back of his head, but he was still breathing. Once home they doused him with cold water and he woke up.

Fergal said, "What the fuck just happened?"

Thomas said, "Fucking UDA bastards."

Martin looked at Fergal laughing and said, "You earned that gouge on your noggin."

Thomas said, "Fucksake Fergal, you left two of them hurting worse than you."

Martin said, "Aye."

Fergal said, "Well, it was all I could do not to kill the bastard after he hit Martin unawares like that."

As scared and beat up as they were they laughed and for a moment temporarily erase the nightmare, they cleaned themselves up the best they could and went to bed.

The next morning Sean O'Kane and his brother-in-law, Dermot Brennan, sat at the breakfast table having coffee when the three boys walked into the kitchen. Martin was wincing with every step; Fergal was seeing double with the ache in his head and Thomas was black and blue around both eyes.

Sean said, "Jaysus, lads, what the hell is this all about?"

Fergal said, "Nothing Da, some Protestant boys jumped us from behind last night and ended up getting the best of us."

Sean said, "You three can take better care of yourselves than this. How many were there?"

Fergal said, "After a few swings we lost count, Da."

Dermot Brennan stood up and said, "So they did all this to you lads with nothing but their fists? Thomas, come with me."

They went to his bedroom and shut the door. Dermot said, "Tell me the truth. You and your cousins are worthless liars."

Thomas told his father everything that happened and finished by saying, "They were lads from the UDA."

"Mason and his crew?"

"Aye."

"Was it Mason who pulled you up by the hair?"

"Sure as Mary gave birth to Jesus."

"That chicken shit. I'll take care of this."

When they arrived at the table Sean was looking at his boys, checking the back of Fergal's head and making Martin pull up his shirt. When he saw the divot in Fergal's head and the large black bruises that covered Martin's side he said, "Jaysus, lads, I'm taking you both to the hospital."

Martin stared down at his father and waited until he'd made sure he'd gotten his attention and said, "No Da, if Fergal wants to go fine, but I'm not going, these wounds will heal."

Fergal said, "Aye, Da. It's nothing more than a scratch."

Sean said, "Scratch my arse, you haven't seen it lad, it needs stitches."

Dermot told Sean what had happened and Sean looked at his brother-in-law and said, "The goddamn loyalist bastards."

Dermot looked at the boys and said, "You lads okay?"

They all nodded.

He said, "I'll take care of this."

Martin said, "Thanks, Uncle Dermot, but I'll get mine back in me own time."

Dermot, impressed with the boy's toughness looked down at Fergal, who looked up and locked his eyes upon his uncle with a knowing stare and said, "Where do we sign up?"

Sean, once more in a quandary, could say nothing, knowing somehow, someway both of his lads would join the fight. And they, like their Grandda, would be lost to him forever.

The following week retaliation was quick, neat and merciless, letting the UDA know they had crossed the line. Each of the men in Mason's crew was quietly rounded up one by one, taken to the countryside, knee capped and told to tell Benji that Dermot wanted to talk to him. By the end of the week Benji Mason was so wound up that he left Portadown and was not seen anywhere for six months.

The call was made to Eamon Gainey in Belfast and the contact was made. At ages seventeen and sixteen, Martin and Fergal O'Kane had joined the Republican Brotherhood in the fight for one free Ireland. In three years time, the O'Kane brothers would be the most wanted men in Northern Ireland.

Chapter 37
The Green Book

One week later

The Falls Road

Belfast, Northern Ireland

The wind blew cold down the Falls Road in Belfast, and all was quiet at two a.m. Martin and Fergal O'Kane road nervously in the back of an unfamiliar sedan while two voices spoke in low Irish whispers in the front seat.

The car rolled to a stop and as they got out to the stinging cold winter's wind no one said a word.

The safehouse was on The Falls Road but looked no different than any other house on the road. The brothers had the idea that they were going to some secret hide out and it was, in a sense, but secret in plain sight. The front door creaked open and they stepped into the front room.

A woman came out of a shut door in a robe and curlers. She said, "I've got some soup on, you must be starved."

Fergal shrugged and said, "I've always got room, ma'am."

When she left Martin whispered, "What kind of safehouse is this? She could have been our mum."

Fergal shrugged again and then looked to their left into the dining room where they recognized their uncle Dermot Brennan sitting with two other men who sat smoking cigarettes and drinking strong, hot tea that steamed from mugs before them.

The brothers stood for a moment wondering if they had made the right decision, not daring to look at one another.

Dermot stood and said, "Welcome, lads. Come in and sit down."

The brothers took seats and Eamon Gainey said, "Would you care for some tea?"

Both wanting to shake the cold that they felt said, "Aye."

The tea was poured and Fergal lit a cigarette.

Dermot said, "Jaysus, Fergal, is that a Park Drive?" a Park Drive being a particularly deleterious cigarette preferential to old men in Belfast's Catholic ghettos because they were cheap and available.

Fergal, a bit embarrassed, said, "Aye."

Dermot said, "Why don't you just light up some dried dog shit and do us all a favor."

The men around the table, as well as the guards who stood behind them, laughed while Fergal quickly put it out and cleared his throat. Martin nudged him and grinned.

Eamon said, “Well at least we know which side the lads are on.”

They all chuckled in agreement and Eamon continued, “Lads, this is Daithi O’Connor.”

They nodded.

“It's his wife you met on your way in. Obviously you know your Uncle Dermot. And I'm Eamon Gainey.”

The brothers nodded nervously.

“Your uncle tells us that you’re ready to join our ranks?”

They nodded again.

He threw a manual on the table in front of them.

Eamon continued, “This is The Green Book. It is the official manual of the standing IRA, and it is now your bible. Read it, memorize it, and know it. It is now everything that you are.

“I’m going to highlight a few things for you right now. The moral position of the Irish Republican Army and its right to engage in warfare is based on three basic rights. Number one is the right to resist foreign aggression. Second, the right to revolt against tyranny and oppression and third, we are in direct lineal succession with the provincial government of 1916, the First Dail of 1919 and the second Dail of 1921. Any questions so far?”

Both had questions but neither had the courage to speak up.

Eamon said, “Good. At the beginning of the manual you will notice the section on loose talk. This is no bullshit lads, men are dying every day because gits can’t keep their fucking mouths shut. No one knows that you are members of the IRA, no one. Not your family, friends, girlfriends, workmates, no one. Do not speak of it in taxis, elevators, phones, public or private, clubs, pubs, or football matches. Whatever you say – say nothing. These English bastards are everywhere and they especially take advantage of our lads after they had too many pints. Be very aware.

“If you're a member of the IRA you will be involved in killing, it’s what a soldier does, and if you can’t take an order to kill then you cannot be part of this organization. It's the same in any army in the world, no different here. The chances are very good that you'll one day be arrested and interned. Please read the sections on arrest, interrogation and torture because when you are arrested, and you will be arrested, you will be interrogated and you will be tortured. Read in detail this section and the three kinds of torture they use; physical, psychological and humiliation.

“Lastly, gentleman please read thoroughly the procedures for court martial. This is deadly serious. There are and will be informers and they will be dealt with severely. We are an army and if you break the rules there will be serious consequences. I'm not worried about you two, but this is a technicality that needs mentioning.

"Listen lads, if you're going to pursue this fight, chances are you're going to end up in The Kesh. If you get arrested the first place they'll take you to is Castlereagh, and it isn't a nice place. It's there that they'll beat the shyte out of you trying to get a confession out of you. And when the time comes, and you'll know when that is, you'll ask yourself if it's worth fighting for, is it worth dying for? At that point in your life, remember the words of the Republican Terence McSweeney when he said, 'It is not those who inflict the most but those who endure the most who will conquer in the end.'"

Chapter 38
Setanta

Four Clovers Ranch

Polson Montana

1976

Michael Patrick "Mick" Quinlan was raised in the lap of luxury, but because of a firm hand from his father, the rigid discipline from Ms. Gonzaga, his nanny, and hard work on the ranch, he was far from spoiled. But he never took life too seriously and found that he was constantly seeking fun and adventure to eliminate a void that existed within him that he could not quite express.

Consuelo Gonzaga kept close supervision on Mick until he was out of grade school. As a result of her harsh discipline at times, he had excellent manners, did well in school and could speak Spanish fluently. But Mick had a gregarious personality, a contagious laugh, a need to make people laugh and was constantly finding himself in trouble.

By the time he was in high school his father had taken over much of his supervision, making sure he was kept busy on the ranch, kept out of trouble and insisted on him knowing about all things Irish. The Irish thing irritated the hell out of Mick at times, and he took no more pleasure than when making fun of the old man's brogue behind his back at every chance he could.

He had to admit, if only to himself, that he did love some of the stories his Dad told him, especially when he was younger, out riding shotgun on his dad's horse. But the times he loved the most were Uncle Dinty's visits from Ireland. Dinty was a Seanachie, an Irish historian and storyteller, and Mick loved the complex and entertaining yarns he spun as effortlessly as the spider preparing her intricate web. You never knew if he was speaking fact or fiction, but his brogue had a way of pulling you in so that his audiences hung on every word. He would come to visit the Four Clovers Ranch for at least a month each year. The first couple of years Mick remembered Dinty fighting it because he hated to fly. But as usual Paddy would get his way. Mick remembered phone conversations in which his father would question the size of his uncle's stones. Paddy would hang up after winning over his brother and say to Mick, "I knew it would be enough. Question Dinty's courage and he'd swan dive off the Cliffs of Moor just to spite you." And then he would laugh and laugh.

But after a while, Mick noticed that Dinty seemed to look forward to his trips to Montana. Dinty always told him, "Lad, I don't know how the hell they get ten tons of steel in the air, but they do. And I'll tell you, boyo, my fear of flying has been replaced by gorgeous stewardesses on Aer Lingus and a wee bit of the drink on the way."

But, Mick noticed that no matter how much Dinty enjoyed the ranch, his brother, nephew, and the beauty of it all, the shores of old Eire would call him home once more.

When Dinty was on the ranch there was never a dull moment. When he was telling stories he always had an audience and Paddy had to constantly prod his ranch hands to get back to work after, once again, being mesmerized by some outlandish tale. But what Mick remembered most were the times when just he, his dad and his Uncle Dinty would ride together.

Before Dinty ever set foot on the ranch and before Mick was old enough to go to grade school, he would ride in front on his dad's horse. As he grew he would ride on the back and soon he had his own steed and rode side by side with his father.

When Paddy and Mick rode together, from the time Mick could comprehend, Paddy was passing on stories from Ireland, talking about the troubles in Northern Ireland, singing Irish ballads and would, on occasion, recite an Irish poem or two. At night before bed his dad would read him Irish stories, poetry and sing Irish tunes to get him to sleep. Those were good but his dad didn't have the storytelling talent of his brother. Mick never told his dad this, but Paddy knew.

Mick remembered the very first time he had met Dinty, and every story he ever heard him tell, the wondrous stories about the ancient Kings, like Conor MacNessa and Cormac MacArt or Niall of the nine hostages, ancient patriarch of all the O'Neill clan. He also loved to hear the stories of the learned poets and the great Saints. And, of course, Dinty always told him that tales of ancient Ireland would not be complete without the mention of Brian Boru or the druids. But Mick's favorite stories of all were the tales of the mighty and ancient Irish warrior hero, Cuchullain.

One day, as Paddy and his men were herding cattle; Mick and Dinty fell behind and rode at a leisurely pace. Getting bored in the saddle, Mick said, "Uncle Dinty, would you tell me again the story of how Cuchullain got his name."

"Absolutely. Now, of course, the thing about Cuchullain that differentiated him from other mythic heroes was that, unlike the ancient Greek and Roman Gods, Cuchullain actually lived and breathed."

Mick said, "What do you mean?"

"I mean that the ancient Greek and Romans gods were fictitious characters made up to tell a story, but Cuchullain was actual flesh and blood. Just like you and me.

"When Cuchullain was a young lad, maybe a few years older than you are now, he went by the name Setanta. One day, while on an errand, he went to the house of a great silversmith named Cullan, but before he could get to the door Cullan's vicious dog attacked him. Now most lads his age would have gone to their grave in the jaws of the wild beast. But instead Setanta went on the offensive and destroyed the animal with his bare hands. When Cullan came from his shop and saw what had happened he was heartbroken at the loss of his beloved brute. Setanta, moved with pity, looked upon the smithy and said, 'I shall, from this day forward, be your hound, Oh Cullan.' And thus the name Cuchullain, which translated from the Irish language means Cullan's hound. Cuchullain went on to be the greatest Irish warrior of all time. And that, lad, is saying something."

"Dinty, I love that story. But how do you know whether you have courage?"

"Well, lad, most people find courage when they least expect it. They're thrown into a situation where they have to make a sudden choice and they either stand up or cower. Courage isn't a lack of fear, it's having fear and facing it rather than running from it."

"Like?"

"Like Setanta, he walked to the house of the great smithy and the ferocious dog attacked. He had a choice and his was to stand and fight. He then had the choice to run away or face the silversmith and his decision was to stay and own up to what he did."

Mick thought things over for a few moments and said, "The men you talk about in the Easter Uprising like Plunkett, Pearse and Connelly, they had courage?"

"If your definition of courage is to stand up against a mighty oppressor, even to your death, for freedom and your principles, then yes, they had unrivaled courage."

At age eighteen, like his unknown identical twin, Martin O'Kane, six thousand miles away, something was missing in Mick's life. He had all the material wealth one could be provided with and yet, he yearned for something he knew money could not buy, but did not know what that something was. Some days hurt worse than others did. He had a desire that he couldn't define and it was insatiable.

When the hard days came on him, he knew before he was even out of bed. Those were the days he would engage himself in work on the ranch or his studies to keep his mind off the pain. He wished he had a brother or sister, but he was to grow up as an only child. When the loneliness and the hurt enveloped him, and he realized he could physically work and study no more to escape the pain, he found himself once again around the campfire with the ranch hands. He started smoking cigarettes and experimenting with the bourbon they passed around as they sang cowboy songs.

Chapter 39
The Proving Ground

1979 Four Clovers Ranch

Polson, Montana

For Mick Quinlan, the ranch was a constant proving ground. Even though he spent evenings around the campfire with the ranch hands, days on cattle drives, early springs cutting and branding calves, summers mending fence in oppressive heat, and working long days with no complaint, the general consensus amongst the hands was that Mick was born with a silver spoon in his mouth. Mac Brown, a loud mouth ranch hand who was always causing trouble, exacerbated this feeling. And because of his own insecurities he felt the need to beleaguer Mick, who for his own part was quiet and let it go.

One Friday evening in early summer, just after the cutting and branding was done for the year, Mick was sitting around the campfire with the rest of the ranch hands enjoying the evening, listening to the music being played and pulling on the jug of sour mash.

After a few pulls, in an uncharacteristic moment he said to Corky Johns, the ranch manager, sitting next to him, "Corky, I think I want to try my hand at bull riding during this summer's rodeo."

Corky smiled, one of the few who didn't share the consensus that Mick was soft. He knew better; he had watched this kid work like a plow horse, never mouthed off and always did what he was told. He thought, "Sure his dad was wealthy, but that wasn't his fault and he was far from spoiled."

Corky said, "Mick, that's a tough way to go, you sure? Calf roping would be a better use of your skills."

Mac Brown overhearing this conversation and, as usual, with a belly full of whiskey said, "Corky, he ain't got no skill to rope no calves and he ain't tough enough to get on no bull. He's a mama's boy, still on the teat."

That was it.

Mick stood and said, "Mac, I've heard enough out of you. You're a loud-mouthed son of a bitch and I've sat quiet long enough. I've often wondered why one of the other hands hadn't kicked your sorry ass before."

The ranch hands began too hoot and holler.

Mac stood to meet him and Mick hit him so hard that Mac flew back and landed on his rear, the hooting and hollering rang louder.

Used to being knocked down, kicked and drug threw the dirt by much larger animals than Mick Quinlan, Mac Brown stood up, spit out a tooth, bleeding from his mouth, smiled and said, "And I've been wondering when I'd get a chance to whip your sorry ass."

Mick said, "At least my mother doesn't look like a raggedy assed mountain goat."

"At least I got a mom."

The ranch hands were stunned at first, then they roared with laughter. They had never heard Mick talk tough, they had never even seen him lose his temper and they never *ever* thought he had enough gumption to throw a punch at anyone. The fire blazed in Mac Brown's eyes and he attacked Mick with a fury, tackling him next to the blaze of the campfire.

Corky Johns stood to ensure that there was no interference and let Mick establish what he'd known all along and had waited patiently to happen. The two combatants beat each other into submission and when each man could no longer raise an arm to strike and were barely able to keep their balance, Corky stepped in to break it up.

He said, "Fella's, get Mac over to the watering tank and dunk him, then see him to his bunk."

He put an arm under Mick and began to walk him to the house. Mick shrugged off the help, walked over to the watering tank, cleaned himself up and said, "Mac, you ready to finish this?"

The ranch hands started all over again laughing uproariously now and exchanging money as to who would finish on top.

Mac pulled himself up to stand, looked at Mick under puffy black eyes, water dripping from his face, smiled and fell to the ground, out cold. The ranch hands roared once more, the losers not worried because they just paid for some great entertainment, as Mick walked himself to the bunkhouse and crawled into the bunk that they had designated his when he wanted it.

At 5:30 the next morning Paddy Quinlan walked into the bunkhouse looking for Mick. He thought, "If that son of a bitch was too drunk to get back to the house last night, by God, he's getting his sorry ass out of bed and working it off."

When he saw Mick lying there barely recognizable he said so loud that ranch hands were jumping, "Blessed be Jaysus, Mary and Joseph. Corky, what the hell happened here?"

Corky who had just walked in from putting coffee on the fire and using the head said, "Boss, let's take this outside."

They walked out on to the wooden stoop in front of the bunkhouse and Paddy said, "Jaysus, he looks like he's barely breathing, why didn't you come get me?"

"Because it was the best thing that could've happened to him."

"That needs some explaining and it better be damn good."

When Corky was done explaining, Paddy's chest was ready to burst with pride and he was smiling.

Paddy said, "So, he finally stood up for himself did he?"

Corky said, "Yes sir, and from the looks of it, there ain't a man in there that don't now respect him and who wouldn't think twice before stepping in with him."

"How's that loud mouth Brown?"

"Looks like he's been rode hard and put up wet, he'll be hard pressed today."

"Tell him to pack his gear, collect his pay and get the hell out."

"That'd be a mistake, boss."

"Why?"

"Then every man here'd think if he looked crosswise at Mick he'd be given his marching papers, that's why. Mick held his own, proved himself, if Mac Brown didn't learn his lesson and is still shooting off his mouth, we'll let him go for that, not fighting with Mick."

"You're right, as usual, Corky, thanks for keeping an eye on the boy."

"He don't need me keeping no eye on him, boss, he can take care of hisself."

Two weeks later a storm hit Polson, Montana that would be talked about for years to come. Hail the size of a large man's fist was crashing into the roof of the bunkhouse so hard that it was taking pieces of the wood shingles with it. The seventy-mile an hour winds were knocking fence and barns to the ground. Lightning bolts were leaving large shadows as they split one hundred-year-old black oak trees, like they were cork board, leaving them to rot. And the thunder rolled so close and loud that the men could feel their chests rattle and their hearts jump.

Mick came running into the bunkhouse, Paddy on his heels, and screamed, "Fence is down and the cattle are running!"

The men jumped up and out of their bunks and as they were throwing on their boots and slickers, Paddy started screaming orders.

They all had their horses saddled and mounted in minutes. Not thinking of their own safety, just that of the valued livestock. These worn and experienced cowhands were going out to do another day's work, only this time, in the middle of the night.

Corky screamed, "She's a gullywasher boys, you know what to do."

As they rode out they couldn't see the head of their horses as the rainwater cascaded so furiously off their hats that it was sometimes hard to breathe, their horses, at times, getting so stuck in the mud that they had to jump off to pull them out.

The thunder and lightning continued to crash around them, so loud and often that it forced the cowboys to hold their horse's reins tighter to keep them steady, when their natural tendency was to bolt.

Daybreak came slowly. The ranch hands were relieved to finally have rounded up all the wandering livestock. They were herding them east toward the mountains back to the pens that some of them had worked feverishly throughout the night to fix, when their surroundings became uncomfortably still. The cattle went quiet knowing what was coming. All that was heard were the hooves of the large animals crashing into the soft earth. The sky became thick and yellow and they felt as if they were riding through honey. Paddy turned his horse back to the Northwest and a large black wall cloud was dropping like a giant waterfall crashing over a two hundred-foot crag.

Mick stopped his horse and looked around. He saw a wandering steer just over a knoll to the northwest and screamed, "We missed one!"

Paddy and Corky looked at one another. Both men knew the weather and knew what was coming and Corky said, "Mick, let her go. That's a wall cloud, a twister could drop out any time. Let's get the rest of these in and go look for her later."

"Forget it Corky, I'm going after it."

Paddy screamed, "Get your arse back hear, now!"

It was too late; Mick took off like a bolt heading into the eye of the storm. When Mac Brown saw what was happening he went after Mick.

Corky screamed, "You stupid sons a bitches get back here!"

Paddy looked at Corky and said, "When those two idiots get back, if they do get back, give 'em both their pay and walking papers, they're fired."

"You can't do that."

"Why not?"

"One's a good hand and the other's your son."

Paddy screamed over the oncoming wind and said, "It's my ranch and I can do whatever the hell I want!"

The two young cowboys were not paying attention to the two boss men when the twister dropped out of the sky.

Corky turned around and said, "Boys, let's get these cattle east, now!"

Mac was trying to outrun Mick who didn't know he had company. Mac caught him and was overtaking him with a laugh when the twister appeared. Mac's horse reared on him and he bounced out of his saddle and then slid off the back of his horse and hit the ground as the horse bolted. Without thinking, Mick stopped, grabbed Mac by the shirt collar and pulled him up on to his horse; Mac Brown was white with fear.

Mac screamed, "We must be the dumbest sons a bitches alive."

Mick screamed over his shoulder, "Speak for yourself, you didn't have to come, now hold on and shut up."

They ran over the knoll and came up on the steer that was looking up at the twister as it moved southeast, tearing up everything in its path and sounding like a locomotive bearing down on them.

Mick grabbed his lasso and found the steers horns on his second throw and screamed, "Would've made it on the first throw if it hadn't been for this fucking wind."

They found a low-lying ditch and made for it. Together they wrestled Mick's horse to the ground and did the same with the steer using his horns. Once they got the two large animals down on their sides they lay in between them.

After they were settled waiting for the tornado to take their lives, Mick screamed at Mac, "Now, grab your ankles."

Mac screamed back, "What?"

Mick said, "Grab your ankles!"

"Mac said, "Why?"

"It'll be easier to kiss your ass goodbye that way."

In spite of the frenzy and fear around him, Mac couldn't help but to laugh.

In the blink of an eye it was quiet again and within five minutes the sun was coming up in the east and the familiar blue summer sky of Montana was covering them.

Mick stood, looked around and then screamed in elation, never feeling anything like this in his life. He challenged death. He stared the villain in the face and smiled. He survived and he had never felt so alive in his life.

As they rode back on Mick's horse, like two wet rats out of a local mountain stream, Mac said, "I'll be a son of a bitch. Ain't never seen anything like that in my life. Now where's that nag of mine got to?"

"I've never seen anything like that either and neither has your horse, she's probably still running. But I ain't worried about that just now."

"What're you talking about?"

"Corky and Pa are going to have our asses for riding away like that after they told us not to."

"I didn't hear a damn thing."

Mick said, "Come to think of it, neither did I."

They rode into camp like a couple of schoolboys caught cheating on a test and put the steer in the pen with the rest of the cattle.

Corky came out of the bunkhouse almost at a run trying to control Paddy Quinlan who was in a fury, Paddy pulled Mick off his horse and held him up by his shirt and said, "When I tell one of my men to do something I mean for it to be done, that includes you. As for you, Mac Brown, gather your gear, go on up to the house and draw your pay, then get the hell out. I don't need any goddamn mustangs on my ranch."

Mac started to walk away and Mick said, “Mac, wait.”

The cowboy turned around and stared. Mick turned and looked at his dad and said, “He just saved a five hundred dollar steer for your sorry ass and this is how you treat him?”

Paddy came at him and Mick stood his ground. The two men glared at one another and Paddy said, “This is my ranch and it’ll be run the way I say, not you or anybody else. And if I say Mac Brown is fired, the son of a bitch is fired.”

Mick said, “If he’s fired then so am I.”

Paddy said, “Fine. Pack your gear and get the hell out.”

Mick stared at his dad, memorizing his face, his stubborn Irish pride telling him it would be a long time before he would see it again.

Chapter 40
As The Seanachie goes

Upperchurch, County Tipperary, Ireland

1981

As far back as Paddy Quinlan could remember, his brother Dinty, ten years his elder, was telling stories, writing poetry, studying clan genealogy and immersing himself in Irish history. As a result Dinty became one of the greatest modern day Seanachie in all of Ireland.

The country itself helped him along as she was loath to move into the twentieth century, especially rural Ireland where Dinty practiced his trade. Television was common enough but it wasn't difficult to find the village here or there where there was no television at all.

The Seanachie, when one would come around, would be a great source of entertainment and news from the outside world for a small rural village.

The first night's telling told the villager whether he was any good and if it was thumbs down then he could be on their way that night. The difference between the good and the great was not the facts and the history but the art of telling the tale. Great Seanachie would spin such wonderful yarns with so little effort that after two weeks they would have to secretly disappear from a village late at night if they were ever to get away.

It was not unusual for the gifted storytellers to have four hundred stories in their repertoire which they could pull from their mental library at a moment's notice.

Word would spread and when these noted celebrities would come around, the village would welcome them with open arms. In the evening they would all gather around the bonfire, give the Seanachie a place of honor and a jug of poteen to slake his thirst after too many words, and let him begin. Usually after a good night, the last stragglers in the village were slipping home just before sun up.

Dinty Quinlan was one such Seanachie, so when they found him dead of a massive heart attack in the countryside at the age of sixty-five, on his way to tell one more tale, news spread like wildfire. People came from all over the south and the west of Ireland to see the legend sent off properly.

* * *

Paddy Quinlan sat at his big desk, in his big study, surrounded by his big mansion, on his huge ranch and felt as insignificant as a grain of sand in a vast desert and as lonely as a traveler in a strange land. He lost the love of his life and then his son ran off and he had not heard from him since.

His grandfather clock rang twelve times on the midnight hour, and the only thing moving was the pen in his hand, tapping on a tablet of paper in rhythm to the great clock's second hand.

He stared aimlessly out the window and listened as the breeze allowed the pines to whisper to one another. His heart ached. It had been almost two years since he had lost his temper with Mick, causing his departure. He sorely missed the boy and longed to hear from him so he could apologize for being such a damned fool. And he knew the worst of it was that he had been too proud and stubborn to admit he was wrong. And to make matters worse, the lad had become as proud and stubborn as him..

The phone burst into the silence of his study. He jumped and thought, "Who the hell is calling me at this time of the night?"

Paddy answered the line and said, "Hello."

The Irish brogue on the other end said, "Paddy Quinlan, please."

"Speaking."

"Cousin Paddy, its Packy Purcell in Upperchurch."

"Packy?"

"Aye. Listen, Paddy, I'm sorry for calling you so late, but I'm afraid the call couldn't wait."

"What is it Packy?"

"We found Dinty."

"I didn't know Dinty was lost."

"Paddy, let me finish. We found Dinty dead."

"What?"

"He fell from a heart attack. He's got away from us, Paddy."

* * *

Within seconds of hanging up the call from Ireland Paddy called Corky Johns up to the house. The ranch manager walked into his boss's office ten minutes later in a rough mood, irritated to be called out of bed at this hour. He mumbled, "This better be good."

Paddy poured two whiskeys and handed one to Corky who declined. Paddy said, "Just hold on to it, you may need it."

Corky, who had just sat down, looked curiously at his boss for a second or two in wonder and then grabbed the glass.

Paddy staring back at Corky said, "Dinty died."

Corky, who had grown quite fond of Dinty over the past several years, said, “Well, for the love of Christ, Paddy. How?”

“Heart attack,” Then shot down his whiskey in an effort to kill the sudden pain of saying it out loud.

“I’m sorry for your loss, Paddy.”

“Corky, do you know where Mick is?”

“No. But I know who might.”

“Who?”

“Mac Brown. He went to Butte.”

“Butte?”

“Yep, he's a deputy sheriff.”

“Never thought the lad would leave his horse.”

“He always wanted to be a sheriff.”

“Didn't know that. So what about him?”

“Well, when Mick took the fall with Mac Brown, Brown grew rather fond of Mick. I hear they stayed in touch.”

“How do you know all this?”

“Paddy, you know this valley has ears. But as far as Mick’s whereabouts, you know Sheriff Power in Butte?”

“By reputation only.”

“Well he comes from up around here, we was drinking buddies in our younger years.”

“Hmm.”

“You want, I’ll call him, see if he knows anything. Maybe Brown said something to him about Mick.”

“Aye, I do. I’ve got to go back home to bury Dinty and I’m not going without Michael Patrick. He’d never forgive me.”

“I’ll see to it, boss.”

Paddy spent the rest of the night on his all-consuming couch polishing off the fifth of Irish and staring at the beautiful O’Connor nude that hung in honor in his great room and passed out thinking about Cassie Kenny and feeling as lonely as he had ever felt in his life.

Chapter 41
The Royal Gorge

Canyon City, Colorado

1981

Mick Quinlan, as stubborn an Irishman as his Irish immigrant father, packed his gear that day in 1979, cleared out his savings account and left. He figured that he had earned enough money on the ranch to last him a couple of years at least and then, as the prodigal son, he would return to work with the old man once again.

Leaving wasn't as hard as he thought it would be. His father had told him that his mother had died giving birth to him, so Mick never knew her. Consuela Gonzaga, the Mexican housekeeper who raised him, had done so with such an iron fist that he was glad to be rid of her. And his dad was getting to be a pain in his ass, always telling him what to do. It was always his way or the highway. Well, he thought with a coy smile, there's the highway, never giving much thought to the fact that the Ford F-250 pick up truck with the camper on back he was driving on *that* highway, and all the gear he had stored in it, were given to him by *that* pain in the ass.

What neither man had taken into consideration, upon their parting, were the arrangements that fate had made for both of them. She laughed aloud at their plans. Not only was she pleased with her plans for the father and son, but she smiled demurely as she saw the collision course on which she had set the Irish twins, both living distinct, oblivious and separate lives, and yet co-mingled through one woman. A woman that yearned so intently for them both that their union was destiny.

Mick Quinlan stood looking down and smiled. He had spent the last two years in search of that elusive buzz, the adrenaline rush that he had found in the dangers on the ranch. Rock climbing, dangerous white water rafting and sky diving paled by comparison. They were good, but his addiction called for more, always more and he had found it.

The wind blew his hair in all directions. It rocked the bridge that swung 1,053 feet above the three million-year-old Arkansas River. The high he felt looking down reminded Mick of how he felt when the twister was coming down on he and Mac Brown, death defying. He held the railing to keep his balance as the bridge swayed on the howling wind, and looked at the man standing next to him and smiled.

From this height the river looked more like a thread woven through a fantastic fabric of reds and dark browns than the fierce white water it really was, certain death if anything failed.

So this was the Royal Gorge. The sublime view sent a shiver down his spine and he felt his stomach tighten up as it always did at the thought of all those endorphins being released into his system en masse. This was the pinnacle and they were going to pull it off.

Tourists passed him on the bridge as he went over in his mind a quick rundown of the procedures to be used later, after dark. He thought, the single access road made necessary the radios, they had their headsets, Thomas would be first to jump, I'll pull him up and then I go.

Thomas Higgins, Mick's best buddy since kindergarten, standing next to him on the bridge said, "What?"

"What? What?"

"You just pumped your fist. You must be getting fired up."

Mick laughed. He always got so caught up in his daydreams that he would act them out with some minor physical gesture without even realizing it.

Mick said, "You got a stopwatch?"

Thomas said, "Always."

Mick produced a palm sized rock and said, "Time this."

Thomas said, "Are you nuts?"

"What?"

"First of all, dude, it's totally illegal to drop anything from this bridge. Second of all what am I timing? It's so far down that you'd have to toss a boulder and even then you might not hear it hit the ground, especially in this shitty wind."

Mick said, "Got caught up in the moment. Sorry."

"Trust me, bro, its going to be a L.A.J."

"L.A.J.?"

"Long ass jump."

"Gotcha. But keep your voice down."

"Right. Sorry."

Mick smiled as he made a mark on the railing where he wanted the anchor harnessed to the bridge then said, "Let's go."

The two men drove the twelve miles back to the St. Cloud Motel in Canyon City in silence. Mick was going over all the aspects of the jump in his head while Thomas smoked a joint. They went to their shared room, showered, napped, ate and then began to articulate their whole plan.

"Okay, let's see," Mick said, "I'd love to use a three hundred foot cord for this one but it'll be too damn heavy to carry half a mile up to the bridge. "Hundred and fifty foot cord will have to do and that will be a tough haul as it is."

Thomas said, "Son of a bitch, dude, that'll be a four hundred and fifty foot jump, almost half the distance."

Mick did some quick math and laughed out loud and said, "Shit, that'll be like a seven second descent, which'll feel like a week in the air."

He felt himself getting giddy, had to take a deep breath said, "Okay, Thomas, this is serious shit. If we're not careful we could die or worse, be arrested for felony trespassing."

"Right," then laughed and said, "We can celebrate when this is over."

"That means no more weed until we jump. I want your head clear, understand?"

Thomas said, "Take it easy, Mick, I'm good."

Mick said, "Okay, midnight we head up, get all the equipment secured to the bridge and then its go time."

Thomas smiled.

Mick said, "You go first. I'll pull you up and then I'll jump. Then we get the hell out of there."

Thomas said, "No way, dude. This is your gig, your grand scheme. You jump first."

Mick hesitated, smiled at the thought, and said, "Okay, yeah that works."

At half past midnight the two men got out of the vehicle, pulled off their street clothes and stuffed them in the truck. Underneath were their black wind resistant body suits along with black sneakers, black stocking caps, and radio headsets with portable battery packs. They shouldered their gear and headed into the pitch black.

Trudging uphill, with a hundred pounds of gear on their backs at ten thousand feet in altitude, they were out of breath half way to their destination. When they reached the bridge, the sky, against the bright lights of every single star in the heavens, looked coal black. The wind was vicious, making it scary just to be on the bridge.

Thomas said, "Are you sure this is a good idea tonight?"

Mick said, "This is about as good as it's going to get up here. So I'm going. You do what you want."

Gear in place, Mick rechecked his harness, his carabineers, his bungee cord and finally the yoke connected to the bridge. The wind had picked up considerably and the bridge swayed like a rope lying across the deep crevasse. Satisfied that all was secure, he stepped over the railing, pulled his cord over to the outside, took a deep breathe, made the sign of the cross, counted to three and leaped from the ledge in a perfect swan dive into the gorge.

The wind buffeted Mick's body and tossed him about as he dove into utter darkness; the bungee chord protracted to its maximum and capitulated as if in deference to the laws of physics. He rocketed back toward the bridge and looked up to see the flash light that Thomas held, seeming miles away."

Thomas said, "Mick, you okay?"

Mick didn't hear a word of it as endorphins raced euphoria through his veins. His scream of orgasmic delight that rang through the canyon answered Thomas.

He began his second fall. And could no more control his movement than the ancient river below him would stop its journey to some unknown promised land.

He hung suspended in the dark chasm that surrounded him and screamed again.

Thomas said, "Mick, you ready?"

Mick said, "Yeah, get me out of here."

Thomas said, "Okay, dude. Don't forget to pull down on the chord."

Back on the bridge, Mick was so filled with endorphins and adrenaline after his jump that he wanted to do jumping jacks. He needed a cold beer and he needed it now, but it would have to wait until Thomas made his jump. He needed to be sharp until Thomas was done, reminding himself of the seriousness of it all.

Mick went to hook the carabineer to the Thomas' harness and smelled the weed on his friends breath. He said, "Thomas, I thought I told you. . ."

"Lighten up, dude, everything's cool."

Gear fastened, Thomas began stepping over the railing on the bridge. As he lifted his second leg over a sixty mile an hour wind buffeted the bridge and a devastating wind gust howled down the canyon and rocked the bridge mercilessly. Mick, both feet planted firmly on the bridge, instinctively put both hands on the railing.

Thomas lost his footing on his first leg and his second leg came down on canyon air. Both feet kicked up and his head came crashing down on the bridge and he was gone.

Mick looked down at the blood and hair that his best friend left on the bridge and watched in horror as he continued to fall into the black abyss, recoiled, fell again, recoiled and fell for a last time, mortally wounded.

He then heard tires on gravel and as he looked up he found himself engulfed in the bright headlights of the county sheriff's patrol car.

Chapter 42
Manslaughter

Canyon City Jail

The next morning

The phone rang, and Paddy lifted his fifty pound head off the couch pillow and squinted at his watch, 6:30 a.m. He thought, "What the hell?"

He picked up the receiver and said, "Hello."

The voice came back, "Dad?"

The silenced boomed loudly in his great room and his heart leapt at the sound of his son's voice. It had been two long years.

"Mick!"

There was a pause.

"Mick?"

"Dad. . ." His voice cracked and Paddy's moment of celebration crashed.

"Mick, what's wrong? Where are you?"

"I'm in jail, in Colorado."

"What the hell?"

"They think I did it."

"Wait a minute, back up. Who thinks you did what?"

"We decided to bungee jump off the Royal Gorge Bridge."

"The Royal Gorge? You're shitting me right?"

"No, Dad."

Paddy said, "Who's we?"

"Me and Thomas Higgins," Mick said and then burst into tears.

Paddy said, "Mick, listen to me. What happened? What do they think you did?"

"Thomas lost his balance in a strong wind gust as he stepped over the railing to jump. He slipped and smashed his head against the bridge and then fell."

"Jaysus, Mick. Was he attached to something, or did he fall to his death?"

"He was secure and had the bungee cord hooked up. When he hit his head, he hit it hard and I think that's what killed him."

Paddy thought for a moment and said, "What're you being charged with?"

"Manslaughter."

"So when is your arraignment?"

Mick said, "My what?"

"When do you have to appear in court?"

"Three days. Next Tuesday."

"I'll be down there no later than tomorrow and I'll bring my attorney. Will you be okay until then?"

"Dad, please hurry. Thomas is laying in the morgue somewhere and they won't let me out of here to see him. Holy shit dad, get here quick!"

* * *

"All rise for the honorable Franklin Stipes." Mick's heart skipped a beat and his breath caught in his throat.

The judged, who had traveled from Denver to be here, looked through his reading glasses at the cases on his docket, picked up the first and said, "The State of Colorado vs Quinlan, charge: Manslaughter. How do you plead?"

The Quinlan attorney stood and said, "Not guilty, Your Honor."

"Bail is set at $500,000.00."

The attorney said, "Isn't that a little high for manslaughter charges when my client clearly was innocent of any wrongdoing?"

"Councilor, this isn't a trial, it's an arraignment. The boy's home is fifteen hundred miles away. My guess is he's going there to his family and we sure would like to see him back here in two weeks."

He then looked directly at Mick and said, "Oh, and, please don't leave the country."

Paddy's head fell to this chest.

The three of them walked out of the courtroom and posted $50,000.00, ten percent of $500,000.00, to cover Mick's bail and walked out into the bright mountain sunshine. Mick looked across the street and froze. Paddy took a few steps and when he realized that Mick was not with him he turned around. He followed Mick's frozen gaze across the street to where Thomas Higgins' mother and father, Butch and Jane, walked out of the town café, hunched over in grief and visibly shaken.

Butch was the son of Hank Higgins, whose land Paddy had purchased some twenty-five years earlier.

Paddy said to his attorney standing next to him, "Jaysus, I was so worried about Mick that I forgot completely about Butch and Jane Higgins."

He began to walk toward them and Mick followed with more trepidation at every footfall. In an uncharacteristic moment for a stoic Irishman, Paddy put his arms around them and they all cried together.

When Paddy stepped away Mick had walked up and the Higgins seemed to step back in an almost cold gesture. Mick stopped and the crushing accusatory stares ground him into a fine powder of guilt and remorse.

Jane Higgins glared at Mick, the stare feeling like large, heavy icicles crashing off a winter's gutter on Mick's soft flesh below.

She said, "How could you have done this?"

Paddy looked at Mick and seeing the look of helplessness on his face stepped in and said, "Jane, it was an accident."

"I know that, Paddy. But he had to go sow his wild damn oats and insisted on taking my son with him."

Paddy said, "Jane, that's unfair."

She said, "Who said anything about fair? We're on our way to the morgue to identify our only son."

Paddy wouldn't back down, not even at that. He said, "Jane, the lads were best friends since they could walk. 'Tis a difficult situation at best. But Thomas was no follower, he went with Mick because he wanted to be there."

Butch said, "That's all well and good, but it don't bring him back now does it?"

Paddy said, "No Butch, it doesn't."

"Well, Jane and I agree with the manslaughter charges. I think Mick was careless on that bridge. A bridge they shouldn't have been on in the first place."

Mick suddenly heard Thomas say, *"Are you sure you want to do this tonight?"*

He said, "Mr. and Mrs. Higgins, you're right, I deserve what I'm being charged with and more."

Paddy said, "I've heard quite enough. Butch and Jane, I couldn't be more sorry for your loss. But Mick did not and never would kill your son; he was his best friend. Thomas knew the risks going in. I know you want to blame somebody for your loss, so would I. But you're looking in the wrong place."

Butch Higgins put an arm under his wife's and said, "Why don't we let the courts make that decision."

They jumped into Paddy's rental car and drove the hundred and ten miles back to Denver where they caught a flight back to Montana.

The airplane was not full and weight needed to be distributed evenly in the small United Express Turbo Prop, so the three men on board were asked to sit in the last row. After a bit of grumbling by Paddy, who was getting spoiled in his wealthy old age, it worked out well, because now they could talk in private without talking across the aisle.

After they reached cruising altitude and the beverage cart had made the rounds, Paddy said, "Mick, there's something else I need to talk to you about."

The seriousness in his father's eyes told Mick it wasn't good. It was the same look he'd gotten before being punished as a child for some stupid thing he'd done.

Mick said, "What?"

Paddy took a deep breath and said, "Your Uncle Dinty died."

Mick stopped for a moment, wallowing in the split second before his mind grabbed a hold of what was just said.

Chapter 43
The Shillelagh

March 1981

From the bunkhouse to the great house, the Four Clovers Ranch was quiet in the early morning. Paddy Quinlan sat on his large couch and rubbed his aching foot. He knew deep in his heart that much of his success could be contributed to this deformed appendage, his club foot. It forced him to prove himself time and again; what surrounded him now was the result.

But he cursed the foot at this early morning hour. Pushing it as hard as he had, for as long as he had, and at the moment it felt like hot nails were being pushed through his ankle and toe joints. He rubbed his foot with ointment and winced.

And yet another pain began to tear through his body as he thought of his son sleeping upstairs. Paddy was leaving for Ireland later that morning and Mick had to be left behind. His original intention was to take Mick with him and reveal the truth of his birth. Show him where he was born; tell him about his biological mother and father. Introduce him to Sister Mary de Angels, the first woman to welcome him to this planet.

He had debated about whether to get into the twin thing with Mick or not. During the adoption process he had innocently questioned his cousin, Sister Mary, and asked her where the other twin was going. He remembered that she had hesitated and then acquiesced, he guessed she rationalized that it couldn't hurt, him being so far away and all.

Through contacts back in Ireland he had kept tabs on the family and on the lad. And seeing the independent and fiery temperament of his own adoptive son and knowing the second apple probably didn't fall far from the same tree, he wasn't surprised at the reputation the Irish twin had made for himself. And he wasn't so sure he wanted Mick getting mixed up in that dangerous game, and knew sure that Mick would go looking for his brother immediately upon being told; there would be no stopping him.

Paddy suddenly felt a presence in the room and looked up to find Mick standing over his left shoulder looking pale as a vapor floating above a morning pond. The black bags under his eyes looked as if he was kin to the walrus and his red eyes looked allergic.

Mick said, "Hey."

Paddy said, "Mick."

"That judge can kiss my ass, I'm going to Ireland with you."

"I understand how you feel, but you know I can't let you do that."

Mick came around the couch, anger flared from his eyes. No longer pale and tired, only furious.

"Screw the judge, screw it all dad, I'm coming to bury Dinty with you and then I'm staying in Ireland. Let them come get me there."

Paddy stood slowly using a shillelagh for help. Mick looked at him and the anger turned to puzzlement. For the first time in Mick's life his father looked beaten and tired, like an old bull put out to pasture. It seemed to Mick as if the weight of Dinty's death, Thomas Higgins death and now this trial were the last straws.

"Dad, what's with the cane?"

"It's not a cane, it's a shillelagh."

"What's the difference?"

Paddy not pleased with the flippant answer said, "I'll tell you the difference."

Mick rolled his eyes; Paddy ignored him and continued, "Any fool can manufacture a cane. It takes a true artist to create a shillelagh.

"This," he said raising the walking stick, "is a masterpiece. 'Tis a badge of honor for any Irishman. It comes from the Shillelagh forest in Wicklow."

"Dad I. . ."

"It's made from the wood of an obstinate, stubborn and thorny bush called the Blackthorn. Does that remind you of anyone?"

"Dad, I. . ."

"The handle here, or knob, is actually a root attached to the thick base branch. At one time it was a fighting stick that the Celts branded a 'Bata.'"

Mick was back to angry again, pissed off at these ridiculous tantrums his dad typically threw over nothing more than an innocent question.

Mick said, "Are you finished?"

Paddy said, "I guess so."

"Thank God. *Why* are you *using* this stick?" Refusing to call it anything but a stick.

Paddy said, as if he were innocent in all this, "The Doc told me I've got arthritis in me good foot," Mick knew his dad always called his club foot the good foot, "And that a Shillelagh would help."

"Oh, Doc Smith told you specifically that you needed a shillelagh?"

"Well. . ."

They stared at each other for a moment and Mick said, "Dad, we need to talk."

Paddy said, "I know. I'm sure we woke up Consuelo. Would you go see if she put the coffee on?"

"Sure, dad."

Mick blew cool air into the scalding heat of his cup, sipped carefully and said, “Dad, I’m going.”

Paddy said, “It’s a bad idea.”

“Why?”

“Why?”

“Yeah, why?”

“Because you’re running. You’ve got responsibilities you have to take care of. You didn’t do anything wrong other than a damned illegal jump. But Thomas Higgins is dead and that needs closure lad. If for no other reason than to make sure his parents get what they need. He was your best friend and you can’t let him down now, you owe him that much.”

Mick, knowing he lost, said, “What time do you leave?”

“Corky’s running me down to Missoula at eight.”

“This morning?”

“Aye.”

Mick hung his head and began to walk from the room when an intense chill invaded his spine. It stopped him in his tracks. He turned to look at his father who had turned to watch his son walk away. Their eyes met and they somehow knew.

Paddy said, “What?”

Mick said, “Have a safe trip. I’ll see you when you get back.”

Chapter 44
The Vigilante

Belfast

January – February 1981

It all happened quite by accident. Martin O'Kane had been running some errands and taking care of some personal business when he found himself on the Crumlin Road southeast of his Ardoyne neighborhood. He stood on the corner where Agnes Street meets Crumlin when a taxi pulled to a stop. The taxi was parked at a light when some men jumped out into the street and blocked the taxi, while several others pulled a man out and hit him over the head with a metal rod. They dragged him to a car nearby and threw him in the backseat. One of the men looked around and said, "Just getting rid of another fucking Taig." He got in and they drove away.

Martin jumped in the back of the taxi and said, "Follow that car."

The driver said, "Not on your life"

Martin pulled a handgun from his pocket and said, "How about on yours?"

The driver said, "Fucksake, put that thing away, I'm driving, I'm driving." And they drove away.

Just before they got to the Shankill Road, which ran parallel to the Crumlin Road, Martin said, "Pull over here."

They watched as the men pulled the man they had kidnapped from the car and took him into a pub known as a UVF and UDA hangout called, The Lawnbrook Social Club.

The taxi driver said, "He's a dead man. They're going to romper that poor sot."

Martin knew that rompering was a form of public torture used by some sadist on the Loyalist side. They would grab an unsuspecting Catholic citizen, drag them into a club where they would beat the man, cut him with knives and ultimately kill him and dump his body.

"Get me the hell out of here."

"Where to?"

"The Shamrock Club in Ardoyne."

Martin walked in and Fergal was holding court and looked so much like their father that Martin stopped for a minute. If he hadn't just witnessed the pure evil that had happened in Belfast, he might've smiled. Fergal turned and the smile left his face. Martin nodded and they took a table in the back.

Fergal said, "What's eating you?"

"I just saw something that changes things for me. I struggled with the killing before, but not anymore."

"Why?"

"The Loyalists aren't targeting anyone. They're randomly grabbing Catholic civilians."

"How would they be able to tell?"

"They're watching people coming southwest out of Ardoyne on the Crumlin Road. Chances are pretty good that they're Catholic. I saw the bastards pull a guy out of a cab, hit him over the head, drag him to a car and take him down to the Lawnbrook Club."

"That Proddy pub off Shankill Road?"

"That's it. He's a fucking dead man."

"And just try calling the RUC in."

"Aye."

Fergal and Martin O'Kane remembered every story their father had told all those nights of their youth. It was those nights they went back to as they disciplined themselves as soldiers and honed their skills in hand-to-hand combat. That afternoon on Agnes street and Crumlin Road changed Martin, and when he told Fergal the plan was laid, and revenge was in their hearts.

They would move Southeast out of Ardoyne to the Shankill neighborhood, where they would trawl the pubs frequented by the Loyalist paramilitaries. Waiting patiently for a group to emerge and recognizing one or two, Martin would walk right into it as if an unaware civilian.

"What've we here lads? If I'm not mistaken it's a fucking Taig. What's the best kind of Taig Lads?"

"A dead fucking Taig." They would respond in a well rehearsed chorus.

Martin said, "Whoa there lads, I'm just going to work, I want no trouble here."

The five men circled around him, lead by Fane Taylor, who walked closer and said, "You're going nowhere. Taigs don't work. Taigs are lazy bastards who do nothing but get drunk, fuck, have too many kids and live off the government dole."

The others laughed. Martin put his head down and with one lightning quick move put a nine inch blade through the closest man's Adams apple and said, "Now what were you saying?"

The man began to stagger and while the others looked on still unaware in the dark that one of their gang was nearing death, Fergal walked up, grabbed another one and snapped his neck.

Fane looked at the brothers while the other two ran for their lives.

He said, “So you're the two Taigs running roughshod over our neighborhood, hurting women and children. Running around in the dark as if you might be afraid.”

Fergal stepped up and said, “We've never touched a woman or a child, unlike your Shankill butchers skinning innocent civilians. But I have to admit, you’re the first Proddy Bastard we've come across who hasn't run away like a wee lass on the play ground.”

“That's because I'm not afraid of you.”

Martin stepped forward and said, “You should be.”

Fane smiled and said, “I know who you and your brother are. Take a good look at this face, because it’s the face of the lad who's going to take you down. It won't be tonight and it probably won't be tomorrow. But it will happen, count on it.”

“You just tell your lads to think twice before they grab another innocent civilian off the street.”

Fane said, “Funny that. You talk as if the IRA has never killed an innocent civilian.”

“We don't target them like you lads. Most of our innocents are casualties of war.”

“Aye, you keep telling yourself that.”

Martin said, “Oh and one last thing, you ever threaten me like that again and you won't be walking away.”

Fane then turned and grabbed the two dead men by their collars and pulled them into a nearby alley so they wouldn't be seen on the street. Then, as the O'Kane brothers watched, he walked slowly back into the dark of Shankill road.

Fergal said, “The lad has stones, I'll give him that.”

Martin said, “Aye, I'll give him that.”

This nightly activity of Martin and Fergal was becoming an addiction. The adrenaline high was better than a drinking session at the Shamrock and they felt like they were keeping their community safe. And the intention was met as Loyalist paramilitary men were thinking twice before they grabbed some innocent civilian. No one in the IRA community knew it was Martin and Fergal who were wreaking havoc in the Shankill, but Dermot began to suspect them and put some men on them to check his hunch.

* * *

It was midnight and the RUC station at Castlereagh was quiet for a bit. The conference room where they were to meet was smoke filled and the air was charged.

William Gray, commander of Northern Ireland for England's MI5, tapped his fingers on the table, glaring at the man smoking across the table from him.

Gray said, “Wright, can you worthless bastards in the RUC do anything properly?”

Wright said, “Fuck off Gray.”

“I'd expect as much from a worthless shit who can't keep these Paddy vigilantes from cutting whoever's throat they please whenever they please.”

“We don't know who in the hell they are but the bastards have been doing us a favor, offing illegal paramilitary jag offs that are a pain in our arses.”

“You know damn well it's those fucking O'Kanes.”

“So what if it is?”

“You've heard of informants you stupid pratt? They've gotten two of my best already this month. You have any idea how hard it is to establish one of these agents and how much money it costs. I want these sons a bitches caught before they screw up any more of our network."

Wright said, “I’ve got somebody to take care of it.”

Benji Mason walked in and Gray laughed in spite of his best efforts and said, “Oh, now that is fucking priceless, just fucking priceless. Did you hear what I said?”

“What?”

“I want the O'Kane brothers and I don't care if their dead or alive, but I want them. You send this wee bastard and they'll chew him up and spit him out.”

Benji stuck his chest out and said, “Not just me, but my crew as well.”

Gray chuckled and said, “Well you and your crew better pack a lunch.”

Then he looked at Wright and said, “Don't fuck this up.”

* * *

The brother’s reputation swept through the UDR and RUC, as well as the illegal paramilitary UDA, UFF, LVF and the UVF communities. Never admitting fear, the challenge went up in the Loyalist pubs throughout Northern Ireland, that the man who killed Martin or Fergal O'Kane would receive a thousand pound bonus.

The brothers heard that Benji Mason was on it, and they actually went looking for him and his crew of bunglers, but didn't have much luck. But their nightly rendezvous continued to hone their skills. The addiction was adrenaline and the mission was death.

One evening after a night of violence, Martin and Fergal arrived home as the sun was coming up, and were confronted by their Uncle Dermot.

Dermot said, “Lads, this ends now.”

Martin said, “What does?”

“Don’t be a smart ass with me; I’m your unit commander.”

“I’m not trying to be a smart ass.”

“I've suspected you two were the mighty vigilantes keeping the Nationalist community safe from the big bad wolf, so I put some of the lads on you."

Martin looked at Fergal and they grinned at one another.

“You’ve both proven your worth to me. But this macho bullshit ends now. Those bastards will put an army on you to finish this and I'll lose two of my best men. I can’t afford to lose either of you over something like this.”

Martin said, “It wasn't for nothing. I watched these bastard pick up innocent people, whose only mistake was being at the wrong place at the wrong time. Those fucks rompered them, humiliated them and killed them just because they were Catholic. They'll think twice before that shit starts up again. And if it does, you or anyone else won't be able to stop me.”

“Don't start that crap. This is an army. We need discipline, otherwise we end up just like them. You do what I tell you, understand?"

“Aye.”

“Good. Now listen, both of you. We need you on a job down in Dublin, it’s high profile. You pull this off the way we have it planned, and then we have some business for you in Dublin.”

“Aye?”

“Aye. So when I ask you to knock off the middle of the night vigilante crap I mean it.”

“So is that an order sir?”

“‘Tis an order.”

During the day the O’Kanes had been an integral part of the fight, working closely with the Short Strand Unit and taking orders from Eamon and Dermot. The Short Strand Unit targeted local businesses loyal to the Crown in England. They looked for Loyalist paramilitary units who caused trouble for the Nationalists and met them anytime anywhere. They considered themselves mercenaries, soldiers at war. Lives were lost in these skirmishes and in the businesses they targeted and bombed, sometimes innocent civilians. They refused to see their victims as human beings, they could not. In their minds they had to be statistics, making their justification complete.

Chapter 45
Martin Goes it Alone

IRA Safehouse, Falls Road

Belfast, Northern Ireland

February 1981

Ghosts of steam rose from mugs of hot tea to float with cigarette smoke and whispered words that hung in the air. Eamon Gainey, Daithi O'Connor and Dermot Brennan waited for word when Martin walked in.

He looked at the three men and they noticed the pale and tired look he wore like a nocturnal animal coming in at dawn.

Martin said, "Fergal was arrested with three others. Someone called the police, we heard the sirens and we scattered. I ran out and saw a car blocking the getaway car so I headed east and then north into an alley and jumped into a dumpster."

Eamon said, "How the hell did they get arrested?"

Martin said, "When we ran out of the building I thought they followed me. When I realized they hadn't I peeked out seeing Fergal and the other two were just sitting in the car acting like they were just innocent bystanders or something. The fucking RUC walked up, questioned them, and it looked like they were going to get to walk. Then he turned around, you know, like he had a fucking hunch. He decided to search the car, and found a gun, and they were taken off."

Daithi said, "Fergal and the other lads are headed to Long Kesh. That handgun means ten years and no trial."

Dermot said, "I hate to make it worse, but they'll go to Castlereagh first."

Martin said, "The interrogation center didn't even enter my mind. If they don't sign the confession they're going to get the shyte beat out of them."

Daithi said, "It's the hard part of running an army, lad"

Eamon said, "Not one of those lads will break, so the next few weeks for them may be difficult. But it means now more than ever that we have to stick to the plan and show those British bastards we mean what we say when we tell them we want them the fuck out of Ireland."

Eamon looked at each of his brigade commanders and then looked at Martin and said, “Martin, Dermot talked to you about a job in Dublin after a week or so back?”

Martin said, “Aye, but what about Fergal?”

Eamon said, “What did I tell you lads the day you joined? It's the price we pay. Sometimes it’s higher than we like. We can’t do anything for the lads inside except to keep up the pressure on the outside.”

Eamon pulled out a map Dublin and laid it on the table in front of the men. Ash from his cigarette landed on the map, he quickly brushed it aside and said, “Here’s the British Embassy on Marion Road and here’s Canal Street, both in the Ballsbridge area, and here’s The Grand Canal Hotel.”

He pointed to the exact location of the hotel and continued, “Attached to the hotel here is Kitty’s Pub. They have an outdoor patio here on Canal Street, and we have it on very good information that Basil Millington, the English Ambassador to Ireland, has agreed to a private interview to be held here with a newspaper woman.”

Martin said, “Anyone Da knows?”

“Cassie Kenny.”

“Right, I’ve seen her bylines in the Irish Times and I’ve heard Da speak of her.”

“Anyway, Thatcher has her bloomers in a twist over the blanket protest and the dirty protest, and now we’ve let it slip that we may be working towards a hunger strike. Thatcher’s never understood us, the English never will, but they have to do everything by the bloody fucking book so they’ve set up this interview to get their message out.”

Martin said, “If the nasty old bag would let our lads wear their own clothes, there would be no blanket protest or dirty protest now would there? What’s the plan?”

“Across Canal Street from the hotel there are some condominiums. The one on the second floor here is empty; the realtor is one of our boys. It faces the patio of Kitty's Pub across the street. And because this is a low key affair, and no one is supposed to know about it, they will be expecting nothing.”

Eamon looked at Martin and said, “Okay so far?”

Martin nodded and said, “Aye.”

Eamon dropped keys into Martin's hand

“What are these?”

“Keys to a condo in Dublin. One week from tonight, at 7:00 p.m., Millington’s driver will drop him at the Grand Canal Hotel. One of our guys will drive you to Dublin where you’ll switch your car for a janitorial van. You’ll be dropped at the condo by noon where you’ll stake out the area and be ready by 7:00p.m. so you’re watching when he arrives. Your weapon will be waiting for you in the condo. When you first get there take the weapon apart and put it back together like you've been trained to make sure everything is working properly. Make sure you pack your latex gloves, the weapon stays when your done.

"A half block east here is Barrow Street. Your driver will be waiting for you in the van. We don't want you getting lost, he'll get you to the docks. Here you take a steamer to Glasgow where you'll catch a flight to New York."

Eamon looked at Martin, then threw a fake passport and a one-way ticket to New York on the table and said, "Dan Mulroy in New York will be notified and he'll take care of everything from that side of the pond. Unless something comes up, you won't be back for at least six months, probably a year. You've been chosen for this because you're reliable, you keep your mouth shut, you've got the stones to pull the trigger and the brains to get out of there without anyone noticing. So no mistakes, no fuck ups, hit Millington and get the hell out."

Chapter 46
Fergal

Castlereagh Interrogation Center

Belfast, Northern Ireland

February 1981

The phone rang at 10:30 p.m. William Gray looked at his watch and rubbed his eyes. He picked up the cigarette burning in the ashtray next to his glass of scotch, grabbed the phone and said, "Gray."

Ian Wright said, "We picked up O'Kane's brother."

"Fergal?"

"Aye."

"Where's Martin?"

Wright, thinking he finally was going to score a few points said, "Dunno."

"They always work together…always."

"He must've got away then."

"The ineptitude of the RUC shines again. Feet away from the most wanted man in all of Northern Ireland and he gets away. This is fucking amazing."

"We got his fucking brother, doesn't that count for something? Goddamn it, how 'bout a little something for the effort, here."

"Have you read Fergal O'Kane's file?"

He waited a second too long.

Gray said, "I didn't think so, no. He's genius level intelligence. He's small but is as tough a Fenian bastard as they come. We could bring in a team of fucking Viet Cong and get nothing. So, no, you get nothing for the effort."

"And you think if we got his brother it would be different?"

"Yes, if we made him watch us interrogate Fergal."

Wright sighed and said, "So what do you want to do?"

"I presume you're at Castlereagh?"

"Right."

"I'll be down."

* * *

Ian Wright said, "Sign the confession you Fenian Fuck!"

Fergal said, “Fuck You.”

He grabbed his hair and slammed his head against the cement wall and said,

“Just admit that you blew up the Baltrand furniture building and it’ll be over.”

“Fuck off.”

He viciously slapped him across the face. Fergal looked up at him and smiled.

Fergal's interrogators were frustrated, as they had totally failed in breaking the Republican who stood for hour before them. They left the room for a ten minute break, leaving Fergal handcuffed.

William Gray watched through the two way mirror, things going as he had suspected.

Wright walked into the room and said, “This could take a while.”

“This could take a very long while, if we succeed at all, which I doubt. But I want you to handle it personally.”

“What happens if he dies?”

“We bury him and move you to The Himalayans. It will give you more time before Martin O'Kane finds you.”

Fergal would never give them the satisfaction of seeing his tears. They wouldn't be so much from the pain and the humiliation as not being with Martin, who he sorely missed. He had never been away from him for this long. He then shored up his resolve. He thought, "Martin wouldn’t break, Eamon wouldn’t break. Fuck these bastards, I won’t sign shyte.".

Then he heard Eamon Gainey’s voice in his mind as he had spoken to he and Martin the day they joined, “*Listen lads, if you’re going to pursue this fight chances are you’re going to end up in The Kesh. If you get arrested the first place they’ll take you to is Castlereagh and it isn’t a nice place. It’s there that they’ll beat the shyte out of you trying to get a confession. And when the time comes, and you’ll know when that is, you’ll ask yourself if it’s worth fighting for, is it worth dying for? At that point in your life remember the words of the Republican Terence McSweeney when he said, ‘It is not those who inflict the most but those who endure the most who will conquer in the end.’*”

The door to the room swung open and Ian Wright walked back in. Fergal took a deep breath. Wright didn't say a word, he just stared at Fergal standing in front of him in nothing but his underwear. Fergal shivered from the cold cement and lack of sleep. .

Ian said, “Get on the chair you worthless Taig Fuck.”

Fergal's muscles were so stiff and cramped from standing there for the past twenty-four hours that he could not move.

"I said, get on the fucking chair!"

Wright grabbed him by his hair and dragged him to the chair, Fergal felt his scalp rip and felt the blood drip down his cheeks. He was thrown against the hard wooden chair and slipped back to the floor still unable to move. The kick connected full force with his ribs and he heard the snap, the pain so unbearable that he finally passed out cold.

He came to as Wright doused his face in ice water. He was sitting upright in the chair with his hands tied behind his back so tightly that with his broken ribs he couldn't catch his breath.

Suddenly the lights in the room went out and it became so dark he couldn't tell if his eyes were open or shut.

Wright said, "Did you participate in the bombing of the Baltrand Furniture building?

Fergal whispered, "Fuck you."

The fist landed squarely on his broken rib and he passed out again.

Ice water over his head, the lights went out and Wright said, "Are you a member of the outlawed, illegal, terrorist organization called the Irish Republican Army?"

"Aye, and proud of it."

"What?"

"Fuck off."

After two hours of torture, passing out and cold water showers Wright had had enough and unlocked the handcuffs, and watched as Fergal O'Kane fell to the cold cement floor and convulsed. His blood flowed to the floor from his ears, mouth and nose and his breath came in gasps, as if his head were being held under water and then pulled up at the last minute.

Wright squatted down on his haunches and said, "One more unrepentant Fenian bastard, huh? You sad bastard, what do you have to say for yourself."

With no little resolve Fergal lifted his head and stared directly at his adversary. Wright saw a power in those resolute eyes that was unsettling.

Fergal working hard to breath said, "Come closer."

Wright put his ear closer to Fergal who said, "You got me now and you won this battle, but the war is long from over. So please remember this. One day peace will settle on my homeland again. And one day Jesus Christ will come on a cloud to pass judgment on all our actions. But before those things happen, I am going to hunt you down and kill you like the dog that you are. You won't know when and you won't know where. But you'll know who and you'll know why."

Fergal then smiled a bloody smile and put his head back on the cold floor. A shiver shook Ian Wright with a fear he had never known in all his life. Even in the condition of this man who lay before him, the threat was so real he wanted to run.

Chapter 47
The By-Line

February 1981

The Boeing 747 dropped effortlessly out of the sky and touched down at 7:30 a.m. Dublin time. Paddy woke, yawned, stretched and looked out the window. He had left here thirty six years ago on a merchant marine ship. He was flying back now, first class. He shook his head and said, "Not bad for a shanty Mick."

Dinty's wake was Sunday evening and the funeral Mass was Monday morning in Upperchurch. He guessed he would barely make it out alive. The Irish wake was a long drawn out process, especially when one of the revered elders passed on.

He stood in line for half-hour or so to get through customs, grabbed his bags from the baggage claim and headed for the car rental. He found a diner nearby, grabbed a Dublin newspaper, ordered rashers, scrambled eggs and a hot mug of tea. Jaysus, he thought, it's good to be back. He opened the newspaper and the headline read:

PRISONERS TO START SECOND HUNGER STRIKE
By Cassie Kenny

He froze for a moment. His hands began to shake. He had loved this woman since he had met her. He had never gotten over her, just once in a while quit thinking about her. But when the occasional loneliness dogged him, her memory would come screaming back and haunt his fantasies. He had been lonely for female companionship over the years, and had developed relationships here and there. But he had measured them all against Cassie and none of them ever made the grade.

He read the article and was all at once impressed with her writing and impressed with the lads in Long Kesh with the stones to go to the mat with Margaret Thatcher. Not that it would do any good, because she was ruthless, but the effort was impressive.

It had not even occurred to him to look up Cassie. Thinking of Dinty and Mick, his mind had been elsewhere. But now his mind was squarely on Cassie.

Cassie Kenny had spent most of her morning trying to get through to Basil Millington's secretary on the phone. This would be the icing on the cake before she had to leave for Belfast. His assistant kept promising a return call but she got nothing, when the knock came on the door.

Paddy Quinlan stood in the doorway with a single red rose. Cassie stared at him with the disbelief of seeing a dead relative appearing unexpectedly. After an awkward half a moment Paddy said, "Hello, Cassie."

"Jaysus, Paddy Quinlan in the flesh."

"Aye, may I come in?"

"Yes, yes, of course. Come in, come in."

Paddy walked into the quaint, yet well appointed flat. Cassie took the rose, put it on the coffee table in front of her couch and said, "Please, sit."

"No hug?"

"Oh, yes, of course."

They fell easily into each other's arms and it felt good.

Cassie said, "Would you like some tea?"

"Sure."

"I'd offer something a little stronger but I've got work to do."

"No problem."

While the kettle was put on the boil Paddy looked up on the wall he faced, and to his astonishment he saw three framed posters of three paintings with which he was very familiar. Royle's *Blue Bell,* Osborne's *Apple Gatherings* and, lastly, O'Connor's *La Femme Au Drap Rouge,* and the memory of the last painting sent a nervous yearning through his entire body.

He would make love to this woman right here, right now if she were willing. And he didn't know if he was being pretentious or not, but why else would she have these prints here? They had to remind her, as well, of their time together. Or, idiot, he thought, she is a lover of art and has them innocently. Or maybe it was Mick she wanted to be reminded of?

His pragmatist told him otherwise, but wisdom be damned. When Cassie walked back in he rose, went to her and kissed her passionately and she responded in kind. In short order they were making love on the couch.

"Oh," he said, "I missed you."

She smiled at him and he smiled back, leaned closer and kissed her once again.

When they had finished making love, they rested comfortably next to one another well sated, a novel feeling for lonely professional people as driven as these two.

He said, "I know you were between a rock and a hard spot. And I think you did the right thing, as far as your friend is concerned. But God I've missed you."

She looked at him, not surprised at his words and said, "Thank you for understanding, I've missed you too."

He looked at her with surprise and said, "Really?"

"Aye."

"You seemed so unhappy, glad to get the hell out of there."

"I was confused. I couldn't get comfortable there. Every time I looked at that beautiful little boy I saw his mother and the betrayal. I couldn't stand it anymore. And I knew that I would pay dearly for that mistake if I didn't make it right."

"I understand. What happened when you came back, I mean with you and Clare?"

"When I got back I went to see Clare, and we had it out. She tried to kick me out of her life, just like I would've done to her, but I wouldn't let her. We made up, but as stubborn as she is it took a while to regain her trust. But I did, I immersed myself in my work, and haven't looked back. But I've got to tell you he's never been far from my mind, nor Clare's."

"Who?"

"Who do you think? Michael Padraig Quinlan, of course. Now there's a lad."

They both stopped for a moment lost in their thoughts thinking about Mick. Cassie said, "Paddy, you haven't told me why you've come back."

"Dinty got away from us last week."

"Blessed be Jesus, Mary and Joseph, Paddy, I'm so sorry to hear that."

"Aye, thanks lass, I am too."

"Where's Mick then?"

Paddy told Cassie about the fight, Mick leaving, the two lonely years, the bungee jumping and the manslaughter charges. She stared in awe, then smiled and said, "Like father like son."

"Aye, I guess. When I told him about Dinty he wanted to come to Ireland and never go back home. I told him running was no way out. Plus I haven't gotten around to telling him about his twin yet."

"Jaysus, Paddy why not?"

"Because there'd be no stopping him from running off to Belfast, and Martin and Fergal are dangerous men playing at a dangerous game. This isn't Sunday afternoon rugby. I just didn't want him getting hurt."

"How did you know about them?"

"Clan na Gael. We stayed in touch with the lads in the north and we raised a lot of money for them."

Clare walked into the flat carrying a sack of groceries and instinctively knew who this man was. She stopped and stared at him and, before Cassie could make a formal introduction, said, "Tell me Mick is okay, he's fine?"

Paddy said, "He's fine."

Paddy then stared at Mick's mother and she stared back wonderingly.

"You must be Clare."

"Aye."

She put out her hand but Paddy walked to her and gave her a hug.

He said, "I owe you that much for allowing your son to come live with me. My God Clare, he's a mirror image of you."

Cassie said, "Isn't he?"

Clare said, "Where is he then?"

Paddy said, "Back in Montana."

Cassie, giving up the idea of getting any work done now, poured them all a drink as Paddy went through the whole spiel again.

Clare stared out the window and visualized the lad in her mind, aching to hold him, like she had so many times. The rare winter sun shone and the cool breeze blew over the stone pavers on the road outside.

The phone rang and Cassie quickly grabbed it and said, "Yes…yes…okay. Good, I'll be there at seven p.m. on Monday. Thank you."

Clare stared at her roommate who stood there smiling and Clare said, "What? Did you just get an interview with Tin Knickers or some such thing?"

"No, but this is going to work out marvelously. I got the next best thing?"

Clare said, "Who, then?"

"Basil Millington, the English Ambassador to Ireland."

Cassie shook with delight and continued, "Margaret Thatcher, if it's possible for her to like anyone Irish, likes me. She's up to her ass with these Republican prisoners, their Blanket protest, their Dirty protest and now the hunger strike. The Catholic Hierarchy of Ireland is on her ass, powerful Irish American politicians are on her ass, Sinn Fein, Amnesty International and the list goes on. She wants to get a message out and she wants me to do it."

Paddy stood, leaned on his cane and said, "Cassie, that's great, it couldn't have happened to a better person. But I've got to get to Upperchurch."

Cassie said, "Not so fast lad, I'm coming with you."

Paddy said, "Seriously?"

Cassie said, "Aye, do you think any reporter worth her salt would miss covering the wake and funeral of one of Ireland's last great Seanachie."

"Well, put like that."

Clare said, "What are you two on about?"

They explained and she said, "I've got the week off, let's go."

Chapter 48
Goodbye Story Teller

Saturday afternoon Paddy, Cassie and Clare headed southwest out of Dublin on highway N1 heading toward the small village of Upperchurch in Tipperary. Thirty or so miles into their journey, he took a side road for a mile or so and got out to smell the rural Ireland of his youth.

Clare said, "What are you doing?"

Paddy said, "The breeze is never so soft as in Ireland. Why did I ever leave?"

Clare said, "Because you were poor, hungry and had no work?"

Paddy, looking through those beautiful rose color glasses all Irish Americans did when it came to Ireland, smiled and said, "Aye, that I'd forgotten."

An eerie feeling crawled over his skin without warning and he quickly turned around to see who was standing there, but found it was nothing but the wind playing tricks and whistling by as if mocking him. He swore he heard Dinty talking, probably telling a story. Paddy smiled.

Cassie said, "What?"

"I think Dinty just passed by."

Clare said, "You lads from Tipperary are all a bit crazy."

Cassie said, "Aye, but Upperchurch. I've never met a livelier group, but they're all a bit mad there."

Paddy stared at her and said, "When were you ever in Upperchurch?"

"After I got back from America your lads in NORTIP caused a raucous there."

"Aye, the Northern Tipperary Irish Brigade, and a bit of gunrunning I presume?"

"Aye. The bloody peelers caught wind of it and there was a bit of a rising. But you being from there I had to go have a look see for myself."

They climbed back into the car. And with a firm belief that Dinty had whistled overhead, Paddy had a renewed sense of urgency to get to the home of his youth, his birth, a village of ancient history.

Pulling off N1 he took a road south to a town named Templemore, and as he drove southwest of Templemore, maybe fifteen or twenty minutes on he saw his village on the horizon

When Paddy and his companions walked into the home of the life long bachelor and Seanachie, Dinty Quinlan, a small roar went up as if a celebrity had just walked into the room. Cassie and Clare stood and watched as Paddy Quinlan worked the room with the magic he possessed. After a shot or two of poteen he began to move toward his brother who was laid out on a table in the living room.

Before he could reach him a hand caught his wrist and turned him around. There smiling at him was his cousin and friend, Sister Mary de Angels.

He said, “Maggie O’Meara dear, how are you?”

He reached out and hugged his cousin who had been instrumental in bringing him his greatest joy, Mick.”

“Paddy Quinlan, the world has been good to you. Now where is that lad of yours?”

Paddy looked down and said, “He’s not here, darling,” and went on to explain.

She clucked and said, “He’s a Quinlan all right. And as a Quinlan, he’ll be just fine, now no worries lad.”

She then went to Clare, hugged her, and kissed her on the cheek. Neither could speak for a moment.

Finally, Sister Mary said, “Clare Eva White, I am so glad to see you. I’m still mad at you, but I still love you!”

The two women hugged and laughed. Then she turned to Cassie and said, “Cassie, it is so good to see you darling cousin of mine. How are you, dear heart? Are you going to the family reunion this summer?”

“I’m good Maggie, other than, you know? What family reunion, no one tells me shyte?”

“Oh yes, I almost forgot. I’ll tell you about it later.”

The pudgy absent-minded nun took Paddy’s hand and walked him toward Dinty as if he needed an escort to keep his admirers away. Paddy stopped and chatted for a moment with Niebh Kinnane and Siobhan Butler, sisters and proprietors of the local pub who put on the wake. He then stopped and had a quick drink with Jimmy Butler, a friend in his youth. The cousin nun finally dragged him away or he might never have made it to his brother.

Paddy knew that a normal wake would go on for days, but the wake of a celebrity Seanachie may be a weeklong event, so he tried to stay reasonably sober that evening and failed miserably.

After midnight, he stood over the body of his older brother, best friend and mentor. The trembling began in his shoulders and spread through his entire body, and he wept. The next morning Cassie and Clare found him passed out from grief in a fetal position prostrate before the Seanachie himself.

After the requiem Mass and the burial it seemed to Paddy that he walked in a long black veil witnessing everything in blacks, grays and whites, a kind of surreal slow motion, as if questioning its validity and the reality of all that had happened to him in recent weeks.

Dinty was dead and gone forever, Mick was most probably going to jail, Thomas Higgins was dead and gone forever, and he stood in Kinnane's Pub in Upperchurch on the other side of the world, mourning his mentor and best friend.

He looked around the pub; his heart started to pound faster and sweat began to form on his upper lip as if he were having a panic attack, a novel feeling for the likes of Paddy Quinlan. He heard a shot, his head snapped around, the burst sounded as if from a high powered rifle, waiting for the slug to slam into someone or something.

Cassie said, "What?"

Paddy said, "Did you hear that?"

Clare said, "Hear what?"

"Oh, never mind."

The music continued, the talk, the drink, the smoke, the laughter, the stories all continued and so did his fast heartbeat, in cadence with the omen that just hit him right between the eyes.

Chapter 49
The Singalong House

Mindanao, The Philippines

New Year's Eve 1980

It was New Year's Eve 1980 and Father Ruari O'Keefe found himself alone and staring up at the sky as happy as he had been in recent memory. He was entering his twentieth year in the Priesthood and soon after would be the twentieth anniversary of his exile. There were few days that went by that he didn't wonder about Clare White and the twin boys she bore. In the church he would be absolved but his mind would never forgive him.

The endless lonely nights, the heat and humidity of the rainy season, the large rats, the desire to hear the laughter in an Irish pub, all of it gave way to a peace and acceptance and he had begun to love it in the Philippines. As he enjoyed the beautiful stars in the inky black sky, with the warm breeze about him, he hoped to stay for another twenty New Year's.

The next morning he got a call from Father Hennessy in Manila calling him to the Singalong House, the Columban Order's headquarters in Mindanao.

He arrived a few days later and Father Hennessy called him in to his office.

"It doesn't seem like twenty years, does it Ruari?"

"No it doesn't Bill, but I'm hoping to continue my work here."

"Well the Lord may have different plans."

"What do you mean?"

"Cardinal Byrne. . ."

"John Byrne?"

"Aye."

"He's a Cardinal now?"

"Aye. He's been appointed to The See of St. Patrick in Armagh, the High See of Ireland."

"What've I been living under a rock?"

"Well, you could say that. I got a letter from the Cardinal and he wants you back."

Ruari stared at the letter with dismay and obvious irritation.

"Ruari, can I ask you a question?"

"Sure, Bill."

"Why did they send you here in the first place?"

Ruari looked at Father Bill Hennessy and sighed aloud.

"That bad huh?"

"Aye."

They spent the night in quiet talk as Ruari came clean with his past for the first time since he had done with John Byrne twenty years before.

Ruari was in tears, still in pain from what he'd done and Bill said, "Ruari, you've done your penance, it's time to put this behind you. False pride is keeping you from forgiving yourself. God has a plan for all of us and yours is to go back to Belfast and continue your ministry. I talked with Cardinal Byrne on the phone about this. He thinks the world of you and I think he has some plans for you."

"Bill, I don't want to go back. I want to stay here."

"God obviously has other plans."

"Did he mention what I'd be doing?"

"Aye. You're going to Holy Cross Parish in Ardoyne."

"So he's got me going to Belfast?"

"Well it's not as if you haven't seen your share of violence and hard times in the past twenty years. If anyone is ready for an assignment like that, you are Ruari."

"But I don't want to leave my mission."

"It's not our will but the will of the Father."

"I know. But why wouldn't the will of the Father be that I stay and do his work here?"

"Because he needs you in Belfast more than he needs you here. Don't fight it, accept it and realize that now you'll be doing missionary work there as well. You don't have to be in a jungle to do this work. You know that."

Chapter 50
Holy Cross

Ardoyne, North Belfast

January 1981

Gray sky spit down on brownstone homes lined up to do battle with one another. His heart sunk when he thought of the madness that had settled on this neighborhood and in the north for so long. Father Ruari O'Keefe walked down Ardoyne Road in the north Belfast community of Ardoyne where, he thought, nowhere else in all of Ireland was sectarianism more apparent than right here, on this road, which separated Catholics from Protestants, both sides keeping track, Protestants running Catholics out of their end and Catholics retaliating with the same. Other parts of Belfast were segregated by neighborhoods, Ardoyne by street.

He looked to one side of the road, where the Catholics flew the tricolors flag of the Republic, then to the other side where a large Union Jack snapped defiantly in the brisk wind for the UK, one side, Catholic Nationalists, the other, Protestant Loyalists. One side sang the rebel songs of the Irish Republican Army; the other side raising a glass to King William of Orange and his glorious victory at the battle of the Boyne. One side sent emissaries to Boston and New York to raise money for the IRA, in an effort to unite Ireland. The other sent lads to Toronto and Montreal to further the interests of the Orange order and its anti-Catholic and Unionist agenda. One side was orange. One side was green. The Orange wanted the rule of the British Government, and to continue on as part of the United Kingdom, while the Green wanted Irish independence and home rule with no outside interference. Sinn Fein was Irish for 'Ourselves, Alone' the motto of the political arm of the IRA. Both sides had a few things in common however. They both lived in fear; they both garnered generations of hatred toward one another, and the working classes not involved in the paramilitary fight were sick and tired of it all.

In the two weeks since he had arrived, Fr. Ruari O'Keefe had personally witnessed the fear. He had witnessed open street fighting on this very road, blood running in the gutter, plastic bullets flying, Molotov cocktails landing on homes and the sadness that billowed like the smoke from smoldering remains when it was over. Military vehicles moving in to try to break it up but only made matters worse.

Ruari knew that Long Kesh was brimming with prisoners both Republican and Loyalist paramilitary, and it looked like the Republicans were now going to start a hunger strike. The church was dead set against the strike, but he personally was all for it. Ruari grew up in The Bogside neighborhood of Derry and if it were not for the hurling he'd most likely be sitting in Long Kesh. He understood. He had lived in the oppression, experienced the hatred each marching season as it culminated with Apprentice Boys Day each August 12th in his home town of Derry.

He walked further south to where Ardoyne Road met Crumlin Road and looked up the hill to his new home. The two tall towers of Holy Cross, the eighty year old Catholic Church that he likened to a Celtic warrior, standing guard over a bloody battlefield, a wound that would not seem to heal.

He shook his head and began the last leg of his morning walk. He came to the junction of Crumlin road and Woodvale Road, stopped and looked up at the church, which looked as if it were swaying as the clouds passed overhead. He sighed and walked toward it.

Cardinal Byrne had just returned from his College of Bishops meeting in Rome and waited in Ruari's office for him. The Cardinal stood and embraced the prodigal son and said, "Fr. O'Keefe, it's good to see you back on Irish soil."

"Eminence, I wish I could say it's good to be back."

"Look, lad, this is the reason we join the priesthood. Nobody said it was going to be easy."

"The hard part for me is not to hate the Loyalists and Unionists."

"Well, you're going to have to put your feelings on the back burner because I need your to help with a couple of things."

"Such as?"

"Well, first of all, I want you to be the chaplain for the lads in Long Kesh. I want you to be my emissary to the prisoners. The first hunger strike that was called off last October was a blow to them because they feel like they were double-crossed by the Church and the Brits. The word that I'm getting is that they're going to have another go at it and this time they won't be calling anything off until they see real results. We are going to have to get involved and I want you right there with me on this, cara."

Ruari smiled at the term *cara*, friend in Gaelic. The Columbans in the Philippines used it as a term of endearment when they were far from home.

"Lastly, if they do go ahead and strike again, I'm getting personally involved."

"Such as."

"I will be insisting on a meeting with Mrs. Thatcher and I want you to be part of those meetings."

Ruari's eyes widened and he said, "Why me?"

"I figure that if you can handle twenty years in the jungle a meeting with Thatcher will be a walk in the park."

The clock in his office ticked and Fr. Ruari O'Keefe shook his head, smiled and said, "You know that I'd do anything you asked me."

Chapter 51
It's Time to Go North

Dublin

February 1981

Cassie walked in as Clare was getting ready to go work.

Clare said, "How was your day?"

"I've had better, I've got news."

"And what would that be?"

"My editor wants me to go to Belfast to cover the Hunger Strike."

"I thought the Hunger Strike got called."

"Aye, the first one last October. But when they got the lads eating again The Brits reneged on their original agreement."

"And who is surprised by that?"

"No one."

"So now what?"

"I called Sean O'Kane."

Clare froze and said, "Who's that?"

"Reporter for The Andersontown News and the Republican Newspaper An Phoblacht in Belfast."

"Aye?"

"Aye, he told me that the IRA has approved a second strike and that a lad named Bobby Sands will be the first to go on this one. I told my editor about it and he's sending me there until this thing is concluded. He doesn't think that Thatcher is going to back down. He says she doesn't understand the Irish psyche and he's betting that the hunger strike will go to the end."

The two women stood and stared off into their own thoughts for a long moment. Clare thinking about Eamon Gainey and Cassie thinking about a Pulitzer prize.

Suddenly breaking their silence, Clare said, "I'm going with you."

"And just how do you propose to do that?"

Clare just smiled.

That smile took Cassie's breath away and she said, "Jaysus, Clare, the last time I saw that smile you ended up with twins."

Ignoring her best friend she said, "When are you leaving?"

"A week from Monday, I've got to finish up a couple of assignments, I've got this interview with Millington and some other loose ends. Sands is supposed to go on strike March 1st. That gives us a month to get a place and get settled in."

"That's okay by me. There's nothing keeping me here. I'll talk with Jack Baggot and I'll get the apartment rented."

Cassie, thinking more about a glass of wine now, said, "Okay."

Then she stopped dead in her tracks when it hit her and said, "Wait a minute. What are we going to come home to? I mean when this thing is over."

Clare looked at Cassie and said without thinking, "I don't think I'm coming back."

Chapter 52
The Interview

Two days later

The British Embassy in Dublin, at 29 Marion Road in Ballsbridge, was a stone's throw from The Grand Canal Hotel. The interview was at 7:00 p.m and Basil Millington had just finished his phone conversation with Prime Minister Thatcher, who spent the first thirty minutes chewing his ass and then gave him specific instructions on the message she wanted to get across in the interview.

James Hornsby, Millington's bodyguard, rang his office and said, "I'll bring the Landrover around, sir. We should leave in five minutes."

"Thanks Hornsby, I'll be right out."

As he was getting ready to leave when his phone rang again and the Ambassador said, "Lord, does this ever end?"

"Millington here."

"Basil, William Gray here."

"William, good to hear your voice, how are you my good man."

"I'm fine. Listen, I know you're busy and I'm glad I caught you. Linda and I were talking about you and Jen. Can you clear the decks a week from this weekend, we'll catch up a bit."

"I can't think of anything I'd rather do. I need a break, it has been rather hectic here. But listen, I've got to run. Have Linda call Jen and make the arrangements, she knows my schedule better than I do."

"Good man, we'll see you soon."

"Great, thanks William."

Paddy, Cassie and Clare spent a lazy afternoon together, one of the few in all of Paddy's life, but it felt good. Cassie was preparing for the interview, Clare making arrangements to move to Belfast and Paddy making calls back to the ranch to check on Mick, as well as business.

When Paddy had finished, Clare couldn't help herself, "How's Mick?"

Paddy said, "Great news, he was found innocent of manslaughter charges and he wants to come over and spend a few weeks. He'll fly out this afternoon."

Cassie said, "That's fantastic."

Clare had the nervous pit in her stomach of someone finally meeting the love of her life. She was happy and excited for the first time in recent memory.

At 5:00, they all left the flat, Clare off to work and Cassie and Paddy off to dinner at Kitty O'Shea's where she would meet the ambassador for the interview.

When they reached the street Clare said, "Good luck with the interview, Cass, give 'em hell."

She then turned to Paddy and looked him in the eye for a moment longer than was comfortable, hugged him and said, "I'll see you later."

As Clare rounded the corner Cassie laughed and said, "I think she's become quite fond of you."

"You think so?"

"Aye."

"Well, I've become quite fond of her."

"It's a beautiful afternoon. Shall we walk or is your foot bothering you?"

"Let's walk, it'll be good for it."

Martin O'Kane made it to Dublin from Belfast without incident and spent the afternoon familiarizing himself with the Ballsbridge neighborhood. He made sure his driver would be waiting in the van when he got there and then went back to the condominium, where he checked his weapon several times and then steeled himself against the worst part of the operation for him, the waiting.

Paddy and Cassie strolled casually and chatted as they made their way to the eatery a few blocks away. Paddy's foot hurt more than usual, but he refrained from complaining. After all, he was in Ireland, with the love of his life, on a magnificently soft mid February day, and his son was on his way. And yet the seeds of despair had somehow been planted in his stomach and grew more urgent with every step he took.

By the time they reached the restaurant, he had lost his appetite and he was glad to get off his feet. They sat down and Cassie said, "What's wrong, Love? You look suddenly pale."

Paddy annoyed said, "I'm not sure what's come over me. Maybe it's finally hitting me that Dinty has got away for good. Whiskey should help."

"Then whiskey it is. I'll wait to join you when I'm done working."

Cassie ordered dinner while Paddy nursed two fingers of John Power's finest, and they both spent the next hour whiling away in their own thoughts, comfortable in their silence.

Martin paced the front room of the condo, looked out the window, checked and re-checked his weapon, took it apart, put it back together, smoked a cigarette, then another, sighed as time passed as if it were frozen in ice and he said, “Jaysus, at least now I know what purgatory must be like.”

He looked out the window again and breathed heavy as the Landrover turned on to Canal Street, crossed over the Grand Canal Bridge and came to a stop in front of the hotel. The hair rose on the back of his neck, he put his field glasses to his eyes and watched as Millington disappeared into the lobby of the hotel, which Martin knew, was connected to the pub. The vehicle disappeared into the hotel parking lot and within five minutes James Hornsby appeared once more, this time on foot, alert and aware of his surroundings as he walked into Kitty O’Shea’s to keep an eye on his boss.

Martin smiled and said, “Aware of everything but me.”

Then the unexpected knock came on the door. He ignored it thinking it was a door-to-door salesman or unwanted Seventh Day Adventist handing out pamphlets of doom. Then he heard the unanticipated part of every plan, the human element for which there can be no preparation, just steeled nerve reaction. It was a realtor’s key opening the door to show the condominium.

As Basil Millington walked into Kitty O’Shea’s, Cassie, who recognized him immediately, approached him discretely and introduced herself. His bodyguard came in just after and went to secure the patio for an hour of privacy.

They walked back to the table and Cassie said, “Mr. Ambassador, this is my friend Paddy Quinlan.”

Paddy stood shook the ambassador’s hand and said, “Pleasure.”

Millington nodded and being rather congenial for a British emissary said, “Bit of a light dinner then, eh Quinlan?”

Paddy caught unexpected said, “Oh, yes, well a rough day.”

“We all seem to have those now and then don’t we?”

“Aye, we do. But they do seem to be back to back to back recently.”

Small talk finished, the ambassador said to Cassie, “Ms. Kenny, I’d like a bit of privacy for this, and as it is a nice evening for February can we do it on the patio in front? It’s quiet this time of night and my man Hornsby has spoken with management and has managed to quarantine the area for us for an hour or so.”

Cassie said, “That’s fine, sir.”

Paddy said, “I’ll just meet you back at the flat then.”

The ambassador shocked them both when he said, “Quinlan, you’re welcome to join us. I’m about to speak to a reporter on the record. You’ll hear it tonight or you'll see it splashed across the front page of tomorrow's news."

Paddy glanced at Cassie, got the subtle nod, and he said, "Well, if it wouldn't be a bother?"

Martin watched as the three made their way to chairs on the front patio as the keys rattled in the door. He mouthed the word "fuck" as he ran to the back bedroom with his weapon and his knapsack. He put on his black ski-mask and waited. The door opened and the realtor walked into the front room with a young married couple. No time to wait, he walked out and said, "This is not a good time to be showing the condo. Get on your knees, face the wall and if you make one fucking noise you'll all be meeting St. Patrick before you want to. If not you'll all get out of this alive. Do we understand one another?"

They all nodded in shock and knelt down. He tied their hands and feet and put duct tape across their mouths and said, "I won't hurt any of you, so don't panic. Just stay still and quiet."

He walked back to the window and mumbled, "Well fucksake, this is just my luck."

He knelt down and looked across the street at the threesome having a conversation as if they were just three people out for a pint. The bodyguard walked back and forth and kept a watchful eye for any shenanigans. He mumbled to himself, "Who the hell is the odd man out over there? Eamon said only two people would be there. Something doesn't feel right."

The interview was going well until about halfway through, Paddy's foot began to throb and twitch. Unable to sit still any longer he finally said, "I'm sorry to interrupt but I'm afraid I've got to go, my foot is bothering me something fierce. I'll just catch a cab rather than walk."

Martin O'Kane had Ambassador Millington in his cross hairs. He steadied himself, took deep breaths to quiet his pounding heart and pulled the trigger.

Paddy stood with the intention of thanking the ambassador and Cassie for a nice evening and then taking his leave when the high-powered bullet hit him in the back, exploding his heart and exiting his chest, slamming into the brick building just above the ambassador's head. As it erupted from Paddy Quinlan's chest it sprayed his company with bone and blood. The momentum pushed Paddy onto their table with such force that the table, chairs and glasses crashed all around them.

Martin said, "Son of a bitch."

James Hornsby quickly moved to cover his boss but he was too late. Another bullet pierced the night, targeting the chest of the English official. It successfully met its mark and pinned the ambassador to the brick wall behind him, dead before he slid to the ground. Cassie screamed into the night. Paddy looked up at her, smiled weakly, and then died there on Canal Street on a soft February evening in the land he so loved.

* * *

The phone on his desk rang and startled him out of the work he studied intently. He said, "Does this damn thing ever stop ringing?"

The clock on the wall said 11:45p.m. and the ubiquitous cigarette burned down in his ashtray.

He said, "Gray."

The voice said, "Mr. Secretary would like to see you in his office immediately."

Before he could answer there was a click and the line went dead.

"Goddamn it! What now?"

Stormont House, where the government of Northern Ireland was housed, was quiet. Guards met him at the door, but otherwise it was empty.

William Gray knocked and entered the office of the Secretary of State for Northern Ireland, who was smoking a large cigar and working on a glass of scotch whiskey.

He looked up and said, "Gray, thank you for coming on such short notice. But I'm afraid it couldn't be helped. We've got bad news."

"Sir?"

"Basil Millington's been assassinated. He was pronounced dead tonight down in Dublin."

The color drained from Gray's face as acid began erupting in his stomach.

"I just talked to him tonight. Who?"

"Guess?"

"O'Kane."

"And I'll wager he's now out of the country."

"The bloody bastard, he's just made this personal."

"That's right, you and Millington were in the Queen's Navy together."

"I'm going to have Wright's balls on a platter for this."

"Why Wright?"

"I told him we needed this bastard apprehended before he caused some serious trouble and now this."

"He also took out an Irish Ex-Pat by the name of Paddy Quinlan. Republican supporter who had made it rich in the ranching business in the U.S."

"Accident then?"

"Well, one would think so. You wouldn't cut off the hand that feeds you."

"No, you wouldn't. Where did they send him?"

"Our intelligence guess says that he went to a safehouse in New York. It's too soon to tell, but they've been using a fireman in Queens New York recently. "

"Let's go get him."

"Our lads are telling us that they may try to get him back in the country in a few days when we wouldn't be looking for him here."

"So we cover all the ports."

"There is something else."

"What?"

"You're job is on the line."

"What?"

"Politics. We get Martin O'Kane or they get you."

"Oh, bloody hell."

They sat for a moment when Gray said, "Sir, may I use your phone?"

"Surely."

He picked up the phone dialed and said, "Meet me at Castlereagh in thirty minutes. I'll have a car come by and pick you up."

"What? I know what time it is you git."

"Our friend, O'Kane, assassinated the Queens' ambassador in Dublin earlier tonight. Oh, and bring your flak jacket. You're going to need it when I shoot you."

William Gray was sitting in the conference room when Ian Wright walked in.

He said, "Did I not tell you this would happen if we didn't pick up this Republican?"

"Aye, you did. We tried, but he's a right slippery bastard."

"Not hard enough. But let me make this clear, my job has just been threatened at the highest level. If we don't bring him in, I'm done. But let me also make this clear, I am not going down by myself."

The two men stared at one another, the message obvious.

The two then picked up separate lines and began making phone calls to secure all ports in and out of Northern Ireland as well as the Republic, both by air and by sea. When Gray was satisfied they had everything secure he said, "We have it on good intelligence that O'Kane is going to try to come back in soon, when we least expect him. But if this bastard decides to sneak back in I want him. He's mine."

"I'll make sure the RUC are on it and we'll meet with the Garda in the Republic to make sure they are on high alert."

Gray wanted to be a smart ass but he was too tired and said, "Thanks Wright, let's just get him."

After a long night at work, Clare walked into their flat on lower Baggot Street. The room was dark and filled with a gloom she could not identify and a small amount of light from the street lamps outside. She noticed the silhouette of Cassie sitting in the dark at the table in the kitchen, alone.

With a flick of a switch, light permeated the darkness and Clare, barely recognizing her best friend, cried, "Oh my God, Cassie, what happened?"

Splattered dried blood had tattooed her face and best blouse but she wore it in seeming defiance and pride like the war paint of an ancient Celtic warrior after battle. Her truculent green eyes let Clare know she was okay. Cassie sat nursing a small amount of whiskey and said, "Paddy's dead."

"No."

"Aye, he's been shot."

"By who?"

"My best guess is Martin."

"You mean my Martin?"

"Aye, your Martin."

"How do you know?"

"I called Sean O'Kane when I got back from the police station. He said that Martin left Belfast yesterday morning. He said he only leaves town when the brotherhood has him on something."

"Why would he shoot Paddy?"

"He also shot and killed Basil Millington while I was interviewing him. He was sent to take out Millington. The brotherhood wanted to send a message to Thatcher. Paddy was an innocent bystander. He's dead, and it's my fault."

"Cassie, what's that supposed to mean, your fault? That's nonsense."

"It means I was so interested in my interview and bragging about it that I didn't think it through. I shared that with Sean O'Kane, who of course, innocently, let the brotherhood know."

"How could you have known?"

"I should never have allowed Paddy to join us with The Troubles in The North. Well regardless, the empty condo from across the street where the gunman was held up had three people tied up in it."

"What?"

"Aye. Just a bit of bad luck and timing. A realtor was showing a young couple the place and walked in on whoever it was. He had a ski mask on but the general description could very well be Martin, so Scotland Yard is out looking hard for him."

Clare stopped for a minute and then stared at Cassie with a look as if someone was holding her head under water, unable to speak.

"Clare, what is it?"

When she finally was able to speak she said, "Oh Jaysus, Cass, when did Paddy say Mick was coming?"

Now Cassie panicked for the first time, "Fucksake darling, I completely forgot about Michael Patrick. They'll be watching the airport; we've got to get to him before they mistake him for Martin."

Chapter 53
The Irish Riviera

Queens, New York

The next day

The neighborhoods of Breezy Point, Roxbury, Neponsit, Belle Harbor, Rockaway Park, Seaside, Hammels, Arverne, Edgemere, Bayswater, and Far Rockaway in the Queens borough of New York City became known to the locals as the Rockaways. In the 1930s, 1940s and 1950s some of the wealthier New York Irish built cottages for summer getaways in The Rockaways, specifically Rockaway Beach, and it became known as "The Irish Riviera."

The 1960s brought change and with it the cottages were torn down to make way for permanent residences for the generations of Irish to follow. The Rockaways in Queens became the bedrock of an Irish Catholic community, parishes, pubs, Ancient Order of Hibernians halls and the more clandestine RELA, the Robert Emmett Literary Association – named after the great Irish Patriot Robert Emmet – which supported the efforts of Clan Na Gael. The residents were hard working, blue and white collar, but all were interested in keeping their Irish heritage alive and continually concerned with the issues, difficulties and politics of the people who lived on that rock in the north Atlantic, whose blood continued to course hotly through their veins.

Dan Mulroy was a local fire captain who lived in the Sunnyside neighborhood of Queens. When he wasn't putting out fires for a living, he was pouring cement, and when he wasn't pouring cement he was at Sullivan's, one of the many Irish pubs on Queens Blvd, staying connected to the troubles in Northern Ireland.

It was late in the evening and Dan was in the office he kept in the basement of the home he shared with his wife and five kids. He was sending invoices and paying bills when the phone rang.

He picked up the phone and said, "Mulroy."

Eamon Gainey liked Dan Mulroy; he was a man of his word, always followed through on his promises, and could be trusted to handle, with discretion, any business that may come his way from across the pond.

Eamon said, "Slainte."

Mulroy smiled and said, "Hello."

"The Scottish Oak has been cut and is on its way; you can pick it up tomorrow at 2:15. Pull the tarp over it and keep it dry for six months or so, otherwise it'll be no good for the cooper. The harvest did not go as planned so keep a close eye on the wood so it doesn't warp."

"Thanks, we'll take care of it."

The phone went dead. American flight 215 would be arriving tomorrow at JFK in from Glasgow, Scotland. He knew Martin O'Kane would be on the flight and the lad would be troubled. Dan didn't know what went wrong but he would make sure Martin was kept safe and out of sight.

Chapter 54
Irish Soil, Again

Dublin

That same day

William Gray was startled out of his sleep by the ring of the phone on his night stand. The clock there read, 2:12 a.m. He sighed, lifted the receiver and said, "Gray."

The British agent said, "AerLingus flight 713 leaves New York in one hour, our man will be on it. It is scheduled to arrive in Dublin at 9:30 a.m. GST. He's using an American alias."

"Good work. We'll be waiting."

"Sir, I'm sorry to disturb you at this hour but it couldn't wait."

"What is it Gray?"

"As we guessed, he's on a plane back to Ireland in one hour. He flies out of New York and will be landing in Dublin at 9:30 this morning. I'm taking my team there and if all goes well we'll have him back in Belfast by noon."

The Secretary of State of Northern Ireland said, "Good work Gray. I'll call the Prime Minister, she'll be very pleased."

The AerLingus Airbus broke through the blanket of gray that made up the bedclothes of the Irish landscape this time of year.

Mick Quinlan, who slept anytime, anywhere, was waking up to the restlessness that settled on all cabins of overseas flights just before landing; the alacrity of those on their first trip overseas and the lethargy of those dropping down from the umpteenth trip over the pond this month.

He looked out the window and saw below him the ancient land that was the cause of so much pain and suffering, pride and joy, war and remembrance, love and hate; unaware that he was about to become part of all that.

He could hear Paddy's brogue increase in volume and his eyebrow raise in animation at the mere mention of Ireland. The stories that dear old Dinty told around the campfire on his visits to Montana, made even the toughest and most skeptical of the ranch hands sit mesmerized for hours.

As the plane lightly touched down, he felt an odd sensation, as if he were not going for a visit but was finally coming home from a long journey. He shook it off as just the effect the stories he had been told by his dad and

Dinty. The flight attendant said something in Irish he couldn't understand and then said, "Let me be the first to welcome you to Dublin, Ireland where the local time is 9:30 a.m. We hope you enjoy your stay."

Mick grabbed his backpack, his only luggage, and headed to customs. He got through with no problems and looked around for the smiling face of Paddy, when two women approached him.

One had shoulder length auburn hair and fierce green eyes that radiated confidence and purpose and a peculiar familiarity that he could not place.

The other had short blonde hair and blue eyes that were misting over. He did not know if they were tears of sorrow or tears of joy but either way he had this overwhelming desire to comfort her.

Cassie Said, "Clare, there he is, thank God they didn't see him at customs."

Clare said, "Oh my God."

"Quick, follow me."

Gray said, "That's him. Let's make this seamless. I don't want anyone hurt. There are a lot of civilians around here."

Mick Quinlan, as happy as he could remember, suddenly found himself surrounded by five men in dark suits.

William Gray said, "Martin O'Kane?"

Mick said, "Excuse me?"

Gray pulled his badge and said, "You're under arrest for the assassination of Ambassador Basil Millington."

"Is this some kind of joke?"

"Nice try at the Yank accent, asshole. You're mine now."

"Where's my dad? Is he behind this?"

Gray smiled and said, "Your dad is in a basement somewhere in Belfast writing his drivel. Cuff him gentlemen and read him his rights."

"Cuff me? What for?"

"First of all, for the assassination of Her Majesty's Ambassador to Ireland."

"What the hell are you talking about. I didn't kill anybody."

"Nice try, O'Kane. Knock of the act."

"What act?"

Cassie and Clare were ten yards from Mick when the suits surrounded him. The two women stopped dead in their tracks and froze. One of the men caught their eye and they quickly turned around and walked to a nearby souvenir shop where they watched the scene unfold.

The conversation erupted when one of the men pulled out his MI5 badge and Mick's eyes grew large.

Clare said, "Cassie, what're we going to do? They're going to arrest him. They think he's Martin."

Clare began to walk when Cassie grabbed her and turned her around. She said, "There's not a damn thing we can do, Clare. We walk up there now and they'll take us too."

"So we're just going to watch? We've got to tell them who he is."

"Oh, and you think they'll believe us? Hell no. They'll take us with him and then we'll be no good to anyone."

"Well then what the hell do you suggest?"

"I'm not sure, I'll think of something."

The five men walked Mick Quinlan out to the curb where two black sedans waited. His first breath of Irish air was in handcuffs. They put him in the back of a black sedan and the two drove away.

Cassie said, "Didn't you tell me that you met Eamon Gainey at Big Jack's one night?"

Clare said, "Aye, I did."

"Then you know who he is?"

"Aye, Chief of Staff for the Provos, so?"

"Sean O'Kane can get us to him or at least get this info to him. Time to go North."

Clare said, "I'm glad to hear you say that. My son needs our help and I want to get as close to him as I can."

"You know we're jumping from the frying pan…"

"…into the fire? Yes, I do and I can't wait."

Cassie sighed at her best friend and they walked quickly from the airport, the soles of their shoes getting hotter with each step.

Chapter 55
The Shamrock Club

The corner of Ardoyne and Flak Street

Ardoyne, Belfast, Northern Ireland

February 1981

Sean O'Kane was covering the Republican news of the hunger strike for An Phoblacht and because of his son, Fergal, Sean would be the only reporter that Bobby Sands and Francis Hughes, the first Republicans to strike, would allow in to see them.

At the end of a long day of packing fast and driving even faster to Belfast from Dublin, Cassie and Clare walked into the Shamrock Pub, which was more of a social hall, for a pint, when they came upon Sean O'Kane sitting at the bar holding court. Finishing up a joke he said, "No Father, I haven't made a novena, but if you've got the plans I've got the lumber." And the crowd around him roared with laughter while someone bought another round.

Sean turned to look at what the lads in front of him were looking at as the two beautiful women walked in.

Sean stood and said, "Cassie Kenny, it's about time you got here lass, it's grand to see you."

Cassie smiled, although her mind was racing and she wanted to talk to Sean in private with Clare. Instead, with all the eyes on them, she said, "Sean it's grand to see you as well. Sean O'Kane meet Clare White."

The two stared at one another, both aware of who the other was. Before it became too uncomfortable Sean said, "Clare 'tis a pleasure, welcome to The Shamrock and to Belfast."

They shook hands warmly and Clare's heart beat fast realizing this was Martin's adopted father. She said, "Oh, the pleasure is all mine, Sean, I'm a big fan."

Cassie said, "She reads An Phoblacht."

Sean raised an eyebrow and Clare said, "And the Andersontown News. My way of keeping an eye out for Martin without getting in the way."

Sean said, "He and Fergal have the fight in them alright. But Clare, he's a grand lad and no mistake. And you've got to meet Fergal one day."

Clare said, "Aye, that would be grand."

Cassie said, "We need to have a chat in private if you don't mind."

"Sure. What'll you have?"

Clare said, "Power's."

He nodded and looked at Cassie who said, "Pint of Smithwicks, thanks."

He turned to Hugh Reilly, owner and bartender for the night and said, "Hugh?"

Hugh said, "Right, Sean."

Sean said, "Ladies, follow me."

They went to the back of the pub where it was dark and quiet on a February night in Belfast.

Their drinks came and Cassie said, "Sean, we've got trouble."

He said, "Who doesn't?"

"No, I mean real trouble."

"Okay, talk to me."

Cassie spent the next hour explaining everything that had happened in the last forty-eight hours, Sean's eyes widening by the minute. When she was finished he said, "Let me get this straight."

They both nodded.

He said, "Martin shot the father of his biological twin brother, and one of our largest contributors from overseas, by accident. And in the meantime Martin's twin came to visit his dad, who is now dead, and he was picked up mistakenly as Martin?"

Cassie said, "Aye. And to make matters worse, the American lad knows nothing about his father's death, his twin or anything that is going on around him."

"Do you think he's in Long Kesh?"

"Well the men that picked him up were English. Probably MI5 from the North."

Sean said, "Fucksake Cassie, no."

"What?"

"If he was mistaken for Martin, he would've been taken to Castlereagh first for questioning?"

"I thought that was an RUC station?"

"Aye, MI5 will turn him over to the local police."

Cassie said, "Jaysus, no Sean."

Clare said, "What?"

Sean said, "Clare, welcome to the North. Castlereagh is a police station and is the place they take these lads they pick up for some fairly brutal interrogation."

Cassie said, "Sean, we need to get a message to Eamon Gainey and it had better be quick."

Sean said, "I can do that tonight."

Clare suddenly looked at Cassie and then at Sean in a weird sort of way.

Cassie said, "What is it?"

Clare said, "I know this is way off our subject, but do you think Mr. Reilly would hire me? I was worried about what I would do for money. The Shamrock would be the perfect place for me to keep busy and I think it would be a great place for me to stay in touch with what's going on here.."

Sean said, "Well, we won't know until we ask will we? If you like I'll introduce you to Hugh Reilly."

"That would be grand."

They walked to the front of the pub and Sean said, "Hugh Reilly, meet Clare White."

He reached across the bar and shook her hand firmly and said, "Pleasure."

Clare said, "Thanks, it's nice to meet you."

Sean said, "Clare's new in town and is looking for work."

"Welcome to Belfast and welcome to The Shamrock. Do you have any experience in a pub?"

"Loads, I worked for Jack Tobin at Big Jack's in Dublin."

"You worked for Jack Tobin?"

"Aye. For over twenty-years."

"You're not that old, lass."

"You're a sweet talker, Mr. Reilly."

"That's what some say."

"How about it?"

"Sure, lass, I can always use the help. When can you start?"

"How about tomorrow?"

"Come on in around noon and I'll show you around."

Clare and Cassie found a flat in Ardoyne. Cassie could get around the city easily from there and get to Long Kesh to cover any news that might be breaking regarding the impending hunger strike. They were also close to Sean and Patricia O'Kane for both work and pleasure.

Cassie knew that Sean O'Kane was visiting his son Fergal in Long Kesh prison regularly and delivering "comms," for the brotherhood. Comms were the way that the brotherhood on the inside communicated with those on the outside, and vice versa. They were ingenious in their smuggling the comms in and out, making sure to inform everyone as to what was going on.

Chapter 56
The Poet's Call

Belfast

Later that night

Eamon Gainey, chief of staff for the IRA, lived on the run most of the time. There were safehouses in West Belfast, Millstown, Andersontown, Ardoyne, Derry and Potadown but they were moved month in and month out, sometimes sooner depending on recent events. When his second in command, Dermot Brennan, was in town he stayed with his boss, mostly planning next moves and strategizing.

Sean O'Kane was the one they counted on to deliver any media messages, and because his sons were active soldiers, he had access to the High Council of the brotherhood in the north.

The phone rang at two o'clock in the morning, the two men looked up from their map as Dermot went to answer it.

"Aye."

Sean said, "This is the poet with some new verse I'd like to share."

Dermot said, "You damn phone pranksters, don't you know what time it is?"

He hung up and said, "Sean is on his way over."

Within a half hour Sean O'Kane walked into the flat. He threw a pack of cigarettes on the table and said, "Lads, we got real trouble."

Eamon said, "Jaysus, Sean, tell me something I don't know."

"Listen, I wouldn't have come at this hour unless this was something serious."

The two men across the table looked at one another and then nodded.

Sean said, "When we brought Martin home twenty years ago. . ."

Chapter 57
A Change

The Shamrock

The next day

The next day, just after the lunch crowd died down and Clare was getting the lay of the land, Eamon Gainey surprised her as he walked into The Shamrock and strolled to a room at the back of the club. She stared at him, never forgetting that face and he stared back, unable to place her face but knowing it from somewhere. After an hour or so he emerged from the room and took a booth by himself to the back of the pub.

Hugh Reilly said, “Clare, come here.”

She walked over and said, “Aye?”

“That’s Eamon Gainey.”

Playing dumb she said, “Who’s Eamon Gainey?”

“The man in the booth back there.”

“No, I mean, *who’s* Eamon Gainey?”

“Are you serious, lass?”

“As serious as a mortician.”

Reilly laughed and said, “Lean over the bar.”

As she leaned closer, Hugh enjoyed a healthy view of Clare’s cleavage and had a momentary lapse of thought.

“Keep your eyes off of me chest and tell me what this is about.”

He laughed at being caught and whispered, “Chief of Staff of the Provos.”

Acting surprised at what she already knew she said, “Eamon Gainey?”

“Aye. Take good care of him.”

She walked back to his table and said, “What’ll it be?”

Eamon Gainey looked up, startled out of a deep thought, and stared blankly for a moment. It finally came to him and he recognized her as the waitress he had seen a month earlier in Dublin. How could he forget? He also knew now that this woman was Martin’s biological mother. His eyes devoured her once more and said, “Big Jack’s in Dublin.”

“Very good.”

“So?”

“You were the one who couldn’t make up your mind.”

“It’s not typical of me. I usually know what I want and I get it.”

“Well, what do you want tonight?”

"Well, for starters, Power's."

"Coming up."

She returned and stared at him, he held her gaze she then put the glass on the table.

"What is it?"

She wanted to ask him about her boys but couldn't bring herself.

"I don't know, not sure."

"What brings you to the North?"

She stuttered something under her breath and before he could engage her further she walked away and he stared after her. He had a nagging thought in the back of his mind that the last thing he needed now was a woman, but he could not stop staring at her, something he had not done in a while.

Chapter 58
A Soldier First

Eamon Gainey was a soldier first and only. He had come up through the ranks of the brotherhood in Ireland. He liked to tell people he was born to see Ireland freed from the bondage of another country and united as one. At fourteen he joined the Eire Na, the Republican Youth, and by the time he was sixteen he was fighting for one united Ireland and had an innate ability to lead men. He found early in his career that men would follow him and that they trusted him. He was smart and was able to anticipate the enemy and thus, his long and decorated career in the fight for a united Ireland.

He had no personal life, he had no real home and had never known the true love of a woman. Women were at his doorstep with a great deal of regularity, but he usually refused their advances; he was not to be distracted from his mission. He trusted no one and felt the enemy had ways of using women to get information from weak men. His discipline called for many lonely nights, but he would not be diverted from the cause.

Few men had his passion and drive. He would never have been satisfied with anything less than commander-in-chief and the loneliness, to which he had become accustomed, served him well at the top of the organization. Eamon Gainey, a hard man, was as hard on himself as he was on his men. He expected nothing short of excellence and was disappointed time and again; but he never quit; the word did not exist for him.

That night he lay awake in this strange room in another safehouse that he would use for a week and then move on. He could not get that woman out of his mind. God she was gorgeous and he wanted her. What was her name? Clare? "Damnation," he said to himself. He kept picturing her in his mind's eye, and wasn't sure if it was her eyes, her smile, her short blond hair, her personality or her great ass. Whatever it was he was furious with himself, she was an unwanted distraction, or so he thought. "This is all bullshit," he thought, "It was the whiskey." He'd see her again and feel different, feel nothing.

Clare walked out of the Shamrock pub that evening at eleven and skipped down Flax Street like a schoolgirl. She lay in bed that night and rather than thinking about what Ruari O'Keefe was doing at that precise moment, like she had done every night for the last twenty years since he'd left, she was thinking about something else. She could not get Eamon Gainey out of her mind, but she knew this was a mistake, a man like that would lead to nothing but heartache. She wanted no more heartache; she'd had enough. That was the pragmatist in her and she knew that the sensible thing to do was to forget him. But a voice deep within her told her she wouldn't. She couldn't. Love was no sensible thing anyway. She would have him… whatever the cost.

Eamon Gainey walked into the Shamrock the following night for another meeting. He went straight away to the backroom without acknowledging anyone. Three hours later the room emptied and he emerged, walking across the pub floor on his way home, when he stopped. He saw Clare standing there waiting on a table of customers; he felt a stirring in his chest that he'd never felt before.

Dermot Brennan, who had been in the meeting with Eamon said, "What is it Eamon?"

"Nothing."

Dermot looked over at the woman standing there and frowned. Eamon threw Dermot an unfamiliar look and said, "I'll meet up with you later, I need a drink."

Dermot said, "Aye."

Staying with Eamon during his visits to Belfast, Dermot walked quickly from the pub. Eamon sat down in the back of the pub at his table and waited.

Hugh Reilly said, "Clare," as he jerked his head in the direction of the man sitting at the back of the public house. She looked that way and felt a jolt shoot through her body. She walked slowly to the table and said, "What can I get you, sir?"

"You."

"Pardon me?"

"I want you. Look, I know this is a mistake."

"Why?"

"Because. . . never mind. What time do you get off work, maybe we can get a cup of tea?"

"That would be grand. Eleven O'clock."

"I'll be back."

With that he slipped out of his booth and left the pub. Eamon Gainey's driver picked him up outside the pub and drove around the neighborhood several blocks to make sure no one was following. He drove quietly down an alley and stopped. Eamon got out and slipped through a back yard and up the stairs to the most recent residence. Dermot was studying a map of some barracks of British soldiers that had been stirring up trouble, which they planned to attack.

He looked up as Gainey walked in and said, "You've got a look on your face that's troubling."

"Why's that?"

"It's that woman look."

"That what? Jaysus, Dermot, can I hide nothing from you, man?"

"How long have we been friends?"

"Too long."

"She's Martin biological mother, this could get messy."

"And this coming from a married man."

"That has nothing to do with it. Besides Siobhan and I grew up together, she knew what she was getting into."

"Aye, I know. I'll be careful. Sometimes it just gets bloody lonely."

Dermot was stunned. He'd never heard Eamon Gainey say anything quite so personal and it struck him. He'd never thought of his friend and leader as anything other than a soldier, totally committed to the cause. He looked at him and realized just how alone in the world he was. Eamon's grandfather faced the firing squad in prison after the rising in 1916, his father and two brothers died on raids and his mother died of cancer three years ago. He was utterly alone in the world and his life was the brotherhood, a bottle of Power's and the occasional one-night stand. Eamon Gainey never looked to anyone for help; he had been entirely self-sufficient.

Dermot said, "Be careful."

Chapter 59
The Mother's Blond Hair

Cassie drove to Dublin to meet with her editor and would be away for a couple of days. The door to their flat creaked open as Clare and Eamon walked in. She went to the kitchenette, filled the teakettle, and put it over the open blue gas flame that shot up from the small stove.

Eamon sat on the couch and rested his head on its back as he stared at her silhouette against the soft back-lit kitchenette.

The walls of the flat were stark and bare with the exception of a beautiful watercolor painting. Above the painting was a lamp attached to the frame that cast a soft yellow light upon it. The position of the painting and the spot light gave it the significance its owner had intended.

It was a painting of twin boys playing in a sandbox on a playground as a mother, sitting on a picnic table, looked on lovingly.

Eamon was drawn to the work and stood, crossed the living room, and stared. Then he reached out and touched it as if he couldn't help himself. His fingers caressed the mother's blond hair that waved in the wind as the leaves blew in their autumn colors. It struck him how much the woman looked like Clare. And he guessed the boys were her twins, rather than closely resembling siblings, because of their identical outfits.

She came in from putting on the water to boil and stood next to him and he looked at her as she wiped a tear away.

He said, "What is it?"

She said, "Oh, nothing, just a memory."

"This is beautiful and obviously means a great deal to you. Where did you get it?"

"I painted it."

"Seriously?"

"Aye."

"You're very good."

"Thank you."

"The woman could be you."

"'Tis."

He looked at her quizzically and said, "Then who are the lads?"

"My sons."

"Twins?"

"Aye,"

Eamon pictured the tall blonde haired soldier he sent to Dublin.

"So it's true, you're Martin's mother."

Tears welled in her eyes and she said, "I wanted to tell you earlier but I couldn't bring myself to. Initially I was coming north to be with Cassie as she covered the strike. But I also wanted to keep track of Martin. But suddenly Paddy Quinlan shows up to bury his brother and tells us his son Mick is coming shortly."

"I was informed of all this in meetings the last day and half."

"Well Cassie and I figured it out and made a mad dash for the airport knowing they'd have it covered. We saw Mick get arrested and that's why we came when we did. We figured you needed to know what was going on."

He winced.

"What is?"

"That Martin's twin is probably in Castlereagh being tortured by those British bastards, who will be convinced that he's Martin with a fake passport and fake accent. And to make it worse he has no idea what the hell is going on."

"He must be scared."

"Aye. Do we know how tough this lad is?"

"Well, he grew up on a ranch and everything I've ever heard was that the apple didn't fall too far from the tree."

"His biological father?"

"Well, both actually. I met his adoptive father before. . ."

"Before Martin shot him. Fucksake, Paddy Quinlan was hugely successful in the states and very generous with us. But it's way too strange that Martin shot him."

"Yes it is, and he didn't seem like someone to be messed with."

"Well, the lad's biological father was a mean bastard in his day. I saw him play. You know where he is now?"

"Aye, somewhere in the Philippines."

"Nay, no more, he's back."

She said with more surprise than she wanted, "What? Where?"

"Right here in Ardoyne, Holy Cross Church."

"Jaysus, no. How do you know?"

"The Cardinal and I are friends, he grew up near me in Crossmaglen in South Armagh, know his whole family. He called old Ruari back because we discussed the strike, and the Cardinal knows where Ruari's loyalties are, and he wants him as chaplain for our lads in Long Kesh. He also knows how tough O'Keefe is and he wants him as back up when he has to go visit old Tin Knickers on Downing Street."

"Seriously?"

"Aye. She's one tough bird and the Cardinal is convinced she'll let one or more of them die before she gives in, so he'll have to go and try to talk some sense in to her."

Clare looked nervous and said, "What are we going to do for the American twin? His father's dead, he's in Castlereagh getting the shyte beat out of him and will be heading to Long Kesh. He's got to be confused and a bit pissed off. Nice welcome to Ireland."

"I've got some ideas but it really is bad luck and timing for the lad, because he's stuck for a while."

"What do you mean stuck?"

"Well we don't get an opportunity very often to stick it up the arses of those limey bastards. But when the Brits realize that they've arrested, tortured and imprisoned an innocent citizen of America, their closest ally, and we are the ones who'll tell them, they'll realize there'll be no saving face, and there'll be hell to pay. And to the British sensibility there's few things worse than not saving face. I'm also counting on Fergal O'Kane telling the lad what's what to see if he'll be willing to help us out. If he's anything like his brother we'll be holding the red hot poker a bit too close for comfort to their hairy white British arses."

"You are a devious man aren't you?"

"We've been trying to expose the torture tactics of those bastards over at Castlereagh for quite some time now. It'll be interesting to hear what the U.S. has to say about it after one of their own starts shouting."

"Don't kid yourself. The American Government is up to the same tricks and are as good at hiding the shit as the British. Why do you think they are such close allies?"

Chapter 60
Castlereagh

The black government sedan cruised comfortably north on the Dublin to Belfast road, M1, heading to the British occupied six counties in the north.

Mick Quinlan sat in the back squeezed between two taut Englishmen who could not have been more serious or stern.

He said, "You fellas mind telling me where we're going?"

A blackjack drove into his ribs from the left and a forehead smashed into his right ear, he winced and said, "A yes would've sufficed."

Within two hours, Mick found himself sitting in a cement block room in the Castlereagh Royal Ulster Constabulary station, the interrogation center in Belfast, with a hot bright light on his face, hands cuffed behind his back, looking at a two-way mirror and facing an extremely menacing looking interrogator.

Ian Wright said, "Are you Martin O'Kane?"

"No."

Wright's opened hand slapped Mick so hard across his face his neck snapped back and blood rolled down his chin.

Mick said, "What the fuck?"

"Are you Martin O'Kane?"

"No, I'm. . ."

Wright's fist came out of nowhere and broke his nose.

Mick tried to stand and Ian Wright laughed and pushed him back down in his chair.

Mick said, "You son of a bitch, take these cuffs off and do that!"

"Are you Martin O'Kane?"

"Are you a dumb fuck or just deaf?"

This time a blackjack hit him so hard in the back of the head that he went out.

He awoke and found himself sitting in what he supposed was the same chair in the same room with a hot wet towel fastened to his entire head completely covering his face and he felt like he was suffocating. He struggled a half hour or so to get a decent breath and then passed out again.

He woke up again on the floor of a jail type cell. The door suddenly opened and he was pulled to his feet and dragged back to the interrogation room. For the next twenty-four hours he was punched, kicked, slapped, physically thrown, burnt with a cigar, burnt with a light bulb, put back under the hot wet towel and whipped with a knotted nylon rope at intervals of two hours on, ten minutes off. After they viciously questioned him for two hours, they then threw him in his cell for ten minutes, and then a fresh team of interrogators would take over.

After a night of rest Ian Wright walked back into the interrogation room that now smelled of sweat, vomit and blood.

He said, "Just sign the fucking confession Taig, admit that you're Martin O'Kane the murderous fucking Republican Taig cocksucker that we all know you are. Admit that you killed an Irish ex-pat, and that you murdered in cold blood the English Ambassador to this toilet of a fucking country you fight for and we'll be done with this. We'll take you before the judge and then we can get your sorry fucking Paddy ass locked up where you belong. It's that easy."

Mick's mouth was so swollen he could barely talk when he looked up and said, "Fuck you."

After twenty-four hours the interrogation team gave him some time off while they met.

Ian Wright looked at William Gray and said, "We may have a problem here."

Gray said, "What's that?"

"He says he's an American. He has a legitimate American passport. And even in the last throes of the first twenty-fours, he didn't lose the Yankee western type drawl. Either Martin O'Kane is one hell of an actor, or he has a twin brother."

Gray said, "Bullshit. Martin O'Kane is just like all the rest of those lying, cheating, thieving, shameless Fenian bastards. But listen; when he gets to The Maze I want him in the same cell as his brother. We've got it wired, maybe we can learn something."

Before the week was out Mick found himself in a court with no attorney and no jury. He stood, face black and blue, nose broken, eyes swollen, before a judge and next to a prosecuting barrister.

The Judge said, "Martin Peder O'Kane you have been found guilty of the murder of a British official and possession of an illegal firearm. Before I sentence you, do you have anything to say for yourself?"

Mick smiled incredulously at the nightmare he was in, ready to wake up at any moment. He said, "Your honor, you are making a grave mistake here. First of all, I'm an American citizen, like my passport says. Secondly I don't even know who this Martin O'Kane is. Thirdly, I thought England was a democracy with a fair judicial system. Where the hell is my attorney and where are the jurors and where the hell are my rights, goddamn it!"

The judge responded calmly, “You lost your rights when you decided to lead the life of a terrorist. You are a murderer and I hereby sentence you to a life sentence in Long Kesh prison to start immediately.”

As Mick was being dragged out he screamed, “This is a joke, right? Come on you’re kidding, tell me you’re kidding! This isn’t a court this is a fucking joke!”

Great Britain's Diplock Court system door slammed in the face of Mick Quinlan, locked it tightly and threw away the key.

Chapter 61
Long Kesh Prison

The Next Day

Mick had never felt so all alone in his life, nothing made any sense to him. All he had ever heard all his life were wondrous stories about this magical land across the sea; how the people were gracious and friendly. He could hear Uncle Dinty's melodious voice telling grand stories of Ireland. He had waited his lifetime to make this trip, and now this. He found himself so homesick he was nauseous.

He sat in the back of a dreary orange van that smelled like an old wet dead dog. His feet and hands shackled. He looked out the window at the drab, colorless city. The end of February was nearing and the clouds broke for a bit to let the sunshine reign, if only temporarily, something that would have normally made him smile.

He wondered why his dad was not helping. Where was he? And who were those ladies at the airport? He could have sworn they were walking toward him when MI5 intercepted him. And who in the hell was this Martin O'Kane they kept talking about? And why did they insist that he was Martin O'Kane? Not just insist but knew with absolute certainty that he was. He knew none of the answers to these questions, but he was about to get some answers he did not necessarily want, about what life was like on the inside of Long Kesh Prison.

He looked up and his heart sunk as he saw the gray cement mass up ahead. A twenty-foot gray cement wall ran the entire perimeter of the prison. Guard Towers stood defiantly at different spots around the prison and reminded him of a large alien robots from some 1950's Sci-Fi movie.

They went through the main gate and took a right on a road that was in between the perimeter wall and a large fence with razor sharp barbed wire. Great Britain had built a modern prison facility with eight blocks each containing four wings, A,B,C and D. From the air they looked like a capitol H and thus the term H-Block was born. Each block had four wings of cells and the center bar on the H was the administration.

The van driver put on the brakes and Martin slid uncomfortably forward in his seat. The gate to H-4 opened and they drove into the U at the top of the H for the 4th block. When he had put the van in park the driver turned in his seat, smiled a brown crooked smile and said, "Hope you enjoyed your freedom, lad, because you're fucked now."

The side door of the van opened and a prison guard said, "Harry, what have we here, another Fenian prick who hasn't learned his lesson?"

The loyalist driving the van coughed from brewer's drip after thousands of pints of heavy English brew and in a gagging sort of laugh and said, "'ats right Joey, 'ats right."

Mick was pulled roughly from the van and lost his balance in his shackles and fell to the black top scraping his face and hands. Pulled roughly to his feet, they walked into the H4 block through gate wing entry 161, which consisted of two sliding iron gates that were typical in any modern penitentiary. When they slammed shut behind him this boy from the big sky Montana ranch country suddenly felt like he had just been locked into a car trunk for a long trip. He found his heart beating rapidly and he was taking long deep breaths to keep from panicking.

Two prison guards now escorted him and, as they entered the C wing, their steps echoed down the smooth cement floor and off the pink flesh colored walls. There were solid iron doors painted white and located every twenty feet or so, with a metal flap that opened to a crevice in the door at eye level to look in and out. Centered on the wall in between each door was another larger metal flap, which swung open to a thick plated window so prisoners were able to received food and water

Suddenly, in the thick accent of the uneducated Northern Irish, Mick heard, "Bear in the air, Bear in the air," and the wing erupted into a cacophony of metal on metal, bed pans and coffee cups banging on the thick metal doors that stood between these men and their freedom.

Mick began to gag and one of the guards laughed at him and said, "Come on now lad, don't tell me a big shot IRA man like yourself wouldn't recognize the smell of your lads dirty protest now would you? You'll get used to it. Or maybe you won't."

The guards were still laughing as they got to cell 210, opened it, and pushed Mick inside. One guard took off the shackles while the other held his high powered rifle on Mick. As the door shut behind him Mick stood in a puddle of urine and vomited.

One of the guards laughed and said, "Not so tough now are you?"

They slammed the door shut and Mick screamed, "Wait a minute there's shit on the fucking walls! You're not leaving me in here, for Christ's sake!"

The floor went deadly silent and the guards looked at one another. It was eerie, like a morgue when one is identifying a next of kin. Each man in each cell heard the American accent and knew it was not one of their brothers trying on a lark. These street smart Republicans knew something was not right. One of them was Bobby Sands, a week away from his hunger strike.

Chapter 62
The Blanket Protest

Mick pulled his blanket to his mouth and nose and looked around this cell. There was human excrement smeared on the walls, he stood in puddles of human urine and there was a bucket in the corner that over flowed. He did not know what to do so he just stood where he was. He had never seen anything like this in his young life and was confused and scared beyond reason, when the door to his cell opened and a man walked in followed by a guard who released him from his shackles. The man then took off his prison uniform and handed them to the guard who left the cell. As the door clanged shut the man walked naked to his bed, took the blanket on his bed and wrapped himself in it.

Mick stared at Fergal O'Kane and Fergal stared back. Mick had him by at least a head but by the look in his eye and his wiry build, Mick's instincts told him that this man should not be provoked.

The red hair that rested on his shoulders, and the beard on his chest, were matted and filthy. He stood in a brown blanket so threadbare that it looked as if it did little more than cover the naked body beneath it.

The man said, "So it's true."

Mick said, "What's true."

"Martin really does have a twin."

"What do you mean Martin has a twin?"

"My older brother Martin O'Kane. And if you're not his twin then St. Patrick never drove a single snake out of Ireland."

"For Christ sake will somebody please tell who in the hell Martin O'Kane is?"

"The most wanted Fenian bastard in Northern Ireland, that's who."

"So the British think I'm him?"

"That's right, cowboy."

"So I'm fucked."

"Aye, that's about right."

"How do you know any of this?"

"Me Da, Sean O'Kane. I just came back from me monthly visit and they pieced it all together."

"Who's they?"

"Da said two women went to meet you at the airport and saw the whole thing?"

"Yeah, come to think of it, I did see two women walking toward me before the English welcoming committee met me. They walked away in a hurry. Who were they and where the hell is my dad?"

"The women were Cassie Kenny, a good friend of your Da, and Clare White, your mother."

"My what?"

"Your mum."

"My mom is dead, my dad told me so. Look I need to get a hold of my dad, how come I didn't get a fucking phone call."

"Welcome to the North, Yank."

"So I don't get a call?"

"It wouldn't do you any good anyway."

""'What's that suppose to mean?"

"Look lad, I'm not sure I'm the one to be telling you this."

"Tell me what?"

"Your Da's dead."

"What? Give me a break, my dad's not dead."

Fergal nodded and said, "He died in an accident, the night before your plane landed. No one has had a chance to tell you until now."

"You're serious."

"Aye, and I'm sorry to be the one to tell you."

He screamed, "No," which could be heard down the wing.

The next morning Mick woke, all was quiet and Fergal was reading psalms out of his bible when he heard, "Youse 'tenshun!"

He said, "What's that?"

Fergal said, "Wing shift and head count."

"Wing shift and head count?"

"Aye, changing of the night guard and counting us to make sure we didn't escape in the night. Sometimes they'll rush in, slam you across a wooden table, spread your legs and shove a hand up your arse to check for comms and they're none too gentle. When you hear a scuffle you'll know."

Then the same voice screamed, "Wing Shift."

Boots were heard walking down the hall and the same voice again, "Two, two, one, two, two, one, two."

Their window opened up and the voice said, "Two."

It was over shortly and Mick said, "Check your ass for comms, what the hell are you talking about?"

Fergal looked at Mick and said, "I keep forgetting who you are. Fucksake, you're identical to Martin and it makes me miss the bastard all the more. Sit down, let's have a chat."

Before they got started, morning breakfast arrived, cold porridge for the third day, cold toast and cold tea. Fergal put a slab of margarine that came with breakfast on the window seal and Mick said, "What the hell?"

Fergal said, "I've got to grease my arse with something."

Mick said, "Okay, enough about arses, would you explain to me what the hell is going on?"

"The only way we can communicate with one another and with the brotherhood outside is through 'comms,' which is short for communications. We smuggle them in and out of the prison on our monthly visits. We write them on cigarette paper, roll them tight, put them in cellophane, grease the arse and shove them up. So the screws, the rotten limey bastards, will give us the unexpected rectal exam, and none to delicate I can tell you, to make sure we're not carrying any comms."

"Screws?"

"Aye, that's what we call the guards, because they're always putting the screws to us."

"What happens if you get caught?"

"You go to the boards."

"What?"

"Solitary confinement where they'll beat the shyte out of you for fun. And then they'll leave you in a five by five cell with no windows for a week. Nice of them, eh?"

"So how long will you carry a comm up your ass?"

"Until someone has a visit and then we pass them along."

"So what's with you guys wearing blankets and the shit on the wall?"

"Fucking Yanks, you know nothing."

"How would we?"

"You wouldn't. In 1976 the Brits decided that we were no longer prisoners of war. Now, by their backwards laws, we're considered criminals. They did this to try and make us look bad to the rest of the world. Anyway, before 1976, IRA inmates were able to wear their own clothes, didn't have to do prison work, could organize their own exercise and education, associate freely with our own lads, and had a right to remission of sentence due to good behavior, we were considered prisoners of war. Well, they took these rights away because they said we were not soldiers but criminals. So we started the blanket protest. If we couldn't wear our own clothes we refused to wear prison clothes, so we wear blankets. Then we started the dirty protest, which happened by accident."

"What do you mean?"

"We take care of our business during the day in these buckets. When it was bath time, we'd take them with us, dump them and get a new one. To go to wash we'd wrap a towel around us and leave the blankets in the cell. The bloody fucking screws started harassing us for wearing our towels, saying that if we were on the blanket then wear the fucking blankets. We told them to piss off. They dumped the buckets in our cells and the dirty protest was on. We refused to bathe."

"Doesn't that hurt you more than them?"

"No, the bloody bastards have to live with the smell; it makes their lives hell too."

"Huh."

"Anyway, we weren't getting anywhere with the bastards so we're starting another hunger strike, and it seems to be getting some worldwide attention."

"You mean you've got guys willing to die for a few rights as political prisoners in prison?"

"No, we've got lads willing to take on the British government for eight hundred years of hatred, injustice and oppression. Bobby Sands starts next week, Francis Hughes, Ray McCreesh and Patsy O'Hara will go in the next weeks after and we've got lads lined up to go after that."

"Guys are lining up to die for their country? A long, slow, and painful death?"

"Aye, it's an ancient form of protest for the Irish. In ancient times if a wealthy man did a poor man dirt, the poor man could protest by hunger striking at the rich man's door. And by Irish law, if the wealthy man let the poor man die he would have to be responsible for his widow and children."

Mick sat and thought about it all, the death of his dad, that he had a twin brother and a birth mother, his situation, and these men.

"Bears in the air, bears in the air."

Their cell door opened and the prison class officer walked in and looked at Fergal, who sat on his bed, and said, "Do you want to put on prison clothes?"

Fergal said, "No."

Mick looked on.

The class officer said, "Do you want to do prison work?"

"No."

"Do you want to exercise?"

"No."

"Wash?"

"No."

"Shave?"

"No."

"Shit?"

"No."

He left without a word.

Mick said, “What was that?”

“Lad, you'll learn, the Brits do everything by the book. Every fourteen days from the day a lad went on protest they show up and do this.”

Two hours past and Mick heard, “Big bear in the air.”

Suddenly their door opened again and in walked an Assistant Governor, and following him into the tiny cell was the Chief Officer, Principal Officer, Class Officer, and the two floor guards. Mick had no idea what was going on but he thought this was trouble.

The Assistant governor stood at attention in a crisp uniform and said, “Class Officer, please prefer the charges against said prisoner.”

The Class Officer, crisply dressed, pulled his reading glasses to the tip of his long nose, squinted down at his clip board and said, “I state, sir, that I did, on the 25th day of the this month, charge said prisoner with refusal to wear prison uniform, refusal to do prison work, contrary to rule forty-four and contrary to rule sixty-three. I preferred the charges to the prisoner at breakfast time this morning. The prisoner refused on all accounts.”

The Assistant Governor looked down his nose at Fergal, who sat reading his bible and paying no more attention to them than if they were not there at all. He said, “Have you anything further to say in your defense?”

Mick looked at Fergal and Fergal smiled back at Mick and said nothing.

The Assistant Governor said, “In the absence of a plea from you I order you, prison officer, to enter a plea of not guilty on his behalf.”

The screw standing there trying to make a name for himself said, “I have entered a plea of not guilty for said prisoner, sir.”

The assistant Governor said, “Have you anything to say on your behalf?’

Fergal yawned.

“Having heard the evidence against you I make you an award of fourteen days’ loss of privileges, fourteen days’ loss of parcels, fourteen days’ loss of visits, fourteen days’ loss of exercise. Good Morning.” With that they all turned around and left.

Mick said, “What the hell was that?”

“The Brits. They completely miss the boat. It’s been eight hundred years of them meddling in Irish lives and they still don’t understand us.”

Chapter 63
Underground

Queens, New York City

One Week Later

Traffic on Canal Street was nonexistent as he walked its yellow lines without interference. Life was dead, no one except the three people on the veranda of the pub up ahead in celebration over a pint, laughing loudly and carrying on.

He stopped before the bridge over the Grand Canal. Knowingly he looked toward the window across the street as it slid discreetly open and the cold blue steel slid silently to its rest on the ledge. A reflection of himself in the window but dressed like a Yank. The shot echoed down the water in the canal and startled him, when he looked up the bullet flew past in slow motion as he stood, amazed.

He looked past the sound wave moving up and down as the bullet headed toward its target. One of the men on the patio stood unexpectedly and the bullet slammed into his back, sending him hurdling on to the table, which crashed around him as he landed, drinks flying all around them. The woman stood and screamed for help as a third man ran to help. Another bullet let fly and this one slammed into the chest of the second man, landing him against the wall before he slid to his death. Drops of blood spread in the air like mercury from a broken thermometer.

He walked calmly to the scene and turned the first dead man around to check his pulse, when he noticed it was his father, Sean O'Kane, who had the blood of the mortally wounded running out of his mouth and down his chin. He gasped when his father looked up at him with blood on his teeth and laughed odiously and kept saying over and over again, "Now look what you've gone and done lad, now look what you've gone and done." He then looked over at the man who sat bloodied and dead against the wall and saw that it was the Irishman, with a hole the size of his fist in his chest, his heart still pumping blood, when he suddenly opened his eyes and laughed as he said, "You got the wrong man, lad, the wrong fucking man."

Martin O'Kane awoke with a scream, in a reservoir of sweat. He looked around and didn't recognize his surroundings. Then he realized he was in his flat above Sullivan's Pub on Queens Boulevard, digs arranged by Dan Mulroy. Martin didn't know how long it had been since he left Ireland but it was the same thing night after night. He would spend all day and night in the pub where the Yanks refused to let him buy a drink and refused to let his glass run dry. He would finally stumble to his room, fall into a restless sleep, and awake with a start, which usually meant he would be up for the rest of the night trying to figure out the dream. Who was the Irishman and why was he there? Why was he haunting his dreams?

This particular night Martin trudged his way to the kitchenette, where he found Dan Mulroy nursing a few fingers of Power's. Martin stopped, a bit startled, and then walked in and said, "Dan, what brings you here in the middle of the night?"

"Just got off shift at the firehouse and came by to check in on you. I've been hearing things."

"Aye? Like what?"

" Like you've been drinking hard from sun up to sun down. Eamon tells me that is unusual behavior for the likes of you."

Martin lit a cigarette and poured himself a glass of water from the sink.

"What am I suppose to do? You Yanks expect an Irishman to drink and won't leave me or my glass alone."

"Look son, I know there's trouble back home. We all do, but if you ever need someone to talk to."

Martin looked at the man sitting across the table from him. He thought of Fergal sitting in Long Kesh. He thought of his Mother and Father, and his cousin Thomas fighting with his Uncle Dermot. He thought of the constant struggle of the troubles in the north and the brotherhood that he cherished. He thought of his hatred of the Unionist and Loyalist bastards harassing his people as the bloody RUC watched, and then he thought of the innocent man pulled from his cab on the Crumlin Road just because he was in the wrong place at the wrong time, much like the innocent man he had shot, and he got weak in the legs for the first time in his life.

Dan got up and left the room; he returned a moment later and threw a copy of the Montana Standard, Butte's Newspaper, on the table. The headline read, "Local Irish National dead during assassination."

Dan said, "A friend of mine in Butte sent this to me."

Martin studied it.

Dan said, "I didn't know if you knew who he was."

Martin said, "This is the man who was with the English Ambassador."

"Right."

"What I don't know is why he was there."

"We think he had a relationship with the reporter."

"That still doesn't answer why he'd be at this interview."

"Maybe he had met the reporter for a drink before the interview and maybe the ambassador didn't mind him joining them. After all he was an ex-pat Yank and everything the ambassador said in the interview was going to be on the front page the next day anyway."

"So he was from Montana?"

"Yeah. His name was Paddy Quinlan. He was President of the Irish American Clan in Montana. Lot of Micks settled there because of the copper mines. He sent you lads a load of money."

"Fucksake, Dan, how was I to know?"

"You weren't, Quinlan being one of us and all. But this thing happens in a war."

"Easy for you to say, Dan, while you're living in a suburb in New York a long way away from all The Troubles. When I'm sent to do a job, it's hard, but to kill an innocent bystander, it's eating me up. Knowing he was one of us sure as hell doesn't make it any easier."

The tears ran down his cheeks and were soaked up by the newspaper below him. He began to shake and thought he might pass out.

Chapter 64
Surprising Meeting

Armagh

The Next Day

Cardinal John Byrne sat in his office running his hands through his hair and struggling with some budgetary issues that he hated, when his secretary rang through.

"Excellency, there is an Eamon Gainey on the line."

Cardinal John Byrne said, "Thanks, Mrs. Ryan, ring him through."

"Hello."

"Do you have plans to meet with Thatcher?"

"About?"

"The strike."

"Aye. She'll let these men die if someone doesn't interfere."

"Then I've got a message I want to get to her."

"And you think that an Irish Cardinal is going to deliver a message for the IRA?"

"It's not a message from the IRA, it's a message from the Irish people and the American people."

"What would that be?"

"You know who Martin O'Kane is."

"Aye, the lad they arrested recently."

"The lad they *think* they arrested recently."

There was a silence on the phone.

"What do you mean *think*? Either they arrested him or not."

"They arrested his American twin brother."

"Is this some kind of joke, because. . ."

"It's no joke. Make time to meet with us and I'll bring proof."

The Cardinal thought for a moment. It was risky business meeting with the IRA, even though he and Gainey grew up together, were mates who went opposite directions.

"Okay, I'll also have Fr. O'Keefe join us, he's the man I've put in charge of IRA matters for the Church in Northern Ireland."

Eamon, Clare, and Cassie pulled into the circular drive behind St. Patrick's Cathedral in Armagh. The Cathedral stood on Tealach Na Licci, or Sandy Hill, where St. Patrick walked some fifteen hundred years ago.

The grounds were immaculately manicured, as expected of the home of the High See of Ireland. When they arrived the stars shone brightly in the black sky and there was a chill in the night air.

Clare said, "It's hard for me to believe that the great saint himself once walked these grounds."

Cassie said, "Not only walked these grounds, but after traveling the length and width of the island chose this place for his office. I can see why he loved it here."

The large gray stone home, known as The Archbishop's House, was located behind the cathedral. The housekeeper, Mrs. Cavanaugh, was tough and very protective of the Cardinal. Looking irritated that people were bothering the man at this late hour, she showed the trio into his office. Father Ruari O'Keefe had his back to them as they entered the room, bending over the desk discussing church business with his boss. When he turned around and saw Clare, he stopped, as if a bolt of electricity temporarily paralyzed his movements.

Eamon had not told Clare that Ruari was going to be here, not sure if she would come. He needed to play on both of their sympathies to get the job he needed done.

The Cardinal, unaware of all the unspoken conversation bantering silently around the room, walked around his desk and introduced himself to both Clare and Cassie. He then introduced Ruari to his guests. Ruari and Clare shook hands last while Eamon and Cassie looked on knowingly. Ruari's mind raced back to Clare's apartment the night they said goodbye, the door shutting and the sinking despair he felt standing in the hall. It had taken him forever to travel from the West Coast of Ireland to the Philippines and he needed every minute of that journey to pull himself back together.

Clare stared at the leathery hand of the tanned man in front of her, whose ring of hair around his bald pate was now fully white, his eyes penetrating her as they had done some twenty years before, as if they could see her secrets and read her thoughts. She smiled at him and he, as if coming out of some deep thought, suddenly smiled back and said, "It's good to see you again, Clare. You look lovely."

She said, "Thank you, Father, it's good to see you as well."

The Cardinal, antsy to get started, said, "It's late, let's get started."

They sat at a large meeting table and the housekeeper brought in tea. She left and Eamon stared at the Prelate and his Direct Report longer than was comfortable and then said, "Everything said here tonight stays here. I'm going to share some information that I normally would not. But because we have a certain situation we're dealing with, I have to. If men's lives weren't at stake I'd take this information to the grave. Do we all understand?"

They all nodded, knowing the IRA man that sat across from them could be no more serious than if he held a gun on them.

"Thatcher's people reign down terror, prejudice, violence and death on our people in The North and when we fight back they call us criminals. She says that if she gives in to the demands of the men on the blanket or their dirty protests in The Kesh it'll be labeled political and that it will give our lads respectability, even nobility, as she put it. First of all, we are not criminals; criminals do what they do because they stand to gain something from it. By standing up and asking for the political status as a POW, or by fighting for our ancient lands, we gain nothing more than torture, internment, humiliation and death."

Ruari said, "I understand all that, but what gain was there in killing the ambassador?"

"Margaret Thatcher is sending us tough messages and we wanted to send her one back. Let her know that we are serious."

Ruari said, "It's the death of an innocent man. What about his wife and children?"

Eamon stared at Ruari and said, "He was a protégé of Airy Neave, he hated the Irish and was working against any reunification. He was put in place because Thatcher was pissed that Neave was assassinated and she wanted to send a message that she would not be intimidated. And, while we're on it, what about the widows and children of all the Irishmen whose blood has soaked Irish soil, slaughtered by English soldiers, for the past eight hundred fucking years? I'm not concerned about the blood of one Englishman who should've known better than to fuck with us."

Cardinal Byrne put up his hand and said, "Let's not, lads."

Cassie and Clare glanced at one another as the discussion heated up.

Eamon said, "Okay, fair enough, Father, I know you're just doing your job. But let's call a spade a spade, shall we? Anyway, Cassie, who's here off the record, was there when the hit took place. As sometimes happens during a war, innocent people die. Cassie had no idea what was coming, otherwise it may have been prevented."

The Cardinal said, "You mean the Yank who was killed next to the ambassador?"

"Technically he was an Irish National, but aye, that's the one. He left his home in Ireland in his twenties. His name was Paddy Quinlan and he was accidentally shot by the biological twin brother of his adopted son."

The clergymen both said, "What?" Simultaneously.

The explanation was made and Ruari went pale. He thought he might be sick. He looked at Clare who nodded slightly, acknowledging his assumption to be correct.

Their subtle communication was not lost on the Cardinal; he now understood who Clare was.

Cardinal Byrne said, "And this is the lad they arrested."

"Aye, the American twin came to Ireland to be with his Da, who was here for a funeral. After the assassination, MI5 was on high alert for Martin. We knew that would be the case so we got him out of the country that night."

The Cardinal said, "Lord help us all."

"Aye, I'm afraid so. The American twin was apprehended by MI5 agents at the Dublin airport, mistaken for Martin O'Kane, and is now in a cell at Long Kesh."

Ruari said, "God save us, I've got an appointment with the lad tomorrow. As their chaplain I visit all the new prisoners."

The Cardinal said, "So the Brits have an American citizen in custody in Long Kesh, who they think is a wanted IRA man?"

Eamon said, "Aye, not only that but before they took him to Long Kesh, they had him in Castlereagh."

The Cardinal groaned and said, "They tortured him?"

Eamon said, "Well, we don't know that for sure. But we don't know that they do anything else there to suspected Fenians."

"This could get very interesting for Mrs. Thatcher before this is through."

"My thoughts exactly."

The Cardinal looked at the Chief of Staff for the standing IRA and said, "Where is the Irish Twin?"

"Therein lies the answer to all this."

"What did you have in mind?"

"It's time to let the twins in on exactly what's going on. Your Excellency, can I borrow Fr. O'Keefe for a week?"

"I'm afraid to ask why?"

"We need to take a little trip to New York to see Martin. I've got a plan to get the Yank out of the Kesh and Martin off but I'm not going to say anymore than that now."

The Cardinal said, "It'll have to be the week after next, Father O'Keefe and I have a meeting with Mrs. Thatcher next Tuesday evening."

Eamon said, "You do?"

The Cardinal nodded and said, "The timing couldn't have been any better. I've been trying to get in to see her since Bobby Sands announced his hunger strike. Her secretary called me this evening before you got here to set up the meeting."

Chapter 65
Brother Meet Your Father

Long Kesh Prison, Maze, Northern Ireland

The Next Day

Since his boss appointed him chaplain to the Republicans, Ruari O'Keefe had become a fairly regular visitor to the inmates, visiting the new prisoners, hearing confessions, saying mass and supporting the lads in whatever way was needed. But this morning, as he walked with his prison guard escort down the long, rancid smelling corridor of the C wing in H4, to which he still had not yet become accustomed and never thought he would, his trepidation was palpable.

They stopped in front of door to the room where the chaplain met the inmates. The guard unlocked the door, stood aside to let the priest in and then shut the door behind him. There was a table in the middle of the room. Ruari took a seat and waited.

Within ten minutes two men walked in to the room wearing the prison uniforms they exchanged for their blankets for visits. Both men were shackled and shuffled to take a seat. The guard stood at the door and they both immediately lit cigarettes from a pack that Ruari had put on the table.

Ruari stared into the eyes of his biological son and had to fight back the emotion that was welling in him. He wanted to hug him but couldn't. Mick had two black eyes and a fat lip.

Fergal O'Kane, who had met Ruari on his last visit, reached out to shake the chaplain's hand and said, "Dia duit, cara."

"Dia Duit."

Mick said, "Okay, what the hell was that?"

Fergal laughed and said, "I said, 'hello friend' and he responded 'hello.'"

"That's Irish I take it?"

"Aye."

Ruari said, "And what would your name be?"

"Mick Quinlan."

They all shook hands.

Ruari looked at the skin under Fergal's prison uniform that looked like raw steak, spotty red blotches, crusted bloody scratches and chunks of his red beard missing.

"What happened to you two? Why is your skin scratched and raw? And why is Mick all black and blue?"

Mick, unable to contain himself, said, "I'll tell you why, Father. These bastards opened our cell late last night and surprised Fergal with a bucket of scalding hot water. They doused him with it. I just got a few sprinkles on me and it hurt like hell. Then the bastards tossed some awful smelling soap on him, four of them held him down while two of those bastards took these hard bristled brushes to him and scrubbed him raw from head to toe. I couldn't just stand by so I jumped in and they beat the shit out of me."

Fergal said, "And he was still black and blue from his week at Castlereagh."

Mick and Fergal looked at one another with a newfound respect.

Mick continued, "Then a few minutes later they came in with a high powered hose and pressure washed the whole cell. Hell we about drowned while they laughed saying shit like, 'You want a dirty fucking protest, we'll give you a dirty protest.' Then they started tossing around chlorine bleach like it was water. It got in my eyes and burned like hell; it landed on my skin and burnt a hole in my blanket."

Fergal smiled and said, "It's the way the screws deal with the dirty protest."

Ruari said, "It's a dirty business, all of it."

Mick said, "You can say that again. Say, Father, I don't know if you know anything about my case but these damn English fellas have mistaken me for an IRA man that people are telling me is my long lost twin. Now I don't know much about that but I do know that I'm an American and have no business in here. Can you help me out? Make some of these idiots listen to the truth?"

Ruari looked at Fergal and said, "Fergal, your Martin's brother, is that right?"

"Aye."

He said, "Okay, good. Both of you lads sit down. We need to have a chat."

Chapter 66
Crossing the Pond

One week later

Sean O'Kane, Ruari O'Keefe, Dermot Brennan, and Eamon Gainey ran for their gate, late for their flight from Dublin to New York. Out of breath, they handed the gate attendant their tickets and boarded the large jet. Cardinal Byrne and Ruari had arrived late from England and their meeting with the Prime Minister, so the foursome was late getting out of Belfast.

The plane taxied down the run way as everyone aboard settled in for the long trip to the U.S. Ruari and Eamon sat together while Sean and Dermot sat four rows behind them. Ruari and Eamon had made peace, understanding that each of them played a role in trying to unite Ireland. Ruari especially felt this after the meeting with Margaret Thatcher.

Eamon was anxious to find out how that meeting went. He looked around the Aerlingus Airbus, which was three quarters full, and saw two window seats toward the front, which would give them some needed privacy. Once they were well on their way, the fasten seat belt sign had gone off, and before the beverage cart made its rounds Eamon said, "Father, follow me."

They sat down and before Ruari had his seatbelt fastened Eamon said, "So how'd the meeting at 10 Downing go?"

Ruari looked around to make sure they were alone and said, "Interesting. We waited an hour and a half past our scheduled appointment to get into her office."

"What time was your appointment?"

"Six thirty."

"So you got in at eight?"

"Aye. Cardinal Byrne doesn't like to wait for anyone and I'm talking the Holy Pontiff himself. He takes pride in seeing people when he is scheduled to and he expects the same in return."

"Thatcher can't always control her schedule; she's the Prime Minister of Great Britain, for Christ sake."

"Watch your language."

"Don't start, Father."

"Anyway, the tension was thick from the get go."

"How so?"

"She asked us what we'd like to drink and the Cardinal asked for Irish. All I've got is Scotch, says she."

"Does that astonish you?"

"I know, so he asked why she wouldn't stock whiskey from all of her provinces."

"He did?"

"Aye. The first shot was then sent over the bow when she said she didn't care for the Irish…whiskey that is. Unable to contain myself, especially when she laid it so neatly in front of me I said, well that's okay Madame Prime Minister I, at least, like the Scotch…whiskey that is. Her sour smile could've curdled milk. Then the Prelate himself said he was being obdurate and that Scotch Whiskey was fine, especially after the ninety minute wait."

Eamon laughed out and said, "That is beautiful, absolutely beautiful."

"At any rate, being well aware of how you lads were angry at the clergy and the Church after the fiasco at the end of the last hunger strike, he went right to it. The second strike was to begin shortly, says he. How is that my problem? Says she. Since your government reneged on the verbal agreement reached after the first strike, it sure is your problem, says he. Her response was the same old horse shit of not being aware of any agreement."

"And you're surprised by that?"

"No, but it was an eye opener. The Cardinal told her he wasn't there to argue that point and that he figured as much, because the English government had been reneging on deals with Ireland for eight hundred years."

"The man has balls."

"Considerable, Aye. So he says he's come to appeal to her more moderate sensibilities, which I now know she has none. He then said that the power of her pen could save the lives of the hunger strikers, and that he was certain the lads would die on this second strike."

"But of course there's no trying to be reasonable with the unreasonable. How did she respond to that?"

"There must be some confusion here, says she. That this matter had nothing to do with any decision that she did or did not make and everything to do with the decision made by these criminals."

"No revelation there, why do you think we call her Tin Knickers?"

"They're not criminals, says the Cardinal. All they're asking for is five simple demands. Yes, those demands and trying to make Great Britain out to be the big, bad bully, says she. Yet she could still not acquiesce because then it becomes political and the same crap about this not being political and that these men are criminals and murderers.

"That's when I finally stepped in, unable to keep quiet a second longer. So Great Britain's occupation of Ulster is not political? Says I. Well of course it is, says she. Then why would men who see you as invaders and occupiers of their sacred and ancient ancestral land, who are willing to fight for their freedom from a foreign oppressor, be labeled criminal? Says I."

Eamon said, "Good for you."

"Because they are murderers breaking the laws of the land, says she. What are your RUC and the bloody UDR if not murderers, lads who work with the UVF and UDA to plan the assassination of Catholic businessmen, if not murderers, says I. They are peace keepers, says she, doing their jobs to keep criminals like these Republicans from breaking the laws of the land. And what about the Loyalist businesses targeted by the IRA? Is that not the same? We didn't come to open old wounds, says the Cardinal. We simply want to save the men on hunger strike and you can do that.'"

"And she calls us criminals. But we knew all of this before your going in."

"Eamon, I haven't told you anything you really didn't already know, yet. So we sit there sipping our whiskey like the next one to speak loses. Then the Prelate himself speaks up again. Ireland has been a thorn in the side of the English for the last eight hundred years, says he, so why not pull out and let the Irish take care of Ireland. That is the most ridiculous thing I've ever heard, says she, that would be similar to the US giving Texas back to Mexico."

The two men, eyes wide, stared at one another and Ruari said, "Lad, the Cardinal and I stared at each other like you and I are now, knowing sure now that our lads are certain to die."

Eamon sat very still as if the weight of all those men on hunger strike weighed heavily on his very soul. He sighed and said. "We really shouldn't be surprised by any of this. Why the hell do you think that the lads are hunger striking again? To fight this sort of ignorance at the highest levels and to expose it to the world."

"I know, I know, but one of the greatest experiences of my life was watching the Prelate himself drop the stink bomb in old tin knickers office that would permeate the fabric of that high office for years to come."

"Madame Prime Minister we have a bit of a problem that we think you should be made aware of, says he. And what would that be? Says she. Your people have arrested an American citizen, mistaking him for a Republican. He was interrogated and tortured in Castlereagh, put before the Diplock court, and sent to Long Kesh for life, says he. Is this some kind of Irish trickery, says she. I assure you Madame Prime Minister this is no trick, says he. His name is Mick Quinlan, he's from a ranch in Montana and the twin brother of Martin O'Kane, says he. You mean the assassin we arrested in

Dublin last week, says she. I mean the Republican you *think* you arrested in Dublin last week, says he. Excellency, says she, let's not mince words here. What you are saying may have very dour consequences. The Cardinal himself, unable to stay seated stood and walked to the Prime Minister's desk and looked down at her. No, Madame Prime Minister, says he, what I am saying *will* have dour consequences. He then went on to explain that the American twin had quite innocently and unexpectedly walked right into this mess."

Eamon said, "How did she respond?"

"Never one to be intimidated by anyone, anywhere, she stood to meet her adversary. If this is some kind of cheap trick, says she, to get one of Northern Irelands most heinous criminals released from a life sentence he so justly deserves, you will rue the day."

"She said that to a Cardinal?

"Aye. But did the man back down? No, nay, never. He looked her square in the eye and they stared for an uncomfortable moment. No, Madame Prime Minister, 'tis no cheap trick, says he, 'tis the truth. 'Tis a grave mistake made by a British Government that is unable to yield or bend and unable to admit when they have made mistakes, grave mistakes. But my words will have proof within the week. This meeting is over, says she. I'll be back one week from tonight, says he, and I expect to be seen on time. With that we walked out without another word."

Eamon smiled and said, "Well then it's Plan A. I don't think she'll bite on Plan A, but at least she'll know the truth."

Ruari asked the stewardess for a whiskey and said, "Plan B is what scares me."

"Don't worry Padre, Martin O'Kane is slick, he'll take care of you."

"One can only hope, cara."

They sat lost in their thoughts as the giant air craft glided effortlessly above the clouds, soaring across the North Atlantic with ease and grace.

Ruari said, "Anyway, as we got back to The Archbishop House and just before you lads picked me up the Cardinal received a phone call. It turns out he has a mole somewhere inside Ten Downing, not a big deal, just another set of ears and eyes, I guess an Irish sympathizer. So he calls and tells the Cardinal that a half hour after we left the Secretary to Northern Ireland comes walking in disheveled, hair sticking up and got his arse chewed.

Eamon laughed and said, "Wish I could've been a fly on the wall."

"Aye."

"I think your meeting was a success."

"We got the message delivered."

* * *

“Gray here.”

“Did you arrest the wrong man, Mr. Gray?”

“Excuse me, sir?”

“Mr. Gray I am getting sick and tired of taking the brunt of your foul ups.”

“Sir?”

“The Prime Minister has it on good authority, Mr. Gray, that you arrested the wrong man. As this gets stranger, apparently O'Kane is the Irish Twin of a bloody Yank. And your team arrested the American brother.”

“I’ve never heard so much hogwash. I personally participated in the interrogation. O’Kane is a bloody chameleon, but we have got Martin O’Kane.”

“Oh bloody hell, Gray, you had better or it’s your ass!”

William Gray set the phone down and was visibly shaking. They had arrested the wrong man, he knew it then, but he refused to believe it. The scotch that burned his throat never served the medicinal purpose it did now.

Chapter 67
The Hard Cold Truth

The next day

Martin O'Kane was drunk when Dan Mulroy, Eamon Gainey, Sean O'Kane and Ruari O'Keefe walked into Sullivan's. Eamon, who had no time for over consumption said, "Dan, what the hell is going on here?"

Martin looked up with bloodshot eyes.

Dan said, "Eamon, it's been hard on him since he found out who Paddy Quinlan was. Plus, he can't walk a foot in this place without one of the regulars buying him a drink. Hell, I'd have trouble staying sober."

Eamon said, "Let's get the lad upstairs to bed. We need him sober and moving. He's been like this since I've known him."

Ruari said, "How's that?"

"He can keep more balls in the air at one time than anyone I've ever met. But when he's idle he takes up with the very devil himself."

Sean took his son under one arm and Ruari under the other and lifted him off his seat.

Martin said, "Da?"

Sean said, "Don't lad, let's get you to bed."

Martin said, "No Da, would you tell me a story? You know like you use to when Fergal and I were wee."

Sean smiled with a mist in his eye and said, "Aye, lad, anything to get you to sleep."

The next morning, over strong cups of hot coffee, the five men sat around Mulroy's kitchen table.

Eamon said, "Lad…"

Sean raised a hand and said, "Eamon, let me do this."

Eamon nodded at his friend and Sean said, "Martin, I should've done this a long time ago."

He looked across the table at the pale, hungover young man, who looked lost and confused sitting opposite him and tears welled in his eyes seeing his son this disheveled.

Martin, seeing this, said, "Da, what is it?"

Sean lit a cigarette and said, "Twenty years ago, your mother and I weren't able to have children. A childhood friend of your mum's, a nun in Dublin, called and asked if we wanted to adopt."

Ruari sighed aloud at the memory of the whole period, still as painful today as a gaping wound.

"And?"

"We adopted you."

Silence hung in the kitchen like the rain soaked roof of a canvass tent.

"So I'm not your son?"

"Of course you are, lad."

"I am?"

Ruari said, "Have you known any other Da?'

"No I haven't. But why wasn't I told."

Sean said, "I don't know, lad. There was just never a good time. I guess we just kept putting it off for a better time."

The four men looked at one another silently, deciding who was to proceed.

The aspersion surfaced like foam on a violent seashore, Martin said, "So you just decided to tell me now, here, three thousand miles from home, in front of other men, some strangers."

Sean cleared his throat, knowing this wasn't going to be easy said, "Martin, there's more."

Martin said, "I could've guessed as much."

Sean looked at the other men as if for help and said, "Lad, you've got a brother."

"Da? Of course I have a brother."

"No lad, I don't mean Fergal. I mean another brother, you have a twin brother who was adopted by an Irish National in America at the same time we brought you home."

Martin said, "What the fuck?"

The room around them seemed to inhale and then exhale, allowing a bit of relief for the building pressure.

"Where is he?"

"Where's who?"

"My twin Da, my fucking twin."

Eamon stepped in and said, "Take it easy Martin, your Da did his best and if it wasn't good enough for you then tough shyte."

"Tough shyte is it? Well then fuck all of you."

Martin began to slide his chair back, Eamon said in the low menacing voice of a commander-in-chief to a mutinous subordinate, "We're not finished here soldier so slide that chair back to the table now."

"Aye, sir," a soldier once again.

"To answer your question, your twin is a lad named Mick Quinlan and he sits now in your place in Long Kesh."

"What? Mick Quinlan? Why's that name so familiar? Da, did we know some Quinlans growing up?"

The four men looked at one another once again, moving delicately, not wishing to be the one to trip on one of the emotional land mines that dotted the current landscape.

Eamon said, "Martin, Paddy Quinlan. . ."

The look in Martin's eye registered recognition and he physically gasped. A sick moan left his lips, he ran to the kitchen sink, and the bile in his throat did the rest as he realized he had killed his brother's father. When he finished, he stood, resting his hands on the kitchen sink, bent over in anguish.

Eamon said, "Lad, its war and sometimes innocent people are killed. I know this brings little relief but it's a dirty fucking job some days.

"Mick Quinlan was coming to Ireland to join his father when you shot him along with Millington. You were following orders like any good soldier and the man accidentally got in the way. It's fate. You left the country as ordered to and your brother came in at nearly the same time. The key suspect on this was you, as we predicted it would be, and that's why we were having you leave until things cooled down. His luck and timing couldn't have been worse. They had the airport covered and he walked right into their net. This is not the way I wanted this played out but it is what it is."

Martin turned with blood shot eyes and a putrid taste in his mouth and said, "It is what it is? Are you serious?"

Eamon, ignoring the outburst, said, "You've met Father Ruari O'Keefe?"

"Aye, so?"

"The good Father here is the Chaplain for the brotherhood at Long Kesh. We have a plan A and a plan B, and the British will decide for us which we run with."

Martin said, "I'm listening."

Chapter 68
The Hunger Strike

Prisoners Announce New Strike

By Cassie Kenny

(UPI) Feb 5,1981 Republican political prisoners today announced that they will begin a new hunger strike starting March 1, 1981. The prisoners maintained that they were "morally blackmailed" by local politicians and the Catholic Church during and after the last hunger strike. A spokesman for the prisoners, who has chosen to remain anonymous, said to the politicians and the Church hierarchy, "What did your recommended ending of the last hunger strike gain for us? Where is the peace in the prisons which, like a promise, was held before dying men's eyes?"

The first man to go on strike will be Bobby Sands on March 1, 1981. He will be followed in two weeks by Francis Hughes and Raymond McCreesh, all of the provisional IRA. Then Patsy O'Hara, commanding officer in Long Kesh prison of the INLA, Irish National Liberation Army, a radical branch of the Provisional IRA.

In 1976, Great Britain brought a policy of criminalization to Northern Ireland in which they took POW status away from all prisoners whom they deemed paramilitary, both Republican and Loyalists. These prisoners were no longer considered prisoners of war, but common criminal inmates. With the POW status gone, so were the rights that went with it.

The initial hunger strike and the one recently announced to follow March 1st by Republican prisoners in Long Kesh prison is to protest the fact that they do not believe themselves criminals, but prisoners of war, and that they want certain rights restored. The five demands that they are striking for are: 1) The right to their own clothing. 2) The right not to do prison work. 3) The right of free association with other prisoners. 4) The right to organize their own educational and recreational facilities. 5) The right to one visit, one letter and one parcel per week.

Paisley's Response to Republican Hunger strike

By Sean O'Kane

(UPI) Feb 6, 1981 Ian Paisley, the leader of the second largest Unionist party in Northern Ireland, invited five journalists to the hills north of Belfast yesterday morning for a secret meeting to unearth his most recent plans to fight any sort of reunification of Ireland on which the governments of Ireland and Great Britain may be working.

The journalists were in the back of a van whose only rear windows were covered in black. When they came to a stop hooded men unloaded them and walked them to a scene in which Dr. Paisley, in a booming voice, was addressing five hundred men. A whistle blew and the five hundred men each held up a firearms certificate which would allow them to legally carry a weapon, even though they were not soldiers in the British army, a certificate that is illegal for any soldier of the IRA or any other citizen in Northern Ireland to obtain.

Dr Paisley then led the journalists on an inspection of his troops and he was quoted as saying, "The British and Irish governments are conspiring in secret towards Irish reunification, and these 500 men are representative of the thousands prepared to defend their province and their rights in exactly the same way as Lord Carson and his Ulster Volunteer Force.

"We will shortly challenge the Government to interfere with us and our province if they dare and we will, with equanimity, await the result. We will do this regardless of the consequences of all personal loss or of all inconvenience. They may tell us if they like that that is treason. It is not for men who have such stake as we have to trouble with the costs."

Paisley was referring to the army of 100,000 Loyalist volunteers Lord Carson raised in 1916 to combat any chance of a reunified Ireland during the Irish War for Independence.

Chapter 69
The Revelation

English Embassy, New York City

March 14, 1981

The first hunger strike that ended in December of 1980 due to an agreement broken by the British Government, started and ended with seven men. None of those men died.

The Republican Prisoners within Long Kesh knew that in order to succeed they had to plan the new strike differently to maximize pressure on Great Britain. The plan was to start the strike with one man and add men every few days or weeks in order to lengthen the process.

Bobby Sands was in his fourteenth day when his cousin, Francis Hughes, joined him on hunger strike. The British government, through The Northern Ireland Secretary of State, made it clear that they had no intentions of making any concessions to those on hunger strike, even as international pressure to end the strike was mounting. The sense was that the Republicans were going to finish the job this time and the people of good will around the globe were incensed.

The protesters outside the British Embassy in New York City were growing daily.

Martin said, "This looks like a good spot, Dan."

Dan said, "Okay Martin, stand over here so we have the embassy in the background with the protesters. Are you ready to do this?"

Martin nodded, held his notes like a street reporter and began speaking as the camera began recording, "Prime Minister Thatcher. My name is Martin Peder O'Kane, a proud member of the Irish Republican Army in the struggle to rid Ireland of all foreign oppressors. Please note the date at the bottom right hand side of your screen. It is March 14th and I am standing in front of your embassy in New York City."

The camera scanned the building and the protesters so there was no misunderstanding or doubt.

"I'm participating in the video so that you'll understand that your government made a grand mistake when you arrested me long lost twin brother. It has come to our attention that he was ruthlessly tortured and has since been incarcerated in Her Majesty's prison at Long Kesh. And when your lads in MI5 were told time and again that he was not who you thought he was, they scoffed.

"So your situation, as a ruthless intellectual like yourself will certainly surmise, is delicate. Not only do you have high powered Irish American officials breathing down your neck to end the hunger strike, but now you have jailed one of their innocent citizens who came to Ireland on holiday."

* * *

Father Ruari O'Keefe and Cardinal Byrne sat and watched the faces of The Prime Minister and Secretary of State for Northern Ireland as their faces grew more pale, a trick the Irish Prelate didn't think possible.

When the video had finished Prime Minister Thatcher said, "Cardinal Byrne this is beneath you."

The Cardinal said, "Excuse me."

"Any fool can manipulate film. This meeting is over, Good day, gentleman."

"There was no manipulation of film, that is a preposterous accusation. You have an innocent man in jail and I want him released."

"I said, good day gentlemen."

Ruari felt weak in his knees as the thought came to him that plan A didn't work and that plan B wouldn't work and as a result he'd probably be sitting in Long Kesh with the Republicans by this time next week. It was a damn good thing the Cardinal knew nothing of plan B.

The clergymen left the office and Mrs. Thatcher looked at the Secretary of Northern Ireland, who really did not want to be there right now, and said, "Did you know this?"

"I suspected."

"That's not what I asked."

"I didn't know for sure, how could I?"

"How do you propose that we wriggle out of this?"

"I don't know."

"Well by this time tomorrow you better know."

Chapter 70
The Angst of the Mothers

The next day

Clare had the day off. Eamon had left that morning with Ruari for America. Cassie was working long hard days covering the troubles in the North and now the hunger strike. Clare felt alone, in the way, left out and very vulnerable.

She rented a car and drove south out of County Antrim into County Down, with all its rolling glens and drumlins that locals described as looking at a basket of eggs.

With no plans for a final destination she decided to head east and maybe a catharsis of salt water, cleansing her mind and soul. She came to the village of Strangford and stopped for a cup of tea before heading to the water's edge.

She pulled into a parking lot for public use and got out. The smell of the salty sea air filled her senses and she knew then that she had made the right decision. A ferry was just leaving and an old man sitting on a nearby bench looked up at her and said, "The next one leaves at half ten."

She said, "What?"

"The ferry. The next one leaves at half ten."

"Oh no, I just came to sit by the water."

Friendly and lonely he patted the bench and said, "Well then have a seat."

Not what she had intended and yet not wanting to offend the lonely old man she sat down.

He said, "You're not from around here, are you?"

"No."

"I'm guessing Kilkenny or maybe Tipperary."

She smiled and said, "Kilkenny."

"Aye, lovely county, Kilkenny."

"Aye, I do miss it."

"Well, welcome to Strangifjorthi."

"Excuse me?"

"Strangifjorthi."

"Aye, I heard you, what does that mean?"

"When the Norsemen sailed into this inlet a thousand years ago that's what they named it."

"You mean the Vikings?"

"Aye. It means *lake of the strong currents* in Danish."

She chuckled and said as if to herself, "Sounds like my life, except maybe it should be named violent currents, or better yet, what's Danish for lake of the constant tempest?"

She lit a cigarette and offered him one. He gladly accepted it and thanked her as she lit it for him.

She pointed to the ferry as she exhaled and said, "I thought this was the ocean, the sea."

"Technically, it's Strangford Loch, the largest tidal inlet in Ireland. So it's fed by the ocean. The ferry runs across to Portaferry, and from there, the coast is minutes away."

"Well it's gorgeous here."

"Aye, 'tis."

The old man tossed his cigarette to the wind and folded the newspaper he was reading and set it down on the bench between them. She looked down and noticed at the top the letters 'LACHT' and knew them to be the last five letters in An Phoblacht, the republican newspaper, and now knew his leanings.

She said, "My roommate is Cassie Kenny."

He nodded and said, "Just finished her article on the lads starting the second hunger strike. Up Ireland! So you live in Belfast now?"

"Aye. I just needed a break from the craziness and ended up here at the water's edge, trying for a bit of peace and serenity."

"Aye, I don't blame you. But I've always felt for those who can't get out even for a bit."

"Who do you mean?"

"The unemployed Nationalists standing around because they're Catholic and can't get work, those people who live in the middle of The Troubles not out of choice but circumstance, and don't have the wherewithal to pull out for a break once in a while."

She looked at him and a light went on. The last thing she wanted was conversation and yet without this wise old man with Republican leanings she'd still feel vulnerable and directionless.

She said, "What's your name, sir?"

"What does it matter?"

"I'd like to thank you properly."

"That I've helped you in any way is thanks enough. What matters more than my name is that you get to who you need to get to and soon."

"How did you know?"

"I've been around a very long time and I've learned to keep more than just my eyes open."

* * *

The Nationalists of the Short Strand Neighborhood in North Belfast were like an island in a sea of Loyalist. Brick, cement and metal fences were erected as if to keep them caged in. The Post Office, Grocery store, pharmacy and clothing shops were all located outside the Short Strand, as if daring those Nationalists to spend their dole on the necessities of life. During marching season they paid an exceptionally heavy price to gain access to their daily bread, especially the elderly.

Clare's rental car rolled uneasily down Beechfield Street and came to a stop outside a humble home that rested anxiously inside the Short Strand. She got out of her car and the kids playing kick ball on the street stopped and stared at the outsider, the stranger that invaded their fortress. The look was of unfriendly suspicion, as if wondering what strife the stranger brought to interrupt their play.

She waved to them and smiled to let them know she meant no harm, and she walked to the door of the intended home. She knocked and Patricia Brennan O'Kane opened it a crack with the thick chain holding the other side. She stared for a moment and then it opened a bit wider and finally said, "May I help you?"

"Patricia O'Kane?"

Nothing.

"Look, me name's Clare White. I'm a friend of Martin's."

"My Martin?"

"Aye."

"How?"

"Can I come in? I mean no harm. I'm also a friend of Father Ruari O'Keefe."

The door was opened and Patricia finally smiled and said, "I'm sorry to be so rude. But we never know who to trust living here. Especially when a stranger knocks."

The home was humble but immaculate with a bloody crucifix hanging just above a black jack on the kitchen wall.

Patricia said, "Please sit, I'll make tea."

Clare said, "I'd be grateful."

The teakettle whistled and Patricia came back with steaming mugs of black tea and sugar cookies.

Clare smiled and said, "Can I ask you a question, or maybe more of an observation?"

"What's that?"

"It's not everyday that you see the black jack of an RUC man hanging below a Crucifix."

"You've seen the murals up and down the Crumlin Road?"

"Aye.

"This is me own private mural. It represents the injustice we live with everyday for the beliefs we hold and the freedom we fight for."

She then went on to tell the story of how she had come by the baton. Clare smiled at this small woman who looked as tough as two men. She was glad that Martin was raised in this home.

Patricia said, "So what brings you to The Short Strand?"

"You. It was brought to my attention, quite by accident, how you must be feeling now with both of your lads gone."

"It's a price we pay in our fight for freedom from a foreign oppressor, but how did you know?"

Clare looked at her and said, "I gave birth to twin boys twenty years ago last September in a convent in Dublin."

Patricia stared at the woman sitting across from her. She had lived in Northern Ireland her entire life. She had grown up in Portadown in the heart of the Devil's Triangle, she had moved to Derry's infamous Bogside neighborhood during the 1968 civil rights movement and now she married into The Short Strand. She had seen a lot and was not afraid of a fight and was rarely rattled. She was now rattled.

The tears rolled down her cheeks and Clare continued, "I've kept up on these two lads ever since, never interfering, mind, but just staying aware of where they were and what they were doing. Cassie Kenny is my roommate."

"The Cassie Kenny who works with my Sean on stories?"

"The very same. So I knew that they got Fergal and I know now that Martin has been sent abroad and it suddenly dawned on me that you had lost your two lads."

More tears.

Clare said, "Well, I lost two lads twenty years ago and I remembered how much I hurt. Then I realized that I didn't even really know them. But just carrying them for nine months and losing them was bad. Then it dawned on me that you raised these lads and lost them and that you may need a friend or at least someone to talk to so I've come."

Patricia Brennan O'Kane reached across the table and put her hands on Clare's and said, "You've no idea how lonely I've been and the pain of really losing my lads."

"No I don't, but I've got an idea and that's why I came."

Chapter 71
Hunger Strike Accelerates

Sean O'Kane
March 15, 1981

(UPI) The Republican prisoners at Long Kesh announced today that Francis Hughes will join Bobby Sands on hunger strike. The British Government's only comment after fifteen days of this strike was, "The government will not surrender control of what goes on in the prisons to a particular group of prisoners. It will not concede the demand for the political status, or recognize that murder and violence are less culpable because they are claimed to be committed for political motives."

Bobby Sands, on the fourteenth day of his hunger strike, said, "They (The British) have nothing in their whole imperial arsenal that can break the spirit of one Irishman who doesn't want to be broken."

According to a source inside the IRA command outside the Kesh, "The hunger strike is and always will be the plan of the men inside the Kesh. They requested the strike, they organized the strike and each man on the strike is doing so of his own volition. We do, however, support them fully and have given them our approval. Hunger striking is an ancient, time-honored Irish form of protest against one's oppressors."

Sands up in Fermanagh/South Tyrone

By Cassie Kenny
March 26, 1981

(UPI) Irish politics have always been full of surprises with unexpected twists and turns but this may be one of the most unexpected surprises of all. Bobby Sands, Republican prisoner in Long Kesh prison on hunger strike, was nominated today as a candidate in the by-election in Fermanagh/South Tyrone due to the sudden death of Frank Maguire, Independent MP in that district. Sands will run on the Anti-H Block/Armagh political prisoner ticket.

Trying to eliminate any propaganda by the British Government that Sinn Fein or the IRA have no public support, they put up Bobby Sands for the seat. Noel Maguire, brother of the deceased MP, said that he would not run against a Republican prisoner, let alone one on hunger strike. And Owen Carron, the Socialist Democratic and Labor Party member who was up for the seat, was embarrassed into withdrawing after the statement from

Maguire. This clears the way for Sands to go head-to-head with Harry West, running on the Ulster Unionist party ticket.

Sands Taken to Hospital Ward
By Sean O'Kane
March 28, 1981

(UPI) While Ian Paisley, the head of the Democratic Unionist Party (DUP) addressed thirty thousand of his faithful at a rally held at Stormont today, protesting talks being held by the Irish and British governments, Bobby Sands, Republican hunger striker on his 28th Day without food, was taken to the hospital ward at Long Kesh to be watched by the medical staff.

Bobby Sands Elected to Parliament
By Cassie Kenny
April 9, 1981

(UPI) Bobby Sands, on his thirty-eighth day of a hunger strike that started on March 1, 1981, was elected as a Member of Parliament for the district of Fermanagh/South Tyrone by the slimmest of margins. Sands beat Harry West the Unionist party member 30,492 votes to 29,046 with 86.9% of the district turning out, its largest ever.

Thatcher Won't Meet
By Sean O'Kane
April 21, 1981

(UPI) Margaret Thatcher, during a press conference in Saudi Arabia today, said that she had no interest in meeting with the three Teachtai Dalas, members of the Irish Parliament, stating that she had no intentions of talks with members of a foreign nation about problems dealing with citizens of Great Britain. She then added, "We are not prepared to consider special category status for certain groups of people serving sentences for crime. Crime is crime is crime, it is not political."

Chapter 72
From A to B

New York

March 28, 1981

It had been two weeks since the video had been made and the men had left New York to go back to Ireland. Martin, left behind, was at the end of his tether. He was homesick, restless and he needed to be active once again, if for no other reason than to save himself from himself. Dan Mulroy asked him to meet him at his house.

Dan had a wood working shop in the back of his garage and in his spare time he worked on building beautiful wood furniture with ornate wood carvings. With all the other activity in his life, it might take him a year to finish a piece, but it would usually fetch ten, sometimes fifteen thousand dollars, and it all began as therapy to help him relax.

He walked into the kitchen from his workshop and put a brown paper sack on the kitchen table. He then pulled an envelope from the inside pocket of his jean jacket and threw it on the table hard enough so it would slide to where Martin sat.

Dan said, "Plan A failed. Thatcher didn't bite, but then again we didn't think she would. All we really wanted to do was make sure she had proof that her boys fucked up."

Martin nodded and said, "Aye."

Dan said, "So it's plan B now."

"Which is?"

"I don't know. I just take care of the business they want done on this side of the pond."

Martin opened the envelope and saw a one-way ticket to Glasgow, Scotland. He quickly scanned the itinerary and saw that he was in Glasgow for a ninety-minute layover and then it was a puddle jumper to Ayr, Scotland. It also contained a fake passport for a Liam Dolan.

Dan gave him a chance to digest the contents of the package and said, "You fly tonight at 9:30 p.m. By noon tomorrow you'll be in Ayr, Scotland. When you walk out of the airport to the taxi stand you'll see a man standing in front of taxi #5581 smoking a cigarette and reading the newspaper. He'll be wearing a jersey for the Scots National Rugby team. If he's not wearing the jersey, walk away. When you meet him you'll say, 'Where can a lad get a drop of good Irish whiskey around here.' He'll respond, 'He can't. But I'll show you where a lad might get some good Scotch whiskey if he has a mind.' And you'll answer, 'That'll have to do then.'

"He'll drive you to the docks on the Firth of Clyde where you'll board *The Hercules,* a merchant ship headed to Derry. Once docked you'll be contacted."

"By who? And what if I'm recognized?"

"The people who you want to meet will know who you are and the people who you don't won't have a clue because you'll be wearing this."

Dan held up the white soutanis worn by the Columban Missionary Fathers in the Philippines. Ruari had left it behind.

He said, "You'll also be wearing these."

He held up some sandals and a large brimmed straw hat.

Martin could do nothing but smile and then said, "Well, then what's in the bag?"

Dan pulled out an authentic looking German Walther pistol that he had carved out of wood in his shop. It had been sanded, painted and looked to be the real thing until you picked it up.

Martin said, "What's that for?"

Dan shrugged and said, "Don't know. The lads know I'm good with wood and I was told to carve this, make it look good and make sure you packed it."

By noon, forty-eight hours later, Martin O'Kane sat in the office of Father Ruari O'Keefe in the rectory of Holy Cross Parish in the Ardoyne neighborhood of Belfast.

Unlike the rural members of the standing IRA, the urban members of the brotherhood were skeptical of the Catholic Church and its clergy. Martin was no exception, especially after they intervened to help stop the last hunger strike only to find out later that the English Government had no intentions of living by their verbal agreement.

Martin said, "What am I doing here? And where the hell's Eamon?"

Ruari said, "I asked him if I could meet with you first and spend a bit of time with you."

Martin shrugged and said, "All right, what's on your mind?"

Ruari said, "I know the distrust that you and your Belfast comrades have for the clergy. But I need you to trust me if we're to succeed."

"Succeed at what?"

"That's for Eamon to go over with you when he gets here tonight."

Martin tired and out of sorts from his recent travels and in no mood to wait for Eamon, said, "Jaysus, what next?"

Ruari said, "But you need to know something."

Martin said, "Look Father, I'm weak from travel and would like to lay down a bit. So if you could get on with it."

Ruari said, "I'm your biological father."

Martin said, "Right, and for an encore monkeys will now fly out your arse."

Ruari just stared and said no more. The message was clear and Martin, a man unable to sit still for long under normal circumstances, stood and said, "This is too much for me right now. Can you show me to a bed. . .Father?"

At seven o'clock that evening Martin walked into Ruari's office, where he was talking with Eamon and his uncle Dermot. Even after sleep and food he looked like Atlas ready to crumble under the weight.

By midnight they had adjourned with Plan B scheduled for May 7, 1981.

Chapter 73
Mick's Turn

Long Kesh Prison

Mid February 1981

Fergal O'Kane, by all accounts, had the IQ of a genius. Raised in The Short Strand, his education was spotty at best.

He and Martin were subjected to ridicule and harassment in public school and their parents were unable to afford parochial school.

As a result they both dropped out in high school, but Fergal's education was far from over. He was a voracious reader and he spent as much time listening to the tales of his father and other Seanachie as he could. He absorbed the oral history as if his mind was a patch of dry earth welcoming the long awaited rain. He also read as many books of Irish history as he could get his hands on. Where Martin joined the IRA for emotional reasons, Fergal looked at it from a historical perspective. In doing so he knew that it was his time to join the fight to rid the land of the eight hundred-year-old monster that had haunted his homeland.

Fergal was not only a student but a teacher as well and was a talented storyteller, a gift handed down by his father and grandfather. Thus, it was that Mick Quinlan was to gain his associates degree in Irish history from the University of Long Kesh.

The days that had previously gone on forever for Fergal were now filled with lectures to his new and eager student. It all began with a question, as Bobby Sands and the nine others all contemplated a hunger strike that was to begin in two weeks. Mick had to understand what drove them to do this.

He said, "Fergal, why would a man hunger strike to death? It just seems crazy to me."

Fergal, covered in nothing more than a threadbare brown blanket, held class. He said, "Mick, it's not a question answered so easily, you have to fully understand the history of Ireland. Then and only then will you understand why these men are willing to put their lives on the line to unmask their oppressor to the world outside."

For the next seven weeks Fergal paced six steps up and six steps back, six steps up and six steps back in their small cell and lectured Mick on Ireland's history. He stopped occasionally to drink some water or answer a question by Mick. But most days, for twelve or so hours he went on. Being a

Seanachie in his own right he was an outstanding storyteller and a magnificent historian. Mick, being a captive audience, in the truest sense of the word, enjoyed every minute of it.

Fergal started with the Tuatha de Danaan, some of Ireland's earliest occupants.

He said, "We're not sure where exactly they came from. We think they're Norse, but they came to Ireland on flying ships."

Mick said, "What?"

The hostile glare he received from Fergal put an end to the verbal skepticism.

"The ships flew around the world nine times to find the perfect spot to land. They decided it was Ireland so they then burned their ships. With them they brought the Lia Fall."

"Burned their ships?"

"Aye. They found the island so enticing that they had no need to leave ever again."

"What is a Lia Fall?"

"The Stone of Destiny, which they laid on the Mound of Tara, also known as the Mound of Kings in County Meath. The Stone called out to the rightful Kings of Ireland, thus choosing them."

Mick hung his head and thought, holy shit, if this is going to be a bunch of mythology.

Fergal then spoke of the great early kings like Conor MacNessa, Cormac MacArt and Finn MacCool, the Fenian patriarch, all chosen by the Lia Fall.

To Mick's great delight he told stories of Cuchulain, Ireland's greatest soldier, and then Niall of the Nine Hostages, the father of the O'Neill clan. He went into all of the Irish Saints, specifically her patrons Patrick and his staff, Kevin and his thumb and Bridget with her cross. He told Mick the story of Colm Cille, the poet Saint, and of his exile.

He spoke in great detail of the storied past of the Celts and the Gaels, the Irish poets and the Viking invasion. He told of Brian Boru, the last High King of Ireland and the father of the O'Brien clan.

By now they had spent three weeks, day in and day out, and soon other prisoners were listening down the walls and asking questions as well. The only difference now was that Fergal was wearing prison clothing and the walls in their cell were immaculate. As of March 1, 1981 Bobby Sands had gone on hunger strike and as a show of complete solidarity, all other protests had been called off.

Mick had never enjoyed school as much in his life. He would lie on his bed, then sit on its edge, then pace with Fergal and ask questions, and then he might sit in the corner and then back to the bed. All day long changing positions and listening intently. He grew to love Fergal like the brother he never had growing up and they became fast friends. This also allowed Mick to immerse himself in something other than the loss of his father, thus enabling him to avoid thinking of his dad and the despair that awaited him there.

One day, into the fourth week of lecturing, Fergal said, "Mick, remember how you asked me why a man would go on hunger strike?'

"Yeah."

Fergal said, "It all started in 1171 when England invaded Ireland using a Papal Bull from an English Pope given under false pretense."

"What the hell is a Papal Bull?"

"It's a decree from The Pope."

"Why did they need that?"

"To justify invading Ireland, Henry II, who was the King of England at the time, wanted Ireland for himself so he went to Pope Adrian IV and told him that Ireland had lapsed into moral despair due to the centuries of invasion and influence of the Viking Danes, who were, according to him, nothing more than a bunch of savage pagans."

"So?"

"So he told the Pope he was going to Ireland to bring her back to the one true faith which was so much bullshit. Henry II hated the Church as much as he hated the Irish. He simply needed justification to invade and was given it by the Papal Bull that he lied to get."

From there he told Mick about the illegal midnight parliament held by Henry VIII to declare himself King of Ireland and head of the Church of England, all the while outlawing the Catholic Church in Ireland, a decision that held for the next three hundred years.

He spoke of the Catholic and Irish blood that ran red in the fields due to the Battle of the Boyne, Oliver Cromwell's invasion of Ireland, and of the Williamite Wars. He spoke of the great Irish patriots like Theobold Wolfe Tone, martyred when he rose up against his English oppressor with his United Irishman in 1798. He spoke of Robert Emmett's failed rising in 1803 and his infamous courtroom speech before he went to the gallows.

Fergal stopped, turned around, and stared out the window as if in a sudden trance and said, " 'Let no man write my epitaph; for no man who knows my motives dares now to vindicate them. Let not prejudice or ignorance asperse them. When my country takes her place among nations of the earth, then and only then, let my epitaph be written.'"

Mick said, "Was that Emmett?"

Fergal said, "Aye. Patriots like Wolf Tone and Emmett were the inspiration for the likes of The Young Irelanders and their rising in 1848 and The Fenians and their rising in 1867."

Mick said, “So that's why those assholes kept calling me a Fenian bastard when I was at Castlereagh.”

Fergal couldn't help but smile while he winced at the reminder and said, “That's right, because the direct descendants of the Fenians were the Irish Republican Brotherhood, which was the group that rose up in 1916 and we, today's IRA, are direct descendants of the IRB, making us proud Fenians as well. They paid you a compliment calling you a Fenian”

He spoke of the Catholic Emancipation, led by Daniel O’Connell. He said, “After three hundred years of illegal Masses said in caves by priests considered outlaws, hunted down and hung, O'Connell helped pass a bill meant for Home Rule and Catholic Emancipation, but received only the latter.”

He talked about Michael Collins who led the IRA to a stalemate against the English in the war of Irish Independence. He spoke of Charles Stewart Parnell and his political fight for the common Irish.

Fergal said, “Some of these Irish patriots were Catholic, some Protestant but all were unrepentant Fenian bastards fighting for a wholly United Ireland.”

Close to being done now, he started in on the land struggles, English Ascendancy in Ireland, landlordism, and The Land League, a political group developed to protect the rights of poor tenant farmers in the nineteenth century from their greedy English landlords. Then he spoke eloquently of the Great Hunger that held the land in its grip for five years while the English government and its ascendancy in Ireland sat back and watched as one million died and three million left. And he finished by telling Mick of Arthur Griffith’s brainchild, Sinn Fein, the political arm of the IRA, the Easter Rising of 1916 that started the war that ended with the Treaty of 1921, which gave Ireland a Republic for the first time in eight hundred years, but not without a price, a huge price.

Fergal said, “Mick, Eamon DeValera was an Irishman who declared himself the President of the Republic after the rising of 1916, and then he went to America to raise funds for the Irish War of Independence. Michael Collins, his second in command, stayed at home, and led the troops in a guerilla war that successfully forced England into treaty talks.

“Now, DeValera comes back to Ireland and he sends Michael Collins and Arthur Griffith, with a contingent, to England to negotiate this treaty for Ireland, knowing full well that they would be negotiating with their hands tied behind their backs. There was a rift between DeValera and Collins because Collins felt like he was the lamb offered up for slaughter while DeValera, who was gone to America for the majority of the fighting, was now distancing himself from the treaty process for political reasons.

"When the lads got to the negotiating table, Winston Churchill told them that there were to be four non-negotiable clauses in the treaty: 1) The six counties in the North were to be partitioned. 2) Inclusion of an oath to the allegiance of the King of England. 3) The Appointment of a Governor General to represent the British King in Dublin. 4) Certain Irish ports to be retained by England for Her Majesty's Service Navy.

"He said if we didn't like these terms there would be all out war. The Irish lads sitting at the table were the same ones who led the Irish Republican Army against the English army. The IRA was a ragtag lot of mostly farmers who fought brave and won. But if they didn't accept these terms, how were they to put up an army? There was no way for Ireland to fund a war. On the other hand, there would be a Republic for the first time in eight hundred years for a vast majority of Ireland, and they felt like this would be better than nothing at all. They were ultimately damned if they did and damned if they didn't. Collins said that when he signed the treaty, he was signing his death warrant and he spoke the truth.

"But the crux of it for us is the partitioning bit and that's why we're sitting here. After the treaty was signed and the six counties in the North were partitioned, civil war broke out between the pro-treaty factions, or what became known as The Free State Party, and the anti-treaty factions, known as The Republicans.

"The Republicans said, 'Fuck the British,' it was all or nothing and that they would never take an oath of allegiance to a foreign king. And the Free State lads were saying something is better than nothing at all. But after the treaty was signed and the six counties in the North were partitioned it was open season on Republicans and Catholics here. You see, there was a powerful Ulster leader named Sir Edward Carson who hated the Nationalists, was loyal to the English, and saw that the war began to go Ireland's way. So he raised an army of over one hundred thousand men made up of Protestant Loyalists, in anticipation of having to fight Ireland when the English were gone. Even with the partitioned six counties, Lord Carson was angry that the British even negotiated with the Irish.

"As a result, by mid 1922, reports were coming in daily of harassment of Republicans in the North by Carson's Ulster Constabulary and Orangemen. The Republicans that said they would die before they would take an oath to a foreign king and were outraged at the harassment of their brothers in the North, and so civil war broke out between the Republicans and the Free Staters, in which Michael Collins own men killed him, the hero of the war of independence.

"Mick, it's now 1981 and this shyte is still going on and we've had enough. We recognized that the blanket and the dirty protests haven't worked, so it's time to gain world support by taking this to the street with a hunger strike to show the Brits for being the oppressive bastards that they are."

Fergal had finished his history class on April 6, 1981. Bobby Sands had been on hunger strike now for thirty-seven days, Francis Hughes, twenty-two days, Raymond McCreesh, and Patsy O'Hara for sixteen days respectively.

Once Fergal finished, there was too much silence and it became disquieting for Mick. The walls closed in on him as he had too much time to think. He despaired at the loss of his dad and missed him terribly. He had been such a fool, he thought, for leaving the ranch when he could have spent that time with him. He did not even know where they buried him. Did they take him back to the ranch or bury him in Upperchurch?

He missed Thomas Higgins and experienced dreadful pangs of remorse and regret at the loss of his best friend. He kept thinking of Mr. and Mrs. Higgins, which made it all worse.

He missed Montana, the ranch, his friends, the mountains, Flathead Lake, all things he took for granted before. He even missed the stern Consuelo Gonzaga; he would give anything to get his ass chewed in Spanish, just to be home again.

Now he sat in a prison cell in Ireland, mistaken for his twin brother that, he realized, he had felt but had never met. He felt cheated, cheated that they took his freedom, that his dad was taken from him, and cheated that he had a twin brother that he had never known.

But with all that, he felt very much a part of all that was around him now. He had learned much of Irish history just being around his dad growing up, but to hear it in such wondrous detail from a brilliant storyteller like Fergal, who had grown up in the oppression and violence of Ulster, had changed him. Mick always knew he was Irish, but not like this. Now he felt like he was Irish.

He found himself pacing the cell, back and forth, when he finally stopped at the window and looked out at the birds chirping on the power line.

Fergal broke his train of thought and said, "What's on your mind, Mick? You're restless as hell."

Mick said quietly and deliberately, "It's my time, I have to go."

Fergal said, "Go where, lad?"

"On hunger strike. It's my time to do something about this, to join in."

"Whoa there cowboy, you don't know what you're asking. You don't just go on strike. We have a system in place, not just anybody who feels like it goes. We look at each volunteer carefully to make sure he has what it takes to go to the distance, to die if the Brits keep it up. This isn't a prank or something you just try on, we're talking to the death here lad and that's no joke. It's a bitter ugly way to die, cara. I think Thatcher is going to make a point with some Irish lives here. They've been doing that for eight hundred years and now's no different."

"I know Fergal, but this is my shot. No one ever told me about Martin, I didn't even know I was adopted let alone that I had a brother living in this oppression while I lived in the lap of fucking luxury over there. Actually, I have two brothers."

Fergal smiled.

"I've had a taste of it in Castlereagh and now in here. I haven't lived it as long as you have, but I've never felt so strongly about anything in my life. My dad's dead, I have nothing left for me at home. Sure, there's the money but what good is all that if you guys are over here like this. I couldn't live with myself. It's all here and now for me. If I hadn't been adopted by my dad I'd have been here and doing this anyway."

"Not necessarily."

"Look Fergal, even if they figure out who I really am, I couldn't walk out of here with my head up if I don't try. I'd rather die trying to do something good than live with regret. I want to be with those lads. Fuck Thatcher. Like you said, she'll never understand. I finally do and it's my turn."

Fergal stared at the man in front of him and saw nothing more than the identical twin and identical spirit of his brother, Martin, and knew what had to be done.

Fergal's comm reached Bik McFarland, the leader of the IRA men on the H Block in charge of the strike, at just after ten that evening.

"Greetings Comrade. We've got a bit of a problem. The Yank intends to go on strike day after tomorrow. I'm afraid it's a bit of my fault. As you know I've gone off and taught him a bit of Irish history in the past two months. He was so tore up by it all that he said it was his duty to join the strike. He has Martin's constitution and if I'm any judge of character he'll take it to the end. Please advise. The Historian.

"Comrade Historian, nothing to do now except let history takes its course. You're a powerful storyteller to get a Yank to join the ranks of the strikers. I trust your judgment. And as we know now that Tin Knickers knows that this isn't Martin it may put further pressure on her. I'll let command know. Bik."

"Greetings comrade, historian informs me that the Yank wants to join the strike. At first, I was dead set against it. But a couple of things dawned on me. One, Historian, whose judgment I trust implicitly, says he has the

stones to go all the way with it. Two, Tin Knickers knows who this is and if she is informed the pressure has to increase. Just a heads up. Bik"

A nice padded rocking chair was brought into the cell for Mick, as was done for all the strikers. He had eaten his last meal on the evening of April 7th and the next day his strike was to begin. The first two weeks were tough but doable. He consumed only water and salt and Fergal kept his spirits high by reading him books and singing him Irish rebel songs. After two weeks he became weak, depressed and troubled in spirit. They finally came to get him, by doctor's orders, to take him to a cell in the hospital wing to be watched twenty-four hours a day by medical staff. He was to join Sands, Hughes, McCreesh and O'Hara who were already there. Except like them, no one would be coming to visit Mick, he was on his own.

Fergal knelt next to his chair before they came in and said, "You're going to be alright, you know that don't you?"

Mick shook his head up and down.

"You're a true son of Erin and I'm proud to be your friend."

Mick slowly opened his eyes looked at Fergal and said, "Only because of you."

Fergal said, "God Bless you, lad."

The screws walked in with a wheel chair and took him away while Fergal stared. He hadn't felt this lonely since the day he was arrested and sat in his cell in Castlereagh preparing himself to be interrogated by his British captors.

He whispered, "May God have Mercy on all their souls."

Chapter 74
The Tragic Beginning

European Commission Will Not Proceed

By Cassie Kenny

(UPI) May 4, 1981 On April 23rd of this year Marcella Sands, sister of hunger striker Bobby Sands, brought before the European Commission on Human Rights a case against the British Government, stating that the government was abusing the rights of Republican prisoners in Long Kesh and, in particular, those on hunger strike.

The commission ruled today that it had no power to proceed with a case against the British government. Bobby Sands has since dropped into a coma and today marks the 65th day of his hunger strike. He is not expected to live past this week and his family, who has agreed not to obstruct the striker's wishes to the death, has not interfered.

Bobby Sands Dead after 66 days!

By Sean O'Kane

(UPI) May 5, 1981 On March 1, 1981 Republican prisoners in Long Kesh prison southwest of Belfast in Northern Ireland started their second hunger strike after a failed attempt was aborted just before Christmas last.

Determined that this strike would succeed even at the cost of his own life, Bobby Sands died this morning at 1:17 a.m. after sixty-six days without food.

Margaret Thatcher, addressing the British Parliament today concerning one of her own elected peers in Sands, said, "This government will never grant political status no matter how much hunger strike their may be, we are on the side of protecting law-abiding and innocent citizens, and we shall continue in our efforts to stamp out terrorism. Mr. Sands was a convicted criminal. He chose to take his own life. It was a choice his organization did not allow to any of their victims."

Chapter 75
Plan B

May 7, 1981

Fr. Ruari O'Keefe stared out his office window at the 1979 V.W. parked in the lot of the Holy Cross rectory, provided by the brotherhood for the upcoming trip. His sadness was evident. He could not believe, even forty-eight hours later, that Margaret Thatcher actually allowed it to happen. Three more men were coming close to death and now Joe McDonnell was scheduled to take Bobby Sand's place tomorrow. How many more lives will be lost? Martin walked in wearing the white soutanis of a Columban Missionary, sandals with black socks and holding a wide brimmed straw hat.

Ruari said, "Good, let's go. The Sands' funeral procession is this morning and it's going to be huge. We need to get out of town before they begin to gather."

As they drove south out of Belfast, Ruari's heart continued to sink, his melancholy palpable. He did not sleep last night, could not sleep. He had not slept for a while. Bobby Sands' death was a burden on him as well as the entire Irish nation. And now as they drove he knew they were like two men on an icy mountain road sliding precariously close to the edge and there was no guard rail. All that Cardinal Byrne had done for him and this was how he was paying him back? But he knew he had to be part of this, he just could not walk away.

Martin had not slept well either. He had been very careful to avoid Long Kesh, and of all the free men in all of Ireland, he was the one who the British felt deserved a seat there more than anyone. But by a twist of outrageous fate his twin brother had taken the fall for him. He had not intended for that to happen. He also knew Mick had to be released, but the Brits would never release him and admit their mistake. So the way he looked at it he had two options, turn himself in and take his brother's place or break Mick out. He much preferred the latter.

But now the Yank had decided to go on hunger strike. Of all the unexpected happenings, this was the greatest to his mind. After mulling it over he had to admit he was impressed with the lad's stones, but he also knew he could not let him die. He had to break him out.

And, as much as he distrusted men of the cloth, Martin was also impressed with Ruari. This man was putting it all on the line for what he deemed family. He could have walked away but he did not. Martin said, "Does the dark make-up look realistic?"

Ruari glanced over and said, “Aye. It’ll work. They’re not going to look too closely at you. Besides the guard at the main gate likes me for some reason and I’m a bloody Taig. You okay?”

“No. But I’ve got to do this for Mick. He’s sitting in my cell.”

“You’d have joined the strike then?”

Martin almost winced at the question. After a moment he said, “I don't know. I don't think anyone knows until you're faced with it. I could go on some bullshit macho rant about how I would. But I don't know, I hope I would have the guts to.”

“That's fair. What do you think motivated the lad?”

“Who, Mick?”

“Aye, to go on strike.”

“I was thinking that myself and I came to the conclusion that Fergal had a hand in it.”

“Seriously?”

“Aye, the lad is too smart for his own good. He’s a born storyteller and he knows his Irish history, couldn’t help it being raised by our Da. I just hope he didn’t take the lad too far into the Tuath de Danaan. A Yank would think we’re nuts with that stuff.”

Ruari laughed, an unexpected gift.

“Anyway, with nothing else to do in that cell all day long I’m guessing he got the lad all worked up with his stories. If for nothing else, he did it for the craic.”

“Well, you know Mick’s in the hospital wing now and getting weak. If we waited another week it might be too late. It’s going to be touch and go as it is, plus he doesn’t know a thing about any of this.”

“Have you visited him?”

“Aye, I’ve met all the men in the hospital, Bobby, Frank, Ray and Patsy. I’ve tried to talk them all out of it.”

“What? I thought you were behind them?”

“I am. I just think there has to be a better way. I knew Thatcher wouldn’t understand nor let up and I still think that. More of these lads are going to die before this is over, count on it.”

“Aye.”

“Prepare yourself. Seeing a man die from the hunger is not pretty.”

An unintended tear came to his eye and dropped harmlessly down his cheek. Those were his mates in there.

Martin said, “Will I get a chance to see some of the lads?”

“No. They’re each in separate cells. We have to get in and out. Now, when we go in there'll be a guard that’ll chaperone but they won’t post a guard at the door like they do with a prisoner.”

“So we only have to deal with the one guard.”

"Aye, like we discussed, he'll be right in the room with us. You got the duct tape, rope and wooden gun?"

Martin felt under his robe and said, "Aye."

Ruari said, "A change of clothes for you and your brother and your battery razor?"

"Aye, in me bag in the back."

"Okay then, take a deep breath, and relax. In a couple of hours, God willing, we'll join the throngs for Bobby's funeral and they'll never find us."

"Easier said than done. What about you after this is over? You don't think they'll come around asking?"

"Sure they will. But you're a bloody terrorist remember? You held me hostage. I had nothing to do with any of this."

Martin smirked and said, "Might as well throw me under the bus, I've got nothing to lose."

"You're going to be so far gone no one will know where to look."

"I wish I could've seen me Mum and Da."

"You will."

"Aye?"

"The rendezvous point is a pub in Upperchurch called Paddy Kinnane's. Mick's adoptive father was from there. It's a quiet village in Tipperary that Eamon thought appropriate. Republicanism runs deep there. The Brits will never suspect a thing. Your Mum and Da, Cassie Kenny and Clare White will meet you and your brother there if God wills it."

Martin frowned and said, "I know everyone but Clare White. Who's she?"

Ruari said, "Oh, you'll find out soon enough."

They reached the prison and rolled to a stop at the main gate.

Ruari said, "Grand morning John Lyttle."

The guard at the gate, John Lyttle, was raised to hate Catholics. He was Scots-Irish Presbyterian, his loyalties were Orange and British, and yet he could find no reason to hate this papist. In fact, he found that he really liked the man. He would never admit it to anyone but he always liked it when the priest paid a visit and could chat for a moment, break things up in a boring job and Ruari planned to take full advantage this morning.

The guard said, "Fr. Ruari O'Keefe, well if it wasn't it is now. How are the likes of you?"

Ruari said, "Lad, if I were any better I'd be twins." He winked at Martin whose heart was pounding so hard he was shocked the guard couldn't see his chest vibrate.

The guard said, "Driving a different car today there Father?"

"Aye, my jalopy is in the shop."

"They're a money pit, they are."

Ruari said, "John, I've got a guest with me this morning. Fr. Liam Dolan, you should have him on the ledger for a scheduled visit, a Columban missionary in from the Philippines. He wanted to join me today."

Martin handed over his passport from the passenger side.

The guard said, "Awfully tan for an Irishman."

Martin laughed and said, "Aye, that's what twenty years in the sun'll do to you."

The three laughed and he waved Ruari through.

Ruari said, "Smooth as silk, nice job."

Martin said, "I thought me heart was going to jump out of me chest."

Once inside the main gate and the outer wall they took a right on the road that ran between the exterior wall and a fence that surrounded the H-Block. After a few hundred yards, they came to a fence gate marked H3, stopped and checked in once more and then the guard waved them through to a blacktop parking lot. The two got out and walked into the prison where a guard sat behind a desk in front of two double iron gates.

The guard said, "Who?"

Ruari said, "Martin O'Kane in the hospital wing."

Another guard appeared out of nowhere. Ruari almost visibly winced. The screw was a hard ass named Melvin Page. He stared at them both and said, "Follow me."

Martin's heart began to pound again. Page opened a heavy metal door and said, "Step in here. The search guard will be with you shortly."

They walked in and the door shut behind them. Martin went to say something and Ruari shook his head subtly.

The door opened and Seamus McCullough, a guard on the Provisional Irish Republican Army's payroll stepped in. Behind him, they heard Page say, "Make it quick McCullough, we don't have all day."

Seamus said, under his breath, "Smile for the camera, lads."

He threw them both against the wall and roughly searched them. He opened the door and said, "Visitors are good to go."

The gates opened and Page moved to escort them down the corridor of H-3 cell block. Suddenly they heard, "Bear in the air," reverberate down the corridor as it went. Then the corridor went up in a cacophony of bedpans and tin cups slammed against the iron doors that held the prisoners.

They moved further down the hall where he suddenly stopped when the small crevice window hinge in the door of cell # 210 squeezed open and all Martin could see were the two eyes of the prisoner behind the thick iron door but he knew them immediately and he almost cried out.

Fergal's fingers came through the opening and Martin put his hand up to touch the warm finger tips of his brother and had to do everything in his power not to react in recognition.

He said, "I'll pray for you."

The response from the other side was, "Our day will come."

Martin's heart suddenly swam in a sea of anguish. They were here to break out his twin, a lad he did not even know. Then what, leaving Fergal in this hell to rot?

Martin snapped out of it when the guard slammed the hinge down hard on Fergal's fingers. Martin could hear him wince in pain. Ruari gave him a look of warning and it was all he could do not to attack the man. They began to walk again and Martin thought, *his* time will come, and quickly.

They finally reached the hospital wing and walked into Mick's cell where he was in his thirtieth day on hunger strike. He was weak but strong enough to sit up. The only one who ever came to visit was Ruari and he began to look forward to seeing him, both for company and because he was scared.

The guard took his place, standing at the foot of the bed, making it impossible for private conversation between prisoner and visitor. Martin looked around the room and noticed the metal table in the corner with a pitcher of water and cups.

Ruari sat on Mick's bed and said, "How are you doing, lad?"

The guard said, "Would you like some nice cold milk? How about some cereal, eggs and toast, how about some nice moist yellow cake?"

Mick said, "No, just water."

Martin, ready to kill after the bastard slammed the door on Fergal and now this bit of cheek to a dying man, held his temper and said, "I'll get it."

He walked to the corner of the room as if to get the water, pulled the wooden gun from under his robe, and put it to the unsuspecting guard's head and said, "Don't make a move screw or I'll blow your bloody fucking head off."

He said, "Don't shoot."

"Shut the fuck up, screw. Now slowly give me your black jack and be very glad I don't break your fingers for what you did back there."

The guard handed him the black jack and Martin put it under his chin and tugged, cutting off the man's air and said, "Who the fuck do you think you are talking to a dying man like that?'

The guard tried to talk and Martin pulled the large stick tighter and said, "I thought I told you to shut the fuck up."

He let go and the guard dropped to his knees gasping for air.

Martin said, "Now strip down to your birthday suit."

"Even me undies?"

"Even those, then you'll know how my comrades have felt being humiliated by you fucks for the last five years on the blanket. You're lucky I don't shove this night stick up your arse. How many times have you done that to me comrades? Huh?"

Before the guard could make any more noise or say anything Martin duct taped his mouth and within two minutes had his hands and feet tied behind his back, resting his kneecaps on the hard cement floor.

Martin squatted down and said in a low venomous whisper, "I know where you live and I know what you do there. If one of these lads in here feels even the least bit of repercussion because of what we're doing here, every Orange Lodge in Ulster will receive pictures of you and your friend doing the hairy hump."

Mick, weak and sick, said, "What's going on here?"

Ruari said, "Don't ask lad, just follow our lead."

Martin stripped to his underwear, put on the guard's clothes, and then slipped on the soutanis over the head of his weak brother. While Ruari helped Mick with the sandals Martin shaved off his beard with his battery powered clippers and then razor. Mick kept staring at his brother in disbelief.

Ruari then pulled out some tan make up, looked at Martin and said, "Use that pitcher of water to wash your face as best you can." Then he began to apply the make up to Mick.

Mick said, "What're you doing, Father?"

Ruari said, "Don't ask. Can you walk, lad?"

"Sure, but I don't know how far."

Ruari said, "Okay lad, put on this hat and keep your head down."

The guard did not make a sound as they slammed the hospital cell door shut and locked it behind them.

They made it down the corridor and once again the noise rattled endlessly. They got to the double gates without a problem and the guard at the desk pushed a button to open the gates.

As they walked through he noticed the priest in white was limping and said, "Are you okay there?"

Ruari said, "Seeing the strikers upset his stomach."

The guard stood up and said, "Hey, your not…"

The black jack split his skull and he was dead before he sat back down.

Ruari turned his head, not anticipating the sudden and bloody violence.

The three walked out to the car.

Martin said, "Don't run, as a matter of fact don't even walk fast. The guards in the tower will be watching us. Now, when we get to the car I'm going to give the car the once over like I'm searching it. Open the trunk before you get in the car. I'll look like I'm searching it and then the back seat when I jump in. Then you just start driving and hope they don't notice. If they do hit the gas and stop for nobody."

Ruari nodded and said, "Mick, when we get to the car just walk around and sit in the front seat. Can you do that?"

"Sure, anything to sit down."

The guards in the main tower watched as the three men walked out to the car.

Guard 1 said, "What's Melvin doing?"

Guard 2 said, "He hates the papal bastards. He's just harassing them for fun, searching the car."

They both laughed and went back to their coffee and morning paper, not paying any more attention.

Martin squeezed into the back seat and tried to get on the floor of the small car. He said, "Jaysus lads, can you move your seats up?" He pulled the blanket over himself and they casually drove through both gates and to freedom.

At around noon the same day, The Secretary of Northern Ireland sat in his office reading reports from Northern Ireland and fed up with the Irish and the headaches they had been to him since he took office. He had his administrator place a call for William Gray and was getting irritated when his phone rang. He picked it up and said, "Yes."

"Sir, William Gray is on the line."

"Put him through."

With no pleasantries he said, "So is it true?"

"Is what true?"

"That one hundred thousand Irish have lined the streets for the funeral procession of Bobby Sands? The bloody terrorist that you insisted had no support."

"Oh, you know how the bloody Irish exaggerate…."

"Even if it were a half of that, it would be considered huge you bloody idiot; the President of the United States wouldn't get that many people at *his* funeral! These bloody Republicans have a hell of a lot more support than you or your advisers have been telling me, what with Sands getting elected to Parliament from his cell in Long Kesh and now this."

A second phone line rang signaling an urgent call from his secretary.

"Gray, hold the line, another call is coming that I have to take."

A bead of sweat began to appear on his upper lip as he waited and wondered why he did this shit for a living

He came back on the line and said, “Do you have a bloody inkling of what you’re doing in Northern Ireland?”

He suddenly wished he were anywhere else than where he sat.

He said, “Yes, I would like to think so.”

“Well I’m glad someone does. And of course, I’m sure you’ll have a plausible explanation as to why the *real* Martin O’Kane, the most *wanted* man in all of The United Kingdom, just waltzed into Long Kesh, tied up one of our guards, bashed in the head of another and waltzed out with his bloody twin brother. No one had a clue and they are now gone, long gone?”

Gray lost all the color in his face as his boss breathed hard on the line waiting for an answer for which he had none.

“You mean to tell me that the Prime Minister in London knows that Martin O'Kane busted his brother out of Long Kesh and you don't?”

“Sir, I…”

“So you did arrest the wrong man, you git, you knew it and you lied to me.”

“How the hell, I…”

“Don't Gray. Martin O'Kane just went into Long Kesh with a Catholic Priest he supposedly kidnapped. He tied up one guard, killed another and then just bloody drove away. Do you have an explanation for that?”

“We've had our hands full with this Sands funeral…”

“No more bullshit, Gray. We are done mincing words. You find O'Kane and his brother and then you come to my office. This is not over by a long shot. Do we understand one another?”

“Yes sir.”

“Good, because *if* we had O’Kane and his brother, I would fire you now. But now I’m going to wait until you bring them in to fire you. And if you fuck with me on this Gray, I’ll bring you up on so many charges your grandchildren will be visiting you in the gaol.”

Chapter 76
The Funeral

Ruari, Mick and Martin were on the A3 Motorway leaving Maze, Northern Ireland where Long Kesh Prison was located, and heading toward Lisburn, where they would change cars at a local petrol station.

Martin said, "Watch your speed, we don't want to get pulled over."

Ruari said, "But I'd also like to get the hell out of here."

"Me too. But let's not get pulled over for speeding."

"Plus, we've got to get Mick some medical attention, he doesn't look so good."

Martin tossed some pants, a t-shirt and some black Doc Marten boots to the front seat and said, "Mick, I know you don't feel well but we've got to get you out of that white robe in case were pulled over."

Mick said, "Guys, quit fussing over me. I'm good, I can do this."

Before Mick turned back to face the front he stared at his twin brother in the back seat for a long moment. Martin, staring back, smiled innocently at his identical twin brother and said, "Is this weird to you, too?"

Mick smiled at his brother and said in a weak voice, "You have no idea."

Martin smiled, if only inwardly. All at once, it was all there in front of him, like it had been all along, but he just couldn't see it. The solitary confinement, the desolation, the insatiable wanting that had all subtly haunted him, the sense of deficiency and privation, it all made sense. The other half had been missing and he had now been made whole.

They reached Lisburn, switched cars, picked up A1, and headed toward Belfast on the Dublin to Belfast road, the M1. Once they were on the M1 and Mick had finally managed to change his clothes in tight quarters he said, "What's the plan now?"

Ruari said, "We're going to a funeral."

Martin said, "Mick, half of Ireland is at Bobby Sands funeral procession. We're going to disappear into the mob. How are you feeling, lad?"

Mick said, "Thirsty and tired. I could take a nap."

"No appetite?"

"No, haven't for a while."

Ruari said, "You're going to head into some serious crowds up ahead. Once things quiet down and enough people leave so we'll able to get around, Eamon has people looking out for you two to take you to a safehouse in Andersontown. A local doctor we can trust will be there to look after Mick. You'll be there for a couple of days. Eamon will contact you there to give you further instructions.

Mick said, "What about you?"

Martin said, "He goes in the trunk."

"What?"

"Aye, we have to make it look like a kidnapping."

"Shit, what happens if nobody finds him?"

"We're in a stolen car lad, they'll find him."

Before local police knew and a roadblock was set up they were at the Monagh By-Pass exit and headed toward Andersontown Road, and took it toward the Falls Road where the funeral procession was in full swing, heading toward the Millstown cemetery. When they could go no further they parked, got out. Five men came up, one said, "Cara." They surrounded the trunk so people wouldn't notice, Ruari slid in and they joined the one hundred thousand mourners come to bury their martyr.

Mick, being from rural America, had never seen so many people in one place. They lined the streets and covered the hillsides. It was an impressive sight, looking down on the city of Belfast in the background. After spending the last three months in Long Kesh, he understood in a way that no American ever would, the oppression and the hatred that these people had lived under for the last eight hundred years. The Republic, at least, got a break in 1921, but not the Nationalists who lived in the six of the nine counties of the Ulster Province known as Northern Ireland. They lived in fear and oppression every day and some readily gave up their lives for freedom.

Six soldiers of the IRA carried the casket and as it came by there was silence. Mick was awestruck by the reverence paid, this many people and not a sound. This many people and he could hear the birds whistling in the trees and the wind blowing softly. This many people and he could hear the soft patter of the rain on the street. This many people and he could hear the soft sob of despair in the crowd around him. Then the solo bagpiper started again and as the casket moved away people filled in behind and walked toward the final resting place of the man who gave his life for their cause, Ireland's most recent martyr.

Ian Wright came in from a long day of baby sitting Republicans as they buried that idiot Sands, who had decided to commit a long painful suicide. The RUC had been on high alert since Sands died. Not only were they dealing with the funeral, which was enormous, but riots were breaking out all over Belfast on both sides. Then O'Kane breaks his brother out of Long Kesh. When he first heard about the breakout, Ian knew they were heading for the funeral crowd, where there was no way in hell anyone would find them. They were one step ahead of his guys all day, slipping through all his road blocks, and they were still out there.

He lit a cigarette and put his feet up on his desk and said, "How in the hell did he get in there and then get out again with his fucking twin brother in tow and not get caught?"

He stood with a pint of the black brew on his mind when his phone rang. He picked it up and said, "Wright, here."

Gray said, "Any word on O'Kane or his brother yet?"

"We talked to the priest, that bastard is guilty as hell, but he swears he was taken at gun point."

"He was found in the trunk of a stolen car and you think he was in on it?"

"Hell yes I do. But with the Catholic community up in arms over this hunger strike, there's no way in hell I'm even bringing him in for questioning. The riots we got now will be nothing to what we would have."

"So what do you suggest?"

"We put surveillance on the priest, twenty four hours. Then we go door to door in Andersontown."

"Why there?"

"I think they disappeared into the funeral and Andersontown would be the closest Catholic community, lots of safe houses."

"Okay. Well I want the biggest manhunt this town has ever seen. RUC, MI5, UDA, everyone. We start in Andersontown and then move to every Catholic neighborhood with known safehouses. Move into some Protestant neighborhoods too so it doesn't cause any more shit than it already will. His brother went on strike, he's got to be weak, so they won't be able to move him easily. Let's not fuck this one up."

Chapter 77
The Instructions

Two days turned into a week. The safehouse was the home of a family whose leanings were with the INLA, the radical wing of the IRA, whose members were also on the Hunger Strike.

When Mick first heard they were going to a safehouse, he thought of a clandestine place out of a James Bond movie. This place had kids running around, a mother making good things to eat in the kitchen, and people coming and going.

They put Mick in a back bedroom and a doctor came in to look at him and put him on an intravenous feeding tube. After a few days of rest, he was fidgety, after a week he was crazy, but he had to admit that he did feel stronger. He then began to take blended foods that were soft and easy to consume, and he gradually gained strength and began to get his health back.

Joe Casey and his wife Nancy were the proprietors of this safehouse and could not have been better hosts. One evening, a week after the twins had been there, things had quieted down, Joe sat down with them and said, "We got word that the UDA bastards will be in our neighborhood tomorrow. They're going door to door looking for you lads. We've had this trouble before. We've hollowed out space underneath the floor boards beneath the throw rug in the front room. When we get word they're on their way, you go underneath."

Mick looked at Martin and Martin said, "Don't tell me you're claustrophobic?"

"I didn't think I was until I went in to The Kesh."

"Can you do this?"

"Don't think I've got much choice. How long we going to be down there?"

Joe said, "Couple hours at the most I'd say."

Martin said, "Fucking Yank."

They all laughed.

The next morning before six Joe came into their rooms and said, "They're on their way, quick lads."

There was at least a bit of light through the floor boards but when the rug was thrown over it was deep, dark and suffocating to Mick. But he didn't have much time to think about it because within a half hour they heard dampened boots pounding the floor. It seemed like an entire army of men entered the house and after a few minutes a scuffle broke out and muffled screaming was heard, then quiet. An hour went by when the rug slid off and the boards were lifted and Mick sat up and breathed fresh air.

Martin sat up with him and noticed his brother was trembling and he said, “Are all Yanks pussies?”

Mick slugged him as hard as he could in the arm, which wasn’t much because he was still weak, and they all laughed, more from relief that the soldiers were gone than anything else.

Two days later Mick, Martin and Joe sat at the kitchen table smoking cigarettes when Eamon Gainey walked in the back kitchen door. They looked up at the imposing figure who seemed to appear out of nowhere.

Before he even sat down he looked at Mick, who he had yet to meet and said, “Michael Patrick, how are you feeling, lad?”

Mick looked up. No one but Paddy had ever referred to him as Michael Patrick and he immediately took to Eamon and said, “Feeling much better, thanks for asking.”

“You ready to travel?”

“Yeah, I think so.”

“What did you think of our welcoming committee?”

“Just glad Joe had the floor boards hollowed out.”

Joe winked at Mick and smiled.

Martin said, “By the way Mick, meet Eamon Gainey.”

He reached a hand out to the man and said, “The pleasure’s mine, sir. My father spoke very highly of you.”

“Paddy Quinlan was a good lad, he’ll be sorely missed.”

“Thank you.”

They shook hands and Martin saw Eamon smile for the first time in a long while.

Martin said, “How’s Ruari?”

Eamon said, “He’s been better. Interpol, MI5, the RUC, all of them got in on the act and hit him hard from all sides but he didn’t cave. He stuck to his story, told the same one repeatedly, and then kept his mouth shut. They’ve got nothing and they know it. Plus there'd be hell to pay taking in a Catholic priest in the current atmosphere.”

“What was his story?”

“You showed up, knew he was the chaplain at The Maze, put a gun to his head and forced him into the whole deal.”

Martin smiled and said, “The bastard told me he was going to do it and he stuck to it, huh?”

“Aye. When I left him he said something funny.”

“What?”

“He said, ‘My penance is finally paid in full.’”

"What do you think he meant?"

"I don't know but you two owe him."

"My only regret is Fergal."

"I know lad, I know. We'll get him."

"Anyway, what's next?"

"A furniture truck is stopping by tomorrow afternoon to drop off a fridge and freezer. You two will be going out in those boxes. The lads will load you in the back with the other furniture heading to Dublin. It won't be first class travel but it'll get you out of here.

"The Truck will head to the warehouse district near the Port of Dublin. When you get there the driver will unlock the truck's overhead door and the overhead door to the dock. You'll wait a half hour or so and then climb out. The warehouse will be dark. Just make sure you lock the truck, the warehouse door and then get the hell out of there. Next to the truck you'll find a blue Ford Marquis, keys will be on the floor.

"Sister Mary de Angels will be awaiting your arrival at the Mercy Convent on Lower Baggot Street. Martin, can you find the convent from the port?"

"Aye, no problem."

"Good, you'll spend the night there and then you'll drive to Upperchurch the next afternoon."

Mick said, "Upperchurch? Is that the same village where my dad grew up?"

"Aye, we thought it appropriate, first in honor of your father, a great man who always helped our cause. Secondly, NORTIP will make sure no one comes nosing around."

Mick smiled.

Martin said, "Where's Upperchurch?"

Eamon lit his pipe, pulled out a map and laid it on the table. His finger slid across the map south and west of Dublin and said, "Here, just west of Thurles."

Martin said, "Hmml."

"You lads had better be thirsty when you get there. Plus I'm counting on the Kinnane sisters to fatten up Mick.

Chapter 78
The Convent Revisited

The trip to Dublin was as uncomfortable as any journey that either man had ever encountered and they had to continually remind themselves that some particularly nasty people wanted them and this was a small price to pay.

The boxes they were loaded in were placed in the back of the trailer, then other boxes were loaded in front. When they got to the border soldiers stopped the truck and pulled it over. They heard the soldier talking to the driver.

"Papers?"

"Aye, here you go."

"Looks good, can you open the trailer for me please?"

Their hearts started to pound. The trailer was opened and two soldiers jumped up and looked in and stood there looking in at all the boxes of appliances.

The driver said, "I got a hand truck, I can start pulling boxes if you want?"

The soldiers didn't say anything for a minute, knowing they probably should but didn't want to hassle with it. Plus cars were beginning to line up to get into the Republic.

"No, you're good. Drive safe."

"Aye, thanks, I will."

They arrived at the dock and waited the requested half hour in the back of the truck. But it paid off as everything was exactly as Eamon had said. They found the car, got in and drove across Dublin to The Mercy Convent.

They found a parking spot and walked to their destination where Sister Mary de Angels was patiently waiting.

They rang the bell, she opened it and said, "Come in, come in before you catch your death."

The twins smiled at one another over the fussy and plump little nun. When they all reached the foyer, they stood and stared at one another, the little nun seemingly lost in a memory.

After an uncomfortable moment Martin said, "Um, Sister we were told to come here?"

She said, "Oh yes, I'm sorry. Just look at the lot of you, tall and handsome. You must be starved."

Mick smiled and said, "We could eat."

She stopped in her tracks at the American accent, as if she had forgotten her cousin in Montana raised Mick.

Then she said, "Follow me, lads."

They entered the kitchen where she put plates heaping with brown bread sandwiches of bacon rashers and broiled tomatoes. She also brought out mugs of hot black tea.

Mick said, "Sister, I've had about as much tea as I can drink. Can I get a glass of milk?"

She smiled at his accent again and said, "Sure, sweetheart."

She came back with the cold milk and sat down with them while they ate. She talked for the entire time they ate. Mick would smile and then Martin, both tickled at this woman and her stories.

She stopped for a moment to catch her breath when Martin said, "So now we know who Clare White is."

She said, "You didn't know?"

"No, everyone kept saying that we'd find out and weren't willing to tell us anything."

Mick said, "Hell, Sister, I didn't even know I had a brother, let alone a twin."

"Well, let me tell you that Clare White is one of the grandest ladies I've ever had the pleasure to take care of."

She then took Mick by the hand and said, "As you know, your Da was my first cousin on my mom's side, a grand man he. He was a big supporter of ours. He was also a big supporter of all things Irish, he'll be sorely missed. I'm sorry for your loss, Michael."

Mick glanced at his brother who had his head hung low and said, "Thank you Sister, that means a lot. By the way, if the old man left me any dough you can continue to count on my support."

Chapter 79
Upperchurch

Mick and Martin got up early and left the Convent in the dark before dawn, heading for the rolling hills of Northern County Tipperary.

Fifteen minutes out of Dublin Mick said, "Martin, I want you to know that I don't blame you for the death of my dad. It was just bad luck and timing and couldn't be helped."

Martin, unable to deal with the issue yet, said, "Thanks."

To make sure they weren't being followed they stopped in Thurles and then Holy Cross, took their time in both places and by mid afternoon they drove into the hushed village of Upperchurch. They walked into Kinnane's Pub. It was quiet, no one was behind the bar and the only person to be seen was Johnny Gleason, who sat at the end of the bar nursing a pint of Guinness and welcomed the lads to Upperchurch.

By five that afternoon the pub was so full it was hard to get around as word spread about the twins who had arrived and one with a Yank accent.

Mick and Martin walked outside for a bit of fresh air and to smoke a cigarette.

Mick said, "Where did all these people come from? They came out of nowhere. There can't be that many people that live here."

Martin smiled said, "The word must've got around that a couple of twins showed up, one Irish, one Yank. That's more than enough to get an Irishman out for a pint."

They both laughed and went back inside.

Chapter 80
Mom

Mick and Martin stayed in the room above the pub and woke on wobbly legs the next morning as the night went into the early morning. They walked downstairs to look for something to eat when Mick stopped at the bottom of the stairs, Martin crashing into his back and said, "What the hell?"

Mick looked across the dining room into the pub where he saw two women and it startled him. He turned around and whispered, "Those are the two ladies that I saw at the airport when those cops surrounded me."

Martin grabbed Mick and pulled him back on to the stairwell and said, "Not another word. We take the back door and get out of here."

The door that led to the Kinnane's home in the back opened up and Siobhan walked out smiled at the boys and said, "What are you two doing?"

Mick pointed, she looked out and saw the women, smiled and said, "I think you two are going to want to meet these women."

They stood, a bit embarrassed and followed Siobhan out of hiding.

Clare was the first to see the two young men together for the first time, as they followed Siobhan, and could only stop and stare. Cassie turned to see why Clare gasped, saw the boys and put her arm on her best friend's shoulder and said, "It's going to be okay, Clare. Take a deep breath."

Cassie exerted herself, something she had always done with ease, walking to the twins and said, "Which one of you lads is Martin?"

Martin turned around and stood up and said, "That would be me."

"I'm Cassie Kenny. I work with your Da on the newspaper."

"Aye, I've seen your work many times. It's grand to finally make your acquaintance."

Then she stared at Mick as if she could tell them apart and for an awkward moment could not move or say anything. The memories came flooding back of this lad as an infant on their trip to Montana and then as a toddler on the ranch, of making love to Paddy, who she now missed terribly. Her heart ached when she remembered how much she had loved this little boy and ached even more when she recalled her transgressions toward her best friend.

Mick, unable to stand it any longer, stood and said, "I'm Mick Quinlan."

She smiled at his accent and said, "Aye, I know who you are."

By now, Clare had mustered enough courage to join the gathering and said, "Yes, she knows who you are because I asked her to escort you to

America when you were a baby, and then asked her to stay a while to make sure you were going to be okay."

Cassie turned and smiled at Clare who smiled back. The twin boys stared at the beautiful woman with short blond hair, unable to speak, as they realized for the first time who she was.

Clare's eyes misted over and her throat knotted up. She opened her arms and the two large men fell into their biological mother's arms for the first time.

Ian Wright's phone rang at his desk, it was just after three p.m. It had been another long day about to get longer.

"Wright here."

"Meeting tonight. Upperchurch. Gainey, Brennan, O'Kane and his brother. Paddy Kinnane's Pub. Put the money where we agreed."

The phone went dead. He picked up another line and dialed.

"Gray here."

"There's a meeting tonight. We need to move fast."

"Hold on there. Who? Where?"

"O'Kane, his brother, Gainey, Brennan. In Upperchurch."

"Where the hell is that?"

"Couple hours southwest of Dublin in Tipperary. It's a Republican hotspot. But we need to move."

"Put a team together, one car, I'll do the same. We'll be in your office in half hour. Wright, I don't know who your mole is but it doesn't get any better than this. Let's not blow this one."

Chapter 81
The Meeting Gone Wrong

Upperchurch, County Tipperary, The Republic of Ireland

May 20, 1981

Kinnane's Pub was half bar, half dining room separated by a door of Irish lace. The restaurant had ten tables or so and was open for business Thursday, Friday and Saturday evenings while the pub side was open every night. The food was so good that the Kinnane sisters usually had every table booked for all three nights every week all year long.

Unlike in America, where restaurants were trying to turn as many tables as possible in an evening, moving the diners in and out. Once you booked your table at Kinnane's Pub, it was yours for the night. The peat fire would burn warmly in the fireplace and once the five-course meal was finished people would sing, tell stories, read poetry and enjoy each other's company all evening long.

But this wasn't a Thursday, Friday or Saturday night. This was a Monday night, a few days after Mick and Martin had arrived. And even though the restaurant was not open for business, the white tablecloth covered the table, the silver, china and crystal were all laid out as the Kinnane sisters, Niebh and Siobhan, welcomed their guests from the north.

Eamon, Dermot, Cassie, Clare, Sean, Patricia, Ruari, Martin and Mick sat around the table and as the dinner was being prepared the black brew flowed and the conversation became more lively and animated.

Dinner was then served and, after everyone was sated, Irish whiskey was poured and Eamon stood and said, "I'd like to toast our hosts, the food was excellent and the company exceptional."

"Here, here."

"Also, Niebh and Siobhan come join us and Siobhan bring that rascal of a husband of yours, Jimmy Butler."

Eamon then raised his glass again and said, "To the hunger strikers."

This time the glasses raised in silence and everyone drank. A tear slipped down Mick's cheek, he had been there, and he missed the men he had met, especially Fergal.

With a choke in his voice Mick stood and said, "I would like to make a toast first to Fergal O'Kane, my cellmate and best friend. One so charming and bright can not be dimmed by the darkness around him."

A small groan fell from Patricia O'Kane's lips as Sean put his arm around her shoulder and they raised their glasses once more.

Mick said, "Next, I'd like to toast Mr. and Mrs. O'Kane for raising two of the finest men I've had the privilege to know."

They raised their glasses.

"Lastly, to the greatest Irishmen I ever knew, who taught me to love this country as if it were my own, my dad Paddy Quinlan and my uncle Dinty."

Martin then stood and said quietly, "I could never replace my mother Patricia O'Kane, never. She gave me the faith, the love of country, the love of freedom and the courage to fight for all three. But had it not been for Clare White, I'd have never had the chance to spend my days with Patricia. So I'd like to raise a toast to my two mothers without whom I would not be here and would not be the man that I am today."

They raised a toast and drank.

Then Martin said, "And to my Da, who night after night, patiently told Fergal and me the tales of this ancient land and patiently answered all of our questions, helping us to understand why we struggle and giving us the courage of our convictions."

Then Eamon took the floor back and said, "Let's start this meeting with a moment of silence for Bobby Sands, Francis Hughes and Ray McCreesh, who have all gotten away from us on hunger strike to expose our oppressors for who they are."

All heads bowed in prayer for a long moment.

He continued, "Joe McDonnell came on two days after Bobby passed, while Kiernan Doherty and Martin Hurson have just joined. The pressure is mounting the world over. We know that Sinn Fein is having secret talks with the British Government and the word is that The Brits want to give in to the five demands, but they're so bloody worried about saving face that they'd rather our lads die."

Sean said, "Why is now any different than the last eight hundred years?"

"It's not, I guess. But there are a couple of things happening here that are against us. First of all, Thatcher is still pissed off about Airy Neaves."

Mick said, "Who is Airy Neaves?"

Martin looked at his brother and said, "Back in 1979, when Margaret Thatcher was running for Prime Minister, Airy Neaves was her right hand man and credited with her rise to power. This wasn't a good thing for Republicans in Northern Ireland because Neaves hated Irish Republicans more than most English politicians, and it was generally felt he had to go. So one day before Thatcher took office, his car suddenly blew up while he was in it."

Mick said, "Who did it?"

Eamon said, "The INLA, they wouldn't be talked down. We all agreed it needed to be done but we didn't know what the repercussions would be. And, of course, now she hasn't forgotten and this may be a little payback time. And now that she knows that Martin, the man she wants most, just walked in to Long Kesh and walked out with his twin brother, she has to be really pissed. I'm sorry that I allowed it now, we did get Mick but at what price?"

Cassie said, "Don't kid yourself, Eamon. She's a mean bitch and really believes these lads are criminals. The strikers dying have nothing to do with Martin and Mick and everything to do with an English Prime Minister who's under the illusion that Northern Ireland is as English as her own damn neighborhood."

Ruari said, "In reality some parts are."

Eamon said, "Father, The North is Ireland, regardless of what the residents want to believe. Thank you Cassie, what's done is done. We're all doing what we can to expose them to the entire world for what they truly are. But I brought you all together to answer questions that everyone has and to discuss plans to get these two lads out of the country."

The next two hours were spent discussing plans. Eamon finally handed Mick and Martin two passports and two one-way plane tickets.

Eamon said, "The lads are to be driven to Limerick tonight where drivers will be waiting to take them to their ports of call. Martin will work on a merchant ship from Galway Bay to Amsterdam in the Netherlands where he will catch a flight to New York. Mick will work a ship from the Port of Dublin to Brussels, Belgium where he will catch a flight to Boston. If all goes well these two lads will be in Omaha, Nebraska in America in two weeks time."

Sean said, "Omaha, Nebraska?"

Eamon said, "Aye. Without going into too much detail, we have Northern Aid members there who will offer safe room and board until further notice. When they arrive safely there, plans will be made to get them to an American operative's home in Butte, Montana."

When they were ready to break up, one the of the NORTIP members that Eamon had watching the village while they met, ran in and said, "Eamon, Dermot there are two black sedans a mile or so down the road heading our way. Looks like MI5, maybe Interpol or Scotland Yard."

Eamon looked around the table and said, "Who's armed?"

Martin had made sure that he and Mick were properly armed just in case and Mick had assured him that he knew how to use it. Dermot nodded at his boss, Patricia Brennan O'Kane pulled a handgun from her purse, and Sean said, "Why am I not surprised?"

Eamon then said, "Niebh, where's the best place to hide, we've got to get the twins out of here."

She said, "The cemetery out back, it's nice and dark."

Eamon looked at the man from NORTIP and said, "Line up your lads around the cemetery as best you can without creating any notice and give us as much cover as you can. There will probably be some shooting but we've got to get these lads out of the country or there'll be hell to pay."

He said, "Aye." And he turned and walked away.

Eamon said, "Everyone except Dermot follow Niebh to the cemetery. Hide behind the gravestones until this is over. Go quickly."

As the last person walked out the back door, the front door to the pub slammed open and William Gray walked in, two men following, all with guns drawn. The pub was suspiciously empty.

The Irish lace curtain hung down on the door that separated the two rooms. Gray walked with caution toward the curtain. His gun was up when he quickly slid the curtain back and was just as quickly less than an inch away from the cold steel barrel of Eamon Gainey's .357 magnum. Dermot walked around him and said, "Drop the guns lads or your boss gets carried out in a box."

Guns dropped to the floor.

Eamon said, "Mr. Gray, did you think you'd just walk in here and start harassing people? You and your flunkies here."

William Gray said, "Mr. Gainey, you'll never get away with this, we've got the place surrounded. All we want is Martin O'Kane and his twin brother and we'll leave, no more problems."

Eamon said, "Well, you came for nothing then. They're not here so you can leave peacefully or we can do this the way we've been doing it for the past eight hundred years."

"We know they're here. Give them up and nobody gets hurt."

"Look lad, even if they were here do you honestly think I'd hand them over to the likes of you. So, we're going to walk outside and you're going to call your dogs off."

"I can't do that."

"You *will* do that, this isn't the fucking UK, this is the Republic of Ireland and you've got no jurisdiction here."

"We're tied with Interpol and we've got jurisdiction throughout all of Europe."

"I don't give a fuck who you're with. You're tied to the English government and so you're my sworn enemy."

Eamon and William Gray walked out into the village square where Eamon said, "Okay, call off your lads or you three are dead men."

The man shouted, “Lads, it’s over, throw down your weapons and come out.”

A shot rang out and ripped through Eamon’s left ear lobe. A second shot hit in front of his right shoe. Eamon turned to put a bullet into Gray who had leapt for cover. Eamon ran back inside where Dermot had taken care of the other two and they ran for the cemetery.

Hearing the shots that rang out, Martin said, “Okay there’s trouble up there so spread out, but not too far and take cover.”

Clare sat close to Mick and said, “I’m scared, Mick.”

He said, “Don’t worry mom, I’ll take care of you.”

The words that she had longed to hear just came from her son’s mouth and she smiled and hugged him. He hugged her back, never having had a hug from a mother, and it felt good.

The hunter's moon hung high above the cemetery casting light and shadows making it difficult to find good cover. As Clare and Mick sat down, Mick looked over, saw two new gravestones, and cried out.

Eamon and Dermot ran toward them and more shots ripped through the quiet night air of the normally sleepy village. They slammed into the nearby headstones spraying uncomfortable razor sharp pieces of stone at the cemetery’s occupants.

Another shot sliced the cool night air only this time it met its mark and slammed into the back of Dermot Brennan’s head; he was dead before he hit the ground. Eamon, ever the battle commander and soldier, grabbed his best friend, pulled him to cover before he felt for a pulse, and recognized he was dead.

Patricia, who sat with Ruari and Sean, saw her brother go down, moaned and ran to his side. As Eamon lay him out of the way, she threw herself on top of him and a bullet grazed her shoulder, though she felt nothing. Eamon tried to get her to safety, but she refused to let go. He suddenly grabbed her, slapped her and said, “Patricia, get a hold of yourself. You’re giving them a target. Be quiet and get down.”

Mick slid over to cover Clare but it was too late. Another shot came from out of nowhere and exploded in her chest. She looked up at her son and he stared down at her with his hand over her bloody wound.

She said, “Lad, I, I…”

He said, “Shush, you’re going to be fine.”

But she struggled to speak, not be denied.

She said, “No, I’m okay now. I’m okay now that I got to spend some time with you and your brother.”

Mick was sobbing now, the dead and dying overwhelming him.

“I love you and tell your brother that I love him too and…”

With that Clare White died in the arms of her son in the cemetery in Upperchurch, as Eamon looked on.

Martin crawled with Cassie, Sean and Ruari to the group gathered. He looked down and saw his uncle Dermot lying motionless and dead. Then he looked at his twin who held their dead mother in his arms, staring at the gravestones in front of him, freshly strafed with enemy fire. Mick stared as if in a stupor of utter grief. Martin moved closer, saw the names of Dinty and Paddy Quinlan glistening in the moonlight off the marble headstones, and winced.

Eamon, curious, looked at the marble slab and then at Martin, who now had a dangerous look of pain and hatred that radiated brightly from his eyes, even in this darkness.

Cassie crawled over and took Clare so Mick could get up and help. She looked down at Clare and wept.

Martin said, “Let’s go, there are some men who need to die.”

Mick, coming out of his trance at the sound of his brother's voice, stood to join them and Eamon said, “Sorry lads, you two stay with the priest, I need you both alive after this.”

Martin said, “Fuck that.”

Eamon said, “Excuse me, soldier?”

Mick said, “I'm with Martin.”

Eamon said, “Goddamn it, I can't have you lads dead too.”

Martin stepped up and said, “These bastards just killed my uncle and our mum. They came for me and it's me there going to get.”

Then Mick stepped up and stood shoulder to shoulder with his brother, taking cover behind a large Oak, and they both stared down their commanding officer in defiance and solidarity.

Patricia stood up and gave the same look of hatred and resolve that Eamon saw in her son. She squeezed herself between the twin boys and said, “The bastards killed my brother and my friend Clare. I’d rather die shooting them than sitting back here like a fucking coward.”

For the first time in his command, Eamon second guessed himself, then said, “Okay, then, lads you two go up on this side of the pub, Patricia and I will go up on the other side and get as many as we can.”

Sean grabbed Dermot, Cassie grabbed Clare and pulled them out of harms way behind Paddy Quinlan’s headstone, as if to protect them.

Unable to contain himself any further Ruari said, “Fuck this.” He grabbed Dermot’s rifle and headed to the fight.

Martin and Mick came up and out of the cemetery along the side of the pub and looked out on to Main Street where the fighting was heaviest. Ruari came up from behind and squatted down behind the twins. He looked up and saw a sniper in the tree across the street with a bead on Martin. He got up and as the sniper pressed the trigger he jumped in front and took the bullet in the chest and collapsed in front of them.

Seeing the priest which exposed the position of the twins, Ian Wright stood raised his rifle and shot. It slammed into the building just above their heads. Seeing that he missed, Wright raised his weapon once more, ready to fire, when a slug slammed into his upper right arm, knocking his gun to the ground.

The fire came from Patricia Brennan across the street. William Gray stood to return fire when a slug slammed into his right thigh knocking him off his feet. Suddenly two large black sedans roared up and the two wounded men crawled in and off they drove into the night.

Seeing that this was going to end badly the second black sedan rolled up and more government men jumped in and took off after the first.

When the smoke had cleared the twins looked down in front of them where they found Fr. Ruari O'Keefe. He lay mortally wounded. He was pale and his body convulsed in spasms and then lay still. Martin grabbed his hand and said, "Try to lay still Father, we'll get help and you'll be fine."

He looked up, blood spilling from his mouth, and smiled and with blood covering his teeth he said, "Not this time, lad. But it's okay; I've made my peace and done my penance. I have no regrets."

Mick said, "What penance, Father? You said that once before."

He said, "Ask your brother, he'll tell you."

Mick said, "Thanks for getting me out of Long Kesh; I'd still be there if it weren't for you."

"That's what I meant when I said I have no regrets."

Martin said, "You're a courageous man, Father and I'm proud to have known you."

"Me too lads, me too."

And with that Ruari O'Keefe breathed his last and died.

Chapter 82
The Aftermath and The Valediction

Patricia Brennan O'Kane had witnessed much violence and death in her life as a Republican in Northern Ireland. Losing Fergal to prison and Martin to a life on the run were crosses she intuitively knew she would bear. But Dermot's death put her over the edge. He was her safety net and had always been. She tried to put the reality, the very keen reality of his death out of her mind, but she failed miserably. This was a dark cross that she was convinced was one ounce too heavy to bear. Staring at her brother, grey and lifeless, brought a moment of insanity. Her safety net came apart at the seams, allowing her to crash to the ground. She felt exposed and lost, angry and bitter as she convulsed in her husband's arms, unable to move.

Eamon, after checking all the dead and wounded, walked back to where they had gathered. Cassie sat next to Patricia and Sean, faced with a stark, bleak reality, unable to move, paralyzed in grief. She stared aimlessly off into the night in an emotional blackout, unable to process the certainty before her, afraid of where it would take her, questioning her strength to go there. She had written about the violence, had seen it, reported it, but all from a safe distance. No one she knew had died or been hurt. But now, within a month, that all changed, her ex-lover, her best friend lay cold and dead and she knew they had to go and go quickly.

Eamon walked out of the pub to the people standing in the square. He looked at Siobhan and said, "Can Jimmy drive us to Limerick City in your station wagon there?"

She said, "I don't see why not."

"Good, I just made some calls and made some arrangements but we've got to move."

Cassie said, "What about Clare?"

Patricia said, "And what about Dermot?"

Martin said, "And Father Ruari has just got away from us as well."

Siobhan said, "You can't worry about this right now; you have to get out of here. But I promise they'll all be well cared for and sent back to their homes to be buried properly."

Eamon said, "What're you going to do?"

Niebh said, "Call the bloody Peelers and when they come, tell them we woke up to this and know nothing. It's not the first time, when the bloody Brits unleashed the Black and Tans on us in 1921, they attacked first right here in the village of Upperchurch. Just a little payback I guess."

They loaded themselves into the wagon and Jimmy Butler drove them through back roads in the middle of the night to Limerick city.

Chapter 83
Godspeed and three Obsequies

It took them an hour to reach Limerick and no one spoke much, everyone still in shock at the sudden violence and loss they had just experienced. The soft sobs of Cassie and Patricia were silent reminders.

There was no time to spare. By the time they reached the safe house the twins had to be moved and moved fast.

Eamon said, "Let's make this quick, drivers and cars are waiting for you two. We don't have much time."

Patricia O'Kane looked at Martin and could say nothing. He saw the suffering in her eyes and grabbed her up in his arms and said, "I love you mum and I'll see you soon."

She stepped away from Martin and then hugged Mick just as tight.

Sean cupped Martin's face in his small hands and said, "Godspeed, lad, Godspeed."

Cassie walked up and hugged both Martin and Mick and then walked away, unable to utter a word.

Eamon said, "You've both got your papers then."

Martin said, "Aye."

Mick felt his breast pocket and nodded.

"Okay then, these men will take you to where we discussed. Any questions?"

They shook their heads no.

"You've got the address in Omaha. I'll call Barry McMahon to tell him you've got off the island when I hear back from my lads here. Send word when you both get there safely so we know. Now off with you."

The two began to walk to their separate cars and they both stopped as if they had the same thought at the same time. They turned and looked at one another and it became an uncomfortable guy moment. Mick walked toward Martin with his hand out and said, "Safe travels, bro."

Martin grabbed Mick's hand and pulled him close in a half hug and said, "Aye, you too. See you in Omaha, wherever the hell that is."

They both got in separate automobiles and drove away. Eamon watched until their tail lights faded to black, his jaw clinched, and finally, unable to hold back the tears, wondering what he was going to do now without Dermot, and cursing himself for falling in love.

* * *

Riots were breaking out all over Northern Ireland, as the hunger strike progressively got worse, and then the news of the shootout in Upperchurch made the papers. It was no different in Portadown in the Devil's Triangle, where they would bury Dermot Brennan. Benji Mason and his crew were well into their pints at The Brown Bear pub in the Shankill district of Belfast as they celebrated the news of Dermot Brennan's death.

Benji said, "Lads, I'm in hopes that those Taig cocksuckers, hunger strike their selves right out of business."

They all laughed and jeered.

"And now that wee bastard Dermot Brennan got what he deserved, here's to just rewards, Aye, Lads?"

They all raised a glass in toast.

"But it ain't over yet. We're going to a funeral march tomorrow lads. We're heading straight into the Devil's Triangle. When we get there we're going to knock his fucking casket to the ground and I'm going to personally piss all over his corpse. One less Taig to worry about."

Six IRA soldiers dressed in army fatigues and black masks, three on each side, chaperoned the pallbearers of Dermot's casket as they made their way down Garvaghy Road to the Catholic Cemetery. Orders were to shoot to kill any Proddy bastard who interrupted the procession.

Close to fifty thousand Irish showed up to see the brigade commander of the IRA laid to rest. But the crowds began to shuffle as clashes erupted throughout and after one temper too many flared it turned into an all out riot. Mason's crew moved in, pushing and squeezing so hard that the pallbearers fell to the ground and the casket crashed to the street. Benji Mason, still stiff from last night's session, ran up to it, carrying a .357 Magnum in one hand and unzipping his trousers with the other. His plan to desecrate the corpse was foiled when the first crack of an IRA rifle cut him down and death bled into the streets of Portadown for the first time that day.

RUC and UDA troops moved in and rubber bullets tagged innocent bystanders in the crowd. People were trampled as fire was met with fire and everyone ran for cover.

By six o'clock that evening two UDA soldiers, Benji Mason, one INLA member and two civilians lay dead, as the IRA soldiers sounded off a three gun salute over the casket of Dermot Brennan, before they laid him in the sod in a salute to their fallen leader. Sean O'Kane stood with Patricia and their nephew Thomas, while Eamon Gainey stood back anonymously in the crowd watching the whole procession.

Behind Patricia and Sean, in the crowd as well, stood Ian Wright, arm in a sling and Perry Young, his CID partner in the RUC Special Branch, staring silently at the casket and the people closest to it.

Ian said, "That's Patricia Brennan O'Kane, she's the mother and she's the one we want. Did you get the photo?"

Perry said, "Aye."

They walked away unnoticed.

* * *

One hundred and fifty Catholic priests from all four corners of Ireland and across the ocean filled the front pews of the St. Eugene's Cathedral in Derry. The rest of the church was filled with family, friends, hurling fans and reporters.

Fr. Ruari O'Keefe's casket lay draped in the white burial cloth at the front of the church, as Cardinal Byrne gave his homily.

"Ruari O'Keefe was a dear friend of mine who got away from us last week. I knew Ruari as a young lad growing up in the streets just outside the doors of this church in the Bogside. I knew him when the whole country fell in love with his athletic prowess. I knew Ruari when he fell from public grace and was unceremoniously kicked off the National Hurling Team. I knew him when he holed up in his flat in Dublin ready to drink himself dead and I knew him when the Mercy nuns gave him the humble job of janitor. I knew him when he was called to the priesthood and I knew him when he was ordained. I was there when it was decided he should go to the Philippines to work with our Columban brothers there and I was here when he came back and took over at Holy Cross in Ardoyne as I had asked him. And as his body lays here before us today, I still know him.

"Ruari O'Keefe was a human being with human frailties that brought him to his knees, but he never ever gave up. Through the good and the bad, the ups and the downs, through the hurt and the humiliation, through the struggle of sin, penance and redemption, he was always an Irishman first.

"He loved you, he loved Ireland and he loved freedom. As many of you know, he assisted me in difficult meetings in London to try and stop the strike, where he showed tremendous poise and courage in the face of frightful odds. I gave him the assignment of Chaplain to the lads in Long Kesh, and he took the assignment seriously and loved those lads as if they were his own family and, as it turned out, he died with them and for them. He never forgot the hardship and harassment he experienced growing up in Derry's Bogside, and so, he felt a true kinship with the prisoners and their cause.

"We talked often of his participation in the civil rights march now known as Bloody Sunday, when innocent people were shot down in cold blood by UK soldiers, and how his perspective changed that day. He often told me that if it wasn't for the sport he'd most definitely have been sitting next to those brothers of ours in Long Kesh. Ruari O'Keefe can rest easy now knowing that he did everything that was asked of him. May God hold him in the palm of his hand."

* * *

Four cars drove slowly into the small village of Ballycraig, followed by a large black hearse. All of Ireland had read about or heard about the shootout in Upperchurch, an incident commonplace in The North but not so in The Republic, and the people of Ballycraig expected Clare's body to come home and rest next to her parents.

Cassie had called her mother and father to make arrangements for Clare's funeral, burial and wake, knowing that both Clare's parents had gotten away from them, they prepared their home for the wake.

The place was spotless and chairs set for a big crowd. Cassie's father went to see the widow Buggy about some jugs of the best poteen in all of Kilkenny County. They anticipated all of that, but what they didn't anticipate what was to happen next.

Four cars and a hearse rolled to a stop in front of Kenny's home. As Cassie got out of the car Colm and Rosemary greeted their daughter with a warm hug, knowing that she could have just as easily been in another casket next to her best friend, not to mention that she was raw with emotion and needed family and friends.

Cassie said, "I'm not sure that I can do this."

Rosemary said, "That's why we're here darling."

The villagers began to gather around as six IRA men in army fatigues and black masks got out of the car, went to the hearse and gently carried Clare Eva White to her wake inside the Kenny house.

For the next three days, they waked Clare. None of them had any idea that she was the mother of Martin O'Kane, and had no idea who these men were who came and went as the three days progressed. Finally Eamon Gainey came in the dark of the night and sat quietly with Clare by himself, something that would be discussed for years to come.

After a long three days, Cassie found herself putting the first shovel of fresh earth on her best friend, and then collapsed in the wet dirt from exhaustion and grief. But she knew in her heart of hearts that Clare could rest comfortably now, knowing that she had finally put her arms around her twins and that she had truly made her contribution to the one free Ireland.

Chapter 84
Omaha

The Atlantic Ocean on the West Coast of Ireland raged as if in anger that ten men were allowed to die for no good reason. The Irish Sea on the East coast of Ireland rose and dropped in a fury over centuries of injustice and misunderstanding of a foreign oppressor.

The twins, hundreds of nautical miles apart by now, both stood holding tightly to the rails as the sea drove itself mercilessly into their vessels and the furious grey blanket above felt as if it were smothering them.

They looked out at the water on different sides of the rock, hearts sinking, tears hid by ocean spray and as lonely as either had ever been in their short lives.

One week later

It was 1:45 a.m. as Frank McGrath and Eddie McMahon made their way home from Barrett's Barleycorn after a monstrous Friday night with pockets stuffed full of tax free tips. They walked across Leavenworth street to their apartment. Frank carried two cases of ice cold Coors and Eddie packed a box of Marlboro Lights in his hand as they walked. This was their ritual after a long Friday night of feeding drunks. It was now their turn. The two cases were just in case their drunk buddies showed up after a night out and conveniently forgot to stop for more beer, which happened regularly.

Eddie said, “I don’t know what’s going on. These Irish guys were supposed to be here yesterday and I haven’t heard shit from anybody.”

Frank said, “Don’t sweat it, Eddie. Can you imagine what they’ve been through? They’re probably laying low and taking their time.”

Eddie said, “I just hope they’re okay, you know, no run-ins with the law. That’s all we need.”

Sweat began to bead on their foreheads and upper lips as they made their way home through the humid summer Omaha weather.

Their place was on the second floor of an old Victorian converted into apartments. The key opened the flimsy door, which creaked into the dark. Concentrating on their conversation, they were unaware that they had visitors.

Mick and Martin sat stock still in the dark and before Eddie and Frank could switch a light on Mick said, “Where in the hell have you guys been?”

Not expecting anyone to be in their apartment, and then not expecting to hear anything but an Irish accent from their visitors, Eddie and Frank froze in their tracks, afraid to breath or even move and wondering what was going on here.

Martin flicked on the floor lamp that rested between him and his twin brother, smiled, and said, "Well at least they brought beer and cigarettes."

Eddie and Frank were now totally confused. What they saw and what they now heard registered nonsense. There were Irish twins sitting in mismatched chairs in their living room, who spoke in mismatched accents, and on the lamb from Ireland.

All Eddie could think of to say was, "How did you guys get in here?"

The twins looked at one another and began to laugh, soon Frank joined in and finally all four of these young men were laughing so hard that they had tears running down their faces. Laughing as if life had been so difficult and stressful lately that to laugh was an unexpected therapy that made them feel immediately better.

Introductions were made, Mick produced a bottle of John Powers and a case of Budweiser he had fetched from Frank's liquor store on 40th and Dodge, after bribing the cab driver with a six pack. The session was now on and would go until the booze ran dry or they passed out or both.

Mick said, "So Eddie, your family's from Butte?"

"Yep."

"Which one of the McMahon clans?"

Eddie said, "My dad's Barry McMahon."

Mick said, "I was going to ask you if you were somehow related to Barry."

"How'd you know who my dad is?"

"My dad's Paddy Quinlan."

Eddie felt his cheeks flush red from embarrassment and said, "I feel like an idiot for not making the connection. My dad speaks very highly of your dad."

Neither Mick nor Martin said anything further; both recognizing the open wound that was festering there.

Frank, totally confused now, said, "What's the connection?"

The explanation was made and Frank said, "So Martin and Mick, until a few months ago you two didn't even know each other existed?"

Martin said, "Less than that, Frank."

Eddie said, "So which one of you was in jail and who busted who out? I'm sorry but we've only gotten bits and pieces."

Mick said, "Eddie, I went to Ireland for the first time last February to spend some time with my dad who was there for a funeral. Just after I got through customs in the Dublin airport these dudes in black suits surrounded me and then arrested me mistaking me for this idiot."

His thumb pointed at Martin, who smiled.

Eddie and Frank nodded, neither smiling.

"These assholes that arrested me dropped me off at a place in Northern Ireland where a team spent a week torturing me, wanting me to sign a confession and admit that I was Martin O'Kane, a name I had never heard of until that moment."

Frank said, "Wait a minute, who arrested you and tortured you?"

Martin said, "The people who arrested him were MI5 Agents, the English government's version of The FBI. They took him to a place that all Republicans shutter thinking about, called Castlereagh in Belfast. It's the equivalent to a police station here, I guess. He was booked and turned over to the RUC, who were the ones who did the actual torturing."

Franks said, "The RUC?"

Martin said, "Aye, The Royal Ulster Constabulary. They're the police force in Belfast."

"The police tortured him?"

"Aye, happens all the time there. Any time a Republican's arrested, they first try to torture a confession out of him. It's a matter of pride in Long Kesh, those who were tortured and didn't talk."

"No shit. And Mick, they did this to you?"

Mick said, "Yeah, it was bad, and then they toss me in Long Kesh prison southwest of Belfast. It was a real hellhole."

Frank and Eddie looked at one another, after having read about the prison in the papers everyday since last March and talking about it every night in the pub, to actually sit across from a man who had been there was mind boggling.

Frank said, "So Mick, did you meet any of the hunger strikers?"

"No. But I joined them."

Eddie said, "You what?"

"I joined them."

Frank said, "You went on hunger strike?"

"Yep."

Eddie said, "Why wasn't it in the papers?"

Martin said, "Because the British government, which was getting some serious pressure from all over the world to end the strike, didn't want anyone to know that they had arrested, tortured and imprisoned a man who was an American citizen. Let alone let the world know that after he was exposed to their form of justice decided to protest with his life."

Frank said, "Their form of justice?"

Mick said, "You're not going to believe this. After they arrested me I told them I wasn't Martin O'Kane but Mick Quinlan, they laughed at me even though I had a legitimate passport and driver's license. After they tortured me for a week and while I continually told them that I wasn't Martin O'Kane, they scoffed at me. Then they put me before a judge in the Diplock court."

Eddie said, "The what?"

Martin said, "Oh, you're going to love this. The British parliament, in order to take care of Republican prisoners in the quickest and most efficient manner possible, invented the Diplock court system. It was named after Lord Kenneth Diplock, after a report that he submitted to Parliament recommending the fastest way to deal with Republican prisoners."

Mick said, "Yeah. So I go before this judge and a lawyer for the government and the lawyer says, 'Your Honor, Martin O'Kane has been accused of killing a government official as well as an American citizen.' Then the judge says, 'Mr. O'Kane, how do you plead?' I said that I wasn't Martin O'Kane, that I was an American citizen and that I wanted to talk to a lawyer. The judge then says, completely ignoring everything I just said, 'Mr. O'Kane, you are a criminal, a terrorist and a murderer. I find you guilty of two counts of first degree murder and sentence you to life in prison without parole.' He then slams his gavel down and just like that I'm heading out the door to a waiting van to be taken to Long Kesh."

Eddie said, "Wait a minute, no lawyer, no jury of your peers?"

"Nope."

"How about evidence and witnesses?"

"All hearsay."

"Son of a bitch."

Frank said, "Okay, so you're an American citizen, mistaken for your brother, the most wanted man in the UK, and you just got sentenced to life in prison without parole. What must've been going through your mind?"

"Frank, there's really no way to describe how homesick I was. It was absolutely hopeless. And to make it worse, I didn't know my dad was dead, and I kept wondering why he didn't come to straighten out this mess and get me the hell out of there."

Eddie said, "Paddy Quinlan's dead?"

Mick glanced quickly at Martin and said, "Yeah."

"How?"

"It's a long story and now's not the time."

Frank said, "What in the world made you go on hunger strike? That is some serious shit, dude. Nine men have died and Mickey Divine is on his last breaths."

Mick simply said, "Fergal O'Kane."

Eddie said, "What? Who's Fergal O'Kane?"

A tear welled in Martin's eye and he said, "He's my baby brother. He's one of the smartest men I know. He's a Seanachie, second to none. It's one thing to know the history, it's a whole other bailiwick to tell it and my wee brother can spin a yarn. He has the gift."

Frank McGrath went into a whole other world at the mention of the Seanachie. His grandfather was a Seanachie and he understood what Martin was saying because his granddad had that same Irish magic. Frank felt his presence here and missed him dearly. But he knew that his granddad was proud of him and glad he was here now with these men, helping in any way he could.

Mick said, "My uncle Dinty was a storyteller and he would come to the ranch in Montana for a month every summer and did the same thing that Fergal does. He started to tell stories and some of the toughest and crustiest ranch hands there would stop and get caught up in it.

"Well, Fergal did the same thing for me in prison. We had nothing else to do so I got my degree in Irish history from Long Kesh University, from a guy who knew the material and could tell the story. By the time he was done I was so tore up that I told him that I was going on strike and I did."

Martin said, "So then I find out I got a twin brother who was wrongly incarcerated in my place and now was in the hospital wing on hunger strike, the decision was made that we had to bust him out before he died. The word from the inside was that he was just stubborn enough to die an Irish martyr. I couldn't let someone do that in my place."

Eddie looked at them both and then said, "So, Mick was put in jail and said to have committed two murders and they had mistaken him for you. And then you, Martin, go in and bust him out. You guys are nuts."

Martin said, "Listen, this was not my plan. When they told me what I was to do, I was not at all excited. I was scared as hell, but I knew it had to be done. And the way it was to be pulled off made sense, so I did it. But there was more than a bit of luck in it."

Frank said what Eddie was thinking, "So, Martin, did you. . ?"

Martin said, "Wait a minute. The less you two lads know the less trouble for you in the long run. You can make a pretty good guess."

The room went silent, cold and heavy as the stark cold truth fell about them like a heavy wet snow in the night.

Eddie, in defense of Frank, who sat in quiet embarrassment, said, "Look guys, we just wanted to know how far we were sticking our necks out here."

Meeting the temper of Martin O'Kane for the first time, Eddie and Frank watched as he stood and said, "Fuck these two Mick, let's get the hell out of here. You two don't have any idea what the fuck it means to stick your neck out."

They all stood now and Eddie said, "Martin, give us a fucking break here. We're just a couple of regular guys wanting to help out. We weren't raised in a fucking war zone, so we don't know about violence and oppression, nobody's arguing that. These were just innocent questions, by a couple of naïve guys, we didn't mean to piss you off."

Mick said, "Martin, they didn't mean anything. It's just been a couple of stressful months, that's all. Eamon said these two were to be trusted and you know they're good for it."

Martin said, "I've been sticking my neck out my entire life. How does it feel?"

Frank smiled and said, "Uncomfortable as hell, but we're in come hell or high water."

Mick said, "Good."

They all sat down

There was a dead silence, Mick sighed audibly and said, "So what's the plan?"

Eddie said, "Frank and I are supposed to drive you two to Butte, Montana. My dad will have instructions for you when we get there."

Mick said, "I can't wait to get to the ranch."

Eddie said, "I bet."

Mick nodded and Martin said, "When do we leave?"

Eddie said, "Monday morning early."

There was a lull in the conversation in which all four men sat lost in their thoughts and their buzz when Mick said, "I'd like to make a toast. To Paddy, Dermot, Clare and Ruari, may you all rest in peace."

Martin said, "Aye."

Seeing the intensity about the twins neither Frank nor Eddie asked, they just raised their beers in toast.

Eddie said, "We leave Monday morning. We'll make it to Rapid City, South Dakota the first day. Then to Butte the second day, so we should be there by Tuesday night."

Chapter 85
The Abduction

Belfast

One week Later

The phone rang on the desk of The Secretary of State for Northern Ireland and his administrator said, "Sir, Mr. William Gray on line one."

"Gray?"

"Sir."

"If you give me one more excuse I'm going to serve your balls to the Prime Minister for tonight's appetizer. Now *my* job is on the line. I want O'Kane back and I want him in Long Kesh and I don't care what it takes."

"Sir, I'm glad you said that."

The Secretary hesitated and then said, "No, I don't want to know. Just get the job done."

* * *

RUC Special Branch agents Ian Wright and Perry Young waited patiently in a room in Castlereagh interrogation center. Young twirled the Polaroid of Patricia O'Kane in his hand when William Gray limped into the room, well-dressed, demeanor severe, as if not giving a thought to the pain he experienced in each step.

He looked at the two men who sat across from him and said "We need Patricia O'Kane picked up. Did you attend the Brennan funeral?"

They both nodded.

"Did you get the picture of Ms. O'Kane?"

Young said, "Aye," as he slid the picture across the table."

Gray looked at the picture.

"It has to be done quietly with no trace back to us. She needs to be taken and placed somewhere where no harm will come to her, depending, of course, on the decision of her son. This is the perfect opportunity to lure this Fenian bastard back to Northern Ireland and Long Kesh where he belongs."

Gray looked directly at both men as if sizing them up.

Wright said, "I don't like any of this. Why don't we put together a hit squad, get with one of our better agents, find out where they are and go take them out."

Gray said, "Are you fucking daft? What, we just waltz into the U.S. and shoot a lad? What don't you like about this?"

Ian said, "Well, for starters we just walk into their flat in the Short Strand neighborhood, where all the good Catholics know one another and know strangers better, and just cart her off? Then where in the hell do we put her to keep her safe? I'm no Taig lover, and I sure as hell want to get at O'Kane, but kidnapping his mother?"

Perry said, "Oh and how about this woman being one of the toughest women in the IRA. She's Brennan's sister for Christsake. She's a trained killer and would take your life without a blink, and by the way how does your fucking leg feel? This bitch shot you. Why don't we just cut our nuts off now and be done with it."

"Sounds like someone already cut your nuts off."

Ian said, "Fuck you, Gray. You sit in your almighty office giving out illegal orders and shoving them up our arses and challenging our manhood. Why the hell don't you go kidnap her you rotten bastard?"

"Pull your head out of your arse will you Wright? I'm not asking *you* to do this, nor any member of the RUC. You know enough of these goddamn Catholic hating, Union Jack waving, Loyalist paramilitary pricks. They'd do it for a pound or two and a couple of cold pints and bragging rights. How in the hell did you two make CID?"

Young stood and said, "We can get this done, we know people. But why should we put our balls on the line for a prick like you?"

"Because there's fifty thousand pounds in it for anyone man enough to take it. I knew there'd be some push back from you two. Now do we have a deal?"

They nodded.

Gray said, "You've got exactly one week."

Wright said, "One week?"

Gray stood up, winced, and the pain and hate in his eyes became black and menacing. He stared back down at them, as if by laser throwing them back in their seats. He leaned over the table resting his hands there and said, "One fucking week. If it's not done on time, to my satisfaction and quietly, they'll find you two cocksuckers floating in the Lagan."

He then smiled at them as if utterly pleased that the meeting had met all his expectations, and he left.

They waited a few minutes to make sure Gray was out of the building and then Wright looked at Young and said, "Fuck Long Kesh. If we're doing this thing we're doing it right."

Perry Young looked at his partner and smiled.

* * *

The soccer field in Woodvale Park in the Woodvale suburb of Northern Belfast was quiet and deserted at midnight. Two men waited at the south goal post looking around nervously making sure no one unexpected showed up.

Fane Taylor walked up behind them and said, “What the fuck is this clandestine shyte all about? Why not meet in my car or in a pub?”

Ian Wright said, “Goddamn it, Fane, keep it down. We can’t take any chances with this one, we don’t need any unknown ears listening in.”

“To what?”

“We need you to do a job for us, but this goes down quickly and quietly. If you get caught, I will hunt you down and put a bullet in you myself. Understand?”

“Okay, Ian. Take it easy. Whatever you want done, I’m in, you know that.”

“Look, I just wanted you to understand how critical this is. We want you and your lads to pick up Patricia O’Kane and hide her away for a week or so.”

“You want I should kidnap Martin O’Kane’s mum?”

Perry Young said, “Aye, we want the bastard back.”

“Well that’s one way to do it.”

“You got a better idea?”

“You know the war this will start.”

“If we do it right, it won’t start anything.”

“What does that mean?”

“It means you and your lads pick her up and treat her like a queen. You don’t pluck one single hair on her head. He’ll come running.”

“Then what?”

“You take her to the house in Londonderry and hold her there. Once we get affirmation that he’s coming back we’ll meet here for the exchange. When we get the exchange scheduled we’ll come to you and give you the rest of it.”

The hair went up on the neck of Fane Taylor, he now knew he was going to get a shot at Martin O’Kane and if that was the case, he thought, O’Kane wasn’t going to Long Kesh he was going to the Millstown Taig Cemetery.

Sean O’Kane and Cassie Kenny had been working eighteen-hour days as the hunger strike was ending. Sean buried himself in the work to keep his mind clear of his sons and to honor the men who had died on strike; Cassie because she was so lonely without Clare that if she didn't put in these kinds of hours she was sure she wouldn't survive.

Mickey Devine just died and was the tenth hunger striker to meet his end. There were six more men on strike currently but their parents had all vowed that once their sons were unconscious they would order nourishment for them. As a result, the ruling council of the IRA as well as the INLA all agreed that the hunger strike was to come to an end.

Sean and Cassie went to the Shamrock Club for drinks and closed it down. Both tipsy and sleep deprived they made their separate ways home.

Sean reached his front stoop and fiddled with the key in the lock. He opened the door slowly to keep the squeak at a minimum and not wake Patricia. When he shut the door he turned around and was surrounded by three men in black masks holding hand guns on him.

The leader said, “Don’t say a fucking word, Taig, and sit down.”

Sean knowing full well the man meant what he said, sat down on the couch under the front picture window covered with drapes. He then looked around to see where Patricia was. He was suddenly stricken with a fear he had never experienced. With all the bullets flying, bombs going off, with all the Orange marching seasons, with every time they had to pack up the newspaper and move it under threat of death, he had never felt the fear that threatened to waylay him at this moment. He knew intuitively that she was either dead or kidnapped. Then it dawned on him, it was the only way the bastards were going to get Martin to give himself up. Damn, he thought, why didn’t I have Eamon’s lads watching her.

The leader looked at him and said, “We’ve got your wife.”

At those words the panic welled up in him like a twister in a jar and he couldn't keep quiet, “For fucksake, why not me?”

The hand came out of nowhere and knocked him senseless.

Fane Taylor looked at the man who struck Sean and said, “You stupid bastard, we need him awake, he needs to deliver the message.”

The third man walked into the kitchen, got a glass of water, and threw it in Sean’s face as he came around.

He said, “What the hell?”

“Shut the fuck up and listen! We’ve got your wife, she’ll go unharmed if your lad turns himself in.”

“What, so your lot can shoot him?”

“No. He’ll turn himself into the RUC.”

“Oh well, now that you say that I’m truly relieved.”

The sarcasm not lost on the leader he said, “It’s either that or us, you pick. I know a few lads who’d love to have a little talk with Martin.”

Sean said, “I’ll get the word to him. But there are no guarantees.”

"Yes there are. I can guarantee you that your wife is a dead woman if the lad doesn't turn himself in."

"What guarantee do I have that you won't hurt Patricia anyway?"

"You don't, you'll just have to trust us. We'll be in touch to make arrangements."

The three masked men walked out of the O'Kane house while Sean sat motionless, unable to move from shock.

Five minutes later, the tiredness that had permeated his body to the very marrow of his bones vanished. He ran out of the house and into the thick August morning air in Belfast.

It was four a.m. by the time he had reached his destination. He knocked twice quickly, counted to ten, knocked again once, then knocked again one time after a count of five. Eamon Gainey opened the door to the flat he was using that week. He saw the panic in Sean's eyes and said, "Sean, what is it?"

"Eamon, they got Patricia, the fucking bastards kidnapped my Patricia."

Within fifteen minutes five men stood in Eamon's living room reviewing a plan.

Eamon said, "My guess is they move her out of Belfast so that means, Derry or Portadown. You know where these lads drink, keep an eye on those watering holes. I know of a couple of safehouses in Portadown and one in Derry, we need to stake them out. If you find her do nothing. Just report back. I want nothing to happen to Patricia."

Colm McGilvery, a red haired freckled face kid of just nineteen, was ready to go stake out some Red Hand safehouses when Eamon said, "Colm, get with Sean. He'll give you the address of Miss Kenny. I want you to roust her out of bed and tell her I need to see her immediately and tell her to bring her passport."

Chapter 86
The Road Trip

Omaha, Nebraska

The next day

Frank McGrath and Eddie McMahon sat across from each other at the old rickety, linoleum kitchen table that came with the small, dank, apartment they barely afforded. Cups of strong coffee steamed out of mugs in front of them, giving them little solace of the relief they sought.

Loud snores floated in on the stale air from the living room reminding them of the surreal guests that slept there.

Eddie, perusing the Sunday New York Times that had arrived earlier that morning, said, “Mickey Devine died last night.”

Frank said, “No shit?”

“No shit, and that makes ten.”

“Wow, ten men dead. When in the hell is this going to end?”

“Looks like very soon. The pressure is mounting.”

“From the UK?”

“Nope, the parents.”

“What?”

“There are six guys on strike right now. According to this article their parents have made it clear to the IRA and the world that when their sons pass out they are going to get them fed. The article also says that the IRA will call the strike before that happens.”

Frank gingerly sipped his hot coffee and said, “Do you think this has helped them or their cause? The Brits don’t seem to give a shit. I know Margaret Thatcher doesn’t.”

“Not necessarily, Frank. I know it’s hard not to hate the Brits. But both sides have stuck to their guns. These ten men didn’t die in vain. The Brits said they wouldn’t negotiate until the strike ended. Now that it looks like it is coming to an end there may be hope.”

“Hope my ass. They reneged on the last strike, they’ll renege on this one too and the shit just continues over and over again. Why would now be any different?”

A thick Irish accent answered saying, “Because now the fucking Brits know once and for all that they cannot break the spirit of an Irishman who doesn’t want to be broken. And that, my friend, is a dangerous foe indeed.”

The tall blonde Irishman, Martin O'Kane, walked into the kitchen and said, "Do you have any tea?"

Frank looked up and said, "Tea? What the hell?"

A fourth voice echoed with laughter as Mick Quinlan followed his brother into the small kitchen.

Martin said, "You fucking Yanks are the only people in the world that don't drink tea."

Eddie said, "You ever heard of the Boston Tea Party?"

Mick laughed harder and Martin said, "Aye, I have. I probably know more American history than any of you Yanks."

Eddie said, "Well then you don't need to ask. We dumped the fooking tea in the harbor and that was that."

Mick was howling now over Eddie's imitation of Martin.

Martin walked over and put Eddie in a half nelson with his right arm with the left on his throat rendering him useless.

Martin said, "Now what were you saying about your fooking tea party?"

He let go and the laughter erupted all around.

Frank looked at the twin brothers and said, "You two look as bad as we feel."

Martin said, "Aye, that was quite the session."

Eddie said, "Remind me why I drink again?"

Frank got up, put some water in a small pan, and pulled some tea down from the pantry.

Eddie said, "What the hell?"

Frank said, "My grandma drinks tea and so of course my mom buys some and brings it over in case grandma stops by. It's Earl Grey, that okay?"

Martin said, "It's fine."

Frank said, "We got news and it's not good."

They both said, "What?"

Eddie said, "Mickey Devine passed away last night. Number ten."

Martin said, "Och, Fucksake, when is it going to end?"

Mick said, "Mickey was coming on just as I was broken out. Shit!"

The water on the stove came to a boil and Frank got up to get the tea for Martin. Mick then got himself a cup of coffee and the four of them sat staring aimlessly in to their own thoughts.

* * *

I-29 North out of Omaha was busy early on a Monday morning, traveling sales people heading to generate company revenue, truckers moving the GNP and families taking late summer vacations. All of whom joined the fearsome foursome heading to Big Sky Country.

Mick said, "So Eddie, what're we talking, eleven hundred miles to Butte?"

Eddie said, "Yep."

Mick said, "And another one hundred and twenty miles north of there to the ranch."

Martin, raised in a country the size of Vermont said, "Wait a minute. Did you say eleven hundred miles?"

Eddies said, "That's what I said."

"How long will it take to drive that?"

"With food and rest stops, fifteen hours door to door. And I've thought about it, we got four drivers here, we don't need to stop in Rapid City, let's drive it straight through. I'll call dad at our first rest stop and tell him to expect us tonight."

Martin lit up a cigarette, looked out the window and whispered, "Fucksake."

Frank, who was sitting in the front passenger seat while Eddie drove, had been quiet, in a bit of a contemplative mood as he stared out the window. This all reminded him of his road trip with his granddad and he missed him. But he knew that he would have insisted that Frank go, that he help his Irish brothers. The sun came up in the east and as it rose above the Council Bluffs and directly into his eyes, Frank came out of his thoughts. He reached over and turned down the radio, turned in his seat to look at the twins in the back and said, "Okay, I know you guys told us your story but that was in a drunken haze. So, now that I am aware of the amount of skin I have in the game…"

Eddie said, "And what would that be?"

Frank said, "Are you serious?"

"Yeah, dead."

"Okay, let's see, let's start with aiding and abetting known fugitives on the lamb from the law the world over for multiple felonies. Oh and, by the way, we just rolled them over state lines. I think those alone would put me in a federal penitentiary for, let's say, oh I think about ten years."

Eddie said, "Oh well, I don't mind sticking my neck out."

He winked at Martin through the rear view mirror and Martin said, "Fuck you, McMahon."

All four laughed.

"Anyway, I want to get all this straight in my head. Okay, Mick and Martin, you two were born in a convent in Dublin and your biological father was a Catholic Priest?"

The miles rolled on and on but there were few dull moments. Four Irishmen, three Yanks and one National, but each had the story in them and a need to tell it. They stopped for burgers and rest areas and Martin whined when they wouldn't pull over to see the Corn Palace as they headed west on I-90 through South Dakota, swearing that no one back home would believe him without a picture, but the car kept rolling on down that highway.

Chapter 87
The McMahon House

Butte, Montana

Late August 1981

They arrived at the Butte exit close to nine o'clock that evening, which Eddie passed without blinking.

Frank Said, "McMahon, where are we going? That was the Butte exit back there."

Eddie said, "Our house is about five miles this way. But you'd never find it unless you knew what you were looking for."

"Why?"

"The family has always kept a low profile. Growing up we had guys like Martin coming around all the time. I didn't know who they were or why they were there, I just knew that they were Irishman from Ireland that had come to visit, and then only because of their thick accents."

Frank said, "That is really cool."

"Well, my granddad came over in 1915 to work in the copper mines. In 1917 he joined the U.S. Army and fought in World War I. He got shot in the leg in Normandy and so they sent him home. They say he was a mean bastard. So get this, in 1918 Ireland was in the middle of an all out war with England and he went back to fight the English."

Frank said, "No shit."

Martin said, "That doesn't surprise me a bit. It happened more than people think."

Eddie said, "Yeah and when the war of independence was over and the civil war had begun, he came home swearing he'd never take an oath to a foreign king and he would never shoot another Irishman."

Mick said, "Yeah, my dad and uncle Dinty would talk quietly about the civil war. They said it was an awful time for Ireland that divided friends and families. They said there are hard feelings even today."

Martin said, "Don't get me started lads, I grew up in county Antrim, one of the six partitioned off in the fucking treaty."

Before Martin could work up a good lather, they pulled into the drive way of Eddie's family. The McMahon place was a secluded five-acre estate five miles outside of Butte. They rolled to a stop and Eddie got out to stretch when a huge Irish wolfhound bounded down the walk and knocked him over licking his face and pinning him to the ground.

The booming voice of Barry McMahon coming from a silhouette under the flood light over the open garage broke the calm of a quiet evening when he said, "Pete! Pete, get your ass off the boy!"

Pete backed up, whined a bit, but stood ready to have his ears itched for the effort.

Eddie said, "Hey, dad."

Barry McMahon said, "Edward, how was the trip?"

"Long."

"I bet."

Introductions were made and Barry said, "I bet you guys are starving."

They all perked up at that.

He smiled and said, "I got some steaks burning on the grill out back. There's cold beer in the fridge."

They followed him inside. All but Eddie and his dad went to use the toilet and wash up before dinner. When they had left Eddie said, "What's up? You look stressed."

"No time to talk now, you'll find out soon enough. Get yourself a drink and help me with these steaks."

"Where's mom?"

"She had a parish council meeting that she couldn't get out of. She was pissed off when she left, I can tell you. She'll be back later."

They had just finished up dinner and were making small talk over coffee and some of Eddie's Mother's homemade chocolate chip cookies when Mick said, "Smelling these pine trees makes me homesick, I can't wait to get to the ranch."

Barry dropped his coffee cup onto the wooden table harder than he meant to and said, "Mick, I got some bad news, lad. I've had some of my lads nosing around at the ranch and the feds have your place staked out in the event that either you or Martin show up. Going there is not an option."

Mick said, "Son of a bitch."

Martin said, "So what the hell do we do now?"

Before Barry could answer, Cassie Kenny walked into the room and stood at the right hand side of Barry's chair.

He looked up at her and then said, "Eddie and Frank, meet Cassie Kenny. Mick and Martin, I think you lads are acquainted."

A bit of fear and question shown in their eyes and both nodded. They both went back to the last time they had seen Cassie which left them both feeling unsettled.

Barry said, "Cassie, can we get you a cup of coffee or tea? Maybe a glass of wine?"

She sat down at the empty chair usually reserved for Mrs. McMahon and said, “No, thank you.”

She then looked at Mick and Martin, ignoring Frank and Eddie and said, “Martin, Eamon has sent me.”

“Why? What’s going on?”

She looked at Barry, then at her long fingers and after an uncomfortable pause said, “Someone has grabbed your mum.”

Martin said, “What do you mean someone grabbed my mum?”

“She was kidnapped out of her home in the Short Strand.”

“Do we know who?”

“Aye, The UVF."”

“Benji Mason’s crew?”

“No, you may not know this because you were heading here. But Benji Mason was killed during the riot that broke out at Dermot’s funeral. Fane Taylor a young upstart in the UVF has taken Mason’s crew. We think the RUC put them up to it with orders from London.”

Martin said, “Fergal and I know him, we had a run in with him and his lads, he told us he’d get us back and I guess he has. This can’t be happening. The filthy bastard grabbed me mum. He’s a dead man.”

“Well, you waltzing into the Kesh to spring your brother was a public embarrassment. You know the Brits don’t take things like that lightly. Oh hell, what am I talking about, Martin. You assassinate their ambassador; leave the country right under their bloody noses, then slip back in, the whole thing, they want you badly and they don’t want to wait for legal channels.”

Frank and Eddie looked at one another with eyes wide open and Barry put a finger to his lips to keep them from saying anything.

Martin said, “Why should that surprise me? It sounds just like the Diplock Court. Anything to skirt the law, the bastards. How do we do this?”

Cassie said, “They want to tell people that you turned yourself in after they make it look like they tracked you down. When in reality there will be a meeting somewhere where you’ll be traded for your mum with no one being the wiser.”

“How is she?”

“She’s being treated very well. Here’s what we’ve been able to piece together. Under pressure from the Secretary of State for Northern Ireland to bring Martin back, William Gray, head of MI5 for Northern Ireland came up with the brainchild of kidnapping Patricia. His flunkies in the RUC, Ian Wright and Perry Thomas, who used their flunkies in the UVF to distance themselves from unlawful activities they want carried out.”

“So nothing gets traced back.”

“Aye.”

Martin lit a cigarette and Barry pushed an ashtray his way. He blew a plume of smoke into the air and they all stared at one another when Barry stood and cranked open a window to let some smoke out and some fresh air in.

Martin said, "So what does Eamon think?"

"He's got some ideas but he wanted us to noodle it around first."

Mick said, "The answer is easy."

They all stared at Mick and as he smiled, Martin said, "What?"

"We dress exactly alike and go back together."

"You'd do that for me?"

"In a heartbeat. Hell, what did you expect? You broke me out of Long Kesh."

Cassie said, "I know Eamon wanted Martin to come back without Mick, one less person in harm's way, but I like it. Sure it's a roll of the dice."

Barry said, "Meaning?"

"The bastards just might take them both out."

Mick said, "Maybe, but it leaves my brother less exposed than if he goes it alone."

Barry said, "Cassie, make sure Eamon is on board with this. Once we hear back we'll get these gents on the next plane out."

Chapter 88
The End

The Shankhill neighborhood was just waking up on Saturday morning when the knock came on the door. Fane Taylor had had a long week at the Rolls plant, plus he had to make sure that Patricia Brennan was being well taken care of in the UVF safe house in Londonderry and as a result had had a long night last night in the pub. He wasn't expecting company.

The knock came on the door again. Coming down the hall in his blanket, chilly from the morning air, Fane said, "Hold your bloody fucking horses."

As he opened the door he said, "All right then, who is it on a bloody Saturday morning?"

Ian Wright stood outside his door and said, "I'm sorry lad it couldn't wait."

"Ian get in here I'm freezing."

Fane ran to the bathroom, splashed water on his face, brushed his teeth and went back to the kitchen where Ian had put some water on to boil. Ten minutes later they sat before tea steeping.

Fane said, "Sorry about the place Ian, long week and longer night last."

"I've seen you look better."

"Aye."

"No worries. I need your help."

* * *

Eamon liked the idea and put all the plans in place for the twins return. Mick and Martin had been given fake passports and IDs. Mick flew into Dublin while Martin flew into Shannon, both dressed as businessmen, both were met at the airport by limo drivers and both were driven to Andersontown in Belfast. On the way, the back seat of the large car was lifted up and they each lay beneath pulling the seat back down covering them so there was no chance for detection at the border crossing. Once they were past border, they each switched vehicles and were driven the rest of the way in less conspicuous cars. They each arrived within half hour of each other, after dark without any problems or delays, all went unusually smooth.

Eamon Gainey awaited their arrival. They had dinner and coffee and talked late into the evening.

Eamon said, "It has been agreed that we will meet at Woodvale Park football field tomorrow night at half eleven."

Mick said, "Clandestine."

Martin smiled at Mick and said, "The bastards don't want anyone to know what the hell they're up to."

Eamon said, "And they don't know Mick's coming."

"Well, I think they want me dead and not in the Kesh, just a gut feel. I don't like the exposure, but I don't want mum getting hurt."

"I wouldn't worry about that. We've checked everything out and it will be a long rifle shot for anyone not wanting to expose their position. To get one of you will be extremely difficult, both damn near impossible. And it'll be fifty-fifty and they won't know who to take a shot at."

* * *

Sean O'Kane drove Martin and Mick to Woodvale Park on the other side of Belfast, tension thick in the silence of the car.

They pulled into the park and drove cautiously to the parking lot closest to the field. There they found a lineup of three vehicles, a sedan in front, police van in the middle and a sedan bringing up the rear. All were eerily empty.

They looked to the middle of the field where Ian Wright stood with Perry Thomas, William Gray and Patricia O'Kane. They got out and walked cautiously toward the group and when it became clear everything seemed all right Sean ran into the arms of Patricia and held her close.

William Gray was the first to break the silence. He said, "So it's true you have a bloody fucking twin."

He looked at Wright as if saying, "Why didn't we know the twin was coming, this could be trouble?"

Ian said, "So what are you playing at? We said nothing about a twin brother tonight."

Mick said, "How did we know you wouldn't have a long range sniper set up somewhere. We're doing this little clandestine thing on your terms, we needed a little insurance."

Gray said, "For what? You think we would shoot your bother and start a war?"

Thomas and Wright looked at one another and then looked around into the dark of the park.

Gray said, "You know we have to arrest both of these lads until we are one hundred percent sure which is which. Then we'll let the Yank go free."

Mick spat, "Like you did last time? I don't think so."

Things heated up quickly.

Patricia walked over to Mick and said, "You'll have to go lad. They won't be foolish enough to make the same mistake twice. I'll make sure of that."

Mick not so easily assuaged said to Gray, "You can't tell by the accent?"

He said, "Easy enough for you two to play at that."

"You mean like I did in Castlereagh station?"

"I'm not taking any chances and I don't give a shit what you think, Yank, if that's who you really are. Cuff them both and put them in the van."

Martin walked over to his mother and father and said his goodbyes, they hugged both the boys and then the boys walked away.

Wright looked around nervously, as if waiting. Patricia and Sean stood holding hands and watching the twins walk to the van, like this would never ever end for them. They watched as the van driver strapped them both into the back seat, Martin nodded to them and smiled. Wright and Thomas got into the lead car while Gray went to the rear sedan. The caravan began to roll toward the park's exit when the explosion lit up the night and the van carrying the twins literally disintegrated as the fiery ball of steal shot into the air and then crashed into the grass off the road.

* * *

Fergal O'Kane went silent. He spoke not a word for over a year. Ten of his best friends, men he respected and looked up to, died on hunger strike and another seven came close. And he felt like they gained nothing. When he was informed of the car bomb it was as if he had reached his tipping point, it was like if he spoke aloud he might fall off the precipice, on which he sat vicariously day and night, into that black abyss that would consume him.

In 1982 the IRA command within Long Kesh agreed to prison work detail for its members. The British, believing they had won, that they had finally beat down the IRA in Long Kesh, used it as a Public Relations coupe. Which, of course, the IRA wanted because they had other plans. What the IRA command in Long Kesh realized was that they knew nothing about the lay out of the prison. Since it was built in 1976 and since the British government instituted their criminalization policy, the Republican prisoners in Long Kesh had been protesting. As a result, they had spent twenty-three hours a day in their cells. They then decided that the only way they could find out about the prison and its weaknesses was to give in and participate in prison work. It was part of a long term escape plan that came together quicker than anyone of them would have ever thought possible.

One day on work detail, Jimmy O'Malley walked up to Fergal and said, "Bik needs your help."

Bik McFarland was the new IRA Commander in Long Kesh, he took the post the day Bobby Sands went on hunger strike.

Fergal looked up from his mop and said nothing. Jimmy said, "Command is forming a committee to put an escape plan together. Bik said you're to be on it and that it was not a request."

Fergal nodded and said, "Tell Bik, I'm in."

Jimmy simply smiled when he realized he was the first person Fergal had said anything to in over a year.

It was exactly what Fergal needed. Then and there he decided it was time to move on. His period of mourning was officially over. Plus the plans that he had formulated in his head the past year would not wait until 1991, the year of his scheduled release. He immersed himself in the escape planning. It went from wild eyed, pie in the sky ideas to something that just might work. And the longer they were on work detail, the more the screws were used to having them around, the more laxed security became, and the better the chance their plan might work. Within six months the plan was set and they reviewed every conceivable detail, nothing was unimportant, until every man on the escape detail knew exactly what they were to do and the date was set for Sunday September 25, 1983.

Barrett's Barleycorn
Omaha, Nebraska
September 26, 1983

Frank McGrath sat watching Monday night football waiting for Eddie McMahon to show up. Since they had heard the news of the car bomb and the death of Martin and Mick, both Frank and Eddie had been down. Life just seemed depressing and they had a pissed off attitude about everything.

Eddie finally walked in and sat down and before Frank could even say hello he said, "You're going to shit."

"What?"

"Thirty-two guys escaped from Long Kesh yesterday afternoon."

"Are you serious?"

"Hell yes I'm serious. Just got off the phone with dad, it's why I'm late. He said that Fergal was one of the escapees."

"You mean Martin's brother?"

"Yep."

"That's awesome."

"Dad said they've rounded up some of the escapees but Fergal is not with them."

"Oh I hope he gets away."

"Me too."

"Did they ever figure out who was behind the car bombing?"

"No. Dad said that the Republicans in the North think it was government ordered and was a cover up. He says, they know who was behind it but aren't saying anything to anyone who doesn't need to know."

They sat sipping their beers, watching the game and lost in their thoughts when they both sat up having the same thought at the same time and said, "Fergal."

Eddie said, "Holy shit batman, I wouldn't want to be anybody who was involved in the car bomb."

* * *

William Gray's phone rang he picked it up and said, "Gray."

"Fergal O'Kane was one of the escapees."

"And they haven't rounded him up?"

"No, he's still out."

"Shit."

"What are we going to do?"

"Not talk about it on the phone for one."

An hour later Ian Wright and William Gray stood on a rural road in a light mist, outside of Belfast.

"So, what are we going to do?"

"What do you mean, Wright, you think he's going to show his face anywhere near Belfast?"

"We kidnapped his fucking mother and killed his brother. What the fuck kind of question is that? Once he finds out who we are, and he will, he'll knock on our fucking doors. He won't rest, he won't care and he won't give one good goddamn about his own safety until we're dead."

"Sounds like you better take a little vacation."

Gray flicked his cigarette into the dark mist, got in his car and drove away.

* * *

The Mill Pub
Outside Upperchurch, County Tipperary
That same night

The Mill was a farmhouse resting in a farmyard in rural northern Tipperary County during the day, but three nights a week it was a popular pub where great local musicians came to play and the locals came to listen and maybe have a pint or two.

Since the escape, people throughout Ireland had been celebrating and government officials had been keeping an eye on Upperchurch, especially after recent events there. As a result, NORTIP, the Northern Tipperary band of Republican brothers were keeping an eye on them.

It was quiet on a Wednesday night, but it was still early and Fergal sat at the bar listening to the traditional Irish music being played. Only a few people knew who he was, they kept his drink full and left him alone.

Within the hour his mother and father walked in. Patricia hugged him and he didn't think she would ever let him go and then his father Sean as well. Once it was dark out Eamon Gainey walked in and John Ryan, the pub owner walked the four of them upstairs to his kitchen and left them alone.

Fergal simply said, "Who?"

Eamon said, "From what we can gather the kidnapping was the brainchild of William Gray, MI5 Northern Ireland. His balls were on the chopping block if they didn't get Martin back. He handed it off to a couple of RUC Special Branch lads named Ian Wright and Perry Thomas. They in turn had a UVF unit do the dirty work, a lad named Fane Taylor."

Patricia stiffened at the memory.

Fergal noticed and said, "Did they disrespect you in anyway?"

She said, "No, other than taking me freedom."

Fergal looked at Eamon and said, "Tell me what you think happened with the car bomb?"

"What do you mean?"

"Well, they also killed one of their own."

"I've thought about that. I think Wright lost control of Taylor. My guess is that he wasn't clear in his instruction, assumed he'd shoot,"

"So Taylor is a loose canon?"

"Aye, after that, I'd say so."

"So do you think Gray had anything to do with Mick and Martin dying?"

"I don't think he cared one way or the other, he just wanted the situation taken care of. His ass was on fire and he needed to put it out."

"So Wright and Perry made the decision and Taylor carried it out the way he saw fit."

"Aye."

"But Gray was the one who made the decision to take mum and forced Martin's hand?"

"Aye."

"And Mick came to try to confuse and distract them?'

"Aye."

He smiled and said, "Doesn't surprise me."

Sean looked at Fergal and said, "Please son, no."

"Da, I have to."

"And what purpose will it serve? We've lost one son, are we to lose another? You'll either die, end up in prison, or on the run for the rest of your life."

He smiled and said, "I won't die and after breaking out I've already earned a life sentence and since when haven't I been looking over my shoulder? There won't be any mercy shown me, just like those bastards didn't show Martin or Mick any, nor *any* of us for the past eight hundred years."

"Fergal, listen to me now."

He held up a hand and said, "Da, please don't. You know I have to do this. I won't be able to live with myself if I let these bastards get away with this."

Patricia nodded understanding as tears ran down her cheeks and Sean stared at his son, looking squarely into the face of his own father and thought, this will never end, it just keeps happening over and over again.

* * *

MI5 Northern Ireland Chief Dead
By Sean O'Kane

AP October 5, 1983 William Gray head of MI5 Northern Ireland died this morning when his car exploded upon ignition in the Woodvale suburb of north Belfast. No group or individual has come forth to take responsibility for the killing, but Northern Ireland officials believe it to be the work of the INLA, the Irish National Liberation Army, a radical off shoot of the Provisional IRA.

* * *

The phone rang in the dark living room. He stared at it and sipped his scotch whiskey. It rang again and he stared, not moving. It continued to ring and would not stop. He picked up the receiver and said nothing.

He heard, “You’re next.”

“Who is this?”

“You know.”

The phone went dead

RUC Special Branch Found Dead
By Cassie Kinney

AP October 9, 1983 On a rural road west of Belfast RUC Special Branch Agent Perry Thomas was found dead in his car from an apparent bullet wound to the head. No one has come forward to accept responsibility but officials believe it to be the work of the INLA. When asked if there was a connection between this assassination and the car bomb in Woodvale, Northern Ireland Officials had no comment.

* * *

Ian Wright hadn’t slept in a week. He went to the pub to blow off some steam and stayed longer than he had intended. He came out with a load on and decided to hail a taxi. He got in the back of the big black sedan and gave the driver his address, put his head back in the seat and closed his eyes. Three bullets cut through the back seat as Wright lunged forward dead. The taxi pulled over, the driver popped the trunk and the two men strolled away.

Second Special Branch Dead
By Sean O’Kane

AP October 14, 1983 RUC Special Branch Agent Ian Wright was found dead this morning in the back of a taxi on the Shankhill Road in Belfast. The INLA has come forward and taken responsibility for this death and the deaths of RUC Special Branch Perry Thomas and MI5 Northern Ireland head William Gray. In a statement they said that these deaths were in retaliation for the car bomb that killed Martin O’Kane and Mick Quinlan. The Prime Minister of Northern Ireland said, “If these terrorist think that government officials had anything to do with a car bomb they are sadly mistaken. These were cold blooded murders and we will bring these murderers to justice."

* * *

Fane Taylor was not one rattled easily. But the deaths of men he respected as street smart law officers had shaken him. He was not sure if the IRA knew he was involved, how could they? He came home late from the bar, opened a bottle of beer from the fridge, sat down and re-read the open letter on the coffee table from Ian:

Lad, Fergal O'Kane, Martin's brother was one of the prisoners who escaped from Long Kesh last month. We haven't caught up with him yet and we don't know what he will do, but he is dangerous and it is best to be wary. We also don't know how much they know about what happened but I suggest you get out of town for a while until things die down. More to come,
Ian

He put the letter down, lit a cigarette inhaled deeply and took a long pull on his bottle of beer. He then felt the cold steel of a large hand gun on the crown of his head.

The last thing he heard was, "You should have listened to Ian."

Epilogue

Eamon Gainey knocked on the door of Cassie Kenny's flat in Killbarrack, North Dublin. Soon after the hunger strike ended she packed up the flat that she and Clare shared in Belfast and moved back to Dublin. She'd had enough of the violence and she wanted to try to get back the normalcy of her previous life if she could. She had been expecting him.

He said, "So what's so important that I had to come to Dublin?"

"I got a letter from Paddy Quinlan's lawyer."

"Aye?"

"Aye. I inherited his ranch and all his money. The letter said that in case something should happen to he and Mick, I was next in line."

"Holy Shyte, Cass. What are you going to do with it?"

"Well, that's what I wanted to talk to you about."

"Okay."

"I'm going to sell the ranch, this is my home and this is where I'm staying. I'll buy a house here, make sure mum and da are taken care of, plus I've got some siblings who are struggling. I'll make sure they're all okay. I also want to take care of Sean and Patricia, I think they deserve a break. Get them out of the Short Strand, maybe see if they want to move out of the north all together."

"I doubt that'll happen."

"I can dream can't I?"

"Sure."

They stared at each other for a moment when Eamon said, "You didn't have me come to Dublin to tell me this did you?"

"Of course not. I want to give money to the cause. But I am sick and tired of the violence, I don't want more people dying."

"I understand. You can do whatever you want, it's your money and I will hold no grudge. But just remember that if we don't push, nothing will change. Our people live in oppression in our own fucking country Cassie."

"Eamon you're preaching to the choir. I'm on your side. Maybe we can set up a fund for the lads on the run and their families."

"There's an idea."

"Speaking of lads on the run, where's Fergal?"

"Can't say."

"I want to take care of him as well, he'll need it now."

"I'll make sure he gets it."

The Dubliner Irish Pub
Omaha, Nebraska
Two days later

Eddie and Frank walked quickly down the cement stairs off Farnam Street to the dark, dank pub in the basement of the nineteenth century office building.

It was quiet at 10:00 a.m. The bartender was icing down the bar and getting ready for the day, he looked up and said, "Back in the corner."

They walked into the next room where the band stand held the instruments of the latest Irish band in town to play for the week. In the back corner the silhouette was slight, but the end of his cigarette burned brightly. They walked tentatively toward the table, not sure of who this was or what to expect.

The thick Irish accent came out of the dark and said, "Eddie and Frank?"

They said, "Yeah."

"Have a seat lads. Something to drink?"

"No thanks."

He sipped his coffee and continued to smoke. His red hair was worn high and tight on his head and he was clean shaven, smelling of clean after shave.

He said, "So you're wondering who I am and what I wanted with you two?

Eddie said, "It had crossed our minds. I think my dad's at work here."

He smiled and said, "You're da has been at work for us for a long time. May God bless him. Look, I just wanted to thank you two for taking care of Mick and Martin when they came here. I heard what you did and it was important for me to do this in person."

Eddie said, "Shit, so you're. . ."

He held up a hand and cut him off saying, "Aye."

Eddie and Frank could only smile.

The End

LaVergne, TN USA
13 December 2010
208471LV00004B/35/P

9 781609 102609